An unclaimed land in the Scottish isles is ruled by the male and female victors in a series of war games every five years. Named Chief and Lady of the land, they rule the vast holding and protect the people by divine right until the next game begins.

After her brother's death, Ceana is named laird. The only way for her clan to survive the ravages of the Highlands is to join in the war games. Bastard son of a powerful earl, Macrath is placed in the games by his vengeful stepmother. He must survive for the ultimate retribution.

Ceana can't stand the arrogant Highlander who seems to be following her, and yet she can't seem to walk away. Macrath wants nothing more than to be rid of the troublesome need to protect the warrior lass. What starts out as a race to survive turns into passion to endure together.

Highland Hunger

Book One: Highland Wars

by

Eliza Knight

****

FIRST EDITION
August 2014

This novel was published previously in serialized "games".

Cover Design: Kimberly Killion @ The Killion Group, Inc.

Edited by Victory Editing

ISBN-10: 0-9903245-5-9
ISBN-13: 978-0-9903245-5-3

Dedication

To my amazing daughters:
Everyday you show me what it is to be a female warrior. You princesses rock and I wish you much love and many victories!

Acknowledgements

Writing a book is not a solitary endeavor. Special thanks to the following amazing people who helped in putting HIGHLAND HUNGER together! Kim Killion and Jennifer Jakes who brainstormed the idea for this book with me over a year ago, and then sat down with me to create the HIGHLAND WARS brand. Many thanks to Stephanie Dray for brainstorming with me. Much gratitude and singing of praises to my amazing beta readers who helped to brainstorm and shape the story: Kate Quinn, Andrea Snider and Angie Hillman. Many thanks to Linda at Victory Editing. And last, but never least, my amazing street team! Thank you for spreading the word about my books! Couldn't have done it without you guys! XOXO

To be married and named Chief and Lady of the land. To live in the grand castle, rule the vast holding, and protect the people by divine right.

May the gods be forever in their favor…

Game on.

Game

One

Chapter One

Late Fall

BLOOD stained the leaf-strewn cave in swirling patterns.

Slashes of crimson lined Dougal's white shirt. His mouth hung slack, eyes stared lifeless at the dimly lit sky. Hair, still damp with sweat, lay in unruly clumps against his forehead.

This was the worst and most terrifying morning of Ceana MacRae's life to date. She dropped to her knees, her hand falling to her brother's motionless arm. How had this happened? And so quickly. They'd only left the castle a few hours past in search of game to feed their starving clan. And now he was… She pressed her fingers against his neck, feeling for the steady bump against her fingertips that would prove life still remained.

Nothing.

She searched again on the other side of his neck. Pressed her ear close to his nose and mouth, hoping for even just a tiny tickle of breath.

Again, nothing.

Ceana shook her head, mouth going dry, her vision blurring. Her brother could not be dead. He could *not*!

She checked him once more, a hard, cold lump settling in her stomach.

Dougal was no more.

Her father had been ripped apart by wolves. Now her brother was killed by marauders. It seemed to be the fate of the men in her family to die badly. Fear circled her heart. An icy chill snaked along her arms and legs. She hissed a breath and bit her lip. Their laird was dead. The chief of their clan—gone.

But who would have dared to harm him?

She gripped the dagger strapped to her hip and wished she'd thought to bring her long, thin sword, not that she would have been able to ward off an attacker for long. Thank goodness she had her bow. She slipped off the bow and nocked an arrow, turning in a circle. *Whoever killed my brother, I will annihilate you.*

Danger wasn't something new. Death was an old pastime. The MacRae's were constantly being picked upon by neighboring clans—like vultures, they were just waiting for them to die.

A hundred years had passed since the king decreed the warring clans should fight against one another in the war games. The declaration made to cease the constant bloodshed. And while the clans near the isles were safer, those smaller clans with fewer men to guard them were still in constant danger. Clans like hers.

Legends abounded regarding those first games. Heroes were made. The opening game, a century ago, was a vicious, unrelenting fight. The first to reign victorious was Gillemorre, son of the great King Olaf who'd been murdered for his lands. Those descended from him now claimed the name Morrison—but only if they won the game. The games had brought a semblance of order to the land, though not to all. Not to the MacRae's. But the ruling council would not waver from its decision.

Even with the war games being designed to keep the peace, small neighboring clans fought against each other. A drought had wiped out many of the crops and killed many of the goats and pigs. Even the streams and lochs seemed to carry less fish.

Aye, danger she was accustomed to. Starvation even. Wasn't that why they'd left today to get food for their clan members?

But this—the vicious murder of her older brother, the chief of their clan…

Tears burned her eyes, and the hair on the back of her neck stood on end.

The death of her brother.

The death of their laird.

What sounded like a branch being stepped on called her attention to outside the cave. Without making a noise, Ceana moved to the back of the cave where she was steeped in dark shadows. She crouched down, shifting the soft plaid of her gown to keep herself balanced. She pointed her arrow toward the mouth of the cave and waited.

And waited.

All the while, she continued to hear the crunch of leaves and sticks. Distinctly a man's steps falling—heavy and hard. And he was alone. Ceana listened intently; her hearing had always been superior. The footsteps paused outside the cave opening. And then she heard the soft sound of his booted feet stepping lightly onto the solid cave floor. The stranger was dressed in a plaid she'd seen before—MacLeod, she thought, but couldn't be sure. Weekly, if not daily, their lands were trespassed by those looking for spoils.

She stared at him, a smile curling her lip at knowing he couldn't see her, but it was wiped off as soon as he nudged the tip of his boot into her brother's ribs. Dougal's prone body barely moved. Anger burned a path to her heart. She'd forever remember the look of pleasure on this stranger's face as he kicked Dougal harder and then laughed loudly as he kicked him as hard as he could.

Without reservation, she let her arrow fly when the man took out a knife and made a move to cut her deceased brother's throat. Her arrow found its mark in his chest, and the man looked toward the back of the cave, eyes squinting in both surprise and pain.

"Who's there?" he cried out, then stumbled to his knees as crimson colored his dirty tunic.

Ceana stood and stepped away from the shadows, shoulders squared, jaw tight, and she assessed the man.

"Who are you?" he asked again, brogue thick and filled with pain. The stranger roved his gaze over her, surprised at what he saw, if she could judge by the widening of his eyes and incredulous press of his lips.

No one expected much from little Ceana. She was slight in frame and shorter than most women, but she was fierce, and that was all that mattered. Her thick red hair was swept into a messy plait down her back, and dirt no doubt smudged her cheeks. The fabric of her plaid gown was worn and torn in spots, mended in others. Dougal himself had teased her for looking like an orphan. But she was no child. She was already nineteen summers.

"Who are you?" she asked him without answering the question herself.

The man gripped the arrow, double-fisted, and broke off the end. His brow dripped sweat down the sides of his cheeks. "I'm a MacLeod."

Just as she'd suspected. "What are you doing here?"

He managed a lecherous smile through his agony. Ceana drew another arrow, nocked it and aimed it at his chest once more. The feathers tickled her cheek, and she let out a breath she didn't know she was holding.

"I asked you a question," she said. One false move and she'd shoot him again. "What are you doing here?"

"Killing your laird." He gave a viscous laugh and then a cough as he clutched at the stump of arrow shaft left in his chest.

"Then 'tis a good thing my laird taught me to protect myself." She let her second arrow fly, watching it once again hit its mark in his chest. The sickening thud of it turned her stomach, but his agony still gave her a thrill of vicious triumph.

The invading warrior clutched at the second arrow buried deep in his chest, his face draining of all color. Perhaps before, he'd thought he may have a chance of escaping death, but now he had to know he would die.

Ceana had been hunting since she could figure out how to clutch a knife and shooting with her bow since before her first word. There was no doubt that she was a skilled hunter. But to kill a man and feel a thrill? There were no words. *I will burn forever in the fires of hell for this.*

But this man had killed her brother. Would have killed her. If the stranger was willing to carve up a dead man, there was no telling what he would have done with her.

I did it to survive.

As far as she knew, this was the first man she'd actually killed. There had been moments when she was close, when enemy clans had invaded their lands and threatened their livelihoods, that she had in fact shot her bow and had her arrow lodge in someone's chest only to watch them gallop away on a horse or be rescued by their men. Most of the time when their holding was laid siege to, she was in charge of taking the women and children to a safer place. Protecting them should the enemy break the lines.

Dougal always told her that since he'd yet to have an heir and she was his only sibling, that the family's modest holding would soon be hers. While it may have been rare for a female to inherit, it wasn't unheard of. But she knew not the first thing of taking care of their meager space of land or politics. How could she ever take his place? Dougal had been a good leader.

Emotion welled inside her, forming a lump in her throat.

I have to.

Blood trickled from her enemy's lips, making a red line from the corner of his mouth to his earlobe. He was dead, and she'd been the cause of it.

But he'd wanted to slit Dougal's throat. Her brother was already dead; there was no need to mutilate his body further.

The man's head lolled to the side, eyes glazing over, mouth opening and closing in silent speech. She suppressed her surprise. She'd thought him dead already, but apparently he still had something to say. Ceana walked briskly forward, ears keen for any noise outside. She bent down beside him.

"You shall be buried," she said. "Even if you don't deserve it. I shall see to it."

"Who are you?" He asked, the same question as before and the same one she'd avoided answering.

She supposed she might as well practice. For as long as she lived, she'd be repeating these words. "I am Laird MacRae."

Ceana stood, the enormity of her new position bringing with it a potent fear. She'd return to her castle and relay to her clan that there was still no food, but even worse that Dougal was dead. They'd all be dead soon unless she could figure out a way to save them.

An idea struck her as she slung her bow over her shoulder and adjusted her knife so it wouldn't get caught on the stave.

The war games. The very games that ensured her clan would never amount to anything. But the coin she could earn if she won—the castle and lands she'd receive—all these would help her protect her people. The winning clans agreed to live in peace and as allies—anyone who went against the law risked execution. It would mean she'd have to marry, but at the end of their five-year rule, the chieftain and lady had the choice of reentering the games to keep their position within Sìtheil, or they could relinquish their position, retain their prize coin, and return to their own clans.

She swallowed hard. *There is no other way.* If she did nothing, her people would starve before the next clan even had a chance to invade their paltry holding.

Stepping out of the cave, she stared up at the graying sky. Joining the games meant she had to cross the stormy Minch to the western isles, that she might die in battle. Meant she'd have to kill many more people in order to win. But such a sacrifice was worth it in the end if she could save her people.

The first thing she'd do as Laird MacRae was join the fight for a throne—and she'd win.

Macrath Mor, bastard son of Chief Campbell, Earl of Argyll, had always been seen as nothing more than a pile of shite to his father's wife. And today was no different.

He stood before her in the great hall of the castle, barely any sunlight filtering through a few narrow windows and only a few candles lit for both light and warmth. 'Twas chilly in the great hall—though not as cold as his stepmother's heart. Leticia stood tall and proud upon the dais, and though she did so for height, even the six-inch-elevated platform only brought her up to his shoulders. Macrath took after his father and was considered a giant among men, though he liked to tease his fellow clansmen he was considered giant for another reason.

"Have you seen the earl, my lady?" Macrath asked, hating the way Leticia's eyes sparkled with ill intent.

His own mother had died in childbirth, and given that his father never turned away a boy of his blood, Macrath had been raised within the castle—though not alongside his father's legitimate children. Leticia had seen to that. She'd also seen to it that every one of Argyll's bastards wished they'd never been born.

"Not as yet. But 'tis a good thing you've come."

Macrath raised a brow.

"You've been chosen." Leticia's too-closely-set eyes narrowed at him, and she smoothed the soft wool of her gown.

Macrath steeled himself for what the woman had in store for him next. There was always something. He supposed he could have left the clan, braved the wilds of the Highlands on his own, but his stepmother would have seen to it that none of their allies housed him. He would have likely ended up an outlaw, and Leticia would have seen him found and his head removed, just as she'd always planned. Besides, he'd risen in the ranks of his father's warriors. Not that the task had been easy, as Argyll had been harder on Macrath than any of his other children. Perhaps it was his size, or maybe it was his skill. It didn't really matter.

"Chosen for what, my lady?" Macrath said.

Where was the earl? The reason he even stood in the great hall instead of out in the fields with his men was that his father had agreed to meet him this morning. Macrath had something important to discuss with him. The captain of the Campbell guard was stepping down, as age and injury had plagued his limbs, and Macrath wanted to replace him.

Leticia smiled. The same smile she'd worn when she'd had him beaten as a child. Not a good sign. "Why, the war games of course. Five years have passed, and so we are called upon to send another of our *beloved* warriors to the cause."

Damn. Had it already been five years? A warrior was eligible to attend the games as soon as they were eighteen summers. Being that he was in his twenty-seventh year, he'd only been eligible the previous time, and Leticia had threatened to send him, but in the end she'd not been able to out-bid his father's choice. What had she done to make his father give in this time? Was this the reason his father had not stepped into the great hall as he'd agreed to do?

Macrath bowed, his weapons chinking in the silence, and a bitter taste filled his mouth. With no one else in the room, he could easily run her through. She deserved as much. He'd once seen her order such a thing herself when a servant made her angry. But killing his stepmother wasn't a way to mete out his vengeance. So instead he met her gaze levelly and said, "An honor."

And if he won, it would indeed be an honor. He'd be named Chief of the Morrison land and clan. He'd rule by divine right for five years. Gain a fortune in coin and the respect of his father. Bastard or no, he'd have a title. Leticia would have to acknowledge him as an equal. But if he didn't win... The woman would have sent him to his death. And so would his father.

A slow clap sounded from the doorway leading to the kitchens. Victor, Macrath's legitimate half brother sauntered into the great hall, his clothes in disarray. No doubt he'd just rutted one of the unwilling kitchen maids. The man had gained more than one beating from Macrath for his behavior toward women—which only made Victor hate him more. The feeling was mutual. Of all Leticia's children, Victor was the cruelest. The most like her. As a team, Victor and Leticia would have been able to convince the earl that Macrath should go.

"So you've heard the news?" Victor worked to straighten his clothes while Macrath worked to keep his temper in line.

Already he felt his neck and face growing hot. It was an effort to keep from bellowing—an effort that had the veins in his neck throbbing. He turned from his brother to face his stepmother, not feeling the need to address the arsehole. Macrath's birth order was another reason Leticia hated him—he was a year younger than Victor, which meant her husband had not been faithful. Hardly an oddity, as many of the chiefs and earls had mistresses, but Leticia was particularly jealous. Macrath was the first of Argyll's bastards. He had always wondered if she'd been the cause of his own mother's death.

A question he'd likely never get answered.

"You can go," Leticia said with a sweetness that stung. "Best pack up your meager things as the games begin in two weeks."

That did not leave him much time. The games were far from Argyll. The fastest way for him to travel would be to pay for passage on a galleon at the Firth of Lorne. From there, he could sail south toward the sea and north into the Minch. He wasn't sure two weeks would be enough time, but that was all she'd given him.

"And the female warrior you've chosen?" Macrath asked.

"Rhona."

Macrath gave a curt nod. Rhona would never make it. She was one of the kitchen maids and the mother of one Victor's bastards, and likely that was the reason she'd been entered. How could his father have allowed that?

Having had enough of his vile family, Macrath turned his back on them. They let him go, not bothering to stop him. After all, they expected he'd be dead within a month's time.

Suddenly the sea and war games looked brighter than anything he could have imagined here. In an odd way, he supposed he should be grateful to his stepmother for entering him.

At the stables, a horse had been prepared for both him and Rhona—not the best of mounts for either of them, but what could he expect? Macrath smoothed a hand down the dark mane of the chestnut mare that had been prepared for him—the furthest thing from a warhorse, *his* warhorse.

"Where is my horse?" he asked the stable master, who suddenly colored so red he was almost purple.

"Her ladyship said ye wished him to be sold yesterday."

And a pretty penny he probably got for him. Macrath's warhorse had been sturdy, strong, and well-trained. He'd seen a number of battles, and it was a great loss for him to have been sold. Sucking his tongue to the back of his teeth, he turned away from the stable master and faced the courtyard filled with clan members—men, women and children.

He may not have been respected by his stepmother and brother, but he was by the remainder of the clan. Rhona rushed toward a short, chubby cherub, hugging him to her breast—Victor's son. She cried and kissed him all over his face, and the child clung to her worn plaid gown. Macrath's heart broke for them both as most everyone knew she would likely not return.

He would do all within his power to protect her, but when she was separated from him, there would be little he could do. He adjusted his saddle and then mounted his horse. There was no need to waste any further time. To the loch he'd go, pay passage on a ship, and arrive at the games in enough time to pull his sword from his scabbard. With skill and luck, he'd win the war and gain the title of Chief.

A few of his siblings who did not share Leticia's hatred stepped forward and wished him luck.

"Macrath." His father's booming voice made those in the crowd settle. The Earl of Argyll never called him son. Never allowed him to sit at the high table or sleep within the castle, but all the same, he did pay him special attention in training and even with the giving of his time.

"My lord." Macrath bowed his head.

"For you." His father pulled his claymore from his back. The hilt of solid steel and studded with jewels, the blade sharp, shiny, and thick with runes down the center. His father had brought many a victory to his people with that weapon. Rightfully, it belonged to Victor. Why was he giving it to Macrath?

Macrath gave a quick shake of his head.

"Take it," the earl growled. "May it protect you."

Macrath swallowed back any emotion that threatened to surface. Never had his father shown him such consideration. He reached forward and wrapped his grip around the cool metal of the hilt. The claymore was solid, sturdy, and he felt a power thrill its way up his arm to hold it. How many warriors in his past had held this sword?

"My thanks," Macrath said. He took his own claymore from his back and replaced it with his father's—*his.*

"My lord!" Leticia called out, rushing forward, eyes darting from the sword to Argyll.

But his father gave her a glare Macrath had never seen turned on her, and Leticia clamped her lips closed, her eyes shooting hatred. If she'd been a witch—which he'd suspected as a child—she would have used magic to turn the blade to his throat.

"We thank you for your sacrifice, Macrath Mor." The earl held out his arm toward him. "Son."

Macrath stared at the extended appendage, shocked that his father had acknowledged him in front of the clan. A fact they all knew, but one that was never spoken of. Macrath struck out his arm, gripping his father's tight. If he never saw the man again, at least he knew in this moment that he was accepted. He ignored Leticia's huff.

Steadying his gaze on the gathered crowd and then back to his father, he said, "I will bring honor to the Campbells."

"I know you will. You're a skilled warrior. One of our best."

Macrath turned to Leticia and smiled, though it didn't quite reach his eyes. "You'll not have seen the last of me, dear stepmother."

Before she could answer, he raised his fist in the air and issued a battle cry that echoed through the clan as they all raised their arms and shouted with him.

Though a fierce battle it would be, Macrath was certain he'd succeed. There was no other way. The ultimate revenge against his bitter stepmother was to survive, and the spoils of war would only be an added bonus. His blood pumped a thrilling race through his veins. Though the news of entering the games and the danger it brought to him had only been announced the hour before, he was looking forward to it. He was ready.

Chapter Two

"I'M here to join the games for Clan MacRae." Ceana stood tall and proud, accompanied by two of her guards—the rest left behind to defend their holding.

Her stomach was still doing the flips it had on the galleon, and she was close to vomiting all over the shoes of the man who assessed her. At least the storms that had rocked her passage had subsided, leaving only a light mist to wet her cheeks. Perhaps the gods had seen fit to give everyone a chill before the games began, sending half of them to the sky from illness before the first arrow could be shot.

"Are you now?" Bloodshot eyes roved over her form, pausing at her breasts and hips.

She bit the inside of her cheek to keep the bile from spilling between her lips. If she never had to see the man again, she would be mightily pleased. Instead of staring at his dirty, overlong beard and pockmarked skin, she focused her gaze beyond him. He stood directly in front of the castle entranceway—a stone arch, the portcullis raised and the doors flung wide, signaling the end of the previous Chief and Lady Morrison's reign and the beginning of a new era.

Through the entranceway was a bridge covering a moat and beyond that the legendary Sìtheil Castle. She peered around the gate steward, catching glimpses of flags and stones but not much else. The thick stone walls surrounding the castle blocked her vision. Would the castle soon be her new home?

I will *call this place home.*

The steward cleared his throat in irritation, and Ceana realized she'd ignored him completely. Hoping that he wouldn't take her disinterest as a sign of weakness, she thrust her chin forward and said, "I am."

A lecherous smile curled his lips, showing yellowed and blackened teeth. "And have you a male to enter?" The man's gaze flicked to her two guards, and Ceana stiffened.

Straightening her back to the point of discomfort, she met his gaze dead on. "Nay."

He made a clucking noise with his tongue and shook his head. "All clans entering must have both a male and female entrant. No quarter given."

"But, sir—"

"Now, lassie." He leaned in close, the scent of whisky strong on his breath. "If you're willing to, eh… come to my tent, I'll be happy to negotiate."

Ceana jerked backward, bumped into her guard, and then quickly righted herself, her face flaming hot with embarrassment. She'd gotten her share of crude offers, but with each ensuing one, the offense never dulled. If anything, her ire was heightened. "Certainly not! I'm Laird MacRae. How dare you speak to me with such vulgarity?" She itched to grab her knife and gut the bastard. But that would not ensure her entry into the games. Then again, would it?

"Och, but you see, I need not dare for here you are just another female entrant, and we'll likely be burying your remains in a day or two. So why not—"

"I'll enter."

Ceana whirled to see her guard, and her brother's best friend, step up beside her. "No, Aaron," she whispered. She'd known Aaron since as long as she could remember. His father had fought alongside her own, and when her brother had taken his seat as Laird and Chief of MacRae, Aaron had been right there to support him. He had skill with a weapon, but he was not the fiercest in her guard. She couldn't let him join. Couldn't watch him die. "As your laird, I forbid it."

Ignoring her, he pressed his lips together and nodded curtly at the gate steward. "I'll enter," he repeated.

Ceana fought the urge to lower her head. Dougal would never forgive her. Behind her, several potential entrants called out their irritation for the time it was taking her to cross through the gate. Boarg, her other guard—an older warrior who had served her father—shouted out a response that made her grit her teeth.

"Boarg, talk some sense into him," she said.

Her guard shook his head. "Made up his mind on the road, my laird."

"Well, now, I suppose you've missed your chance for a piece of this," the vulgar steward said to Ceana, grabbing his man parts beneath his plaid and shaking them at her.

"I'm sure I've missed nothing," she responded, feeling even more ill than when she'd first boarded the galleon a week before.

"Suit yourself."

The steward turned back to his makeshift table and stroked their names on a parchment scroll while saying, "Two entered. One male. One female. Aaron of MacRae, Bitch of MacRae."

Ceana's hands fisted. "Strike that through, sir, and write it again as it should be. I am Ceana, Laird MacRae."

He glared up at her, spittle forming at the corners of his mouth. "I'll do no such thing. Should have warmed my bed when you had the chance."

Aaron nudged her with his elbow. "'Tis not worth the fight. Save your energy for the games," he murmured.

Aaron was right. There was no sense in angering the man in charge of taking names—though with hers now being Bitch of MacRae, she was likely to run into more trouble along the way than she anticipated. Ceana flashed her brother's friend a look of defeat, conceding to the steward—the first concession of which there might be many. "I just hope not all the guards are this way."

Unfortunately, Ceana doubted the likelihood of that taking place. Sensing her upset, Aaron, spoke to the steward for her. "Where do we go from here?"

"Tent steward. Take this." He thrust a signed scroll at them, indicating that they had indeed been entered in the games.

"Our gratitude," Aaron said.

The man huffed, but before he could say anything further, Aaron ushered her forward as did Boarg. However, as soon as she stepped through, she wanted to turn around and run all the way back to MacRae lands to brave the starvation of her people and pray for another way to survive.

Men and women, all unclothed, swam and splashed in the murky waters of the moat, seemingly uncaring that this was the place most chamber pots and rubbish buckets were tossed—along with the holes from the garderobes. The stench of the water, thankfully, did not reach her nose. But beyond this, men and women practiced sword fighting up on the sky-high battlements. And they were good. Experts even.

Immeasurably better than she.

Ceana had skill with a bow. Even up close, she had skill with a knife. But a sword had never been her strong suit. If she were to come up against any of the women above, she would lose. Most Scotswomen weren't trained with a sword, but because of the games, the women growing up in the isles were all taught to handle a sword from the moment they could lift one.

In this game, it was most likely her cunning that would help her win.

"Do not watch, my laird," Aaron said.

"Aye, my laird. Avert your eyes," Boarg added.

But how could she not?

If she'd thought that life on MacRae lands was harsh, she'd just entered an entirely new realm. One it seemed more likely she'd not escape from.

"Tents this way," shouted a scrawny guard near the second gate entrance—complete with another portcullis and opened thick wooden doors. "Hurry now. Let me see your papers."

Ceana couldn't have been more relieved when the man barely glanced at her after reading her name.

"Go on through. Supper's in an hour. Leave your weapons in your tent. Best make haste, lest you miss it. No quarter given."

'Twas the second time she'd heard the term, *no quarter given.* From legends past, she'd known the war games were ferocious, that only the fiercest and mightiest won, but it had not seemed as real as it did now, and even still, she was certain she'd be in for more of a shock come the time to begin. Which would be when?

They were told to arrive today before the sun set. She'd done that. Good gods, could they mean to send them into the first round at night? What would the first round be?

She wavered on her feet, realizing she may not see breakfast the following morning.

Aaron and Boarg gripped the back of her elbows, steadying her before she could make a fool of herself.

"Don't worry, lass. You'll do just fine," Boarg murmured. "I knew your mother, and she was one of the fiercest female warriors I've ever seen. You resemble her greatly."

"Agreed," Aaron grunted. "And fiercer than some men too."

"My mother?"

"Aye, she came close to entering the games herself before your father asked for her hand." Boarg nodded. "Just think. You're practically following in her footsteps."

That brought a smile to her face. How had she not known this? Her mother had died a few years past during one of the neighboring clan raids. Ceana missed her dearly and most days tried not to think about it. Her mother had a hand in the farming for the clan, and none of the crops had been the same since her passing.

Once in the courtyard, they followed the long line of entrants around the side of the imposing castle to the back where a vast amount of land was riddled white with tents, though they appeared to have an order to them. Along the left were four rows of tents, ten deep, and the same on the right, separated in the middle by three large tents. A female side and a male side. Perhaps the dining halls between.

As impressive as the tents were, she found herself turning around to gaze up at Sìtheil Castle. Counted the narrow windows all the way to the top and estimated there had to be at least five stories. Ceana tried to imagine herself living there. Tried to envision herself as Lady Morrison—and Laird MacRae. She'd bring two clans together and rule fairly and justly across the lands. After her five years, she'd have enough coin and allies to keep her clan shored up in the future.

Without realizing her feet had moved, she reached out and touched the stones. They were cold and in some places caught the light of what little sun was left, making it seem enchanted all the more. She could see herself living there. Ruling here alongside the male victor.

"You there, get to your tent!"

Ceana started, turning to the left to see a half dozen guards standing on wide, thick stone steps that led up into the back of the castle. Nodding, she hurried back to her guards who'd waited patiently.

"Papers," a guard, who Ceana assumed had to be the tent steward, held out his hand and glowered at the three of them.

Ceana handed him the parchment, and like the other guard, he barely glanced at her.

"Third row, ninth back. Supper bell will be ringing soon. When it does, go to the middle tent. Leave your weapons."

"We thank you," Ceana said.

The steward grunted and gave her a hard stare. "You'll not be so grateful come the start of the games. Beware. You've come this far. The only way out is death or victory."

Ceana swallowed hard. She'd known this already, but hearing it from his lips sent an icy chill to wrap around her middle. She cocked her head to the side and stared at the guard. "And what is your fate?"

"To see the lot of you buried."

"And to those who win?"

"I serve them well."

Ceana smiled, the first since she'd arrived. "Then you will serve me at the game's end."

"You'll not be the first to have crowed as such."

This time, Ceana grunted and swept past the steward, her two guards following. The little bit of arrogance she boasted made her feel good. If she was going to win this game, she needed to think of herself as victorious. She needed to believe in herself, a feat that would be very difficult, but she was up to the challenge.

Weaving their way through the tents—and equally through the smells of unwashed bodies, sweat, and old ale—they found her new residence easily enough. It looked like the tent on the left side of hers was still empty, but the one on the right housed a woman who looked like she'd been crying. She glanced at Ceana with bloodshot eyes before ducking inside, a subtle reminder that not everyone willingly joined in the games. If your clan chose you, there was no choice but to join—unless a plan of escape could be devised. But more often than not, clan leaders would have taken precaution against it.

With a sigh, Ceana tugged back the flap of her tent and stared into the dark and desolate space. They provided entrants with no comforts, and thank goodness they'd brought their own bedrolls.

"This is home," she said with a weary glance at Aaron and Boarg. "For now."

"Until the title is yours, my laird," Boarg said.

Aaron nodded before looking away, and Ceana felt the weight of his position settling on her shoulders. If he won, they'd be married. For the sake of the clan, if that was what the gods had in store for her, then she would say her vows. Aaron was a skilled fighter, adept at guarding the clan's meager holding, but how would he hold up against a fierce warrior? Maybe just as well as she did. Maybe he'd sustain an injury that disqualified him from the game. Was that possible? Or did everyone have to die?

The thoughts tumbling through her mind were too deep, too heavy, to ruminate on further. She shook them away and eagerly leapt into the task of setting up her bed. Five minutes later, two makeshift beds lined the walls of the tent, Ceana on one side and her guard on the other. Aaron stood with his bedroll in hand.

"I'll have to sleep on the male warriors' side."

Ceana nodded, unsure of how to respond. She still hated the idea that he'd be involved.

"I'm going to splash water on my face," she informed Aaron and Boarg, stepping through the slit in the tent.

"I'm coming with you," Aaron responded, stepping out behind her.

"No. I want to go on my own," she said. "It could only be a few hours' time before I'm alone. Let me have a taste of protecting myself when I still have a tent and my guards to return to."

"Aye, my laird." Aaron bowed his head. "I'll see you at supper then." He ducked his head, giving Ceana the freedom she'd asked for.

Walking between the tents, she encountered an equal number of frightening male and female warriors. The majority ignored her—and those that did pay her attention only did so with assessing looks. The females deciding how they'd kill her, and the males imagining bedding her on their wedding night.

Ceana did her own amount of assessing. There were many women less capable than herself. Some weeping, others looking ill. Still some who looked as though they'd not seen a meal in months and others who'd seen too many. But the ones that made Ceana tremble with fear were either covered in battle scars or bulging with sinew. These women had seen their share of fighting, and if Ceana were to come up against them, she would have a hard time warding them off.

But how could she avoid them? These women would hunt her down and pick her off like a frog did flies.

"What are you looking at?" a particularly masculine-looking woman asked. She crossed her arms over her chest and narrowed her eyes—one of which was milky white. Blind?

"A thousand pardons," Ceana murmured, not realizing she'd been staring.

The woman laughed. "A thousand pardons," she said, mimicking Ceana. "Is that what you'll say when I've got a knife at your throat?"

Ceana took the bait—and also the opportunity to practice. "The chance will never come, because while you're lumbering toward me like some giant who's had one too many swigs of whisky, I'll have nocked my bow and put an arrow through your heart. Just as I did the braggart who killed my brother last week."

She-muscle's eyes widened—including the milky-white one—and she smirked. "So you've killed before?"

"Aye."

"First?"

Ceana huffed. "Hardly." She-muscle didn't need to know that Ceana was including animals in that count.

"A tough one you are, for one so *small*."

"I may be small, but I am quick."

Ceana didn't give the woman a chance to respond. Instead, she turned her back only to come face-to-face with a vision she'd thought never to see—a tent flap was pinned wide open, and several women were engaged in... in...

"Never you mind that. Just a bit of wrestling. They do it in the nude to keep from ruining the clothes they'll need for the games."

Ceana flicked her gaze back to the giant woman. "Wrestling?"

"Aye. Keeps their spirits up. Well, best of luck to you." She turned her back on Ceana this time.

Ceana watched the women a moment longer, mesmerized by the way they moved and their unapologetic nudity.

Having had no luck in finding a well to drink from and wash the dirt from her face—and quite frankly a little unnerved with what she'd find next—Ceana headed toward the center of the tents where the larger tents were erected.

Several wooden and steel barrels lined the front of one tent, and most were occupied by men slurping from ladles. Ceana sucked in a breath, steeling her resolve. She was likely to run into more vulgarity, but thirst won out over her nerves.

Stepping up to a barrel, she grabbed up a ladle that was hooked over the side. She dipped it into the water, sipping with vigor before dipping in again and then pouring it over her head. The strands of hair that had already come free from her plait followed the path of the water and plastered to her forehead and cheeks.

The chill air blew lightly against her wetted hair and skin, making her shiver and raising gooseflesh along her skin.

"'Tis a good look for you."

Ceana swiped the water off her face with her hands, smoothed her hair back into place, and turned deliberately toward the man who'd spoken to her. She rubbed her free hand on her other arm, trying to soothe her chill. Expecting to see another grotesque brute wishing to invite her into his bed, she was surprised to see a rather handsome warrior. He had eyes such a dark blue they could almost be onyx, unruly black hair framed his face, and though he didn't have a beard, his shadowed jaw lent to the idea that he'd not shaven in days. Beneath the shadows were sculpted cheeks and a strong square jaw. A scar curved over the length of one of his eyebrows, and another stroked along his jaw. His linen white shirt was untied at the top, falling open to reveal part of his tanned chest. Overtop his shirt, a plaid of blue, white, and green, and much nicer than her own, was tossed over his shoulder. He looked, and smelled, cleaner than anyone else she'd run into.

"I didn't mean to offend you," he said. And then he smiled, showing mostly even white teeth and a mouth that made her think of kissing.

Thoughts she'd not dwelled on in the past. A little shiver took her, and she realized that the warrior had spoken twice now without her responding. And she was still staring at his mouth. Ceana glanced away, her face heating with embarrassment.

"I'm sorry," she said.

"You do not need to apologize, lass. We're all new here. Well, most of us." He smiled again, and this time Ceana made certain not to fall into his darkened eyes.

"Most?"

"Aye. I've met a past Chief already. He sat on the Morrison seat ten years ago."

"And he wants to sit there again?" Ceana asked.

The man nodded. "'Twould seem so, but I didn't ask him why. Suppose I should have."

"I'm Ceana." She chose not to mention her title.

"Macrath." He held out his arm, also curiously refraining from naming his clan. Leather bracers covered his forearms over his linen shirt. His hand was big and welcoming.

Ceana stuck out her own arm and gripped his bracer. Macrath's fingers wrapped around her flesh, absorbing her into his palm, making her feel small and delicate. She suppressed another shiver but couldn't help staring at his mouth again. If she were to die tomorrow, she would have liked to have a kiss from this man.

"What brings you to Sìtheil Castle?" Macrath asked.

"I heard they had a good cook," Ceana said, surprised at her own response.

Macrath laughed. "And I heard they had a secret storeroom filled with chests of gold and jewels."

Now it was Ceana's turn to laugh. "Are we both to be disappointed then?"

"Nay, lass, we'll both rejoice with sweetmeat pies in one hand and fat rubies in the other."

"If only." The thought made her suddenly sad. Macrath was the first person she'd seen and met at this place who made her feel safe—and she thought she could enjoy spending time with him. Wanted to spend more time with him, in fact.

"My stepmother sent me here, hoping I'd die," he said, running his fingers through his thick hair. "Nice of her, wouldn't you say?"

His confession was harsh. "Extremely so."

His lips curled in a half smile, and he raised his brow. "And you?"

She wasn't sure she wanted to share. Chewing her lip, she hesitated. Disclosing such information would make her vulnerable to him. And she couldn't risk being exposed to anyone. "I was chosen."

"Are we not all?" He dipped his ladle back into the water and took another sip.

"We are." Ceana hooked her ladle back on the barrel, no longer thirsty despite how dry her mouth had turned. One look at a handsome warrior and she was weak-kneed. She'd never survive the games at this rate. "It was good to meet you, Macrath."

He gave her a bow. "It was a pleasure, lass, and I do hope to see you again."

"I'd like that." She'd not the heart to tell him how unlikely it was that they two would ever speak again.

It was then the horn blew. And her heart dropped to her feet.

Chapter Three

"WOMEN left side, men on the right." The tent steward's voice carried over the uproar of the crowd and was echoed by many of the guards as they pointed for the entrants to move into the proper positions. "No weapons!"

Macrath raked his gaze through the throngs of men and women who moved in droves toward their respective spots. The two lines of competitors looked like cattle going to slaughter. None of them had their weapons—and he'd been extremely loath to leave his father's prize sword in his tent. Without anyone to guard it, he was certain it would disappear—that was, if anyone could find it. He'd buried it in the ground beneath his bedroll and prayed anyone looking to loot would do so without the time to dig.

His stomach growled. It'd been a long day of travel for them with only a paltry meal of jerky and stale bannock cakes. There'd not been much time to prepare, and Leticia had seen to it that a meal befitting a man and woman going into battle was not procured. With the stint it took to get to Sìtheil, there'd been no time to hunt. His last meal had been that morning. Thank goodness for the barrels overflowing with water, else his stomach would be eating him alive.

Would the council feed them a meal befitting men and women going to their deaths? Or would they consider it a cost best saved?

Macrath glanced at the men lining up beside him. His assigned place was front and center.

Men as tall as he and some bigger had entered the games, but they were few and far between. Perhaps only a quarter of the entrants would give him a run for victory. It looked like most of the clans sent in men they wished to punish or simply for population control. If—no, *when*—he won these games, one of the first items of concern on his agenda would be to find a means to do away with the entire brutal proceedings.

While he observed all the men he would be going up against for a claim to the Morrison seat—some four dozen at least—his eyes kept sliding over to the female ranks. He tried to tell himself it was because he wanted to see the lot of potential brides. After all, he'd have to wed and bed the woman for five years at least—and for him it might be a lifetime commitment because, if that union were to bear fruit, he'd not leave any child a bastard as he'd been.

No. None of his offspring would ever endure the torment he himself had. So indeed he was examining the women as they passed him and those who were already in line. He was taking note of the weaker ones and the ones who might even be able to take him on in a fight. He searched the lines of women for Rhona from his clan and found her chatting with another woman—perhaps she'd been smart and was connecting with potential allies. Or mayhap she just needed to pretend she was anywhere but here. Rhona was an entrant who'd been sent unwillingly. If there was anything Macrath could have done to be sent off on his own, he would have. But, that was impossible.

Even still, no matter how many allies Rhona had, there were enough behemoth women warriors to crush a half dozen opponents at once. If he found her upon the field he would protect her—pair with her for protection, though she'd likely offer him little. Macrath's gaze roved away from Rhona, guilt souring his countenance. It wasn't his fault that Leticia had chosen Rhona, but it could be his fault they'd sent in entrants at all. It was not required for the clans to send in fighters. But if they did not, they'd have to stay to themselves. No growth in power or coin. Staying stagnant for five years was a lot to ask of an ever-populating holding.

Pain started to throb above his right eyebrow. The way it did whenever he was thinking too hard and long about one thing—and not finding a reasonable solution.

Swallowing away his ire, he again assessed the prospective bride pool.

Aye, he may have been giving the illusion of looking through the throngs and assessing every entrant, but what he was really trying to do was find the gorgeous lass he'd encountered by the water barrels. A spark of interest had ignited within him the moment he laid eyes on her. A tiny flame he'd not yet been able to extinguish. Macrath rarely messed with women—unless the physical need reached a point at which he might engage in brawling in order to release some pent-up energy. But even then, he took precautions to ensure no bastards came of the frenzied unions.

So why now did he find himself desiring Ceana? Why, when nothing could come of it?

A vision of her flashed in his mind as he assessed the faces and hair of the women lining up in a myriad of muted and bright-colored plaid gowns.

Wild auburn hair had framed her face in wet tendrils. Almond-shaped eyes the color of the sea lined with dark long lashes. Skin that was creamy enough to think she'd taken a bath in milk and spice. Though her gown had seen better days—probably years before—she carried herself with all the superiority of a royal. She outranked all the others, not only in beauty, the strength of her shoulders, but also in her wit. He was impressed that she could be wry and funny in a situation as tense and dangerous as theirs.

Another horn blew, vibrating inside Macrath's gut and sending a thrill rushing through him. He curled his fingers against his palm. He was ready for the games to begin.

"All right, you pitiful whelps, get to your lines!" The tent steward was joined by the gate steward and two other men he'd not seen before.

At the man's bellow everyone rushed, several shoving forward and jostling those in front of them—a few fell, getting trampled. Being in the front line, Macrath helped people to right themselves and shouted at those who were shoving. But his warnings to slow down were ignored by those hastened on by the stewards.

As he righted yet another victim, out of the corner of his eye he observed a woman easily as tall as he shove forward, knocking someone else to the ground. The downed female's cries for help were outweighed by the sound of the stewards herding the masses. No one went to her aid, instead walking right over her, happy to see her buried in the dirt.

"Move aside, you horse's arses!" Macrath shouted. When he bent down to help the slight lass, he noted her hair as red as berries and creamy, soft skin. She was the one he'd been looking for. *Ceana.*

His heart pounded against his ribs, breath hitching in a way that made him want to smack sense into himself.

"Och, lass, are ye all right?" he asked, keeping his grip on her arms and tugging her up close. Closer than he needed to. She was tiny and he had the overwhelming urge to keep her against him to protect her. And then he noticed the plushness of her breasts pressed against his chest, and his thoughts turned decidedly southward. She was soft, warm, and gods, but he could picture her lying naked with him beneath the moon and stars. Her skin would glow in the moonlight, and he'd—

Ceana's stormy eyes locked on his, a question, fear, and most of all, strength spinning in their depths. The look was enough alone to halt his wild hunger—well, somewhat anyway.

"As well as I can be," she said with a shaken smile, her gaze darting all around as though she expected to be roughly yanked from his arms and tossed back to the ground.

Macrath smiled back. "Are you hurt?"

She shook her head, her hair loosening all the more and whipping against her cheeks. "I'll live."

"I hope you do." And he meant it in more than just this moment. Out of all the women in the games, he wanted Ceana to win. Because he intended to win. And if they should both raise their arms in victory when the final game was over—they'd be married.

Aye, 'twould be a marriage of convenience, nothing more, but even knowing that, he was willing to dive headlong to the kirk with her. The thought both thrilled and disturbed him. Macrath had always imagined himself marrying at some point for several reasons, one being that he'd like to be able to bed a woman whenever he pleased and not be worried about the bastard born of it. But the other reason was entirely of a more vulnerable nature. He was lonely. He wanted someone to wake up with every morning. Someone who looked forward to him returning after a day's worth of training and a body to pray for him when he was away fighting wars.

And he could picture Ceana—above any of the other women here—being that woman for him. That was all it was. He didn't want to marry any of the other women. She would do. He'd have to make sure she stayed alive.

A warrior pushed from the opposite direction of the throng and gripped Ceana's elbows. Macrath's gut reaction was to tug her back, but the way she looked at the stranger showed she knew him.

He glowered at Macrath as he spoke. "Are you all right, my—"

But Ceana cut the man off before he could finish. "I am not hurt, Aaron." She squared her shoulders and stepped away from Macrath, causing his hands to fall from her arms. "Go back to your spots, and I'll go to mine." She looked first to Aaron and then to Macrath. "I don't want either of you to get into trouble for breaking rank."

Macrath heard her words, but he was still thinking about her friend's speech. She was a lady. He was certain the man was going to call her *my lady*. Or was he going to call her something else—something endearing, like *my darling* or *my sweetheart*? That thought sent a pang of jealousy through him. And not a feeling he wanted to have. Especially not going into a war game. Perhaps distance would do him good. He'd known the lass for less than a few hours, and already he was imagining the sun glistening off her hair as dawn awakened. Not any way to win this thing, with his cock doing the thinking for him.

The man she called Aaron eyed Macrath as though he'd threatened to scoop her up and serve her to his clan for dinner. Was it jealousy he saw in the other man, or was it simply overprotectiveness? Macrath grinned. Truth be told, he'd been thinking about just that. He might scoop her up, but the only one he'd be serving was her—and pleasure would be all he offered.

Hell and damnation. His body reacted quickly to the thought, pumping blood from his limbs to his groin. He refused to shift, which would only draw attention to his discomfort. Instead, he kept his eyes steadily on Aaron a moment longer, then turned to Ceana.

He studied her face, taking in the few freckles that dotted her nose. "I wish you well, Ceana."

"And you," she said. There was a moment of hesitation. A moment where she looked as though she wanted to say something more. She chewed her lip, squinted her eyes.

And he too wanted to say more. To tell her to find him as soon as she could, so he could offer her protection. To tell her that she should hide wherever she could to outlast as many as she could. To offer *something* that would help her survive. Hell, she'd fallen on the walk to supper.

But before he could mouth a coherent thought, she turned her back on both of them and shoved her way into the horde of women. This time around, she did plenty of her own elbowing and cursing as she made her way to her assigned row. Macrath found himself smiling after her, but a grunt to the side of him wiped his smile clean.

"Stay away from her," Aaron growled. "I served her brother, and he'd not take kindly to his sister being devoured by a brute like you."

Macrath raised a brow, not deigning to waste a breath on the jealous man's warning.

"Just leave off." Aaron returned to his spot in the ranks parting from Macrath to search out Ceana in the crowd of women.

The horn blew again, and anyone left in the path between the men's and women's lines was shoved aside by guards as the two strangers he'd seen earlier rode in on horses along with three additional people—one of whom was a woman.

They were all dressed in regal plaids, fully decked out in weapons and with thick gold royal arms pins holding their plaids in place. These were the members of the royal council in charge of the games. And a woman? Macrath had not known there was a woman involved. Though he supposed he should have. These games were all about equality—men and women put to the same tests. It made sense that a previous Lady Morrison would be here to pass the sword on to the next.

She stared at the female side of the warriors, her gaze raking them over yet revealing nothing. When she turned to the men, she did much the same. She was beautiful, and strength emanated from her that made her seat upon the horse and position in the council believable.

"Warriors! Welcome to the twentieth annual war games!" shouted the female council member.

A roar went up in the crowd, and Macrath found himself cheering too, his fist pumping into the air. As before, the thrill of battle rushed through him.

"Quiet!" bellowed several of the guards.

The woman smiled, and there was a harshness to her that Macrath hadn't seen before. "I entered these games once. Won them, in fact, fifteen years ago." He'd not seen from this distance her age, but she had to be in her forties. The passage of time had done her well.

"The rules," she called out and snapped her fingers. A steward rushed forward and handed her a thick leather casing. She opened the case and withdrew a parchment scroll. "As you know, the rules are changed for every game so as to be fair to each entrant. No one can prepare for what is to come—and trust me, none of you are prepared."

Macrath swallowed. He'd been through war. Been tortured and tormented by his stepmother. Been through hell with being repeatedly jumped by his half brother's friends every time they were so deep in their cups they didn't know when to stop. Been left in the woods by his stepmother to suffer the terrors of night before he reached his tenth birthday—she'd hoped he wouldn't make it. But Macrath was a survivor as well as a warrior.

Across the crowd, he caught sight of Ceana. She was staring at him, eyes wide. He wished he could give her some of his strength. Ease the fear he knew she must be feeling inside. He smiled at her, hoping to give her some peace, and was rewarded with a slight lift of her lips.

"There will be no supper. You've all been called here because the games begin tonight!"

At that, a storm of guards weaved through the lines of men and women, patting them up and down in search of any hidden weapons. Men and women were yanked to the center and thrown on the ground in front of the council members, their *sgian dubhs* and whatever other weapons they'd hidden up their sleeves or down their boots tossed beside them.

"Some of you did not follow the rules. No quarter given!" shouted the woman.

The dozen or so entrants who'd not followed the rules were lifted up to their feet and dragged down the line to wooden stakes that were once trees stripped of their branches. They were tied to the stakes, backs exposed with a quick swipe of a knife.

"Rules are important here. We heed them. Live by them. *Die* by them."

At the last of her words, the beatings commenced with those attached to the posts. It was unbearable to watch, even for Macrath who'd seen much. The guards were relentless, brutal. Skin flayed open, blood spraying, screams pummeling the air.

"We'll wait," the woman said, rolling her eyes.

Heartless bitch. He knew his stepmother to be callous, but this woman—she was a hundred times worse. Were all the women who won the games destined to become like her? Hard, cruel, vicious?

Would Ceana?

"Oh, I've had enough. Silence them," she ordered the guards. They stepped up to the victims and slit their throats. Several gasps went up through the ranks. To the rest of the crowd, she turned her implacable gaze and said, "No quarter given."

A cold feeling settled in Macrath's stomach. A feeling of reality that he'd not had before. And the only thing he could do about it was move forward, because to look back was out of the question.

"Each war game has a set of five games—one for every year you will rule. Each of the five games has a set of rules, and rather than waste my breath telling those of you who will not be here to face them, I give out the rules for each game just before we set you loose." Her grin was overexcited, hungry. "At the end of the fifth game, only two of you will be standing here before me. One male. One female. Before you're allowed to rejoice in having survived, you will be wed and a contract signed."

The crowd was silent, not one person wanting to anger this woman who saw to it that anyone not abiding her rules was executed on sight.

"With each game, not only will you fight each other but another common enemy. Only the fiercest and strongest among you shall win." She raised her hand and pointed down the field toward the thick wall that lined the back of Sìtheil Castle's outer courtyard. "You will go through the gate—and we will close the door behind you. No one shall seek safety behind these walls save the guards, stewards, and us on the royal council. We shall blow a horn when you are to exit these walls, and we shall blow the horn when we want you to return. A third horn will blow when those who've survived the round have crossed through the gate. If you hear three horns, best turn your blade on yourself, for we will give no quarter to those who do not return in time."

The female council member turned to the man beside her and inclined her head. He nodded and continued with the rules.

"Through the gate you will go and cross the rear bridge to the field. Strewn among the thick grass are the weapons we've chosen to give you for this round. Seize them. There are not enough for everyone. Cunning plays a part in this game. A ruler must not only be good with strength of body but strength of mind and heart."

The third council member pushed his horse forward and faced the crowd. "Prepare yourselves, for you have enlisted in the sacred war games. Games that have given peace to our lands for a hundred years. You are now a part of this peace, this spiritual reckoning. May the gods protect you and bring us the one male and female who shall rule Sìtheil Castle with iron fists!"

All the ruling council raised their fists in the air, and once they issued a battle cry, the whole of the field did too.

But overshadowing that cry were hundreds of tumultuous thoughts, fears, wishes.

Above all that was the sound of the horn and then the thundering of feet as the crowd of men and women rushed the gates.

The game was on.

Chapter Four

FOR the span of a breath, Ceana stood rooted in place. Her feet would not budge. Her limbs ignored all imploring from her to move. The sound of the horn still echoed in her ears. Around her, women scrambled, and others stood just as immobile as she. The sun was beginning to set, and within the hour they'd all be blanketed in darkness.

That was when the true nightmare would begin. When she was blinded both by darkness and fear.

With her next inhale, her entire body came to life. Ceana leapt forward, arms outstretched as though she'd wade through the sea of people in order to make it to the gate. All happened in impossibly slow motion. With her right hand she gripped one woman's shoulder in front of her and with the left another, propelling herself forward and between them before grabbing on to the next.

"Get off me!" someone shouted.

"Move!" called another.

"What do you think you're doing?"

"Bitch!"

Ceana gritted her teeth through it all, saving her breath, her life's essence. But that last one brought an ironic smile to her face. The Bitch of MacRae. Well, she'd live up to it because, dammit, she was going to *live.*

The gate was within feet of her when she felt arms grabbing at her from behind. She shoved at them, feeling the sharp nails of her assailant dig into her skin.

"No!" Ceana cried. She'd come this far and would not allow someone to yank her back. She was going to get to that field. She was going to find a weapon. She would prevail.

But the hands were strong, tugging, scratching. Anger boiled in her, giving her a feral edge, and she fisted her hands, pummeling at those who grappled with her, emitting a noise from her own throat she'd never heard before. Half growl, half shriek.

At last she broke free and dove through the gate, stumbling with the speed but forcing herself not to lose her ground. Ceana sprinted forward as though the damned MacLeods were on her heels—and they very well could have been. Her feet pounded over the wooden bridge and then sunk into the wetted grass, splashes of water and mud flicking up onto her. But she didn't slow. Didn't look back.

She darted this way and that. Between women and men who scrambled in the grass on hands and knees to find a weapon. Spun away from those who had already procured their weapons and were eager to slice her in two. Leapt over the bodies of those who'd not been so lucky. This was battle. But worse than any battle she'd ever witnessed, for there were no sides. She was her only ally, and everyone else wanted her dead.

Ceana rushed to the left as far afield as she could without gaining attention from anyone wanting to chase after her—including the guards up on the wall who had been ordered to shoot any who deigned to run from the games. Though she looked all around her, making certain not to lose track of her scrambling enemies, she flicked her gaze all around the ground, searching for some sign of difference. A glint of metal off the fading sun. A discoloration in the grass. Something. Anything.

She had to have a weapon.

A couple of dozen paces ahead, there was a disturbance in the grass. Long, brown. Could be a snake. But could also be a bow—and she was damned good with a bow.

"Mine!" shouted She-muscle—a woman Ceana had never wanted to see again. The woman gritted her teeth as she barreled through the grass toward the bow, trying to outrun Ceana. "Better run, little chickie, before I see my arrow through your heart."

Ceana's heart already pumped hard from running for her life, from having to fight through the throng by the gate. And now added to that was her fear. She-muscle would kill her. There was no doubt in her mind. But she couldn't let that happen. Not when she'd not even made it to the wood's edge.

As much as her legs screamed in protest, she pushed harder, faster, reaching the bow just seconds before She-muscle. She ducked low to the ground, grabbing it up and skidding out of the way of She-muscle's outstretched arms.

No arrows.

"Dammit!" Ceana swung the bow over her head and shoulder and kept going, one glance over her shoulder to make sure She-muscle wasn't coming after her. But the behemoth was bent over where she'd stopped running, hands on her knees.

She could make arrows. But she couldn't do it if she were dead.

"We'll meet again, pretty lassie!" the woman shouted.

Ceana gritted her teeth. She certainly hoped not.

Lungs starting to burn, she had to find shelter soon or she'd collapse. Thank goodness she'd been active. Hunting, running, climbing. All because they were constantly being invaded. In a sick sort of way, she had her enemies back home to thank.

Even when they were having a moment of peace, Dougal had made sure the clan was prepared. They often had physical challenges, and though Ceana didn't always come in first, she worked darn hard to get close. Oh, just thinking of her brother made Ceana's heart ache. Life would never be the same without him. Tears started to blur her vision, and she swiped them free. Wouldn't do now to go blind with sorrow. Entering in the games would have been all for naught, and she had a lot of people counting on her to succeed.

She kept her gaze riveted for arrows but saw none.

A few more strides and she'd be within the woods. Ceana pushed herself harder, aware of all the other bodies breaking through the foliage, feet slamming down onto the forest floor. Those that had made it this far were no longer bent on killing anyone they saw. In fact, her gaze connected with several who turned away, ignoring her presence, and she did the same, recalling that though they were all enemies, they would face a common foe within the forest.

A shiver snaked over her, and she stumbled over a thick root jutting from the earth. She crashed hard, hands and knees striking the ground, teeth biting into the tip of her tongue. Ceana cried out, blood coating the inside of her mouth. She spit and pushed herself up, body so sore and tired she nearly collapsed back onto the forest floor. But somehow she found the will to push ahead.

Within the shroud of the forest, the light of the waning sky diminished. Even with her vision lessened, Ceana ran blindly forward, aware of only one thing—finding shelter.

The sound of beating drums caused Ceana's steps to falter. What did the drums mean? She turned in a circle, eyes taking in every inch of bramble, pines, oaks, leaves on the ground, roots jutting up like snakes ready to bite, fallen branches, and trees that gave into age and rot. Animals scurried. Birds took flight. Though she'd been in plenty of forests in her life, somehow this one seemed like a whole new world. Because this forest meant more than any other. This forest was a murdering place. A haunted woodland filled with death and dying.

But the drums? What did they *mean*?

The vile woman atop the horse had mentioned horns. Not drums.

With the beat of the drums, the light of the setting sun slowly faded like the flap of a tent gently folding in on itself until finally all light disappeared, blanketing her in darkness. Ceana felt around blindly, searching for a tree she could put her back up against. Her fingers caught the roughness of bark, and she turned, pressing her spine against it, facing the darkened forest and blinking until her eyes began to adjust.

It didn't really matter how much her eyes adjusted because there was barely a drop of light filtering through from her spot. It was as if she'd found the only corner in all the forest where the leaves had yet to fall. Cursing herself for not paying better attention, she crouched to the ground, searching for anything she could use as a weapon. Rocks, thick sticks. Her fingers slid through leaves and dirt, a few tiny sticks, and equally tiny rocks. Nothing very useful. Nothing she could make an arrow with.

She bit her lip, suppressing a curse that might alert any foe to her whereabouts.

Howls filled the night, making all the blood drain from her face and limbs. She jerked her back against the tree, stomach flipping. Her hands trembled.

Wolves.

Dozens of them.

They cried out into the night sky. It was a warning to all those in the forest that they were on the prowl. That they'd hunt down any who lingered. But also a call to the pack to join together.

Ceana's breath hitched, her heart pounding against her ribs, echoing dully in ears.

This was the first round. Hungry wolves who would tear the flesh from their bodies. And from the sound of it, they'd sent out enough to pick apart at least a third of the entrants.

Tears streamed down her face as fear took hold. To be mauled by a wolf was a horrible death. Worse than being struck down by your enemy who might show you mercy. It was painful. Gory. And how could she outrun a wolf?

Even at her fastest, she'd not be quick enough.

Hopelessness encased her, dragging her down to the ground where she stayed, tears streaming down her face and body shaking. She'd not the ability for this. Aye, she was a trained hunter, had taken down many game in her lifetime. But wolves?

Ceana had had nightmares about wolves since she was a lass.

Her father… The late Laird MacRae had been attacked by a pack of wolves. Shredded from limb to limb along with the guard he'd traveled with.

To come up against one of her darkest fears was unthinkable.

She'd fail.

Deep in her heart, she believed that. How could she have ever thought she'd survive these games? She should have offered herself up to the MacLeod warrior when she'd encountered him in the cave. Should have died beside Dougal. But to have done that would have meant disappointing her clan. Sentencing them to certain death.

A low rumbling growl came from her right. Ceana froze. Eyes widening in the dark, and without moving, she tried to see. Tried to figure out just where that growl was coming from. Imagined thin, black, wolfish lips pulled back, revealing long, sharp teeth glistening with saliva. Eager to tear her apart.

Uncertain of where the growl was coming from as it sounded all around her, inside her, Ceana leapt to her feet, whipped around, and grabbed hold of the tree. She yanked her skirt up, biting the hem so it wouldn't tangle, and jumped into the air, gripping a branch overhead. Wrapping her legs around the thick trunk, her feet pinned to the bark, she pulled herself up, ignoring the scratches to her sensitive skin.

Animal instinct within her bid her to make the leap.

This was survive or die.

Moments before, she'd been immobile, but not now. Not when death growled at her.

Her palms were sweaty, making it hard to grip, but hold tight she did, inch by ever-loving inch. The growl came closer, followed by another. There was more than one wolf ready to make a meal out of her. But not now. Not this minute. Hopefully not this hour. And if she had to sleep in this tree all night and stay up here the remainder of the next day, so help her gods, she would.

Ceana swung her leg up around the first thick tree limb she could find that felt sturdy enough to hold her and was high enough away from the beasts.

She straddled the limb, tucking her legs around it, shaking uncontrollably as sobs escaped her. She was tough, she knew that. But anyone would cry when they came face-to-face with death and their nightmares come to life. *Anyone*, she kept telling herself. She was weak because of the tears. And yet she was strong for having risen up and escaped. For having found a way to survive this.

Three orange, glowing sets of eyes stalked toward the tree where she was perched, their growls vibrating through her insides. Thank goodness for the lack of food, else she would have certainly messed herself by now.

She was shaking so hard she feared she'd fall. Laying her belly down on the branch, she ignored the stabs of tiny twigs against her breasts and abdomen. One of the wolves leapt up into the air, snapping his teeth. She jerked, only held in place by the death grip her arms had around the tree limb. He didn't get close enough, not even by two feet. Even still, the saliva foaming around his snout managed to splat against her cheeks. His fellows took his cue, jumping up into the air, leaping toward her, pawing at the tree. From their shadowed figures, they looked half-starved. This was how the game stewards ensured they would kill many, she mused. They made sure they were hungry.

Well, she was too. Hungry to live.

Damned starving.

A snap of a twig from somewhere below stilled the three wolves, their ears perking. Oh, gods… Someone was there.

"Stay away! Wolves!" Ceana cried, hoping to warn whoever it was off a heinous death, but she was too late. The wolves pounced, and though she could not see who the woman was, her death cries echoed painfully though the forest.

Ceana squeezed her eyes closed, unwilling to lay witness to any of it. The screaming didn't last long, the woman's cries fading to nothing and the only sound that of the wolves feasting on her flesh. Keeping her eyes closed, Ceana whispered prayers to the gods that they protected the woman in her afterlife.

"Protect *me*," she whispered.

No sooner were the words out of her mouth than a blast of air slapped her cheek and a sting sliced her ear. Jolting up, she saw an arrow protruding from the tree and quickly grabbed it before ducking back down.

"Are you dead up there?" It sounded like She-muscle.

"There are wolves!" Ceana called down, swallowing hard. She fumbled to pull her bow over her head and nock the arrow. "And no." Not yet, and gods willing, not at all.

"We'll have to remedy that." A wave of relief flowed through her when the woman stepped under the tree, her arrow pointed upward. It wasn't She-muscle, but a woman half her size. Why she cared, she didn't know. Only one of them could win this.

"There are..." Ceana swallowed, her voice catching on her fear. She pointed her own arrow at the woman. "Wolves. They were just here."

Her attacker wrenched her arm back, prepared to shoot, and Ceana did the same. "Wolves you say? I don't see—"

Her words were strangled on a cry of pain as one of the wolves launched itself at her, knocking her to the ground. Ceana let her arrow fly, sinking it into the wolf's shoulder. The animal howled but only seemed to take his anger out on his victim. Her screams echoed in the darkness. But the sound ebbed, warbling into silence as his mighty jaws wrapped around her throat.

What little moonlight shown through the leaves caught her lifeless eyes directed at Ceana.

She shivered, and tears streamed down her face in earnest. In every victim she saw her father. Saw his death. Saw her own. And yet she lived.

Not wanting to be left out of the spoils, the other two wolves leapt on the dead body below her. But the wolf who'd won this woman's life did not want to share. The animals started to tear into one another, blood splattering up into the tree. Ceana wasn't sure whose it was—the wolves' or their victim's. The stark ferocity of it startled her. She jerked enough to the right when a glob of something flew up that her balance shifted. Hands covered in sweat lost their grip, and her limbs, so tired from running, from climbing, from gripping, seemed to forget how to hold on. She fell sideways and scrambled to grasp, wrapping her arms tight around the trunk, her legs dangling.

"No! Oh, gods, no!" She screamed as she felt herself slipping, preempted the feel of the wolves' teeth on her legs. Clenched her eyes tightly closed and let all her fear out in a scream she hoped toppled trees.

But her grip held tight, and their teeth never came. Instead, painful yowls.

Ceana opened her eyes to see Macrath finish off the last of the wolves with a wicked ax before stepping up to her and wrapping his hands around her waist.

"I've got you, lass."

She opened her mouth to give him her thanks, but no words came, and even if they had, the enormity of what he'd done for her deserved more than a simple thanks.

"You can let go of the tree."

Glancing upward, she saw her hands still wrapped around the limb she'd fallen from. "I don't know that I can."

"Trust me, lass." He was tall enough that, with her hanging from the tree, they were at eye level with each other. She stared into his eyes, felt herself sinking, and then her arms were around his neck, her face pressed to his shoulder and a torrent of tears pouring out.

"I trust you," she sobbed. "Thank you. Thank you. Thank you."

"Hush, now. You don't want to call any more attention to us. We're not wholly safe."

Ceana forced her sobs to quell and nodded. She searched the ground for signs of her opponent's arrows, but found only one broken one.

Macrath's gaze darted around. "We must go." He lifted her into his arms and started to run.

She clung to him, fearing for both their lives and mumbling that he could put her down, but glad when he didn't. If she weren't scared for her life, she might have marveled at his strength in running up a hill encumbered by her weight, but the sounds of death all around them kept her firmly praying they'd make it to higher ground.

Macrath crested a hill, paused, and turned in a circle. Then he darted to the right and gripped her tight as he half ran, half slid down an embankment. At the bottom of the gorge, he raced beneath a niche provided by overhanging tree roots, hiding them both from enemies above.

Their breaths came fast, and still clinging to him, she pulled back, her gaze locking with his once more. "What a miracle it is that you found me. I'd have been dead by now." Her voice shook in a way she wished she could flatten. But it felt like her whole body was wobbly, burning, and so out of control. Even her toes were trembling.

His lips quirked up in a smile that had her imagining they were anywhere but here. "I admit to following you. You're one hell of a runner."

"Oh," she breathed. He still held her tightly, cocooning her in warmth and safety.

"Took me a little while to find you. And I'm glad I did."

"I'm glad you did too."

Macrath set her on her feet, where she swayed until she wrapped her fingers into his shirt to steady herself.

"Why did you follow me?" she asked. Lifting the skirt of her gown, she wiped at the grime on her face and shivered.

"Because..."

He paused for long enough that Ceana wasn't sure if he'd say anything more. Thought maybe he'd heard something and so she tilted her head, hoping to hear what it was. What she did hear made her whimper in the back of her throat. The sounds of death filled the forest.

"I don't know," he whispered.

She glanced down to stare at his hand pressed to her elbow. Heat singed through the fabric of her sleeves to brand her flesh. His touch was light, but so heavy. And she wanted more of it. Desperately needed it.

"I don't know," he said again.

When she looked up at him, their eyes locked, and she sank deeper into him. Wanting in this moment to be anywhere other than where they were. Wanting in this moment for him to kiss her. To stroke her arms, her waist… To touch him.

She slid her hands up his arms, over his shoulders, pressed them to his chest where she felt his heart beat a rapid pace against her palms. A surge of desire encompassed her. The need to celebrate life in the midst of death.

"I'm glad you did," she too repeated her words.

And then she closed her eyes, lifted up on her tiptoes and waited for his kiss to take her to oblivion.

Chapter Five

MACRATH gazed down at Ceana's closed eyes, soft lips waiting for his kiss. And he desperately wanted to kiss her. To escape this moment if only for a breath. To give her the comfort she sought, and take his own in return.

He was shocked by how much he wanted her. Cared about her. Why else would he have followed her? Maybe it was an inner strength he saw that reminded him of himself, or maybe he even wanted to leach some of it, absorb it. Just being near her, he felt like a better man.

But did he deserve her? She was a lady—or at least he was pretty sure she was. He might be the son of a powerful earl, but he was a bastard. Would a lady see it to her advantage to marry him? All his life he'd had it drilled into his head that she would not.

But wasn't that what winning these games was all about? Victory and respect?

And she *wanted* him to kiss her. Perhaps just as much as *he* wanted to kiss her.

What was one kiss? The meeting of lips and the sharing of a moment of pleasure. One kiss couldn't hurt.

Macrath dipped his head, catching the warmth of her soft lips on his. At just that one brush, a fire ignited inside him. Desire flamed by fear and the need to survive, the need to protect her. Macrath slid his hands around her back, splaying one against the small indent above her behind and the other across the top of her spine. He hugged her close, cradling her against him as he continued to softly press his lips on hers.

Her skin was cold and soft and sweet, like cream.

He tilted his head, slanting his lips across hers and gently swiping his tongue across the plush flesh of her mouth. Ceana sighed into him, sinking, tugging. Her fists were wrapping into his shirt at his chest. That small sigh, that one little sign of her pleasure, sent a thrill of yearning through him. She liked him kissing her. And he liked it too. More than liked it. Wanted to stay like this forever.

Macrath nibbled at her lower lip, tugging gently. When she gasped, he teased her teeth and the tip of her tongue with his, giving her a satisfied sigh of his own. He'd never enjoyed a kiss more. Never wanted a lass as much as he wanted Ceana. Tracing a path from her lower back to her hip, he softly massaged the gentle swell. She tucked herself closer to him, a silent message she enjoyed his touch. Wanted more of it.

With his thumb he rubbed her ribs, the tip brushing the underside of her breast. Ceana sucked in a ragged breath, a little whimper escaping on the way out. He stilled his hand, unwilling to move forward, reluctant to break the spell of their pleasure. But then she pressed her breasts closer to him. A silent invitation to explore her further.

Should he take it?

Every fiber in his lust-filled body strained to do so. But his mind warred against it. Thought of the implications. But then again, if they were to make it through the games together, they'd be wed. And if not… One of them would be walking on the other side.

Macrath shifted his hand upward, cupping the warmth of her breast, sliding his thumb over the puckered tip. He groaned, drinking in her soft moan of pleasure and wanting desperately to deepen their kiss, but also not wanting to scare her. Instead, he kept their kiss a light exploration. His touch at her breast a tentative tease. Ceana must have been encouraged by his touch and began a trail of her own up over his neck and through his hair. She tugged on the ends before sliding them down his back, feather-light.

His entire body reacted in a way he found both alarming and enthralling. Every light touch of her fingers was an intense slide of delicious pleasure. Macrath skimmed his mouth from hers to taste the side of her neck, felt the pulse of life in her veins beneath his lips. He gripped her buttocks, and she lifted a leg up, hooking it around his hip. Her back arched, and she pressed her blessed heat against him. Good gods, but he wanted her. Needed to feel the potency of life flowing through him like fire.

Ceana let out a moan that make his cock jerk with the need to be buried deep inside her, and he answered with a feral growl of his own. Tugging at the front of her gown, he freed the tops of her creamy breasts and pressed his face against them, breathing in her scent. When he flicked his tongue over one pink, pert nipple, Ceana cried out, fingernails digging into his shoulders.

And that was when reality came ratcheting back to him. Because he was ready to hike up her gown and thrust wildly inside her, and when their initial frenzy calmed, he wanted to spread out his plaid, lay her down, and show her what the word pleasure truly meant.

But they were in the midst of a war game, about to be gutted by wolves and men. Making love was the last thing they should have been doing. The truth hit him hard. And disappointment too. For he could have kissed and touched her for the rest of his days.

Macrath gently pulled away, staring into Ceana's bemused eyes. Gods how he wished there were more light for him to see her better.

Snarling from above made him stiffen. So entranced by Ceana, he'd not even noticed they were being stalked along the top of the ridge. The spell was most assuredly broken now.

"Stay behind me," he warned, then whipped around, grappling for the battle-ax he had strapped to his back. He tossed it from hand to hand.

A large wolf, bigger than the few he'd had to destroy before kissing Ceana, ran down the embankment. This one was darker too, no hints of silver but more black. His eyes were still yellow, and his teeth glowed white in the moonlight as he bared them. All he had to do was walk in a circle, draw the wolf in, and wait for the animal to pounce so he could raise his ax against him. It didn't take long before the wolf lunged, his big paws reaching for Macrath. Arching his arms back at just the precise moment, he brought the ax down, hitting flesh, muscle, and bone. The contact was accompanied by the cry of the wolf and Ceana's scream.

He'd buried the ax in the animal's chest, killing him instantly. Macrath pulled the weapon free and turned to ease Ceana's fear.

But she was gone.

Macrath whipped around in a circle, scouring every inch of the ravine within eyesight.

Calling out to her would only alert whoever waited on the fringes that she was alone. Hopefully she'd just found a tree nearby to scurry up until it was safe.

"Dammit," he cursed under his breath. He took off in the direction that he thought she'd headed, praying all the while that she'd not been snatched by some foe.

Ceana's cheeks flamed with heat. What had she done? Allowed the Highland warrior to kiss her, touch her intimately, and it had nearly gotten them both killed. As soon as she'd seen the ax hit the wolf, she knew that he would be safe and she could run away.

Run away from how he made her feel.

Run away from possibly endangering him further.

Run away from any hope that his kiss had brought.

Her booted feet crunched through leaves, fingers digging into the dirt as she clawed her way to the top. She was well aware that, without any arrows for her bow, if anyone were to come upon her, she'd be dead. Keen to any noise, she stayed away from the sounds of grappling humans and wolves. She yanked an arrow from a tree and another from someone's body, keeping one tucked into her belt and the other nocked in her bow.

Perhaps a quarter mile from where she'd left Macrath, she found a hollowed tree with an opening just tiny enough to fit inside but not deep enough that she'd be safe from a wolf who wanted to claw at her.

Rather than risk it, she again hiked up her skirts and climbed to a thick branch that she could lay across safely. Lying alone in the tree, the minutes ticked by like hours. She had no concept of time. Only the darkness. She lost count of how many horrid cries she heard. How many people she guessed had been killed.

It gave her plenty of time to feel guilty about leaving Macrath and their heated kiss. In one respect, she hated the way she'd responded, yet in another, she'd loved the curiosity and excitement that his touch brought. The idea that it was right and good. There had been a few lads she'd kissed over the years—even Aaron one late night during the Beltane festival—but none had made a fire ignite within her. None that made her wish for different things and hope for a better future.

Only one that made her want to strip off every inch of clothing until they were both standing nude beneath the moonlight. That was something she'd never even considered before, as she'd always thought to save her virginity for her husband. Perhaps that was what being on the fringe of death brought—the need for passion, for a connection.

While her maidenhood had always been safeguarded, all that was now thrown into the wind. If she won these games, she'd be forced to marry a man who could set her aside after their five years of ruling if he wanted to or if she chose to. Nothing was set in stone anymore.

Macrath had followed her. Wanted to keep her safe. Maybe, in order to make it to the end, they would be stronger if they joined together. But would he want to have her hanging around? Would he consider her to be a burden?

She'd never know if she didn't ask.

If he said yes, then she'd protect him as best she could and endeavor not to be an encumbrance to him. The upside for her was that she'd at least know the man she'd chosen would rule beside her and not some overbearing boar. That was if they made it. If he said no, then she'd leave him be, suffer quietly on the inside, but strive to live all the same.

But she'd never know if she didn't go and find him.

Ceana shimmied down the tree and tried to work her way back from where she'd come, but she'd gotten so turned around that it was impossible to tell if she'd even gone in the right direction. She never passed by the hollowed tree again or the ravine. Overtired, growing weak from lack of food and water, all the running she'd done earlier, her body and senses in a constant state of being hyperaware, Ceana began to slow. To stumble.

To fall asleep while walking.

It was time to resign herself to the fact that she'd not find Macrath. Shelter took precedence. She'd not last the rest of the night if she didn't take a moment to rest. In the morning, if the horns weren't blown, then she'd search for him, for water and berries or crab apples, but not now. Not in the dark. Not when she'd escaped death so many times already.

Not trusting herself to sleep in a tree and resigned to risking the wolves finding her, Ceana must have examined fifty trees before she found one with a hollow. A quick swipe with a stick proved no snakes dwelled inside. Hooking her bow and one arrow in the tree to conceal them, she climbed in, her back against the trunk wall, knees tucked up tight and the second arrow still clutched in her fist as a weapon.

A loud horn startled Ceana awake. She'd not even realized she'd fallen asleep. Light streamed through the opening of the tree hollow.

Game one. It was over! How many horns had been blown?

Fear and panic raced through her. Dear gods, she hoped she hadn't missed the first one. She gripped the sides of the hollow and peered outside. Though she saw no one, she heard the sounds of running feet everywhere. There was still time.

Not wanting to waste a single moment that could mean she missed the second horn, Ceana scrambled out of the tree and stood, stretching her limbs. She grabbed her bow and slung it over her shoulder, tucking the arrows into her belt. Which way should she go? Peering through the trees, it looked like those who were running were headed east.

Ceana ran. She didn't look back but concentrated on making her too-tired legs move as fast as they could. She'd rest later. Her mouth was dry, throat painfully parched. She'd drink later. Stomach twisted in knots. She hoped she'd be able to eat later.

With every step, she prayed she'd make it. Prayed Macrath made it. Prayed Aaron made it.

Even when her feet hit the wood of the drawbridge, she did not breathe a sigh because they had to get under the gate.

Every step took forever. Bodies jostled each other, everyone thinking the same thing—get through the gate. Oddly enough, no one tried to kill the other when they theoretically still had the right to do so. As if they all silently believed that if they'd made it this far they deserved to make it another round.

Under the gate!

She was through the gate, and the guards ordered their weapons to be surrendered. She gladly dropped the bow and arrows and kept on moving. Her footsteps pounded toward the list field where they'd take a count of who remained before… she didn't know what. But hopefully it included making sure the people she cared about were safe, then food, water, and her tent.

As she stood in the list field watching men and women file in looking just as bedraggled as she felt, Ceana realized there would be a moment in the future when either Aaron or Macrath didn't come back, or she didn't.

The thought was sobering. She pressed her hands to her knees and breathed deep, feeling her body shudder, her eyes threatening tears. The first game was over, and she'd made it. But there were no guarantees. No quarter given.

Ceana's eyes raked over every person that stumbled through the gates. Everyone looked worn out, tired. Some wounded, blood seeping from scrapes, gashes. Injured by human or animal, she couldn't tell. It wasn't until then that she paid attention to her own state. Her hands were bloody, arms scraped, and she was sure when she lifted her gown she'd find her legs in much the same condition. Looking at many of the others, she'd escaped with a marginal amount of injury.

All thoughts of her own injuries were banished when she saw a familiar person limping through the gate. 'Twas Aaron. She risked breaking rank to run toward him. His knee was bloody, plaid torn, shirt ripped and bloodstained. A long, jagged gash covered his face from his ear down to the center of his chin.

"What happened?" she asked.

Aaron laughed a little hysterically. "Got into a fight with a wolf. I won."

"Oh, thank the gods." She crashed against him, hugging him tight to her as though he were her own brother. Pulling back, she examined the gash. "You need to get this sewn up."

Aaron grunted. "In time, I suppose. Not sure how they treat their patients when the majority of us are supposed to die."

"But what of a disqualification?" Ceana asked, certain there had to be some way. They couldn't just let those injured suffer and send them back out into the games.

"Do you mean like the men and women strapped to the stakes? No quarter given. Remember?"

Ceana nodded, not having realized it before. No quarter given. Was it the game's motto? Then she hoped the gods *would* be forever in their favor, for they'd get little sympathy here on earth.

"Lassies on the left! Lads on the right!" shouted a guard, a chorus of others taking up the chant behind him.

"I have to go. Be safe." Ceana squeezed his hand, terrified for what was going to happen next.

"You do the same. I had little faith of finding you here," Aaron said, shaking his head and looking toward the ground. "I'm ashamed to admit it. But the way the warriors fight—and the wolves. I'm just glad you made it."

Ceana smiled, keeping any irritation she had at his words deep within her. Aaron didn't know her as well as she thought. And really, she didn't expect him to.

"We were both lucky this round."

Aaron nodded. "Go."

Ceana hurried back to the female side, all too aware that she'd not laid eyes on Macrath. Guilt filled her insides. Was she the reason he'd not returned? Had he still been looking for her? She shouldn't have run away. Dammit. If he didn't come back, it would be her fault.

Once back to her post on the women's side, she kept her gaze focused on the gate.

"Come through," she murmured. "Come through."

No one had walked beneath the stony arch for several heartbeats. The lines were formed on both sides and no sign of Macrath. A guard on horseback rode down the center of the lines toward the gate. The chinking of his horn, slung over his shoulder, as it slapped against his weapons beat like a silent call to all she feared.

"Macrath, where are you?" she said through gritted teeth.

"Hush!" a woman beside her said, elbowing her hard in the ribs.

Ceana pressed her lips together hard, prepared to pummel the woman. But then her eyes caught a figure bolting through the gate. Tall, powerful, dark, and handsome. *Macrath.*

A sob of relief escaped her lips, gaining her another elbow, and this time she reacted, stomping on the woman's foot, which caused her to yelp.

"Hit me again, and I swear I'll make sure we both get put up on the stake." Ceana was bluffing, of course, but the seething tone brooked no argument with the woman beside her who turned straight ahead.

Macrath raced toward the men's lines, his gaze raking over the women. She stared at him, willing him to look her way.

Finally he did. Their eyes locked from across the ranks as he stood front and center and she more toward the back of the female lines. Her knees shook, and gratefulness filled her heart. He'd made it.

As he gazed at her, Macrath's lips twitched. Not quite a smile, but she knew he wanted to. She chanced a smile his way. Quick, so that no one would see.

The horn blew—loud and long—the sound sending chills racing up and down her arms and legs, centering in her middle like a ball of heavy steel. Those who'd not crossed would be sacrificed to the gods. Before her, warriors began to bow their heads, and she did too. They all silently prayed for those who had been killed and for themselves for having made it.

The ground rumbled as several council members trotted their horses into the center of the lines. The former female victor raised her fist in the air, and everyone bent their necks backward to look up at her.

"Congratulations! You have achieved what to some was impossible. You have passed the first round of games. You need only pass four more to take your place on the throne of Sìtheil where you shall rule under His Majesty King Giric of Scotland as the Prince and Princess of the Isles."

This was something entirely new. Up until the previous game, it had been a seat of great honor and title—but to be named as royals? Gasps went up through the crowd. As if they'd not had enough to fight for before—they'd be placed in line for the Scottish throne.

"For now, you shall feast. You shall rest, for at the break of day, the next feat will be upon you."

The woman said no more. She nodded to her fellow council members and turned around to ride back toward the castle.

The tent steward stepped between the lines and raised his hands. "By our count, when there were one hundred sixteen warriors to start, there are now seventy-nine." He paused a moment, letting the numbers sink through. Over a quarter of the people

gone. Dead. "Go and get yourselves cleaned up. Buckets of water have been placed between the tents. You'll also find supplies to mend yourselves if needed. The horn will ring within the hour for the feast. Females in the top tent. Men below. No mingling."

What? His orders sank through Ceana like a sword to the gut. She wouldn't be able to speak with Macrath at all. She stared at him as the women around her began to move. He kept his gaze steady on her, then he nodded. Lips trembling, she wanted to cross the middle, to sink into his arms, to tell him she'd tried to come back to him, but she'd gotten lost. But she couldn't say any of those things, couldn't even mouth them, because a guard hustled Macrath along. With one last longing look at each other, they both made their way toward their tents to get cleaned up.

Ceana spent the day eating, drinking, and resting. The guards made sure that none of the men and women socialized. Even going so far as to send Boarg outside the castle walls to await the end of the games with the other servants.

When dusk settled, horns were blown—by the end of the games, when she won, one of the first things she'd do was banish them from being carried anywhere near her—and then the guards went through each tent to make sure everyone was tucked abed. And Ceana had waited until the last possible minute. Milling by the water barrels so she could see which tent Macrath had gone into. She'd been careful not to catch his eye, so that the guards' attention weren't drawn.

They were both lucky enough to have made it through the first round. Only the strongest survived, and there were still a lot of contenders. What would the next round bring? How would the council deign them fit to be princes and princesses? For they would certainly test them to the extreme.

This could very well be her last night alive. She felt more than lucky to have made it. Her survival was owed to Macrath. If he'd not happened by when the wolves were ready to pounce on her, she would have died.

Tonight she wanted to celebrate being alive, and she wanted to spend it with the one person she'd connected with. The one person who'd ensured that she'd made it. When all sounds outside her tent faded. No more rustling. No more footsteps.

Ceana stood and tiptoed to the tent opening. Heart pounding like a thousand drums, she cracked open the flap and peered out into the night. Torches were lit in the center between the sides, and several guards were posted.

Zounds. She should have known about the guards.

Well, it didn't matter. She'd sneak past them. If she could make it through the night in the woods, she could make it through a maze of guards.

Ceana pulled the plaid of her gown around the back up over her head, hoping to hide any glint of light off her fiery hair. She pulled off her boots, anticipating being barefoot would silence her steps. She slipped outside the tent, keeping her back flat against the fabric and cautiously checked her surroundings. There was no one within this line of tents, so she easily skipped to the very edge by the wall until she could press her back to the stones. She inched her way along until she came to the first of the female tents. There were no guards on the ground here, but they were high upon the wall. If they happened to look down, they'd find her.

There were six guards in the center, but they were all occupied passing around a flask of something—most likely whisky.

Taking a deep breath, she held it in, and when she was certain none of them were looking her way, she lifted her skirts and ran across the lane, ducking behind a tent so the guards on top of the gate wouldn't see her, and nor could those in the center.

She let her breath out slowly, her lungs burning painfully from having held it so long. When no one shouted at her or came running, she took assessment of her placement behind this tent as opposed to the water barrels. Macrath's tent should only be three to the right and two back.

Crossing the lane was the hardest part. Sneaking behind the tents until she was certain to be at the right one was easy. But if it wasn't the right one, she risked being called out by whatever stranger lurked within.

Ceana took one last look at the placement of the tent and was positive this was the one she'd seen him go inside. Taking another deep-drawn breath, she slipped her fingers through the flap and slowly pulled it open. Sprawled on his back with his arm flung over his face was Macrath. His chest was bare, and while he didn't wear his plaid pleated around his hips, it was flung over the tops of his thighs and abdomen.

Ceana let out her breath as she entered the tent. Before she could even draw in another, Macrath had sat up and swung his sword a foot from her throat.

"Ceana," he whispered. "I nearly gutted you." He set the sword back down. "What are you doing here?"

"I…" She stepped forward, her voice faltering. Ceana slipped her plaid from her head and knelt before him, her knees touching his thighs, the heat of his body warming her. "I need you."

Macrath didn't say anything. Simply stared at her, his face tight and filled with angst. But that disquiet quickly turned to hunger. He slipped his hand along her cheek and tugged her forward until his lips met hers. Warmth encompassed her, filling her body with fire, making her so weightless, she thought she could fly. Her insides pulsed, thrumming the same tune she'd experienced in the woods.

Oh, gods, but this was what she'd craved since last they'd parted.

They tumbled down to his bedroll, and she was filled with the scent of him, masculine, dangerous. And she loved every breath of it. If she were to die tomorrow, at least she would have one glorious night.

Game

Two

Chapter Six

IN the pitch black of Macrath's tent, the frenzied heat of their desire was made all the more potent by the danger incurred from sneaking inside.

Ceana was enveloped in warmth and pleasure, certain she never wanted to leave this spot or the fevered sensations filling her. What started as a frantic need to make love slowly turned languid as they both surrendered to pleasure.

Macrath stretched out beside her, smelling of clean, masculine skin and desire. One of his thighs possessively curved over the top of hers, pressing her into his bedroll. His arm curled beneath her head.

Heated lips trailed a searing path over her neck, the shadow of his facial hair scraping deliciously over her skin. A rough palm massaged her hip, and she tilted into him, her free leg hooked over his calf. She fought the need to wrap herself around his hard, hot body.

In complete darkness, their embrace should have felt anonymous, except it was anything but. She'd chosen to come to his tent. Chosen to give herself to him this night. Needed to escape the fear the games wrought on everyone. Death loomed, and right now she needed to feel alive.

She threaded her fingers through his hair, the softness of his locks tickling her palm and between her fingers. With her free hand, she gripped his biceps, marveling at his strength as he held himself slightly over her. He was so much bigger than she, making her feel an exciting thrill but also safe in his arms.

Ceana had never made love. Never done more than kiss a man before she met Macrath. And she was more than pleased to be here with him. If tonight were to be her last night alive—and gods willing it wouldn't be—but if it were, she was going to make the most of it. A soft sigh escaped her lips as his teeth grazed her earlobe. Yes, this one night she was going to give to herself. Saving her maidenhood for a husband who might never be seemed silly now.

She was eager to expand on the taste of pleasure he'd given her in the woods. Keen to let go of all the pain, terror, and anguish the past twenty-four hours had brought.

"Are you trying to seduce me, lass?" His breath tickled over her ear, tongue flicking at the sensitive flesh just below.

She slid her hand down his forearm, her fingers entwining with his. "Aye. Is it working?"

He chuckled, the noise rumbling in his chest, vibrating against her breasts. If only there were more light to admire him by. She could feel the ridges of his muscles, the subtle covering of chest hair beneath her palm as she slid her hand over to where his heart beat.

"I admit that I've never had a woman sneak into my place of rest before." He lifted upward, and she felt, rather than saw, him looking down at her.

She chewed her bottom lip, realizing just how bold she'd been sneaking in here, but she didn't care, nor would she change her mind if given the chance to do it again. "I am your first seductress, then?"

"Aye." There was a teasing lilt in his voice, and she could tell he was pleased.

Ceana smiled. She liked that she wouldn't be the only one with firsts tonight. Though from the way he touched her, she knew he was adept in the art of pleasuring. And oh, how she wanted to feel more. She arched her back, her hardened nipples rubbing against his chest. What would it feel like to tug down the front of her gown and let her bare flesh touch his?

"Och, lass," his lips grazed hers. "You tempt me to madness."

"Madness?" She felt some of that. Sensations whirled inside her that made no sense and that she could not explain, nor did she want them to cease, but to catapult her into another world.

"Aye." He swiveled his hips, pressing the hard length of his arousal against her hip. The feel of it sent a jolt of fire racing through her. "You have no idea..."

Ceana gasped. Theoretically, she did have an idea. Growing up, she'd seen plenty of animals mating, even seen the rocking of bodies beneath blankets when they made camp on journeys. And there was a deep yearning inside her. A need that probed the very edges of her sanity. If that was how he felt, then she could understand. Ceana trailed her bare toes up the back of his calf, the juncture of her thigh pressing hotly against his leg which was settled between both of hers. She stifled a moan of pleasure at the contact and pressed harder. Caressed his bare back, feeling the muscles ripple beneath her fingertips.

He nuzzled her nose. Kissed her temples, then brought their entwined hands to his lips and kissed her knuckles, his breath tickling her skin and sending a shudder through her.

"But we cannot," he murmured.

Ceana froze. Her hand stilled its exploration. Her foot dropped back to the ground. Confusion cleared her haze of desire and pleasure. "What?"

"Lass, why have you come to me?" Macrath still held her, made no move to leave her, only bewildering her more.

"Because I…" Her throat tightened. "Because I wanted to." She tried to tug her hand away, but he wouldn't let go, kept his grasp wound around hers.

"Aye, I gathered you would risk your life for desire, but what has fueled your need?"

She didn't hesitate in her answer. When Ceana made a decision, it was because she'd already had the chance to think about it. "You have."

Macrath chuckled softly. "You flatter me, but I know there is more to it than that."

Ceana huffed a breath and shoved against his chest. "Any man would be glad to take what I offer, but you shun me."

Macrath didn't budge. "I would never shun you." He gripped her hand and pulled it down to cup the long, solid length of his arousal. "Do you feel this? I want you."

Ceana shook her head. His naked length pulsed against her palm. "I don't understand. Why are you pushing me away?" He wanted her. She wanted him. Why did there have to be any question about it?

"I but wonder at your motivation. Did you come to me out of fear? Is that what has fueled your need?"

She faltered, her hand still pressed to his turgid flesh. How could she concentrate with his skin singeing her palm? "You make me feel... safe."

Macrath kissed her lingeringly on the forehead. It was a tender move. She closed her eyes, glad for the lack of light that hid her glistening eyes.

"Ceana, I'd never expect you to return the favor of my protection with... anything."

She huffed. "I did not come to you intent on paying for your protection or repaying you for favors."

Macrath let out a sigh. "And I'd not make love to you because of fear. I'd never take advantage of you." He let go of her hand, and in the shadows she thought she saw him swipe it through his hair. He appeared as frustrated as she was. "I want desperately to take off this gown of yours"—he plucked the fabric—"and ravish you until you scream with pleasure. But I won't. Not yet. We both need something to look forward to, despite our own needs to win this game. Let us save this—*us*—for a future prize."

She retracted her hand from his length and subtly pushed against his chest. It was hard to swallow around the humiliating lump in her throat. No matter what his pretty words meant, he was turning her down. Pushing her away. And despite the chill of knowing that, her body still burned for him. And that only made the sting of rejection worse.

Ceana cleared her throat. "Then I'd best return to my tent."

"Why?" he asked.

"Because you don't want me." She hated the way her voice quivered.

"That's not what I said, lass. I said let us not rush headlong into making love when it is fueled by fear. I'd not have you regret tomorrow that you shared yourself with me tonight."

"I'd never…" She felt her voice grow tight.

"You would. But if it's safety you seek, I can promise that."

Macrath rolled to the side and tucked her against him, one arm protectively draped over her waist and the other beneath her head. She hated the way she felt so safe cuddled in his arms.

She stared out into the void, emotions conflicted between embarrassment, relief and comfort. As much as she regretted admitting it, he was right. They'd known each other only a couple of days, and her fear, the rush of battle, and exhilaration of living had clouded her judgment. He'd saved her today. But that didn't mean she needed to make love to him—even if her body craved his touch.

His arousal pressed against her bottom, sending tremors of need pulsing through her. Despite the rational logic that ruled them both at the moment, it was obvious Macrath still wanted to fulfill their physical cravings just as much as she did.

And as greatly as she wanted to lie here beside him, to drink in his warmth and protection, *if* they were to stick with their convictions, she would need to return to her tent.

"I thank you," she said, lifting his arm away. She rolled up to her knees and turned to face him, finding his cheek with her palm. She leaned down and kissed him gently on the lips. "I wish you luck tomorrow, warrior."

"I cannot let you leave here alone. I will take you back," Macrath said.

Disappointment spread through her like the wind to a flame. Secretly, she'd hoped he would forget honor, throw caution to the wind and ravish her upon the floor.

"No need," Ceana said curtly, not wanting him to offer her protection after his show of restraint.

He sat up, slid his hand behind her head, and pulled her in for another kiss. "I insist. You mean something to me, Ceana, and I intend to see you make it through these games alive. With me."

She tried to ignore everything he'd said and all the implications that went along with it. Was Macrath essentially saying he wanted her to rule beside him?

"You owe me nothing, Macrath. Do not make promises neither one of us can keep."

Macrath stood and tugged her up. She waited for him to dress, glad he'd not responded to her so she didn't have to say anything more.

The return trip to her tent was easier than her arrival. Partly because Ceana knew the lay of the land and also because the guards upon the gate appeared to be in transition while the ones in the center lane were now extremely involved in a game of cards she was certain the council would not approve of.

Macrath's hand rested on the small of her back, and then his fingers entwined with hers. If she closed her eyes, she could almost imagine they were at some far-off castle, running through a garden maze with no worries in the world.

But his sudden stop, and her running smack into his back, was a reminder of exactly where they were. She opened her eyes and saw her tent a few feet ahead. "That one is mine," she whispered.

"I know." Macrath glanced over his shoulders, the moon catching in his eyes.

Even filled with fear, her heart skipped a beat. *He was watching me too.*

Zounds, but she was so confused. Her mind whirled in a hundred different directions, and she couldn't seem to get a good enough grip on what to believe and what to thrust aside as fantasy.

"Sleep well, lass."

Ceana squeezed his hand, wanting to lean up and kiss him, but doing so was wrong on many fronts—especially because when they kissed the world disappeared and they were more likely to be discovered.

She slipped toward her tent, and when she turned around, Macrath was gone.

The following morning, Ceana woke to the sound of horns blaring through the tents. And a headache that raged from temple to temple. Her muscles screamed with tension. Sitting up, she leaned all the way forward, reaching to her toes, stretching the muscles in her back and legs. She couldn't remember the last time she'd been this sore. How would she be able to run again today?

Everything that had happened over the past several days came rushing back with potent clarity. Death, terror, desire.

Whipping back her blanket, she stood and reached her hands to the low ceiling of her tent, her fingertips brushing the fabric. She rolled her neck. Water. She needed it badly. Her mouth was as dry as dirt.

Well, the only way to survive was not to dwell on the past. She had to start every day fresh and learn from her past mistakes. Like the huge one she'd made last night. Ceana pulled back the flap of her tent and stepped outside. A cool breeze lightly blew, and the pink-hued wakening sky was covered in light clouds as though threatening a storm by the end of the day.

Her path to victory was obvious. The only part that wasn't clear-cut was Macrath and how he played into her life. On the one hand, he made mention of them bonding together for the duration of the games, but in the same breath, told her he couldn't make love to her.

Now granted, he didn't say he wouldn't *ever* make love to her.

She rolled her eyes at the sky and decided not to think a moment longer on the warrior, even if he made her heart pound. It was a lot easier to dwell on her sore muscles and aching head.

Outside, women were emerging from their tents, many of them looking just as bad off as she. There was also an equal number of women who seemed in good spirits as though, instead of running and fighting for their lives the day before, they'd simply rested while servants fed them fruit and nuts. Without speaking to anyone, she grabbed her bucket and made her way to the water barrels, prepared to drink and then fill the bucket with water to wash her body.

A light mist brushed her cheeks, and the morning dew clung to the sparse grass. Mud squished, cold and thick, between her toes. She'd forgotten that she'd removed her boots the night before. From the stench that had seemed to grow overnight with the press of so many bodies between tents, she was certain there was more than a little dew mixed with the wet earth that she trod upon.

Ceana picked up her pace, intent on getting to the barrels quickly.

When she arrived, the line was twenty people deep. She hopped from foot to foot, intensely aware that in addition to her boots, she'd forgotten to relieve herself. The lack of forethought was disturbing. Her mind had not been in such shambles since… ever.

Even the death of family members and threats from marauders didn't put her off her common sense this much.

It was all the hulking warrior's fault.

The way he made her feel.

The risks she'd taken in order to feel his hands and lips upon her.

The way he'd pushed her back and made so much sense she could barely fathom it.

He was going to be the death of her. If she could forget her shoes and basic bodily functions, than what would happen when she had a knife at her throat? She couldn't subsist on kisses and touches alone. Wits were essential.

The line moved steadily when a guard stepped forward and began issuing the water himself. With each person that stepped forward, he issued a command, "Break your fast at the lower tent," to the women and, "Break your fast at the upper tent," to the men.

Despite her newfound conviction of avoiding all thought and contact with Macrath, she couldn't help her roving gaze. *Where is he?* Had he made it back to his tent safely?

Aye, she wanted to forget him, but *after* she made certain she'd not been the cause of his death.

By the time she reached the barrels, there was no sign of Macrath, and her lip stung from chewing through the top layer of skin.

"Bloody warrior," she murmured.

"What was that?" the guard said, sloshing water into her bucket.

Ceana shook her head, swallowed. "Nothing. Just..." She didn't feel like explaining.

The guard glowered at her. The skin beneath his eyes was puffy and purple. "Are you giving me cause to punish you?"

She shook her head hard, fearful of what such a punishment would be. The way he leered at her, she was certain it would be unpleasant and meted out within his quarters instead of tied to a stake.

"None, sir. Apologies."

Before he could make another comment, Ceana lowered her eyes and turned to hurry away. But one of the women in line stuck her foot out, tripping her. The bucket flew forward as Ceana thrust out her arms to catch herself, hands slipping in the mud and her chin smacking into the muck.

Laughs broke out all around her. Ceana gritted her teeth and pushed up, sitting back on her heels. Oddly enough, in a humiliating position like this, tears did not come to her eyes, but instead a burning rage settled in her chest, choking her. A woman gazed down at her with a satisfied smirk. Ceana didn't recognize her at first, but there was something subtly familiar.

"Serves you right for pushing past me yesterday," she said, the sneer on her face deepening.

Now she knew who the woman was—one of the people she'd passed when getting through the gate—the one who'd called her a bitch. Ceana wiped at the muck on her face, certain she'd only ended up smearing it.

In her ordinary life, she would have brushed off such a spiteful act. Behaving as a tormenter in retaliation did nothing but make oneself into such, and she usually preferred to take the higher road. Perhaps she should just laugh it off. Call a truce.

It seemed life around them had stopped as people watched to see what would happen next.

She could not laugh it off. Not at the war games. Not when every move she made determined whether she lived or died. Though the woman hadn't come at her with a battle-ax, she was trying to prove that Ceana was weak.

This woman had challenged her, had made her a fool, and if she didn't do something about it now, she'd be a target for the rest of the time she had left.

Ceana slowly stood and rounded on the woman. "They call me the Bitch of MacRae," she said low and clear before shoving both hands hard against the woman's chest.

Her opponent stumbled several feet backward out of the water line, scoffing in surprise and anger. It didn't take her long to recover her footing, and she stared down at the muddy handprints on the front of her gown. With a vicious shriek, she lunged toward Ceana, teeth bared. They grappled on their feet for several moments, both of them grunting and growling, the crowd cheering them on.

Ceana's skin stung where the woman pinched and scratched her, but she pushed through it. Likely the discomfort was the least of her worries for the day.

From behind, someone cleared their throat, but Ceana was too busy trying to grapple with her opponent to pay attention until a stinging slap slammed against her shoulder.

She jumped away from the woman she'd been wrestling and came face-to-face with the female royal council member holding a whip. Blood drained from every place it could within her body to pool in her feet, making her light-headed. "I require the Bitch of MacRae in my chambers."

The line grew silent, and her opponent eased back inch by inch to the line, the horror on her face most likely mirrored Ceana's. Had she really come this far, entered the games and made it through the first round, only to be beaten to death by this witch?

"Now," the woman said, her voice steel.

Finding it hard to breathe, Ceana managed to straighten her shoulders. She swiped at the mud caking her face, her arms, and gown, but it did nothing except smudge.

The councilwoman whipped around and headed straight up the center road toward the castle. It took every ounce of willpower she had to follow, her footsteps heavy and slow.

Ceana flicked her gaze toward the sky, praying that the gods would have mercy on her. *I'm so sorry.* Though her clan would never hear her say it. *I have failed you.* For she was certain she was about to make an appearance at her own execution.

"This way," the woman snapped, turning abruptly and heading toward the steep back stairs to the castle.

The guards bowed to the councilwoman and stepped aside, opening the large wood and iron doors. They creaked on their hinges, raising the hair on Ceana's arms. Inside the castle was dark, and a draft swirled around her ankles.

"Wait here," barked the councilwoman. "You're covered in filth and not fit to cross further."

Ceana nodded and stood proud, filthy or not. She could quaver on the inside.

She was left alone in the back entryway. The only light from a single torch sent shadows dancing around the walls, and she imagined every swift draft tickling against her legs was the fingers of the souls who'd died in the games over the past century.

"Come with me, miss."

A maid stepped from out of the shadows, summoning Ceana down a flight of stairs. She entered into a barren room, save for many steel tubs and linens. The maid beckoned her toward a tub against the far wall.

"'Tis not warm, but we must get you cleaned up, else Lady Beatrice will have my head."

Ceana nodded, guessing that Beatrice was the councilwoman.

"Disrobe," the maid said.

Again, Ceana nodded, not sure where her voice had gone, perhaps stolen by fear. Was she cleaning herself for her own death pyre?

Her fingers shook as she disrobed, her clothes falling in a soggy, mud-covered pile on the floor. When she was finished, she stepped closer to the tub, dipped a finger into the water that filled it one-third of the way. It was cold. Not freezing, but not at all warm either.

"Get in. She'll not want to wait long."

Ceana stepped into the tub, gooseflesh covering her entire body. She wrapped her arms around herself, covering her breasts.

"Don't be shy now, miss," the maid said, prying her arms down and dripping a soaked cloth over her shoulders.

But Ceana wasn't being modest. She was damned cold, and scared out of her wits. Her teeth chattered. Shivering, her nails turning purple, Ceana could do nothing but stand there as the maid washed the grime from her.

"Wait here, now. I need to get you a new gown. Don't mind if we burn this one, do you?"

Ceana turned to stare at her clan's colors, muted by age and mud. Burning it seemed profane almost, like she would be giving up her clan, her soul. "Please don't," she said.

The maid raised her brow. "Wasn't a question, really." She picked up the clothes and tossed them into the hearth that Ceana hadn't even realized was lit. The maid tossed her a linen towel, but it fell short of the tub, landing a few feet away. "Warm yourself if you will. I'll be right back."

Ceana climbed from the tub and tiptoed over the cold stone cellar floor to the linen. The fabric was rough, but clean. She swiped at the water on her body then went to stand before the fire, roaring as it burned her things.

"I knew your mother."

Ceana turned abruptly to see Lady Beatrice standing in the doorway. Her mouth fell open at the woman's words, feet frozen in place, toes going numb.

"She too liked to be called the Bitch of MacRae. Must be a family trait."

Was she supposed to answer? This woman held her fate in her hands, and Ceana didn't know how to respond. What to say or do that would not anger her. She blinked, staring but not really seeing the woman in front of her until Lady Beatrice moved. She took a subtle step in Ceana's direction, glanced down at the simple gown within her own hands, then picked up her pace until she stood not a foot away.

"Here." She handed Ceana the folded fabric. "She and I fought together once. Must have been before you were born."

Ceana nodded. She gripped her towel tighter, knuckles going white. She'd known her mother was a warrior, had seen her return from protecting the clan alongside her father with blood still smeared on her hands. She'd survived many battles, even if in the end she'd succumbed to an enemy knife. It had only been when she arrived at the games that her guards told her about her mother wanting to enter. How much of her mother's life was hidden from her? Why had her mother changed her mind about entering the games? Aaron and Boarg said it was because she was to wed Ceana's father. But was that the only reason?

She wanted to ask but was too afraid her questions wouldn't be welcome. The woman before her was a stranger and had brutally ordered the deaths of many of the contestants in the past few days. She couldn't trust that her questions wouldn't lead to a lashing.

Lady Beatrice shook the fabric until Ceana took hold of it, clutching it to her breast.

"Well. I was sorry to hear that she passed. And 'tis a shame she didn't teach you better. Don't start any more brawls, MacRae, or I'll be forced to punish you. These games are serious, and while I'd like to see you succeed because I respected your mother, I'll not give you any more special treatment."

"My thanks." Ceana let out the breath she'd been holding and met Lady Beatrice's gaze, then curtsied as best she could in a linen towel. She was grateful because she knew she should have been punished. This woman had just given her a huge reprieve—and bathed her, clothed her.

She did not respond to Ceana's gratitude, but quit the room as silently as she'd come, leaving behind a heavy weight on Ceana's shoulders.

Lady Beatrice had given her a gift—her life—and she couldn't squander it.

Ceana let her towel drop. When she unfolded the gown, a strip of MacRae plaid fell free. Was it… Was it possible this was her mother's? How did Lady Beatrice come to be in possession of it?

She lifted the strip of fabric to her face and breathed in any lingering scent, imagining it was her mother's. It gave her strength. She lifted her chin, took the first deep breath of the past hour, and let it out slowly. A renewed sense of pride and guarded courage filled her veins.

This next round would be hers to win.

Chapter Seven

MACRATH felt as though he'd drunk an entire barrel of whisky but got none of the fun out of it. His head was heavy, eyes gritty, and stomach rolling.

He'd slept little after making sure Ceana was tucked safely into her tent. He dunked water over his head by the barrels in an effort to vanquish the cobwebs. It had been difficult to wake, and he'd taken longer than necessary to pleat and don his plaid.

Commotion around the water barrels was high. Lots of chatter, animated hand gestures, and laughter. But having decided to focus only on himself and winning this next round of games, he was able to channel the noise down to a dull roar. Until he heard Ceana's name.

Well, not her name exactly, but—the Bitch of MacRae.

And though she'd not yet told him which clan she came from, or her background, for that matter, he happened to hear it when they'd done the roll call the day before.

Bitch of MacRae.

He doubted it had been what she chose to call herself, rather the cruel insult of the man who registered her. Or maybe she had chosen it, hoping the name would scare anyone away from her. Because she was tough, he'd give her that much, but Ceana was no bitch.

So when he heard her name mentioned, his ears perked up. Every word uttered ratcheted up his uneasiness. He gritted his teeth.

"Aye, saw her go into the castle myself."

"With the councilwoman?"

"Mmhmm. Likely dead by now."

"Else the councilwoman favors cunt over cock."

And then the cackles began and the sounds of slapping flesh as they patted each other on the back for their vulgar jokes.

Macrath turned slowly around, his fists clenched tight, prepared to knock an apology from the bastards who dared speak against Ceana and then to find out where the hell she was. Because if she'd gone into the castle… He had a lot more to fear today than the simple games. And dammit, he wasn't supposed to fear for her. A cold knot formed in his belly, and his teeth ground so tight he was certain those around could hear it.

If he had to, he'd knock every one of the pockmarked bastard guards away from the door and storm the castle himself to find her.

Taking a deep breath, he managed to ask, "Why'd she go into the castle?" without breaking either of their noses, though his fists were going numb from the pressure.

They shrugged. A woman butted between the two men and gazed at Macrath, her eyes hungry as she stared over his shirtless form. When she smiled, her two front teeth were missing, lips swollen. Perhaps an injury from the day before.

"She was fighting," the woman answered.

Macrath raised a skeptical brow. That didn't sound like Ceana at all. She must have been provoked. "Fighting?" he asked.

"Aye. With a woman. They were down in the mud right where you stand."

He glanced down around his feet. Sure enough, the mud was well and disturbed, but he'd only assumed it had been from the number of people coming to the barrels to drink and wash up for the morning. Had it been *this* woman who'd fought with Ceana?

"Her ladyship marched right up to the both of them and whipped the Bitch on her back before demanding her to come inside." She hooked her thumb at the man on her left who was nodding with a lecherous smile on his crude face. "I think he's got the right of it. The lady likes cunt."

They all burst out laughing then, and Macrath was stepping forward to shut them up with his fists when the back doors of the castle flung open and Ceana walked out. Her face was pale, eyes wide and rounded as though she'd seen a ghost. She was dressed in a clean, well-kept gown. Her hair, slightly damp, looked to be plaited down her back, and a strip of plaid was wrapped tightly around her waist. Standing barefoot on the steps and looking down at the crowd that'd gathered to watch her, she looked so innocent, a little nervous. But her shoulders squared as though she already owned the castle.

"Move out of the way, you bastards," Macrath grumbled, shoving past the three who'd insulted her moments before.

He had every intention of walking right up to her to make sure she was all right, but then her friend Aaron rushed forward, his feet hitting the stairs before Macrath had even cleared a path.

Perhaps this was better. He needed to put some distance between them anyway. Hell, he'd been willing to beat the guards and rush into the castle, which would have only served to earn him a battle-ax in the head. He watched as Aaron hammered her with questions. She shook her head and nodded in answer. Her mouth was turned down, brows drawn together, and she looked as though she'd not slept any better than he had. A pang of jealousy gripped him right in the bollocks when Aaron held out his arm and she took it without hesitation. He led her down the stairs and in the opposite direction of where Macrath stood. Most likely taking her to the tent where she could break her fast.

Macrath hesitated for a moment before forcing his feet to move so he could intercept them. However, when the female council member stepped from the back of the castle door, he froze. Her gaze was focused on Ceana's retreating figure, and for a moment he caught a glint of concern—and admitted that for a flash of a breath he thought maybe the vulgar jackanapes had the right of it, that she desired Ceana for her own. But then he realized the look was one he'd never received himself—that of a mother looking fondly on her child. This woman could not be her mother—could she?—but she was obviously concerned all the same. Some deeper connection was held between those two than anyone else in the games. What stake did she have in Ceana? If any at all?

The lady nodded to the guards on the stairs who raised their horns and blew.

"Last call to break your fast before the rules for game two are announced," shouted several guards on horseback riding up the center road.

Macrath's stomach growled. His never-ending appetite. Judging from the past few days, he'd need sustenance today. Needed the energy his body had not received from sleep. Making his way through the crowd, he entered the men's meal tent only to find that the tabletops were loaded merely with men's elbows as they lounged on benches. No food. The trenchers were bare. Cups and jugs littered the surface.

Had they already eaten all the food?

Filthy maggots.

As he made his way to a table, intent on at least grabbing a watered ale, he heard many of the men complaining of the lack of food. A moment later, one of guards came in with two swords drawn and held out before him. He looked as though he was on the defensive, and Macrath's instincts were pricked. He straightened, hand going to his empty belt and cursing the rule of no weapons. He gripped his mug of ale instead. If he had to, he could bash in a man's brain with the cup.

"There's to be no breakfast for the men today," said the guard.

They would starve them. If they couldn't kill them with wolves, they'd let them slowly waste away. No matter, Macrath had gone without meals before, and if his hunger became excruciating, he'd simply forage while in the woods. His stepmother had tried to poison him enough that he knew which plants to stay away from.

Realizing they'd get nothing to eat, the men began to stand. Macrath grabbed several mint leaves to chew from his sporran attached to his belt. They helped to stave off his hunger, but also to freshen his breath.

"Wait!" the guard called out. "You're not to leave the tent until the women are ready for you."

"The women?" Macrath grumbled along with the other men.

"Orders from the council! Anyone to leave the tent before they are summoned will be cut down." The guard swung his swords at the men as he backed slowly out of the tent.

Once he was gone, the men began speculating on what exactly was going on, but Macrath didn't give a rat's ass about all that. He stepped to the side where he had the best view through the opening to the women's tent, hoping for a glance of Ceana. Her friend Aaron had yet to appear.

His earlier jealousy returned with full-on rage. Had they even gone to the women's meal tent, or had she needed the comfort Aaron was willing provide—the comfort he'd refused her the nig before? Were they within her own lodging, soaking up the pleasure that should have been Macrath's and hers alone?

Oh, the pain of that thought. If only he'd taken her when he'd had the chance, then he could have laid claim to her, and she would have not gone near that slimy bastard. But then again, if he'd done that, it would have gone against everything he believed in. Bedding a woman—a lady—simply to ease a fear was not acceptable. Especially one who'd risked her life in coming to him in hopes of repaying him for having saved her life. Hell, he wanted her. That was never in question. But he wouldn't take advantage of her.

Macrath would never expect to rut a woman simply because he'd saved her life. He was not that kind of man. He had honor. He had a moral code. All the things his stepmother and half brother swore he didn't. There would be no bastard sons from him.

And as much as he wanted Ceana—desired her with every damned fiber of his being, grew hard at just the picture of her face in his mind—he was not going to put her at risk.

He swiped a hand through his hair and downed the remainder of his ale. Why was putting her out of his mind so damned hard? He'd never thought of a woman as much as he was ruminating on her. Except for his first. He'd imagined himself in love with that young lass, and she'd let him do all sorts of unimaginable things to her—but she'd also been paid well by his father's soldiers and promised to take care that no babe was conceived. He'd thought about her long and hard after. Knew that he never wanted to have to pay a woman to be in his bed ever again. Thought that he never wanted to feel the way he did after either—as though he'd thoroughly used a woman simply for the pleasure of her body. Back in those days, he'd not known what it meant for a woman to enjoy bedding. Now he knew better.

And *mo chreach*, he wanted to share that blissful oblivion with Ceana.

He stalked forward, slammed his cup on a table, and was about to leave the tent—orders be damned—so he could go and find the two lovebirds and interrupt their reverie when Aaron skidded inside.

As soon as he saw Macrath, he tried to walk the other way, but Macrath grabbed him by the scruff of his neck and yanked him to a stop. "Where are you going? There's no food today."

Aaron glanced up at him, his expression half-annoyed, half-terrified.

Macrath let him go and Aaron adjusted his dingy shirt.

"Macrath," he grumbled.

"Aaron." He crossed his arms over his chest and stared the man down, waiting for him to provide details.

Aaron rolled his eyes. "She's fine."

"What the hell happened?" Macrath spoke under his breath, hoping that no one else in the tent would pay attention to them.

"She wouldn't tell me. Whatever it was scared her half to death."

Macrath scrutinized Aaron's face, looking for signs he was lying. Why he'd lie, Macrath could only guess.

Good gods, what had she been put through inside the castle? The punishment for disruption had to have been harsh. And yet the way the woman had looked after her kept flashing back in his mind. Was it guilt for having had to be punitive, or had she let Ceana off the hook for reasons he was determined to figure out?

Macrath searched Aaron's face for any sign of a lie. "Was she hurt? They said she was whipped."

Aaron's face was grim. "A single lash on her shoulder, but she says that it doesn't pain her."

Macrath had been hit with a whip plenty. Even a single blow could leave a painful mark. "But she was washed." Seemed that more than a single lash would lead to such.

Aaron nodded, his brow wrinkling. He crossed his arms over his chest and stared toward the empty tables. "Odd, isn't it?"

Macrath nodded. Odd. And he wasn't supposed to care. But he did. He wanted to make sense out of it. Knew that the situation would likely keep him guessing and unfocused.

The dreaded horn blew before he could ask Aaron about the plaid belt she'd been wearing. Dammit, there were still so many questions he wanted to ask. He wanted to know how the lady on the council had been in possession of a MacRae plaid. But the alarm for the men to come to order was enough to jolt Aaron into action, and he scurried away from Macrath and toward the door with the rest of the men before Macrath could grab him back.

Shaking his head, Macrath headed for the flap. They were herded like cattle once more to their lines. The sun had fully risen, and though it wasn't warm, the coldness that typically set in when they were so close to winter had yet to hit. Though he was certain it would at some point.

The women were already in their lines across from the men. Though their ranks were substantially less than a day ago. 'Twas the same for the men. Knowing that all those who'd filled the space before were dead was a sobering thought.

Macrath searched the crowd of women for Ceana, finding her easy enough in the back. Her head was bowed, eyes cast to the ground. He stared at her, willing her to look at him. Willing her to make eye contact, but knowing all the same that he'd not get his answers from a shared glance. Ceana made no move to lift her head. She didn't seem browbeaten, rather that she was avoiding him.

Slightly to her left was Rhona. He was surprised and relieved to see her. She was covered in bruises. She smiled in his direction, and Macrath nodded. The woman was tougher than he thought. While he'd searched for Ceana in the woods, he'd also kept his eyes out for Rhona, feeling it his duty to protect her, but she'd been nowhere, perhaps having found a good hiding spot and sticking to it.

The ground trembled slightly as the council members rode into the center of their ranks. The crowd quieted without the need for horns to be blown, everyone's gaze riveted on them. Even Ceana's. The class divide was never more evident than now between the council members and the entrants. The lot of female and male warriors were grimy, their clothes dingy, while the council members were well groomed.

Ceana stuck out in her cleanliness and the way she refused to look at anyone.

Bloody hell, what had happened to her behind closed doors?

This time, the female council member did not take the front. The eldest of the male council members raised his hand until everyone's eyes were on him. After harshly regarding them, he began to speak. "Today the tables are turned. The women will take to the list fields while the male warriors act as their squires."

That bit of news sent a ripple of shock through the men. But it made Macrath snicker. They would starve them and then make them serve the women. For many, this would be a true test of their mental capacity. Many men did not want to serve women, thought the fairer sex inferior. For himself, well, he'd grown up starving, and as his stepmother often banished him to work with the servants, he could handle serving a woman. Besides, this was a team exercise. In a few days' time, when *he* won the final game, he'd have to be a part of a team for five years with one of the female entrants and then the rest of his life if they had a child.

"The women have been randomly given an order in which to choose which squire they would like to work with."

Macrath sent a silent prayer to the gods that Ceana picked him and not Aaron.

But as it turned out, Ceana must have been given a later position, because as the first few were called, she was not named. The guard shouted for Rhona, and she chose Macrath. His name sounded loudly over the crowd. Before he stepped forward, he chanced a glance at Ceana. Her eyes were still cast down, but he swore her shoulders were slumped a little further. Disappointment.

Bloody hell. She would have chosen him.

Macrath stepped forward, and Rhona rushed over to him, her smile tight around lips that were cracked and bleeding. Bruises marred the flesh of her neck, and her gown was torn. She may have survived the first round, but it had not been without pain.

"Macrath. Thank the gods no one chose you before I did."

He nodded. "How do you fare?" he asked.

"I am weakened and sore, but with you by my side, I can weather this next round."

"'Tis the lists, Rhona." He hated to be the bearer of bad news, but she needed to know what she was getting into. "I will help you with weapons. Lift you when you fall, but I cannot fight this battle for you. You must be prepared."

She nodded, tears rushing to her eyes. "I won't make it. I know I won't."

Macrath awkwardly patted her on the shoulder. "Aye, you will. Just be brave as you were in the woods."

"I wasn't brave. Not at all. I was horrible. A bloodthirsty rage took hold of me so I would survive."

"Then that is what you must be, bloodthirsty."

But he didn't want her to be, because eventually she would come up against Ceana, and if Rhona, gods save him, tried to harm her, he'd have a hard time not running out onto that field and cutting his clanswoman down himself.

It was then Macrath heard Ceana's voice—and she was choosing Aaron.

He gritted his teeth. Why couldn't it have been the men against each other? He was ready to beat the bloody MacRae guard down to the ground. He may have been protecting Ceana because he'd served with her brother, but Macrath knew in his bones that Aaron desired her. And if Macrath couldn't have her, no one could.

So much for distance. He was ready to claim her as his own.

Chapter Eight

CEANA discreetly observed Macrath and the woman who'd chosen him. A pang of unexpected and unwelcomed jealousy clung to her center.

She spoke with him in a familiar fashion, and their mannerisms leant to the fact that they knew each other. Was she the reason that he'd pushed her aside the day before? Did they have an understanding?

Ceana's face grew hot. What a fool she'd been.

"Females! To the list field. Instructions will follow!"

Ceana allowed herself to be shoved along the path and through the gate toward the field where two days past they'd fought for weapons. A shudder rushed through her as she passed under the imposing gate. The arching stones and threatening iron portcullis jutting toward her skull resembled so much more than a simple entrance and exit. It represented a line being crossed—life or death.

Shoulder to shoulder they marched, no one shoving today. No one eager to begin the next round of games, for it only meant risking their lives. There would be men and women who did not cross back through this gate when the game ended. A sobering fact. One that gave instinct the push to stall the inevitable.

And yet, if they did not begin, no one would succeed.

Ceana had come to the games with one goal in mind—win.

If she was going to save her clan from starvation, from losing their land to the surrounding clans, then she *had* to win. There was no other way out of it for her. The coin, the land, the power, all of it would bring her clan out of obscurity and poverty. Literally save their lives.

Flashes of home squeezed her chest. Images of happier times. She'd not even had time to properly mourn the death of her brother. But now was not the time to think about it. She had to thrust such heavy remembrances from her mind.

Steeling her emotions—and the softer side of herself that respected humanity—she marched along with every other survivor. But pushing away all contemplations of cherishing life in others was harder than she thought. Ceana wasn't a murderer. And that's what these games were all about—killing.

How did one take life when they didn't want to?

Even in self-defense, it was a hard line to cross. Just like this bridge.

But everyone's path that she walked with led to the same place.

Ceana squared her shoulders. Imagined that if her mother had entered the games she would have walked this same footpath. Her mother had been strong. She would have survived. And so would Ceana.

Their feet sank into the grasses of the field, and they followed the guards on horseback past where they'd fought for weapons and then around to the right of the castle wall. A large arena had been set up. The field—grass cut low—was surrounded by a thick-railed wooden fence. At the head of the field was a large opened tent set upon a dais with chairs for the council members. The opposite end possessed a wide gate for the contestants to enter and exit. The sides were lined with thick wooden logs, and guards shouted out that seating for spectators was on one side and the squires would be on the other. Seated on the spectator side looked to be the servants of the entrants and possibly family members. She spotted Boarg who stared at her intently before nodding and searching out the males, most likely seeking signs of Aaron.

Zounds, but he must have been filled with terror for them both, unsure if either of them would arrive here today. Jostled by several women surrounding her, she pulled her gaze away from Boarg.

The females were lined up two by two in the opposite direction of the positions they've been assigned—those who'd chosen squires first were at the end of the lines. Ceana was close to the front—only three women in front of her. Damn. If she were made to fight all those behind her, she'd tire faster than those who'd been lucky enough to be placed at the end. Mayhap that was the point. Taking a deep breath, she tried for courage, but found that it waxed and waned in her.

The squires were ushered to the logs where they took their seats. She searched for Aaron, finding him on her far left. And without her permission, her gaze sought out Macrath who was on the far right. It'd taken a force of sheer will not to look at him this morning when they'd been lined up within the walls. She'd felt his eyes on her. Had desperately wanted to look up. She reminded herself that she'd not only put him in danger by encouraging any sort of relationship but the uncertain future of her clan as well. Besides, he had his woman with him. That ought to be enough of a deterrent for her.

But then she saw him. And he was looking at her.

She quickly glanced away, not wanting to read into the sentiment she saw in his face, but once more her gaze was drawn. Thank the fates, several guards filed in front of the men, speaking to them with voices not loud enough to carry, but she could see them pointing inside the ring. Weapons were already distributed in great heaping piles on both sides of the field. Wooden staffs that were longer than clubs but shorter than pikes and lacked the pointed iron tips.

"Those cudgels were designed specifically for these games, I heard," a woman behind murmured to another.

"Will hurt like the devil," another whispered.

"Aye. Likely to break bones."

Ceana shuddered. 'Twas a hideous thought, and she could almost hear the sound of breaking bones. Best to tune everything and everyone out and center on just herself. Recall all the training she'd acquired from her brother over the years. She could do this. She *would* do this.

The horn was blown, and the first two women entered the arena. Their squires leapt over the fence and stood, arms behind their backs, neither handing out weapons.

Panic quickened in Ceana's chest. Why weren't the men helping? Had they colluded against the women they were to serve?

The elder council member stepped forward from his place beneath the tent, his arm raised in the air, calling everyone's attention. "The first round will be hand-to-hand combat. The first opponent to fall to the ground without rising for the count of fifteen will lose the round. Discontents will be removed from the ring, their fates to be determined at the end of this first round. Let the game begin!"

There was no mention of the cudgels, and Ceana did not have time to reflect on it. When his arm went down, a horn was blown, and the two women began circling each other. The first fight was brutal as the women swung their fists, grabbed clumps of hair, bit, and kicked. Ceana gaped at the blood pouring from their bloody lips, split eyebrows, and broken noses. Her stomach churned, and she found herself swallowing again and again. One woman's nose was bent in the wrong direction, and still they fought.

Ceana found herself unable to watch. She rubbed at her forearms, and she was certain her face had gone pale. In the chill, her fingers were numb, but it could also have been her dread. The women grunted, cried out. The sounds of their smacks, kicks, and feet scrambling in the dirt echoed in the silence of the spectators. It was odd. Normally at a tournament between warriors, those watching cheered on the combatants they wanted to win.

The silence was a telling cry as to how everyone felt. No one wanted to cheer on the beating of one versus the other. Nor root for a single person to win. For they all knew they'd be in the same place soon. Fighting for their lives. Fighting for the chance to win and rule. Fighting for so much more than that.

At long last, a dull thud sounded, and Ceana raised her eyes to see one of the bloodied women lying on the ground, her eyes staring lifelessly up at the sky. Ceana sucked in a breath, eyes wide as she stared at her prone body. Was the woman… dead?

The woman who still stood staggered backward, clutching at her neck, bloody from both her hands and the cuts streaming from her face. She looked as horrified as Ceana felt. There was a quiet murmur among the spectators but not within the female lines.

A guard rushed forward and knelt beside the woman. He raised his eyes to the line of women waiting their turn for a run in the ring. He gazed at them all in a way that made Ceana shudder. His lip curled and eyes gleamed. He enjoyed his duty entirely too much.

"One. Two. Three. Four. Five…" He counted until he reached, "Fifteen."

Still the woman did not move. She'd not even curled her fingers to indicate life was yet inside her.

He held his hand over her face, then knelt lower, pressing his ear to her chest. When he rose, a smear of blood streaked his cheek. "Dead!" he bellowed, then leapt to his feet and raised the opposing woman's arm in the air and tugged her, arm still high, toward the council tent. "Your victor."

The council members looked on soberly, clapping their hands slowly, until one shouted, "Next."

Dead. Beaten to death.

And she didn't even warrant a moment of silence. Simply a call for the next round of fighters to enter.

Ceana closed her eyes. Blocking out the violence, the sadness, the inhumanity of it. Even though the council members would not issue a prayer to the gods for the poor woman's soul, she would, though she did so inside her mind, unwilling to call attention to what the council had obviously neglected.

She was certain she'd not be able to beat another person to death with her bare hands. Did that mean she was going to be the one to die?

The next two women were ushered into the arena. Their fight was just as brutal but did not end in death, and nor did the two after. The unconscious women were dragged from the list field by their squires. Ceana refused to look and see what happened to them, instead taking a moment to breathe.

"Next!"

It was her. She knew it was, and yet she couldn't make her feet move. Staring down at them, she saw her boots—brown and weathered—sunken into the grass.

She wasn't ready. But they were pushing her. The women in line behind her shoved. And shoved again.

"Go. They have called you! Do not make the rest of us suffer," they yelled at her. "We do not want to wait even longer for our turns because of you."

And still she couldn't make her feet lift. If she refused to go, would they drag her into the arena?

"Bitch of MacRae!" The shout sounded like it came from the guard who'd named her thus when she first arrived.

The name rattled around in her mind, and suddenly her feet were moving. Her blood was boiling through her, and she recalled the faces of her clan members, the hungry children, those wounded from too many raids. She glanced at Board who sat a dozen paces away. Then she looked to Aaron, who nodded, giving her the confidence to do what she must.

This was for her clan.

Her opponent was about the same size—thank goodness she wasn't up against one of the hulking women who could take her down with one thwack. Had her opponent been chosen to enter the games by her clan or had she willingly joined? It was hard to tell something like that. Her gown was torn and dirtied just as everyone else's was from the first round. Her face was thin as was her body. Wrists delicate. A trick of her bloodline, or from circumstance?

"Begin!"

Ceana worked to see past the woman in front of her, to see the person as nothing more than a sack of wool she needed to pound into shape. They circled one another, each assessing the other.

For a moment she wished she'd paid more attention when the females were wrestling in the tents. Though she'd learned a few things from her brawl that morning by the water barrels. But that woman had been much more skilled than she was, and without Lady Beatrice's intervention, Ceana wasn't sure that sheer will alone would have won her that incident. Why hadn't she insisted that beyond climbing trees, fighting with swords, and practicing with arrows that her brother teach her hand-to-hand combat?

The best way to get through this round without killing the other woman would be to hit her in the head to knock her to the ground and hopefully into a deep sleep. On the same note, she'd need to protect her—

The woman swung out, striking Ceana painfully in the shoulder. She recoiled, her eyes flicking to the woman who danced back and forth like a wild, skittish animal. She was terrified, and rather than hit her back, Ceana wanted to pull her into her arms and protect her. She was laird of her own clan, that's what she did. But such was not possible. *I have to retaliate.*

Ceana lashed out, her fist grazing the woman's forehead when she shakily dodged the blow meant for her temple. Her own footsteps faltered at the power she'd put behind the blow that missed, and it was enough for the other woman to wrap her hands around Ceana's waist and tug her to the ground.

Both of them went down hard. This would not do.

Ceana kicked out her legs, shoving the woman off her, and then she rolled on top to have the advantage. She weighed more than the waif beneath her and held her pinned, tucking her hands up over her head.

"I want this to end quickly and without your death, do you not?" Ceana said through gritted teeth.

The woman didn't respond, but her eyes were wide, face pale, lips trembling. She bucked beneath her, but Ceana held on tight.

She leaned down close. "I'm going to hit you. Be prepared. Do not be afraid."

Her opponent continued to wiggle a moment longer, then, when she must have realized that resistance was futile, gazed up at Ceana, perhaps truly for the first time. As soon as the woman gave just the slightest nod, Ceana grabbed the front of her gown and tugged, lifting her slightly from the ground. And then she tried a move that she'd seen her brother do on occasion to a MacLeod that always got the measured result he'd wanted. She reared her head back and slammed the crown against the other woman's forehead. The thundering crack echoed in her head along with the pain that ricocheted around her own skull.

Ceana blinked rapidly, her fingers uncurling from the woman's gown to see her lying unconscious on the ground in front of her. She'd done it. Good gods, it hurt more than she imagined. She grabbed the woman's chin and gave a slight shake, but there was no response, though warm breath drifted over her fingertips. Asleep, but not dead.

She leapt to her feet in time for Aaron to catch her trembling elbow and the guard to count to fifteen. Her opponent's squire picked her up and carried her off the field. This time Ceana did want to see where those who lost were taken. Aaron tugged at her sleeve.

"Come, my laird. You've done well. You must rest until the next round."

"But I want to see—"

"Clear the field! Next!" the guard shouted, giving Ceana a hard glare and shove.

This time she allowed Aaron to pull her along.

She waited on the opposite side of the fence with the other winners and their squires. The discontents were tossed onto the ground until they wakened, their squires watching over them. But they weren't executed as she'd feared. They'd live to fight the next round.

Macrath's woman went down hard, her nose and lips bleeding. When he bent to pick her up, she cringed at the odd angle the woman's arm was bent. A pang of regret and sorrow filled his face. But it lacked anything more—the pain she was most assured he would have if he cared about this woman like he would a lover just wasn't there. The woman had to be from his clan, not his lover. Did he feel just as responsible for her as Ceana felt for Aaron? Or was she just fooling herself?

"Be careful, my laird," Aaron said under his breath, jutting his chin in Macrath's direction.

"Why do you not like the man?"

Aaron smiled. "'Tis not that I dislike him. I just don't trust him."

Ceana tilted her head. "Why is that?"

"He's a hard warrior. I've seen men like him before. Besides, the interest he has in you is of concern. With Dougal gone, I feel like it's my place to protect you."

Ceana waffled with feeling grateful to Aaron for looking out for her and irritated all the same. It was her choice whom she spoke with… whom she kissed.

"Do not fret over it, Aaron. I am a good judge of character, and I believe Macrath is a good man."

Aaron grunted, and she could tell he wanted to say more, but she didn't want to hear it.

Across the field, Macrath glanced up, his gaze falling on hers, and for a few sparking moments he held it there. She wished they were closer so she could see his expression. Aaron was partly right. Macrath was a hard man, and she *should* stay away from him. But not because he was dangerous or unpredictable. He'd only ever been kind and gentlemanly toward her—even with his heated kisses.

She had to stay away from him because thinking about him only distracted her from the task at hand. From winning. But maybe this was the gods' way of giving her a sign. That in order to win, perhaps she needed to side with Macrath. Out of all the men here, he seemed more determined to win than any other. But why? He'd mentioned his stepmother sending him here to die. The woman sounded like a horrid witch. If he won, it would be the best revenge. But she needed more than that from him. Living out of retribution wasn't enough. If they were to partner together, she would need him to want something for their country, for their people.

And why couldn't she partner with Aaron?

She glanced sideways at her brother's friend. He was a good guard, but there was a reason he'd never been Dougal's second-in-command. Aaron was slight and tended to act a lot more with instinct than his mind. Siding with him may not be her choice. He'd only joined the games because she needed him to. And, aye, he had a stake in the clan. He and his family were MacRaes, but that didn't give him the drive to reign supreme. Self-preservation was what would drive Aaron to win.

The horn blew, startling Ceana from her intense thoughts. She'd not even realized how much of what was going on around her she'd drowned out. The final set of women had finished fighting. A total of three were dead. The rest of the rabble ranged from injuries as mild as a headache to broken or dislocated limbs.

The women were ushered forward, those who'd lost paired against each other—and first—while the winners were paired in the back according to the guard's whims.

Ceana sucked in a chilled breath. She was right next to She-muscle. The larger woman grinned down at her, as though Ceana was going to be her next meal. The one milky eye screamed of nightmares and pain to come.

"Round two will begin imminently. This time, you shall each be given a cudgel..."

Ceana found her throat growing tight. She'd made it out easy in the last round—a headache and that was all. Because her first opponent had lost, she was paired in the front. Ceana was now in the back with the rest of the winners—the strongest and fiercest women. The ones who terrified her, and yet she had to be the one to shock them. To send them skittering away from her. Shorter than the average woman, Ceana didn't pose much of a threat on a normal day, and next to none in battle. Especially next to the behemoth.

"Told you we'd meet again, little chickie," She-muscle said under her breath.

Ceana bit the inside of her cheeks to keep from screaming. The only way she was going to get anywhere was by being quick. A feat she'd already proven her superiority at with this woman when they'd both raced for the bow in the first game. Even still, her new opponent's brute strength would be enough to throw her off her feet and into a dark oblivion.

And the way She-muscle leered at her, Ceana was in for a world of pain.

The second round went a bit faster than the first. The weakened women barely had to hit each other before one was knocked to the ground, unable to move. Those with broken limbs barely lasted before the call to begin was sounded.

All too quickly, it was her turn, and She-muscle was already devouring her with her sick grin and eager eye. Damn. This was not going to feel good.

Just as her feet shuffled to the opening gate, Ceana paused, closed her eyes, and looked up at the sky. She imagined her mother, father, and brother looking down on her. Giving her their strength, their courage.

Aaron approached, handed her a cudgel, the wood cool from the autumn breeze. "You can do this," he murmured. "Tire her out."

Exactly as she'd been thinking.

Standing several paces away, She-muscle bobbed on her feet, tossed her cudgel from hand to hand, and leered at Ceana.

"Come on. Don't just stand there, little chickie. It's time for us to battle."

Ceana gripped the cudgel, letting the heat of her body seep into the wood, making it an extension of herself. She took a tentative step forward, keenly watching the expression on She-muscle. The woman expected this to be easy. That was evident in both her speech and her mannerisms. Lucky for Ceana, this woman appeared to lack the cunning that it took to win at some games.

Keeping that realization in the back of her mind, Ceana walked sideways, beginning the courting dance. She-muscle jumped forward, her cudgel bouncing outward and just barely missing Ceana as she dove to the right and ran out of the way of woman's counterattack.

Tire her out. Tire her out.

Ceana ran in a wide circle around her, making the woman turn round and round, and hopefully getting her a little dizzy. She had to duck away from—and leap over—to avoid several hits.

"Stop your running, you little brat," She-muscle yelled out.

But that only made Ceana smile—because though she'd yelled, the tail end of her words had been breathy. Ceana ran one more time, then leapt forward, swinging the cudgel as hard as she could. Her wood cracked against the side of the woman's arm. The howl that elicited from her vibrated Ceana's insides, and the growl the woman issued had her fearing for her life. For a moment, she was too terrified to move as she watched the woman barreling down on her. Bent over, seething, good eye shooting daggers. She reminded Ceana of one of the wolves from the woods.

"Move!" Aaron's—and Macrath's—joint bellow finally reached the sane part of her mind that held her desire to live.

Ceana jumped into action, running full-on away from the woman as though one of the wolves from the woods were chasing after her. The closer she got to the fence, the more she panicked. She didn't want to be trapped there where She-muscle would likely beat her to death. Ceana darted to the left, but her feet flew out from under her. At the last minute she saw that her opponent had thrust her cudgel forward, tripping her.

When she fell, her own cudgel went flying. She scrambled forward to get it, She-muscle's laughter filling her head.

"Now I've got you, little chickie."

She heard the crack before she felt the pain. But it didn't last long as darkness filled in all the little spaces between and she drifted off to someplace warm and safe.

Blinking repeatedly, Ceana tried to pull her hand to her head, but her limbs were so heavy. What happened? Why did her head hurt so damn much?

And then it all came rushing back to her. The fight with the behemoth woman. She'd been hit in the head with a cudgel. But not that hard, obviously, or she'd be dead. The woman had shown her mercy after all, only hitting her hard enough to knock her out. Had she done so on purpose? Part of Ceana wanted to say it didn't matter, that she was alive, and to thank the gods for it. The other part of her knew better. Ceana owed the woman her life—there was no way she could take hers. Not now. Probably not ever.

The blackness began to ebb away, and light came to her eyes—along with the sound of men's voices, raised and angry. She could make out Aaron and Macrath. But their words were warbled, loud, but not pronounced.

"Shh…," she tried to say, but her lips were still a little numb, and dizziness made her want to vomit.

If they didn't stop arguing, Lady Beatrice would hear, and then the female councilor would make certain they were punished for their impudence. *No quarter given.*

An arm filled her vision and then coldness touched her lip. Someone was giving her a drink. She sipped slowly, but then turned to the side to retch, her entire body curling up to purge. This only made Aaron and Macrath yell louder.

"Hush," she tried again, and this time with success.

"Perhaps I shall see the lot of you punished. Cease this at once." Too late. Lady Beatrice was already there. "What is this nonsense? You argue over this puny, insignificant woman?"

Ceana wanted to shout out, "No! Don't argue over me! Listen to the lady," but her lips were still tingling, and her stomach still threatened to spill what was left inside it.

"Perhaps the two of you will end up on the list field before all else. You can battle there instead of here where you distract everyone from the games. This is unacceptable."

Ceana was able to focus her eyes for a moment where she saw both Aaron and Macrath standing a few feet away, each looking contrite in the face of the royal councilwoman, though the loathing glances they shot at one another spoke volumes.

They fought over her. They risked so much. *For me.*

She couldn't allow that. Ceana was already miserable at the thought of having to see people's lives lost in order to save her clan. She'd not be the cause of these men's deaths. She would shun them to save them.

"My lady," she muttered, and this time her voice was heard. "Please do not punish them. 'Tis my fault that they argue. I have given them both cause to..." To what?

But she didn't need to find the word, because Lady Beatrice scoffed. "Do not play the martyr with me, Ceana MacRae." She eyed the two men with disgust. "Leave off, or else I will see you put on the stakes."

Ceana let out the breath she was holding.

"And as for you, my lady, be prepared, for the discontents of round two fight first in the final round."

At that, Ceana sank back against the ground, both relieved the woman had given a reprieve to Aaron and Macrath and terrified of what the third and final round would bring. Would she even be able to walk onto the field?

Chapter Nine

"ROUND three!" the guard called out, and the crowd of men silenced.

Again a council member stood upon the dais and raised his hand in the air to make sure everyone was listening. "In round three, each opponent will be given one dagger with which to fight."

Daggers? Macrath felt the color drain from his face.

"Lassies, be prepared to fight with every ounce of skill you possess. Winners of this round will be granted a request of comfort."

The value of human life had not been a topic Macrath often pondered.

In fact, when he was on the battlefield it was a subject best left untouched.

Sitting on the lumpy log beside a bunch of stinking, whiny brutes, watching the women hack each other to pieces, he'd never considered it more. He scrubbed a hand over his face and contemplated just how he could take on every one of the guards and council members in order to save the rest of the contestants. Doing so would mean there was no winner to the games, and henceforth Sìtheil would be again steeped in war, but that trumped watching another innocent person die for sport.

A scream sounded from the list field as another woman felt the pain of her opponent's knife slicing through her flesh. This time gutting her. Her insides spilled onto the dirt as she fell to her knees, staring up at the sky. She clutched her middle, and the woman who'd done the deed slowly backed away. The humane thing to do would have been to slice the dying woman's throat to ease her passage and pain, but the horror of what had transpired filled the eyes and shaped the silent scream of the winner.

Silence reigned among the male and female entrants.

To him, it appeared that the only ones enjoying the games were those who presided over them. Of course, there were bound to be a few deranged men and women who joined only for the fact that they'd be able to beat and kill people without anyone asking questions. But he had to wonder why the games continued. Why hadn't a single winner in the past hundred years questioned their right to rule longer than five years? The only one to have succeeded was Guillemorre. He'd ruled for fifteen years, and that was purely because he'd entered the games and won his seat three times.

He was a legend among men and warriors. Every young lad grew up, fantasizing about changing their names and charging onto the battlefield with an army behind them chanting on about their prowess and with a woman—or three—at home faithfully waiting for their return. Macrath was willing to bet that none of them, himself included, had ever imagined what they'd be seeing now.

Maybe it was hitting him more viscerally now than before because it was the women fighting. If he was observing the men, he'd probably not think twice as he'd watched and participated in many a tournament before. But the tourneys were also not fought to the death.

The men jabbed each other's ribs and made lewd comments as the broken and bloodied women were brought out to line up two by two. Several of them were not even able to walk of their own accord. He shook his head, subtly knocking the man to his left off the bench when he tried to elbow him. Damned if he was going to join in their ridiculous commenting.

"Were you born an animal, you jackanapes?" Macrath seethed. "Our women are killing each other."

"Aye, and I intend for one of them to be my wife. Imagine what the lass would be like in bed." The maggot guffawed and seated himself back down, not at all concerned with Macrath having knocked him to the ground. "A right wildcat."

Macrath looked at the man, his lip curling in disgust. "*If* by some miracle you win these games, your wife is more likely to gut you and watch you bleed than see to your pleasure."

That shut the man up. Macrath couldn't have been happier about it because another word out of his mouth and he was likely to punch him until every one of his teeth littered the grass like pearls.

But his attention was called away from beating the man to death when Ceana limped out onto the field. Even bruised, she was a beautiful sight. Her fiery hair was wound up atop her head, knotted tendrils curling around her ears and the nape of her neck. The new gown she'd been given was no longer clean, but at least it was not torn. A bruise marred her cheek, and she kept her gaze steady on the women in front of her. His chest tightened, and he itched to leap up and run to her. He longed to thread his fingers through her hair, to untangle the snarls, to take her away from here, pamper her and give her everything she deserved.

Leaning against the fence several feet from him was Aaron, who also intently studied her. The man's expression was grim. Macrath knew that face. Aaron felt responsible for the state in which Ceana found herself. But though he knew not how she'd come to be in the games, Macrath had an idea that she wanted to be here, that no matter how much Aaron would take responsibility for the outcome, it was her choice.

Maybe it was the set of her shoulders or the determined way in which she continued to fight back. There was definitely something about the way she held her head higher than the other women. The way she carried herself despite how tiny she was. Even now as she stood in line, straightening her spine despite the pain she must be feeling. The way she eyed the woman standing beside her…

Bloody hell…

Rhona stood beside her.

Macrath's stomach twisted into knots, and his blood ran cold. There stood the only two women in this entire competition that he gave a whit about. His clanswoman and the woman he… Gods, what? He didn't know. He wanted Ceana to win, to marry her, bed her, and have her bear his children. But it was purely physical. Purely strategic. He knew little about her.

And now she would fight against a woman he'd vowed to protect. Watching this round would be impossible.

What were the odds that the two of them would face off against each other? Was this the Lady's doing? Her way of punishing Macrath for arguing so openly with that sniveling little snake Aaron? Macrath couldn't decide what would have been worse—the stake or watching the two women fight. He would have gladly taken the stake over this. 'Twas a cruel, cruel penance.

Cheering for Rhona meant watching Ceana fall. Cheering for Ceana meant wishing ill to his clanswoman. His stepmother and half brother may have had little faith in him, may have tried to push him aside, but his father let him live amongst the people, and the clan members had always treated him with respect. How could he turn his back on them? On Rhona?

Macrath's head fell to his hands, and he gripped his skull, for the first time actually wishing he wasn't here. To hell with proving himself to Leticia, to Victor. To hell with trying to show his father that he was a man of honor.

This was brutal. Barbaric.

Only half of the women standing in line would walk away today. The discontents would not be rounded up to compete against each other. They'd be piled in a mass pyre and pushed out to sea. And either Rhona or Ceana would be among them. Unless one of them passed out before the round ended. And if they were to pass out, it was likely they'd die from their injuries.

Macrath had barely watched as the first four rounds of women cut at each other with their knives. The dirt-packed ground of the list field had long since turned to red mud as the blood of many spilled. He'd never been one to wilt at the sight of blood, but knowing how the field had turned to sludge twisted his stomach.

Aaron brushed past him toward the field. Ceana was next. And Rhona.

Damn.

"Come on, Macrath," Aaron muttered.

And though he didn't want to, he forced himself to stand, because the only thing he could do was move forward. He didn't want to watch, yet he'd be forced to lest he not provide Rhona with a squire and any assistance she needed—*against* Ceana.

Gods be damned!

Anger boiled through him as he watched the two women enter through the gate. He wracked his brain for a way to put a stop to what was happening, but the only answers he came up with ended with his death and theirs. But staying out of it meant one of the women would die anyway.

He marched past the women, intent on going to the council and begging for a pardon. Of all people, Aaron grabbed his arm, stopping him.

"Don't do it, Macrath. Neither one of us wants the women to fight, but if you go and make a spectacle, all four of us will die. You won't do Ceana or Rhona any good by sentencing them to death."

Macrath gritted his teeth, his feet stuck in place. The guard nearest him eyed him closely, a silent threat written in the corners of his eyes and mouth, his hand touching the hilt of his sword. Macrath drew in a long, jagged breath, glanced up at the sky. Darkening clouds edged the horizon as though the gods were warning him.

Making a decision was damned challenging, but he made it all the same. Macrath turned his back on the guard and took his spot beside Rhona, though he kept his gaze on Ceana for several moments longer than was necessary. The warrior inside him—the one who lead many into battle—tried for logic. Siding with reason was the only way he'd remain strong for both women.

Aaron passed Ceana a long, wicked-looking dagger with a curved blade. He whispered something in her ear, pressed his hand to her shoulder, and she nodded, her knuckles turning white from her tight grip. Macrath wanted to be the one offering her suggestions, words to keep her safe and comforted.

"Macrath?" Rhona's voice was full of fear. He felt like he'd failed her already.

He took a few steps to the weapons pile and picked up a dagger, equally as dreadful as Ceana's, and handed it to Rhona. He gazed into her one good eye—the other too swollen for her to even open—and hoped to calm the sheer terror that glistened there. "'Haps the two of you can agree to a few cuts, and one pretend to fall unconscious?"

Rhona shook her head. "She's little. I can win. I need to win." She looked down at the blade in her hand. "I've cut off many a chicken's head back in Argyll. I know how to use a knife."

"There is no need if you can both agree to bow out," he urged.

"I can't, Macrath. Would you bow to your enemy if you were asked, simply so no one would get hurt?"

She had a point, however much he hated to make note of it. "'Tis different," he said.

"How? This is battle, and though I didn't choose to be here, I will not fall without giving my best."

Macrath curtly nodded, finding it hard to give her any advice as to how to proceed. He'd seen Ceana offer mercy to a woman in the first round. But Rhona wouldn't even consider it. Being able to show mercy was a good trait in a leader, only another reason why he was certain Ceana would be a good match to rule beside him.

"May the gods be with you," Macrath mumbled.

She was going to fight Macrath's woman.

Dizzy from her previous injuries, Ceana managed to find whatever energy she had left inside her and brought it to the surface.

"You can do this, my laird," Aaron said. "Your clan needs you. Do not let this round be the death of you when you've made it thus far with nary a scratch."

Ceana nodded. He was right. She couldn't be defeated now.

In the distant horizon, the sky was turning orange. Night would fall soon. And in good time, since the games wouldn't last long now that the contestants had been given weapons with which to kill each other faster.

She curled her fingers around the hilt of the knife. This she was comfortable with. Thank the gods for that. The guards shouted for them to begin, and she turned her gaze on the woman named Rhona standing opposite her.

Her opponent's eyes were narrowed, one eye swollen shut, and blood streaked her gown. Thick bandages covered one arm, but that didn't seem to bother her as it didn't appear to be her fighting arm. Rhona was in worse shape than Ceana, but the fire in her brown eyes said she was just as determined to win.

Ceana sent up a prayer to the gods and her deceased family that they would watch over her and guide her. She *would* leave this field alive, even if she had to be carried. And she prayed for Rhona's soul because, even though she didn't want to, she had to take her life.

I am not a murderer. I am doing this for my people.

But even if she said it aloud, Ceana wasn't sure it would be convincing enough.

Narrowing her attention solely on Rhona, Ceana bent her knees, feet spread apart, her arms outstretched at the precise angle her brother had shown her. Her fighting stance.

Rhona's eyes widened, and she moved to copy Ceana's stance. The woman may have appeared confident, but that err in judgment showed Ceana that she would be the superior fighter.

Rhona's eye twitched, and sweat beaded on her upper lip and brow. Ceana's nerves weren't much better. Her knees shook a little, and a trickle of sweat was making its way down her spine. But she couldn't let it show. Couldn't think about it either.

Overhead a lone bird cawed, breaking the silence, and Ceana made her move. Shifting a foot forward, she thrust out her arm, cutting a slice along Rhona's injured arm from her shoulder to her elbow.

Rhona cried out, and inside Ceana did too. Her stomach turned, and she wanted to scream. The sensation of her knife breaking through Rhona's flesh reverberated again and again in her fingertips. She ground her teeth, forcing herself not to react. Demon's bollocks, but this was hard. Nonetheless, she couldn't relent. Couldn't deliberate. Ceana forced all thoughts from her mind on who this person was, where she'd come from, and that she felt the pain Ceana was inflicting on her. Instead, she pretended to be using a wooden knife and that she was at home, play-fighting with Dougal.

She went through the motions he'd taught her. Shuffling of feet, strike, retreat. Shuffling of feet, strike, retreat. Again and again. When Rhona retaliated, she ignored the burn on her shoulder, her leg, her hand.

Just kept on moving forward. Intent not to let the other woman win. Intent to be victorious. Exactly as it was when she played with her brother and clansmen and women.

When Rhona fell to the ground with a thump, Ceana's vision blurred. All she saw was red as tears streamed down her face. She stumbled backward, the bloody knife falling from her hand and thudding against the ground. Bile clawed its way up the back of her throat, and she dragged in one heavy breath after another, but no air seemed to reach her burning lungs.

Rhona was dead.

Aaron grabbed her from behind, his hands curling against her arms and forcing her from retreating further. "Come, you've won. We must get you cleaned up," he said.

He didn't congratulate her, and she was glad of that for she didn't feel like celebrating a gruesome victory. She'd taken a life. A life she couldn't give back. A person who would be missed at home. Mourned by many, including Macrath.

Aaron half dragged her on unsteady feet from the field.

Extreme grief filled her as he pulled her toward a tent that had been erected at some point but which she'd never seen before. Beneath it were bedrolls in a row and stacks of supplies for cleaning and tending wounds.

"Lie down," he said. "I have to stitch you up."

Ceana blindly listened, lying down on the ground and staring up at the white canvassed ceiling. Was this the comfort the winners would be provided? Rhona was provided no comforts except to bleed out on a field she'd never wanted to visit. Without the games, they never would have met. Never would have even heard of each other. But today Ceana had given away her soul and viciously murdered another human being. Not really in self-defense either. But purposefully.

While Ceana had watched women die in the woods when the wolves attacked, she'd not been the one to end their lives outright. Even her opponents in the first two rounds of the games had survived. Up until now, perhaps she'd not taken what the rules of the Highland War games meant. To live or die.

It was all the stuff of legends. Of heroism. And she was going to win to save her clan.

Except, in order to do that, she had to take a life. And Rhona's would most likely not be the only one.

She just wanted to curl into herself. To roll over onto her side and cry and sleep and forget about all of it. But she couldn't. It was too close to her face. Reality was a hard hit to stomach. She had someone's death on her hands. That responsibility took away a part of her soul, ripped it right out of her. By the end, she wouldn't be surprised if she was just as bitter and cruel as Lady Beatrice. She could already feel that bitterness sinking in. Shriveling her heart. When—*if*—she returned to her clan, she'd be sure to set them straight about the legends of the war games. There was nothing glamorous. Even if the victors would be named royals.

There was nothing glorious in death. Only darkness.

Aaron tugged on her sleeve, trying at first to roll it and then having to cut at the fabric to get to her wound. Her mother's gown. Ruined just like the last one.

She barely felt the sting of the needle as it entered her skin. Barely noticed the tug of the thread as he sewed the deep gash on her forearm.

"Ceana," Macrath's voice filled her head, but she couldn't look at him. Couldn't face him after what she'd done. Couldn't voice her anguish at the hurt she'd caused him. Surely he'd come seeking retribution.

"Leave this tent at once," Aaron demanded. "You're not supposed to be here."

Macrath ignored him and stood on Ceana's other side. She wanted to beg him to leave, but she was afraid that all that would come out when she opened her mouth was a scream.

"Look at me, please," he said.

"Can't you see she wants you to leave?" Aaron ground out.

Ceana rolled her head toward Macrath. "I'm so sorry," she said, her voice hoarse and tight from the need to sob. "I'm so sorry."

Macrath dropped to his knees beside her, grabbed her hand, and pulled it to his lips. Infinite calm washed over her with that one simple touch. He kissed her hand again, his own eyes closing, and in that moment she felt his forgiveness even if he had yet to speak it. Aaron sputtered, and she was afraid he might try to stab out Macrath's eyes with the sewing needle.

"'Tis all right, Aaron. Would you mind excusing us for a moment?" she asked, though it wasn't a question.

"I... I don't know if I'm allowed to leave your side."

"Tell Lady Beatrice I forced you. Let me take the blame for it."

Aaron stood, sending Macrath a glance filled with hatred. But he left the two of them alone.

Ceana kept her gaze steady on Macrath. Took in his handsome face and the worry lines etched around his eyes and between his brows. He frowned down at her, raking his eyes over her form, resting on the places where she knew she was injured.

"Are you in pain?" he asked.

"None more than I deserve," she replied, guilt making her insides hurt all the more. "I'd gladly increase the pain if it could only wash my soul clean. I took a life. She could have been someone's wife or, gods forbid, someone's mother. How can I ever forgive myself?"

Macrath shook his head. "You survived, Ceana. It is the only thing you could have done."

She shook her head. "That doesn't make me feel any better."

He nodded, his warm breath still caressing her fingertips. "A feeling that will likely never pass but perhaps the pain of which will lesson over time."

As a warrior he would know, and she trusted that.

"Can you show me how?"

Chapter Ten

CEANA watched with interest as Macrath picked up the needle and thread where Aaron had discarded it. The ground was cold beneath her back, and her hands shook from both pain and shock. Her chest welled with unspoken emotion. She knew a lot of it was the rush of battle yet to be released, the soul-wrenching pain of having taken a life, and the unconditional care this warrior bestowed on her.

"I will gladly show you anything you ask," Macrath said softly.

She smiled, liking this tender side of him. His hand was still within hers, and without hesitation she squeezed it, glad for his being there and for pardoning what she thought was unforgiveable. It was confusing and liberating all at once.

"I see that Aaron sewed your arm. Where else are you cut?"

Ceana showed him her other hand where a gash was slashed on top—but not too deep. "I don't think this one needs stitching, just bandages, but I do have one that pains me on my calf."

She tried to sit up, but Macrath gently pushed her back down. "Will you let me do it?"

Nodding, she swallowed and watched the concern flicker over his face as he gripped the hem of her gown and slowly slid it up to her knee. Gooseflesh rose along her leg, and she wasn't sure if it was from the autumn chill or the way Macrath intimately exposed her skin. Maybe a little bit of both.

"'Tis a nasty gash you have here," he murmured. He glanced around, a frown on his face. "There's no whisky."

Ceana smiled. "Need a wee nip?"

Macrath turned to her, a teasing grin curling his lips. "You will."

Though her chin trembled, she said, "I can bear it."

He did not hide his grimace well. "I don't want to hurt you."

"'Tis the price I must pay." She gave a slight shake of her head. "A penance to clean my soul."

Macrath's brows drew together, and his mouth turned down at the corners. He leaned over her, an arm on either side of her head, bracing himself. "You do not deserve pain, Ceana. You did what you were ordered to do. 'Tis the same for any warrior. We do not go willingly into battle simply because we wish to maim and murder. Nay, lass, we do it because we are protecting what is ours."

Ceana swallowed. "What are you protecting?"

"Right now? I'm protecting you from yourself. The better question is, what are *you* protecting, Ceana? Why did you come here?"

She chewed her lip, feeling the heat coming off Macrath's body in waves. The warmth of him, the way he made her feel safe, and eased some of her pain. "I am protecting my people."

He gave a curt nod. "Then do not let yourself fall off the cliff of despair, my lady, because to do so would put those you aim to save at risk, and all you've done would be for naught."

The truth of his words sunk in. She'd known it all along, but it was hard to convince herself. Hearing Macrath say it, however, brought it out in a different light. Yes, she'd killed someone. Yes, she felt terrible about it. Yes, she would remember Rhona for the rest of her days and pray for her soul. Yes, she would likely seek out any family she had and ask for forgiveness. But she would also move on. Carry through the rest of these games with one thing in mind: she had to protect her people.

"Thank you," she whispered.

"You have nothing to thank me for."

"But I have so much. I..." She rolled her head to the side, staring at the tent wall a moment before looking back at him. "I'm not sure I could carry on without your strength."

Macrath chuckled. "Well, I happen to know you would. Strength emanates from your every move. You may be tiny." He plucked her nose. "But you are mighty."

Ceana grinned. "More a nuisance to some."

"Not to me." He leaned back on his heels, his palm pressed to her calf. "Are you ready?"

She nodded and closed her eyes.

"Do you want my belt to bite down on?"

She shook her head. "Nay."

Macrath was gentle, and though it hurt like Hades, she managed to grit her teeth through it. And the reward was worth it. He lightly kissed her knee, his breath warm on her skin, sending a jolt of awareness rushing through her. He stretched out on the grass beside her bedroll.

"Lady Beatrice will come to find you soon. She will want to know what you choose for your comfort. What would you choose, Ceana?" Macrath walked his fingers up and down her uninjured arm. "A new gown? A down pillow?" He grabbed up one of the other bedrolls and rolled it, gently placing it beneath her head. "Or perhaps a lass like you would like a warm bath with fresh herbs strewn in the water. A cup of sweet wine?"

Ceana smiled, her gaze wandering over Macrath's face, studying the angular lines of his jaw and cheekbones. "I fear I'm much simpler than that."

"Is that so?"

She nodded.

"What is simpler than a cup of sweet wine?"

"I would not seek out simple measurable pleasures. I would but wish to spend the rest of my day with you." Her own words shocked her. What happened to her resolve to stay away from Macrath? That had floundered, perhaps the moment she'd thought about it. "Right here."

"Right here?" He looked around. "'Tis rather drab. 'Haps we can convince her ladyship to let us spend the evening in the great hall of the castle."

"I like your way of thinking, warrior."

"Why not get used to the place we shall call home?" He raised a brow.

'Twas not the first time he'd brought up wanting to rule beside her. Ceana brushed his comment aside no matter how it made her stomach flutter. "Indeed, and perhaps they will point us in the direction of the castle's treasure and sweet pudding," she gave him a coy smile as she brought up the topic of their very first conversation.

"And then they shall let us lay upon thick feather-tick mattresses while the servants fill our cups and trenchers."

"I wonder, when you are Prince of Sìtheil, will you spend more time lounging or crusading?"

Macrath gripped her hand and pulled it to his lips. "I suspect it will be neither."

"What will it be?" Ceana's voice came out breathy as tendrils of need unfurled within her.

"I'd rather show you."

Words escaped her. She was breathless, motionless, as Macrath came closer and pressed his lips to hers. Velvet soft, warm. He tasted of spice and smelled of rain and grass and clouds and everything outside that took her mind away from the heaviness of the games. Her heart started to pound, and warmth flooded her, taking away the chill of the ground.

Macrath had the right of it. This was a much better way to spend their days, and she prayed Lady Beatrice would grant her request to spend time with this man.

Ceana caressed Macrath's arms up to his shoulders, to the back of his neck where the ends of his long, dark hair tickled her fingertips. She rolled closer to him, wanting to feel his chest press against hers. He must have known what she wanted and desired the same for he met her halfway. She liked touching like this. The closeness of it made her feel alive and cared for. As though there was some deeper purpose in the world than simply survival.

If she'd not come to the games, she may have never been exposed to this. Nor to Macrath and how his touch quickened her breath and stirred a potent yearning inside her.

"Och, lass." Macrath slid his lips toward her neck, kissing where her heart beat. "I've never known anyone like you. Never wanted to know a lass more."

Ceana cupped the side of his cheek, his stubble scraping her palm. Their foreheads were pressed together, eyes locked. "I feel the same way."

"What is happening?" he asked, nibbling on her lips. His hand caressing over her ribs to palm her breast. "What have you done to me?"

She arched her back. "Not more than you have done to me. You've mesmerized me, taken my sense."

"Aye. First you kiss me in the woods, and then you sneak into my tent. Now you'd have me ravish you when anyone could walk in."

A throaty laugh escaped her. "You make me sound positively sinful."

"Nay, lass, what we share could never be wicked. 'Tis beautiful. Enchanting."

And it was. Like magic. He could take away her pain and fear and make her feel as though nothing could stop them. "'Tis a dream. Don't fight it, Macrath. Let us have these precious moments."

"I cannot deny you." His lips traveled a searing path from her mouth down her neck to hover over her breast. "I want you."

"I need you."

He tugged on her gown, freeing one hardened nipple. His hot mouth captured her aching flesh. A soft moan slipped through her lips, and she arched her back, wanting more of what he was giving her.

Ceana clutched him, her fingers curling into the fabric of his shirt. He was careful not to bump into her injured leg, and so he lay on the opposite side of her. He caressed her unscathed leg, fingers dancing over her calf and behind her knee. Her breath grew ragged, and she kissed the top of his head, fingers threading through his hair. Macrath stroked a little higher on her leg, pausing on her inner thigh. The pressure of his hand on such an intimate spot sent quivers of anticipation zigzagging through her veins.

"*Mo chridhe*, will you let me touch you?" Macrath's raspy voice sent a delicious chill over her.

He'd called her his heart!

"Aye," she said with a smile and tilted her hips.

Macrath groaned softly, his hand sliding delicately up her skirt to the naked crux of her thighs. She held tight to his shoulders, letting her legs fall open and thrilling at the feel of his rough palm cupping her sex. He trailed a finger through her slick folds, stroking over the knot of flesh that ignited a flame inside her center. Ceana arched into him, wanting, needing more.

She moaned softly, keeping her eyes on him. He watched her face as he touched her. Ceana felt color heating her cheeks, but she was too aroused, too ravenous, to care.

"Och, lass, you are so stunning. The way you respond to me...," he murmured, leaning down against her ear.

He claimed her mouth in a deep and demanding kiss. All the while, his fingers continued to work their magic.

"Do you like this?" he asked against her lips.

"Oh, aye," she whimpered.

The flame he'd started sparked into a full-fledged wildfire. Her limbs shook, her breathing was erratic. Heart pounded against her ribcage. Blood roared in her ears. She was dizzy. She was light. She was—

Her world exploded as decadent sensations burst inside her. The pleasure radiated from between her thighs, barreling through her entire body until her toes curled and her fingers tingled.

"Macrath," she murmured, body still quivering.

"Aye, lass?" He pulled back, grinning down at her with sensual self-satisfaction.

She gazed at him in wonderment, her brain still fuzzy from how high she'd seemed to climb and then fall. "That was... amazing."

He winked. "It was beautiful, just as you are."

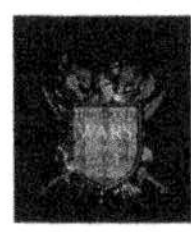

Standing outside the healer's tent, a perfect view through the slit of the writhing bodies inside, Aaron seethed.

Nostrils flared, fists clenched, he'd never felt a more burning rage than he did at that moment. It was hard to breathe. His chest heaved and teeth bared. He wanted to murder someone. To inflict pain in the worst way.

Watching *his* woman in the arms of that barbarian made him sick. It took every ounce of willpower he possessed not to march inside the tent and rip them apart. To slam his fist repeatedly into Macrath's teeth. He could almost hear the crunch, feel the slickness of his blood.

How many times had he warned Ceana away from the man? Warned the man away from Ceana? Neither of them had listened! What sort of spell did that brain-boiled man have on her? Had he poisoned her somehow, given her a witch's love brew? He wouldn't put it past him. Macrath would be the ruin of her. Aaron despised the man. Hated the way her lips opened in pleasure and wanted to strangle the soft moans from her throat.

He tasted blood and realized he'd bitten down hard on the tip of his tongue.

Well, he wasn't going to let that bootlicking churl take his place in Ceana's heart. But he wasn't stupid enough to try to tear them apart just yet. Macrath was a fierce warrior, reminded him a lot of the MacLeods. And Aaron didn't want to get hurt. That wouldn't serve his purpose.

Better to knock him down when the cur least expected it. And then he'd make sure to swoop in and save his lady.

The moment Ceana had kissed him at the Beltane festival, he'd known she was going to be his wife.

Dougal had as much as hinted to it by assigning Aaron as her personal guard. He'd protected her. Even insisted on accompanying her to these games. Before they'd arrived, he knew he was going to sign up to take part. He wouldn't let another man claim what was rightfully his for five years.

The games were theirs to win. He and Ceana would be the Prince and Princess of Sìtheil, not that overbearing varlet.

Macrath leaned in close, his lips moving against Ceana's ear and bringing a satisfied smile to her lips. What was he whispering to her now? Gods be damned, Aaron wanted to know! He'd never seen her look this way before. Wanted to be the man who made her smile. Who brought her pleasure.

"Mosquito-buggering canker blossom."

Macrath had to die.

And Aaron was going to make sure it happened, even if he had to sneak into the blackguard's tent in the middle of the night. Before these games were through, Aaron was going to feel Macrath's blood gliding over his hands.

With that delicious thought in mind, he decided to go in search of a guard. He needed to find out if the squires of the winners were also afforded comforts—and what sort of *dis*comforts the squires of the discontents would be lavished with. For Macrath's discontent was dead, and the more pain the craven suffered the better.

Game

Three

Chapter Eleven

"WHAT do you think you're doing?" Lady Beatrice MacAlpin—formerly Morrison—did not hesitate in approaching the man who stood outside the healing tent.

Anger sharpened every feature of his face, making his flesh only a shade lighter than his red hair. He looked to be wearing a MacRae plaid, though it was in such disrepair, the colors faded and melding together, she couldn't be certain. The dwindling sunlight probably had something to do with that too. However, she wouldn't be entirely surprised, as his plaid was in just as bad of shape as Ceana MacRae's had been before Beatrice took her inside to bathe her that morning.

The man jerked his gaze upward, fiery daggers shooting from his brown eyes.

Beatrice put her hand to the whip coiled at her side, prepared to beat the man if he so much as raised his voice. "Don't make me thrash you, whelp. I asked a question, and I expect an answer."

The resentment was wiped clean from his face. Seeming to come to his senses—though only partway—the man shifted on his feet, bowed his head, and tucked his hands behind his back in a show of respect.

"My lady." His voice shook, either from nerves or residual anger.

Beatrice found her patience growing thin. As if her position wasn't hard enough with having to rein in so many miscreants and watch an equal number of them die. But 'twas the way of things, and she herself knew better than to question the hundred-year-old practice. It had, after all, brought her many riches and a semblance of peace to the northern isles.

He cleared his throat, flicked his gaze up at her then back toward the ground. He hooked his thumb at the tent. "I was but checking on my laird."

"Your laird? He is injured?"

The red-haired man shook his head. "*She* is injured."

Beatrice narrowed her eyes. So this was the MacRae guard Ceana brought with her. Just how did he feel about serving a female? "Your laird is a woman?"

His head jerked in what looked like a nod. "Aye, my lady. Only just been titled, on account of our previous laird being murdered."

From what she could tell, this man was not entirely confident in Ceana's abilities. There was doubt in his voice and shifty eyes. "What is your name?"

"Aaron of MacRae." He puffed out his chest and looked up, staring somewhat toward her face, but not making eye contact.

"Ah, so your laird is the Bitch of MacRae."

That got a rise out of the man she'd been hoping for. His gaze shot to hers, no issue with connecting, despite her superiority. He bared his teeth, and she half expected him to lunge. But he kept his feet rooted, though his fists clenched.

"Best mind that temper, else you'll not have any eyes left to spy on her."

The man sputtered, fingers widening before clenching again. "I was not spying."

"Hmm." Beatrice narrowed her eyes, tapped her foot. Why had Ceana chosen this man to join the games with her?

Lairds did not have to join the games. They sent people in their stead. The fact that Ceana had joined on her own leant more to her courage and sacrifice than many. But knowing that she'd chosen to enter herself, Beatrice would have thought she'd bring along a warrior who she intended to marry. And the man standing before her… well, he was sadly lacking on many fronts.

Aside from that, Beatrice had seen the way the lass had made eyes at the other hulking warrior. Macrath. Bastard son of the Earl of Argyll.

To that end, she frowned fiercely. "What happened to Laird Dougal MacRae?"

Aaron shook his head, regret shadowing his eyes. "He was killed in an ambush by the MacLeods."

"Hmm… Is your clan raided often?"

Aaron nodded, his pallor fading when she took two steps forward.

"'Twould seem the MacRaes have fancy ways of going out of this life." Dougal and Ceana's father had been torn apart by wolves, their mother killed in a raid, now Dougal gone much the same way. And Ceana had chosen to die in the games? Or had she come here to win? To prove that she could take care of her clan?

"Stand aside," Beatrice ordered.

Aaron hesitated a moment before he moved out of her way. 'Twas true she could have walked around him, but she had a feeling he didn't take too kindly to women in authority, and so she needed to put him in his place.

"My lady—" He reached out and grasped her arm as she walked past.

Beatrice swung around, her reflexes still great despite being thirty-four years of age. She gripped her whip, yanking it free, and lashed the man on his arm before he had a chance to think twice about reaching out to her. The snap of leather and his startled cry were sharp, ringing in her ears.

"Do not deign to touch any female, especially your royal councilwoman."

"Apologies, I… I…" He gritted his teeth, eyes wide. Confusion warred on his face.

"What is the problem, Aaron of MacRae?" Beatrice stood at her full height, prepared to lash the man again if he touched her.

"My laird is… has…"

At that moment, Ceana and the bastard Macrath exited the tent. He had his arm around her waist, supporting her weight. They gazed at each other in such a familiar way that Beatrice's heart ached. She'd known love like that once, but it had been ripped away. All love was.

So enamored with each other were they that neither of them noticed Aaron or Beatrice standing there.

Blood stained the gown Beatrice had given her. A slit up the side of one sleeve revealed a bloodstained bandage. There was another on her hand, and her leg was also wrapped. The price of playing in the games. She'd considered not giving her the gown, but the poor lass's garb had been covered in filth from her fight in the mud and years of hardship. As it was, she'd had the strip of MacRae plaid that once belonged to Ceana's mother, Isla. And finding an excuse to hand over the disturbing, guilt-inducing fabric had been liberating. Ceana still wore it tied around her waist.

Just the sight of it brought a pang to Beatrice's gut. And still they'd not noticed they had an audience. When it looked as though they were ready to kiss, Beatrice cleared her throat.

"MacRae, I see you've recovered from your challenge," she said.

Ceana's gaze started on her, and then Macrath's followed. However, he recovered quicker than Ceana and bowed low.

"My lady."

Ceana ducked her head, shifting into an awkward curtsy and mumbled, "My lady."

"Why is your squire not helping you?" Beatrice looked from Aaron to Macrath.

There was a tension between the two men that begged to be explored. They exchanged heated looks—though quite different in demeanor. Aaron looked murderous, and Macrath merely annoyed.

"He was. He did," Ceana began. She gripped tight to Macrath's arm, and Beatrice had a feeling it was more for comfort than the need for support.

"Step away from her," Beatrice ordered Macrath.

Without question, and his expression flat as stone, Macrath patted Ceana on her hand and stepped away. Ceana wavered on her feet. Aaron made a move to take Macrath's place, but Beatrice's whip stopped him. She snapped it against his abdomen, and he sucked in a shocked breath but moved no further. Ceana kept her widened gaze on Beatrice, seeming to only just understand the significance of the situation she now found herself.

"A laird must stand on their own two feet no matter how grave their injury. Is that not right, Bitch?" Beatrice said, every word paining her. But she could not show Ceana special treatment, even if she wanted to. These were harsh games. Coddling her would only hurt her. And so she aimed to teach the lass a hard lesson.

Ceana straightened her shoulders, darted her gaze toward Macrath, who actually looked surprised, though for only the span of a breath.

Beatrice cocked her head and studied the man. What had he to be surprised about?

But like a good lad, he kept his questions to himself. Pity really, because Beatrice wanted to know what could have shocked this man. She'd heard of him before he'd even arrived. Indeed, the letter from his stepmother promised a world of trouble—including that he'd seduced and impregnated many of the young virgin females of their clan. Beatrice liked a virile man. Her own husband had long since passed, and she found that with each ensuing night she was lonelier and lonelier.

"I'll ask only once more, and if I do not receive an answer you will all pay with flayed backs." She looked them each in the eye to make sure they understood she was not jesting. "Why was your squire not attending you?"

Ceana stiffened, growing even taller for her tiny figure, and hobbled forward a step. "'Twas at my request, my lady."

"Your request? You think you get to request anything at the games?"

Ceana had the merit to look contrite. She folded her hands in front of her, though she did not bow her head. "No, my lady."

"We have rules for a reason." Beatrice glanced at Aaron of MacRae. The sappy way he was staring at Ceana made her want to hit him again. Alas, she was afraid he'd either cry or make an attempt to fight back. She didn't have time for such nonsense.

"Aye, my lady."

"Is your squire not capable of stitching?"

Ceana glanced down at her arm—presumably where Aaron had stitched her. "He did fine work, my lady."

"Then why did he leave the tent?"

The lass had the prudence to look guilty. "I asked for a moment with Macrath."

Ah, finally, we're at the root of the matter. "What for?"

Ceana's chin trembled, and her face colored.

"If I may?" Macrath said, his voice void of emotion.

Beatrice flicked her gaze at the warrior. He was big, wide of shoulder, and thick of muscle. His dark hair hung loosely around his face, and his jaw was square and strong. Handsome, rugged. If she was younger, she may have attempted to seduce the man. She could see why Ceana wanted him. And it simply wouldn't do. *Hmm.* 'Haps she *should* still try to seduce him.

"You may not," Beatrice snapped. "In fact, have the guards escort you to the great hall of the castle. Tell them I sent you."

All three of the warriors before her stiffened. Beatrice rather liked that. She missed not being Mistress of Sìtheil, but being a royal council member had its advantages too.

Ceana watched longingly as Macrath walked away from the list field and toward the rear gate where torches were being hung. Within the hour it would be dark. Though he'd been essentially cowed by Lady Beatrice, he walked with confidence, and she had to admire that about him.

What they'd shared inside the tent had been wondrous, and she wished to return again, to live in that moment where he pleasured her, but also to get the chance to pleasure him in turn. Macrath had denied her once more, but only because the sounds of battling had died down and he was certain that they'd be discovered. She'd not agreed to leave the tent though, without the promise that he'd come see her that night.

Ceana wondered if such a promise was too much to ask. Would it even be possible? Would he risk his life to see her? She hoped if the guards were actually alert when darkness fell that he would stay away.

"You are also dismissed." Lady Beatrice gave Aaron a scathing look. "Attend the other winners' squires in the male tent."

Aaron vacillated a moment before nodding at Lady Beatrice. He glanced at Ceana. "Will you be all right?"

Her leg throbbed, and standing there without anything or anyone to lean on only put the pressure on her injury. Her hand stung, and her arm had thankfully gone numb. But she was alive, so she had to be all right, didn't she?

Lady Beatrice scoffed. "She was fine without you a moment ago. She'll be fine without you now *and* in the future. Now be off with you."

Ceana could tell from that exchange that Lady Beatrice did not hold even an ounce of respect for the man. Poor Aaron. That seemed terribly unfair. He'd only done what Ceana had asked. And he only wanted to make sure she was all right. There was no need for the councilwoman to flay him with her tongue. Nor her whip. Her guard was certain to have several welts beneath his shirt and plaid already.

Aaron headed back toward the gate, yet he did not walk away with the same strength as Macrath. Ceana watched as the two men she cared about fell in line with the other squires crossing the bridge.

"What will happen to the discontents' squires?" she asked softly. She hoped it was not too unpleasant, for she was certain they would be punished in some way. Her heart went out to Macrath.

Lady Beatrice seemed taken aback by her question, and then the slightest upturn of her lips appeared before vanishing. A smile? Perhaps. "They will attend their masters' bodies. Injuries need to be taken care of, and the dead require burial."

"How many...?" Ceana couldn't finish her question. There had to be over a dozen dead women. She was certain of it. There'd been nearly four dozen female warriors going into the second game. Perhaps not half of them would have died, but it would be close.

She'd not been the first to fight in the third and final dagger round, but she'd been relatively close, and after—

She could still barely think it. Had to take a deep cleansing breath, and still the images of Rhona's prone, bloody body filled her mind. After Rhona, was without breath—*dead*—Ceana had gone into the tent to be stitched up, so she'd not witnessed the remainder of the round.

"How many what, Ceana?" Beatrice's voice was tight, and she stared hard at Ceana as if willing her to see into her mind exactly what she was thinking.

But Ceana couldn't see inside her head, could not fathom in the slightest what went through such a hard and bitter woman. Lady Beatrice was the epitome of everything she didn't want to become as a ruler. If—*when*—she won the games, Ceana was going to show mercy to those who deserved it.

Steeling her nerves, she said, "How many are dead?"

This time the smile on Lady Beatrice's face was clear, but it was not a gesture that brought about happy thoughts. This woman was cruel. "Dead. Death. Dying. 'Tis a word, a state of being, really, that you'll have to get used to, my sweet. Many have died, and many more will. Over one hundred entrants and only two who will win. This is not some paltry tournament, Laird MacRae, but a game of death. We play with life to see who is the mightiest."

Her words were cruel, her sentiment lacking. Ceana's empty stomach churned. All the beauty she'd shared with Macrath, the pleasure, the way he made her feel less guilty about what had to be done, it was all erased by the callous way in which Lady Beatrice conveyed their imminent and unimportant demise.

Ceana had not played with Rhona's life. She'd not been merry, nor had she made light of the fact that she'd had to take it. That woman's death would always bloody her hands, and she'd never forget it. Ceana would always walk with the guilty knowledge that she'd murdered someone in cold blood, all for the sake of a game—even if winning meant that she'd save hundreds of lives. Her clan depended on her, yes, but all the same. She'd had to kill to make it so.

Having somewhat of an understanding into how Lady Beatrice's mind worked, Ceana jutted her chin and said, "Indeed, you are correct. I purely want to know how many women I have left to fight against. I aim to win the games. I need to know the numbers."

The woman let out a laugh that was short and sharp. "There were thirty-seven women left after the first game. Fifteen women died in the second game. Including yourself, there are twenty-two female contenders remaining."

A staggering number. Thirty-six women had died in the first two rounds alone. It was enough to make Ceana double over. She'd tried to remain strong in front of Lady Beatrice, to act as though she merely wanted to know how many more she had to compete against, but callousness was not in her nature and she mourned every life lost.

"Stand strong, Laird MacRae. In order to win, you must put aside all concerns for human life and seek only to gain victory. You must care nothing for anyone. Your first and only priority is to survive. And if by some miracle you are the female champion, the war does not end there. You will have five years of hardship."

Ceana could guess that even that was not the end of it, for here stood a past female champion and she continued to remain immersed in the games and death. The games were cruel and pointless. They'd been useful in another age when war steeped the islands. And yes, there were still warring clans, and the games had diffused many fights, but what Scotland needed was unity. One powerful leader to rule them all.

How could Ceana make that happen?

She stood up straight. Instead of focusing her gaze on the woman before her, she looked off toward the castle. The place she was determined to call her own.

Ruling Sìtheil was not going to be a solitary post. There would be a male warrior as well. And if he was anything like most men, he wouldn't let her take a lead on anything. He'd probably keep her busy with women's work.

Unless that male victor was Macrath. She couldn't be certain yet that he would allow her to rule beside him, but he'd hinted to as much. He was her best chance at seeing that the poorer clans like her own were given the assistance they needed. That they need not worry over raids and starvation.

"I am prepared for all that comes with being the female champion." Ceana feigned confidence, keeping her voice flat and her face emotionless. There was no need to let this woman see inside her soul.

Lady Beatrice imparted another short burst of bitter laughter. "My dear, you will *never* be prepared for it."

Ceana turned keen eyes on the woman, ignoring her discomforting thoughts. "What is your interest in me? Why do you care? First you bathe me, clothe me, and now you come to offer your advice." She knew her questions could possibly gain her punishment, but she didn't care.

Lady Beatrice pressed her lips together in a firm line, her hands clasped before her. She squinted as she assessed Ceana. "I told you I knew your mother."

"Ah, yes, you knew my mother. And knowing her gives you a vested interest in me? Do you not know the family members of any of the other hundred and sixteen entrants?"

Lady Beatrice smiled. "You should be pleased I have an interest in you, child. But do not flatter yourself. If you were to perish in the next game, I would not shed a tear for you. Nor would I think about it beyond that moment." The woman whirled around, but not before Ceana could see that her words were clearly a lie.

She let it go, not wanting to press her luck with the woman's patience. Not wanting to ruminate for too long on the workings of her mind or why she cared. Going down that tunnel would only lead to darkness, she was certain.

Lady Beatrice marched toward the castle, leaving Ceana alone on the field save for a few straggling discontents and the guards. The spectators had also disappeared.

Ceana watched her go. Preparing herself for the painful walk back. Her respect for warriors had grown tenfold since arriving at Sìtheil.

"Best head back over the bridge afore they bring down the portcullis, forfeiting you from the rest of the games."

She'd been staring so intently after the councilwoman that she'd not realized a guard had approached. His greasy hair was pulled back tightly, secured at the nape of his neck with a leather strap. He grinned at her with rotten, cracked teeth. A long, jagged scar ran over his cheek to the place where his ear should have been. He was not one she'd dealt with before, and instantly she was on alert.

"Might also want to get going quick since many of these guards are not quite chivalrous to the females. Once Lady Beatrice crosses through the gate, it'll be closed and the rest of you left to us to do as we please."

Ceana nodded, fearing for the many that were too injured to cross back through and terrified she may not make it. "My thanks for your kindness."

"Don't mistake it for kindness, lass. Not a one of us is tender. We long since gave up our humanity for this post."

Ceana swallowed, her lips pressed firmly together. Lady Beatrice was halfway to the bridge. She gave another curt nod and turned on her heel, lifting her gown in order to run to the gate no matter how much her leg pained her. The first several steps were excruciating. She felt the stitches tearing, blood pooling in her boot, but she didn't stop.

Couldn't stop.

She'd never cease until she won.

Chapter Twelve

THE guards, who'd been lounging, stood taller as Macrath approached the back of the castle. The swords at their hips scraped against the stone rails gracing the sides of the stairs. Torches flanking the great doors flamed in the waning daylight. Gloaming swiftly approached.

The way the guards fidgeted with their weapons and narrowed their eyes shiftily in Macrath's direction caused him to wonder at their skill. Were they best with weapons? How did they fight? Or was each of them actually nervous at his approach?

Growing up, he'd learned that many of the guards connected with royals fought more like the damned Sassenachs than a true Highland warrior. Not like Macrath. Having to fight for his life nearly every day for as long as he could remember had given him a certain grit. So while he walked with ease and maintained an appearance of all casualness, every fiber in him was ready to pounce should the guards decide he was a threat.

"Stop right there," a guard clipped out. He stepped to the center of the top stair and regarded Macrath with disdain.

Macrath stopped where he stood and held his hands out to the side, showing them he was unarmed. The entrants who'd not yet gone to their respective tents started to turn their attention toward him. A spectacle that didn't involve themselves was addicting to watch.

"What do you want?" the guard asked.

Keeping his arms to the side, Macrath said, "Lady Beatrice asked me to attend her."

All six of the guards burst into laughter. One of them laughed so hard he doubled over.

"Right, and I've got flames shooting out of my arse," the one who'd spoken to him before said, adding an eye roll and purse of his disgruntled lips.

"Might want to get your friend a bucket of water," Macrath said with a confident grin. "For 'twould seem today his arse is on fire."

The men ceased their laughter, their faces taking on menacing glowers. "Best take yourself off, pig fart. The lady has yet to return, and we've an itch to give a man a beating." They clenched their fists as if to show they meant business.

It looked to be more than an itch. These arseholes wanted to pound him into the ground simply for sport.

"Apologies, but I will have to disappoint you." Macrath shrugged. "I spoke with her at the list field, and she asked me to wait in the great hall."

The men exchanged glances. Had the woman asked men to meet her in the great hall before? The way they hesitated gave him cause to believe it was so. And then again, perhaps they just weren't sure how to proceed.

"Come on up. We'll escort you," the guard said, his grin promising much more than a simple escort.

Hell. Macrath had a feeling he was about to get a beating. Only to make matters worse, his stomach growled painfully.

"Let us get on with it then," he said. After what he'd witnessed today, he was more than happy to pound a few of these bastards into the ground.

The guard stepped to the side and bowed slightly, his hands motioning toward the door. "Enter at your own risk, warrior," he said, his voice entirely too sweet.

A tremor of dread circled around Macrath's spine. He was brave, he was strong, but the games were a completely different world. He'd dealt with his cruel stepmother, his evil half brother, but these people—they were without souls. And he had no recourse. No men at his back. He was on his own.

But if he was going to get an arse beating, he was going to damn well take a few of them down with him.

Drawing in a deep breath, cracking his neck, and rolling his shoulders, Macrath put his foot on the first step. The guards' smiles deepened as he ascended the stairs. They reminded him of hungry dogs watching as their master dangled a meaty bone. As soon as he reached the platform, they grabbed his arms. He remained loose, not wanting to fight here where they'd only draw the attention of more guards. There were only six of them; he'd taken on as many men before. And a few more last winter.

"Shall we, gentlemen?" Macrath grinned at them knowingly.

That only seemed to make the guards hungrier for blood. They yanked open the doors and thrust him inside. The shove against his back had been hard, and they obviously wanted him to fall, but he'd been expecting it. He shuffled on his feet, keeping his balance, and whirled around in the darkened entryway.

"You let go of my arms," Macrath taunted, holding out his hands. But the dimly lit vestibule was not the place to fight. He wanted more space, more leverage—like a table and benches. The great hall was perfect.

He ducked when one of the guards swung out his fist—taking note of the stiff metal rings sewn into the knuckles of his leather gloves. He took note that each of the guards had now donned a pair.

Well, that wouldn't feel good connecting. Would likely tear a bit of his flesh too. The guards weren't going to play fair. *No quarter given.* Seemed to be the motto in all things.

Macrath ducked when another man swung, but he did not make contact himself. Didn't even try. That would only aggravate the bears, and he wasn't ready to fight yet. Not until they reached the great hall.

"Come now, I thought you were escorting me to the great hall? Would Lady Beatrice want me to be bloody when she finally returns?"

"You can stop pretending the lady asked for you. We know you came along just for a good buggering." The main guard curled his lips, resembling a silent snarl. He gripped his cock within his plaid and gave a waggle.

Macrath had to keep his foot firmly planted on the stone floors, lest he kick the man right in his bollocks.

"And you could tell that just by me asking to be taken to await her ladyship?" Macrath asked.

The men all nodded, advancing on him from all sides.

Macrath narrowed his eyes, suddenly suspicious that perhaps that was exactly what she'd ordered. A conspiring code.

"I assure you, while you all look like fine lads, I'm simply not in the mood to play cock swords."

The men laughed, their gazes shooting to their leader, who was closest. "But you see, my friend," the man said, "you've not got a choice. Grab him!"

Macrath braced himself as the six guards jumped on him at once. Their hands were rough, but he was rougher. He punched, kicked, rolled and head-butted. He didn't pause for a moment but kept on fighting through the pain of their attempts. But six guards intent on subduing him in small quarters proved to be too much. They pinned him to the ground, their weight holding him down—three on his legs, two on his arms and, one on his abdomen.

"A fighter we've got, lads."

"'Twill make it all the more fun to see him bleed."

"You bastards won't think it so funny when I've got your heads on spikes," Macrath said through gritted teeth. "Let us fight like men. Put me down, cock nibblers."

The main guard smiled and shook his head. "We're going to have a lot of fun with you, bastard of Argyll."

Macrath stilled, the haze of his anger clearing and replaced by apprehension.

"That shut you up, now didn't it?" The man sneered and put his face close enough to Macrath that he could smell whisky and onions on his breath.

"You don't know what you're talking about." Macrath hoped the men were merely guessing at who he was.

Had Lady Beatrice planned to send him here all along?

"Oh, but"—the man slid a leather covered finger down Macrath's cheek—"we do." He stood from where he'd sat on Macrath's chest, making it easier for him to breathe. "Take him to the great hall."

They hoisted him none too gently off the ground and half carried, half dragged Macrath through a second set of doors and down three or four stairs. They tossed him onto the floor, his shoulders hitting the hard wood before his backside. Taking a moment to glean his surroundings, Macrath stared at the torches on the stone walls, the tapestries bearing the clans of victors past, and the waiting feet of a man and woman by the dais behind him.

"Looks like the fun's going to have to wait, bastard," the guard grumbled.

Macrath pushed himself up and turned slowly. Two people he wished to never see again stood with smug expressions on their hated faces.

Leticia. Victor.

Macrath kept his grimace inward and feigned boredom. There was no sign of his father.

"Did you not say we'd meet again, Macrath?" Leticia said, her cruel voice dripping with honeyed vinegar.

Mo chreach. Aye, he'd said it, but he'd hoped it would be after he'd won the games and could flaunt her hatred in her face by the fact that he'd won.

Forcing a smile he was certain resembled more of a grimace, he said, "A pleasure to see you again, my lady. I pray your journey was comfortable?"

Victor snorted, and Leticia shook her head with contempt. "We did not come for idle chatter. We came to watch you die."

And ever so subtle. He resisted the urge to roll his eyes heavenward. "How thoughtful of you," Macrath said. He folded his arms over his chest but refused to say more—especially his burning question—when would that be? Now? In an hour? Tomorrow?

At least he wasn't being buggered by the six guards, though he might have taken that over speaking with his hated family members.

"Where is his lordship?"

A flash of irritation centered in Leticia's eyes. Had she asked him to come and he'd refused? Was Macrath correct in seeing a bit of tension where the subject was concerned?

"He had many duties to attend to," she answered. "Did not see the point in wasting his time on you."

"Ah, but I see you did." He grinned.

Leticia scoffed, displeased that he'd turned her words around.

"Lady Beatrice has informed us you've taken a liking to one of the female warriors." Victor licked his lips, and Macrath could already picture him tearing into Ceana.

But Ceana wasn't a meek maid like many of the women Victor tormented. If he went after her, Macrath had confidence Ceana would cut off his bollocks. All the same, he needed to use caution where she was concerned. How had the lady gleaned the information and shared it with his family so quickly? Had they been here all along? Was he being followed?

Macrath kept his expression grim. "Aye, and now she's dead."

"Dead?" Victor raised a brow while Leticia merely studied him with that cunning and cruel gaze she'd used on him since he was a child.

"Aye. Dead," he repeated. He sent a prayer up to the gods to protect the kitchen maid Leticia had forced into the games.

"Who?" Leticia said coolly, an overplucked brow arched. The bitch was forever trying to keep up with the Sassenachs.

"Rhona, of course."

"Ah, Rhona..." Leticia stepped off the dais and sauntered toward Macrath. "Poor, poor Rhona. What will her boy do now?"

Macrath kept his unsettledness at her approach to himself. He looked his stepmother right in the eye when he said, "Hopefully get as far away from you as possible."

Leticia laughed, pressed her body against Macrath's. Her breasts pushed into his chest, nipples hard, and her bony hips bumped against his thigh. Sourness coated his tongue. "And what about you? What will you do?"

Macrath kept his mouth shut because to tell his stepmother he wanted to rip her limb from limb and feed her head to the wolves would likely get him excluded from the next round of games and ultimately lose him the victory.

She shifted in front of him and gripped his belt. Her claws slid downward, scraping nails over his cock. She gripped his bollocks tight, and revulsion almost had him doubling over. Almost. They'd been in this situation before, and he'd learned to keep still. To not vomit.

"I could rip these off if I wanted to," she said.

He kept his eyes steady on hers. "Likely you should rip off your son's, afore he populates the whole of his clan like his father."

Fury flamed in her eyes, and she tightened her grip painfully. He probably should have stayed silent, but she'd goaded him to the point of no return by putting her vile hands on him. The woman was sick and twisted. Evilness came in all forms. And she'd passed it down to her eldest son.

"Lady Leticia, so good of you to come." The chill voice of Lady Beatrice broke through his stepmother's anger, and she quickly stepped away from Macrath, leaving him with throbbing balls and a hatred that threatened to burn the castle to the ground.

"My lady." Her voice was back to honeyed vinegar. Over the top and discernibly phony. Leticia bent into a low curtsy, and Victor too bowed toward the royal councilwoman.

"I see your stepson and you have already been reacquainted." Lady Beatrice's voice was cold.

Macrath chanced a glance at the woman to see her shrewdly observing them. Had she seen what happened before she interrupted them? Or simply guessed that his stepmother abhorred him? Perhaps she didn't even care. Perhaps her disdain of Leticia stemmed from elsewhere.

"Indeed," Leticia said. "He's still alive."

"'Tis a pleasure to meet you, Lady Beatrice." Victor stepped forward to kiss her knuckles. "We've heard so many admirable stories about you."

Lady Beatrice cocked her head. "Have you? Such as?"

Victor faltered but quickly recovered. "About your victory and rule. You are much revered in the Highlands. My mother has very fondly regaled us of your wisdom."

Lady Beatrice smiled tightly. "Hmm."

Macrath would have given a chest full of silver to see inside Lady Beatrice's mind and to know her thoughts.

"To what do we owe your presence?" Lady Beatrice asked. She flicked her fingers toward a servant who jumped forward to hand her a cup of wine. "Drink?"

Leticia and Victor took the proffered cups, while Macrath was bypassed.

His stepmother and half brother each looked more nervous with every passing moment. "We have come to watch the games," his stepmother said, followed by a charming and calculating smile.

"And to cheer on your entrant?" Lady Beatrice flicked her gaze quickly at Macrath. "I'm afraid your female has already passed on." She casually sipped at her wine as if she'd been relaying something as mundane as the weather.

"Yes, I'm afraid we heard about that," Leticia said. Her voice lacked any remorse.

"Pity," Victor chimed in. He too did not give a fig about Rhona's death or the little boy who'd been orphaned by it. A boy Macrath suspected was fathered by his disgusting half brother.

Macrath wanted to smash their heads together. To watch them bleed. To see them gutted as the women had done to each other.

"Have you been given accommodations?" Lady Beatrice asked. "You'd be considered a guest of honor and housed within the castle."

And whatever rooms they had Macrath would see scoured with flames when he took his seat.

"Indeed, the chatelaine saw us to it." The look of cruel enjoyment that momentarily passed over Victor's face only added to the rage inside Macrath. Seemed his half brother had already availed himself to the help. Vile bastard.

Lady Beatrice held her eyes steadily on Victor. Macrath had the distinct impression that she already knew exactly what had happened. Would she uncoil that whip and see it used on Victor's back?

As much as he wanted her to, Macrath knew in reality it wouldn't do for a council member to lash the son of an earl for a cause that couldn't be proved. No servant would come forward to say they'd been raped by a wealthy nobleman.

"We wish you every comfort," she said. "The council feast will begin shortly. I'll have you notified of when to return to the great hall to join us."

Leticia's eyes widened, her mouth forming a surprised O. She did not hide confoundedness well. Macrath kept his joy at that hidden. The bitch was being dismissed, and she didn't like it. Hadn't seen it coming.

Well, he enjoyed it a hell of a lot.

As much as he disliked Lady Beatrice, he was pleased that she'd so easily batted his relations away.

The same servant who'd served them wine stepped forward and lifted the cups from both Leticia and Victor's hands. They could not hide their dumbfounded faces as they dipped into a bow and curtsy respectively.

"My lady," they each murmured.

And just as they seemed to be doing everything in unison, they each glowered at Macrath as they passed. He felt their hatred all the way to his bones. But it didn't bother him. In fact, the shield of iron he'd set up around himself since he was a boy deflected their blows and turned it back on them. When he was Prince of Sìtheil, he'd find a way to make them suffer for all they'd done to him and the lesser members of the clan.

Just to make them angry, he beamed a smile. "A goodnight to you both," he said.

Victor took a step forward but then thought better of it when Lady Beatrice cleared her throat. Macrath disliked that it appeared he was hiding behind the woman's skirts. Then again, his half brother hated women, so he also liked that a woman was pushing him away. Hard to say, but he thought he just might let her take the lead from now on where his family was concerned. They could care less about Macrath's reactions. But a royal councilwoman? That was a bite in the arse.

"Come with me." Lady Beatrice did not look his way, simply whirled from his relations and walked in the opposite direction past the trestle tables.

She disappeared through a small arched doorway on the far side of the great hall before Macrath could make his feet move. He hastened toward the door and once through was left alone in a darkened stone stairwell.

Had she gone up or down?

"Macrath!" Her voice carried from above.

He took the circular stair two at a time, checking at the first level he reached but not seeing her. On the next, he saw her standing in the corridor waiting. Her foot tapped, and irritation pinched her lips.

"You did not fight today. You should have plenty of strength to traverse the stairs."

He nodded, not entirely sure what it was she wished him to say.

"Do not make me wait again."

"Aye, my lady," he murmured.

Lady Beatrice turned her back on him and walked down the darkened corridor as if by memory. Shadows jumped out at him as they passed thin arrow-slitted windows, curtained alcoves, and several closed doors.

At the end of the corridor, she took out a long key and centered it in the iron lock. His stomach tightened. Was she going to put him in a cell?

He was not shackled. Arms free, he could easily tackle her to the ground if she chose to... What?

The door opened with a creak, and Macrath had no real choice accept to walk through the door. Blackness blanketed the room until he heard the click of the flint stone and saw the spark. She set a fire in the hearth and then moved slowly to light several candelabras around the room, revealing a chamber he wished he'd never stepped into.

He could run.

But he'd only be caught.

"Stand against the wall," she demanded, pointing right behind him.

Macrath turned to see an iron ring up on the wall, a chain ending in shackles dangling from it.

"Is this necessary?" he asked. "I only stitched Ceana MacRae." He prayed the lie was not visible on his face.

"It is entirely necessary. Now turn around and put your arms up."

Macrath did as she asked, his belly against the stone wall. She clicked the shackles into place around his wrists.

"I'm going to undress you." The lady's voice had taken on a throaty note.

Either he was about to be flogged or raped. He wasn't sure which, only knew that this was entirely out of the ordinary and that he wished to take flight.

"And you're going to do exactly what I say."

Macrath nodded. What else could he do? He was shackled to the wall in a locked chamber inside a castle, surrounded by enemies.

He might not have fought on the field today, but he was certain he was about to do battle now.

Chapter Thirteen

THE feast for the winners of game two had been small and quiet.

And lonely.

Ceana felt the loss of Macrath's presence acutely. There was a coldness beside her that could only be warmed by him.

Aaron had done all that he could to make her comfortable, signaling for the servants to fill her trencher with meat, bread and candied fruits. Her cup was never empty of sweet wine. Nevertheless, Ceana had no taste for it. She ate because she needed to replenish her energy. She drank at first because she was thirsty and then because the warmth of the wine had helped to ease her worry over Macrath.

But now, in the quiet of her tent with the fading light casting gray shadows all around her, she stared at the ceiling. Sleep eluded her, and a chill surrounded her heart.

Her wounds throbbed; her mind was clouded with guilt and sadness. She was exhausted. Utterly drained.

But worst of all was the nagging feeling inside that something was wrong. She felt extremely unsettled. On edge.

Where was Macrath now? What did Lady Beatrice want with him in the castle?

She rolled onto her side, unable to get comfortable. Wind blew against her tent, ruffling the fabric and causing a draft to blow over her prone form. Flashes of torch flames mixed with the light of the moon seeped into her tent with each burst of wind. The air smelled like rain and the smoke of banked fires. Judging by the chill and aggressive gusts, they were in for a nasty storm.

"Where are you, Macrath?" she whispered to the tent wall.

The wind picked up, shaking her tent. The wooden stakes holding it up swayed, threatening to collapse. At this rate, she'd be using the tent as a blanket rather than for shelter.

Somehow she'd managed to power through the war games to this point. But lying here in the dark, alone, injured, and having more than just her own life at stake, the trauma of it all was pushing through the wall she'd set up around her heart.

Waiting was the hardest part. They were through two games, three to go, and yet she didn't know when the next game would begin or what it would entail. How long would the war games last? How long did

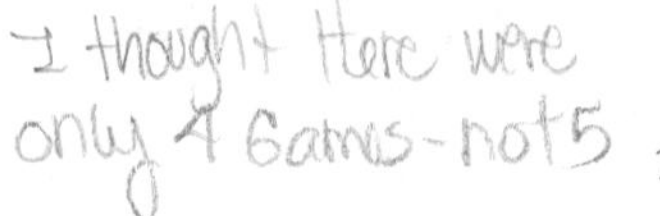

she have left to live? And where in bloody hell was Macrath?

Would they make the males and females fight next, or would the men fight amongst themselves as the women had in the previous game?

She rolled onto her back, flopped her uninjured arm over her eyes, and let out a frustrated sigh.

"Ceana."

She started, lifting her arm and blinking into the darkness. Were her eyes deceiving her?

A tall, muscled shadow stood at the entrance of her tent.

"Macrath?" He looked like an apparition, his face wrecked with emotion, blood dripping from the corner of his lip. Her heart skipped a beat.

"What happened?"

He dropped to his knees, his head bowed. His hair dripped, wet with rain. The opening flap of her tent whipped in the wind.

The man had been broken somehow.

Ceana crawled over to him, placing her hands on his cold, bare knees. She pressed her fingers to his stubbled chin, feeling him tremble beneath her touch. "Macrath, look at me."

Though his head remained bowed, his eyes lifted to hers. Lighting struck outside, momentarily brightening the inside of the tent and illuminating his eyes. She shivered at what she saw inside them.

"They will be looking for me soon," he said.

Panic seized her insides. "What did you do?"

He shook his head, hands gripping hers. "But I had to come see you before."

Ceana glanced away, finding it hard to grasp exactly what he was trying to tell her. "Macrath, you're scaring me. Before what? What *happened*?"

His hands were damp and cold, yet sweat beaded on his upper lip.

"You're the only one I can trust," he whispered.

"Yes, you can trust me." She cupped the side of his face, wiped away the blood on his lips with her thumb, then kissed him quickly, reassuring herself of his presence. "That is not something you'll ever have to question."

He laughed, but it was not a happy sound. It was jaded, dark. He moved suddenly, clasping both her hands in his and bringing her fingers to his lips. "There is much I've questioned in life. Much I've asked the gods for guidance on. Some things were a certainty, and at other times I've been surprised."

Macrath paused and rather than answer, Ceana searched his face, wishing there was some way she could drag him from the mire he was immersed in.

"I have been a fool." He shook his head, let go of her hands. He scrubbed his face with his palms. "They want me to die, Ceana."

"Who?"

"My family. The council."

She was so confused. So afraid. Whatever happened in the castle with Lady Beatrice, he wasn't yet ready to share with her. "You already guessed that your stepmother wanted you dead. But the council?"

"I came to the games with a purpose. Aye, I had no choice in entering, but I had a plan. I was going to win."

Was? Why did he say was? Her heart skipped a beat. "Macrath, you *are* going to win."

He shook his head and said, "No." His voice was filled with such despair it brought stinging tears to her eyes.

"Macrath, yes! You are." She grabbed his arms, squeezing his thickened muscles and wishing she could shake some sense into him. "I cannot win without you."

He shook his head again. "Lady Beatrice favors you to win, lass. But she favors me for something else. I'm so sorry… She… She gave me no choice."

"What choice? If that were true, then you wouldn't be sitting here."

He laughed again, shook some of the rainwater from his hair. "You are naïve if you think my being here means anything other than me needing to be near you."

"What happened in the castle? How did you get here?"

"My stepmother and half brother are here." He'd avoided answering her, but the news he imparted was heavy.

"Why have they come?"

"To watch."

"And what of the council? What did they tell you?"

"Lady Beatrice…" Macrath pressed his hands to either side of her face, pressed his forehead to hers. "She chained me in a room. She undressed me. She flogged me. She touched me…" He stopped abruptly.

A chill ran through her, circling around her spine and threatening to turn her heart to ice. Ceana stood, straightened her shoulders, and gripped his chin, forcing him to look up at her. She couldn't watch the strong, formidable Highlander she knew him to be fall so far into despair. She had to bring him back. "Macrath, do you know what your name means?"

"Son of Fortune. My mother gave me the name because of who my father is. I'm a bastard."

Ceana shook her head. "No, warrior. She gave you that name because you are a champion. You are the son of the gods, and victory is your fortune. Do not let the presence of evil collapse your will to survive and thrive. Do not let *anyone* get in the way of your truth."

He looked up at her with hooded eyes, his lips pressed firmly together. She couldn't let him deny her. Deny himself.

"Stand up." She held out her hand. "Take my hand."

He studied her outstretched hand for several moments, and she was afraid he would ignore her. Outside the storm raged, thunder booming above and lightning sparking. Great drops of rain pelted the tent, and sprays flicked onto them with each flap of the tent's walls. But finally he reached up and took it. A chill still filled his flesh, but there was a renewed strength in his grip. Macrath stood, towering well over a foot taller than her. She craned her neck to look up at him, smiled, and squeezed his hand.

"That wasn't so difficult, was it?" she asked tentatively.

Macrath stepped closer, said in low tones, "I would do anything for you."

His hand was slowly starting to warm inside hers, and the resilient man she'd come to know began to reappear. "I know. But what will you do for yourself?"

He frowned. "I have little choice in the matter."

She poked him in the chest, and he inhaled sharply. "That is where you are wrong, Macrath. You have three choices: win, lose, or run away."

"Running is the same thing as being defeated."

"Then you only have two choices."

Macrath thought on her words a moment. Then he gripped her shoulders and brought his face close to hers. Anger clouded his eyes in sparking, lightning flashes. His brow was wrinkled, lips flattened. For a moment she was frightened, but she knew he wouldn't hurt her. Even still, the pent-up rage churning through him vibrated through his fingers and centered in her chest.

"I don't have a choice. Don't you see? That woman will not let me win. She won't let me leave the next game alive." Rage pulsated in every one of his words.

But anger was better than defeat.

"How do you know this?"

He growled. "When she had me chained to a wall in her secret chamber and her whip on my back, I had a very good idea."

How could Lady Beatrice treat them both so differently? It only made Ceana's confusion more potent. "But—"

"Don't you get it? My stepmother shows up, takes me by the bollocks, and lets me know she's going to enjoy watching me die." He flicked his gaze away. "Moments later the woman who says whether I live or die, controls whether or not I breathe, makes certain I know just that."

Anger and fear laced itself together within Ceana, and she gripped tight onto Macrath's shirt, tugging him into her. "You're blind. When you're in the games, the only one who can say whether you live or die is you. You aren't fighting Lady Beatrice or your stepmother or half brother on the field or in the woods. They are evil, but they will not break a century-old rule."

"What rule? There are no rules."

He had a point. And Lady Beatrice had taken a dozen lives on the first day simply because they didn't follow her rules.

"Every game has rules, even if they change at the whim of the council."

"And how am I supposed to win?"

Ceana stepped away, crossed her arms over her chest, and narrowed her eyes at Macrath. "I like you, Macrath. I trust you. Care for you. I have… taken pleasure with you. The day we met, I noticed a strength in you that is not in many. You captivated me. You saved me. You made me strong again when I was weak. You are a natural-born leader. And when these next three games are done, we will rule together. But I can't do it without you. I can't win without you. You've said it before, but now we make a pact. We do this together. You and I."

"You and I," he repeated, sounding slightly amazed.

"Yes, you and I. Giant rubies, tarts and…" The third thing on their list was—

"This." In one stride, he had her in his arms, hands framing her face, his lips crashing down on hers.

She sank against him, just as eager to fall into this kiss. She wrapped her arms around his waist, careful not to touch his back where Lady Beatrice had whipped him. Hooking her fingers in the back of his belt, she held tight. His warmth seeped into her body, loosening her tight limbs and at the same time sending a rush of chills through her. His mouth slid over hers, tongue teasing the corner of her lips until she opened for him and he swept inside to claim all she offered.

Macrath tasted of raw desire, excitement, and feral rage. She was taken up by it, swirled into the storm of his passion and hunger, feeding the primitive part of her that craved wild abandon.

He bent low and then lifted her into the air, tucking her close against him. Every hard line of his body melded with her softer curves. She wrapped her arms around his neck, threading her fingers in his damp hair.

The storm outside subsided as though it had culminated in their kiss and now everything could be right with the world. Except… Even as they kissed, she could hear marching outside. The chinking of weapons against bodies. The pound of footsteps in the mud.

The guards. They were coming for Macrath. Just as he said they would. She sensed it in every bone in her body.

Pulling back, she held tight to his shoulders and gazed deeply into his eyes. "You have to go," she said. "They are coming."

"I know." But he pressed his lips hard to hers again.

Once more she was swept up in his kiss, wanted to disbelieve what she was hearing outside. Fear at them discovering Macrath within her tent warred with her need to feel his lips on hers, to be safe and warm in his arms. "You have to go now, Macrath. They are close."

He set her down on unsteady feet. "I will fight to win, Ceana. We will rule beside each other."

She nodded. The pain of her injuries had disappeared while in his arms but now started to throb.

"This way!" The guards shouted, perhaps three tents away.

They were looking for her tent. Her heart seized. There was no time left. If Macrath didn't leave now, they'd catch him. "They come from the front. Leave through the back."

Macrath kissed her one last time and then took two long strides to the back. "I'll find you. Whatever these next games bring, I will protect you."

She smiled. "And I will protect you."

Macrath grinned, and Ceana could have melted with joy that, whatever dark place he'd been in, a door had opened letting the light back inside.

"Go," she said when he stayed. "Hurry."

Macrath slipped beneath the back wall of her tent. As soon as she turned her eyes toward the front, the flap whipped outward and several guards filed in with two lanterns, casting a hazy yellow light. Their leering eyes and smiles made her skin crawl. They shifted their gazes, looking for any signs of Macrath, but quickly centered back on her. There was nowhere for anyone to hide in her tent. And thank the gods he'd gotten out as quickly as he had.

Ceana squared her shoulders and fisted her hands at her sides. She'd not let these men see how much they intimidated her. They were armed to the teeth as usual. Eyes were bloodshot from too much whisky, and water dripped from their hair and clothes. The stench of their bodies filled her tent like a muddled cloud.

"Hello, Bitch." She'd recognize the voice of the man anywhere. The game steward who'd named her Bitch of MacRae.

"And whom do I have the pleasure of addressing?" She acted with as much regal bearing as she could bring, pretending she did not recognize him. Wanting him to feel just how insignificant he was to her. She might be an entrant in these games, but she was also a laird and as such required a certain amount of decorum and pride.

"Where is Macrath?" the steward asked, taking a step forward.

"Macrath?" She held her ground and feigned ignorance.

"The overbearing boar you've been letting lift your skirts."

Ceana gasped with outrage, shoved aside their vulgar representations of the beauty of Macrath's touch. She placed her hands on her hips and jutted her jaw forward. "How dare you speak to me like that? Such slander ought to gain you a lashing."

He squinted, not at all touched by her show of anger. "The only one who's going to get a lashing is you, lass."

"What for?" She kept her voice strong, though inside she quaked.

"Harboring a male entrant in your tent."

She held out her arms. "But as you can see, there is no one in my tent."

"'Haps he lies beneath your skirts."

Ceana laughed sharply, but stopped short. She glowered at the man, then gripped her skirts and lifted, baring just below her knees. "No one. You're mistaken."

The move was bold, and in hindsight, she should not have done it. The way their eyes bulged with lecherous interest was enough to make her wish she could run out of the back of her tent as Macrath had. She prayed he was far, that he'd made it back to the safety of his tent.

Thunder cracked outside, and the storm that had subsided raged once more.

The game steward took a swaggering step forward. "You recall my offer?" he asked.

How could she forget the way he'd shaken his limp prick at her and asked if she wanted to join him for a night of unpleasantness? "Do you recall my response?" she said haughtily.

"Nay. Nay I don't, bitch." He reached for her, but she batted his hand away.

"Don't touch me." She took a step back, but he flicked his hand out, and his men surrounded her.

This was not going to end well for her. Alone in her tent with lecherous men who had no qualms… Her heart dropped to her feet.

"Or what?" Another step closer. His rotten breath washed over her face. "Rain's pelting. Thunder's clapping. No one to hear you scream."

Nails digging into her palms, she forced her voice to come out strong. "Lady Beatrice will not be pleased. You will be punished for your threats."

He stroked her cheek, and Ceana had to swallow her revulsion. "Och, sweet lass, you mistake me." His voice was soothing in a chilling sort of way. "I did not make any threats."

Ceana's throat tightened, her eyes burned with tears.

The steward grabbed the plait of her hair at the base of her skull and yanked. She shrieked as pain radiated through her scalp and her head snapped backward.

"You see, bitch," he whispered in her ear, "I don't have to make threats, because I'm a man of action." His nasty, snakelike tongue flicked out to lick along her jaw. She gagged. "And when I see something I want, *nothing*, no ladies, no council, can take it away from me."

He tugged hard on her hair again, forcing her to her knees. Her eyes were at level with his belt, and the way his plaid jutted out made it obvious what fueled his cruel behavior. But Ceana would be damned if she let this filthy pig ravage her.

"And you're going to do exactly what I say without complaint and without a fight, then you're going to do the same for my friends here, else I will make certain Macrath is hung before the sun rises."

She glared up at him, pain centering on the ends of every hair on her head as he still held her tight. "You won't. You can't."

"Oh, can't I?" He sneered. "The bastard is already on Lady Beatrice's shite list. A few kind words from myself and he's as good as dead."

"You won't get away with this." She nearly choked on the last words as bile rose in her throat.

"Och, lass. You naïve, little bitch. I already have." He yanked up his plaid, his red, angry-looking phallus protruding from beneath. "Open your mouth."

Ceana clamped her lips closed and met his eyes with as much contempt as she'd showed the MacLeod who killed her brother.

"You wish to fight me, then?" He touched his decrepit phallus to her mouth.

And Ceana did open, but not in the way he wanted. Her insides rolled, forcing their way up from her stomach and coming out in a deluge of meat, bread, wine, sugared fruit and pure, unadulterated revulsion.

"Fucking whore!" the steward shouted, letting go of her hair and jumping back.

Vomit dripped down his legs, and thank the gods, his plaid had fallen back in place.

The guards surrounding her laughed, slapping their knees, which of course only seemed to fuel the steward's anger even more. He wrenched back his fist and slammed it into the side of her face.

Ceana wavered a moment on her knees, pain shattering inside her skull. She tasted blood. And then she was falling down, hands then elbow and then her head hitting the ground. The last thing she remembered was trying to force herself not to succumb to the blackness surrounding her.

Chapter Fourteen

"WHERE are you taking the lady?" Macrath asked.

He stood in front of Ceana's tent, arms crossed over his chest, leg's braced. His chest was tight, and he was finding it hard to rein in the supreme fury racing through his veins. She was tossed over the game steward's shoulder, eyes closed, though she didn't look peaceful. Even in sleep, she was disturbed by what was happening to her. He kept his face void of emotion as he regarded each of the guards who exited her tent. Though it took an enormous amount of willpower to do so. He raked his gaze from their heads to their toes, counting weapons, assessing their skill.

The steward had what looked like vomit down the front of his plaid. Ceana's?

In the dim light from their lanterns, he could easily see a bruise darkening her cheek that wasn't there before. He wanted to rip the men to shreds. Why had he agreed to leave? This was his fault. Guilt only fueled his need for vengeance.

"None of your business, Macrath. Stand aside," the guard who stood adjacent to the steward answered, taking a menacing step forward but moving no further.

"Well, as it happens, I've seen you take a lifeless entrant from her tent." He stared hard at the steward. "Hence, as a witness, I believe 'tis my business."

"She's not without life," the steward said, "quite the opposite."

That got a rise out of several of the other guards who elbowed each other and laughed. Dammit. He should not have left her alone. Should have protected her. And now she'd had to fend for herself, and gods knew what they had inflicted on her. Oh, games and council be damned, he was going to rip these brutes to shreds.

"I'd put her down if I were you," Macrath said. He rolled his head to one side and the other, cracking the tension. Clenched his fists.

A couple of women poked their heads out of their tents. One behemoth in particular with what appeared to be a milky-white, blind eye, came out.

"What are you doing with MacRae?" She walked toward the group, shoulders stiff with anger.

"Aye, Steward. Tell us all what you're doing with her?" Macrath said, raising a brow.

Six women came to surround the larger woman. Appeared he had some backup now.

"I don't have to answer to the likes of you vagrants," the steward sputtered.

He shifted Ceana on his shoulder. She groaned painfully but did not waken.

Macrath bared his teeth. "Well, as I see it, you do. You're not only outnumbered but likely outranked."

The guards scoffed. "Shut the hell up and move out of the way. You know naught, you lying bastard."

Macrath shook his head. "You hold over your shoulder a laird, and though a bastard I may be, my father's an earl."

"And so is mine," the larger woman said.

"Best leave MacRae to us," Macrath said. "We'll take care of her so you can be on about your duties."

The steward spit at Macrath's feet. "You'll pay for your interference."

"Not before you do, I'm certain. Put her down."

"Don't be so definite in your confidence, bastard. I'll be reporting you to the council for insubordination." The goons surrounding the steward nodded.

Macrath grinned. "Likely they'll give me a good lashing." It wasn't anything he'd not gotten already. In fact, he'd gotten much worse. Beatrice had whipped his back, his buttocks, his thighs. Every inch of him stung from the swelling. But worst of all, she'd done it in the nude. Brushed her breasts against his marred back. Pressed herself between him and the wall, hooked a leg around his hip and rubbed the apex of her thighs against him. Grew angry when his body did not respond…

Ceana groaned again, her eyes blinking open. He was relieved that she'd wakened and pleased to release the unpleasant reminders of his ordeal in the castle from his thoughts.

"'Tis all right. I'll get my piece out of her later." He slapped her hard on the arse.

"Not afore it gets broken off," Macrath growled.

About to step forward and punch the man in his pockmarked nose, the guard tossed Ceana to the ground. Already in motion, Macrath dove forward in enough time to catch her head before it hit, but not before a wicked kick of a boot landed in his ribs. He kept his grunt muted, not wanting to give them the satisfaction of knowing it had stung.

Ceana's eyes opened, the moon reflecting in their depths. "What...?" But she clamped her lips closed as she took in everyone around her. Rain splattered on her pale cheeks, and she shivered in his arms.

A loud horn broke the silence, and everyone stopped what they were doing to momentarily look at the sky.

Then the steward began to chuckle. "Looks like you curs are all about to be beaten." He glanced back at his men. "Let's go."

The guards shouldered their way through the women, not giving a fig when they bumped a little too hard and a slighter female fell.

"We've just finished a game! Haven't even slept a night and now we have to fight again?" one of the women sobbed.

"We are not on holiday. Suck in your tears, wench," the larger, one-eyed woman growled.

"Macrath...," Ceana croaked. She swiped at her mouth with the back of her hand. Clutched at him with her free arm. "I am beaten."

He gathered her in his arms and held her close. The other women dispersed through the tents toward the center lane where they were all to go line up.

"I gather we've both been through hell this evening," he murmured, kissing away a tear that slid over her temple. "The only way to show them that we are not well and truly beaten is to forge ahead, lass. We must not show our weakness."

"But I already have," she choked on a sob. "He put his…"

"Shh…" His chest swelled, and he found his own eyes prickling. They'd both been violated this night. "I should not have left you. I'm so sorry."

Ceana shook her head against his chest. "They would have done worse to you."

"Nay, lass. Nothing is worse than despoiling a woman." Not even the battering Lady Beatrice had given him.

"They were looking for you. They knew you'd be here with me."

He nodded. Lady Beatrice had said as much when she let him go. Warned him not to go to Ceana or she'd send the guards after him. But after the lashing she'd given him, he'd not known where else to go, save for the comfort of the only person he trusted. He needed the security of her innocence and sweetness, the strength of her will to go on. And it had worked.

The horn blew a second time.

The rain fizzled to barely a mist, and somehow when they'd been lying there the clouds had mostly disappeared, a few left to float on the horizon, giving way to the stars and moon.

"We must go," Macrath said. He turned her chin to look at the bruise marring her skin. He vowed right then and there, before the games were over, he was going to see the steward bleed. "Can you stand?"

Ceana nodded, tried to push up, but collapsed against him.

Macrath stood, lifting her as he went. She trembled against him. "I'm so tired. And dizzy."

"Lean on me, *mo chridhe.*"

It wasn't the first time he'd called her his heart, and it wouldn't be the last. She wrapped her arm around his waist, and he tucked his hand around her hip.

"Thank you, Macrath."

"There is no need for gratitude."

"But there is. If you'd done as I suggested and gone back to your own tent, I'd be…"

"You'd be right here because there is no way I would have ever gone back to my tent knowing those jackanapes were with you. I'm only sorry the storm raged loud enough that I couldn't hear what was going on inside. Know this, if I had to do it again, I never would have left. I never should have."

She shook her head as they slowly eased through the tents. "We cannot live with regrets."

"Aye, but we can learn from past mistakes."

She nodded. "'Twas a mistake for me to provoke the guards. I… I vomited on him."

"You what?" That was what had been all over the steward's plaid and legs.

"He tried to put his… And I couldn't stomach it. I vomited all over him."

Macrath tilted his head back and laughed, breaking through even the sound of the thunder. It was as much for relief that the man had not succeeded in his purpose, but also that she'd retaliated.

"Good gods, lass, you're a genius."

"'Twas not planned," she grumbled, though a spark of humor lit in her eyes.

"Aye, I know it, but 'twas just what he deserved for preying on a lass." He pressed a kiss into her damp hair, drawing in her familiar scent.

"I wanted to fight," she grumbled.

"And you would have had it gone further."

"But he was stronger. Hit me so hard the world went black."

"And he'll likely try it again, but this time you'll be prepared."

"How?" Her voice sounded so small.

They were nearing the line. "Aim for his bollocks, lass. And if that doesn't work, his throat. Never stop moving."

"The women, they were standing with you." She seemed amazed.

"Indeed. They did not want to see him leave off with you."

"She-muscle, she continues to protect me." Ceana shook her head as though she couldn't believe it.

"She-muscle?" They stepped out of the line of tents.

Lady Beatrice sat on top of her horse, the torches flickering in the rain and wind. She glared in their direction, and Macrath had to keep himself from shuddering. He was going to pay heavily for having gone to find Ceana.

"The big woman. She's about your size," Ceana said.

"Is that her true name?"

Ceana laughed. "'Tis what I've called her in my mind since day one."

"I bet she appreciates that," Macrath said wryly, ignoring the sharp daggers shooting from the councilwoman's eyes.

"I ought to learn her name in truth since she knows mine."

When heads began to swivel in their direction, and Lady Beatrice shifted in her saddle, Macrath gave Ceana's shoulder a gentle squeeze.

"I'll be all right. Leave me here; this is my place in line." Ceana stared straight ahead, the smile she'd worn a moment before gone.

But he couldn't just leave her. Not after what had happened with the guards. He didn't care how angry it made the council members—Lady Beatrice in particular. "I will stay."

She straightened her back. "Please go. We've already called enough attention to ourselves. I can see you from my place here."

"Aye, but I can better protect you if I'm right next to you."

Ceana pressed her hand to his chest. "Not if she locks you away again."

From the men's side, her guard Aaron looked on with murderous rage.

"I may not be safe away from you." Macrath tried to make a jest of it, but in truth, he was in more danger than most. He not only had to contend with the games, but the many enemies he'd made as well.

"Don't mind Aaron. He is harmless. Now go."

Macrath reluctantly left her. As he crossed the center road toward the men's side, the guards he'd infuriated earlier walked menacingly toward him, issuing threats under their breath that didn't quite carry on the wind.

"Stand down," Lady Beatrice said sternly.

The guards backed off, and Macrath took his place front and center. He kept his gaze steadily on Ceana, and she on him. In the light of the torches, even with her hair a fright and her face bruised, she was the most beautiful thing he'd ever seen. How was he going to keep her safe in game three? Game four? Game five? All the time between?

"There is no rest for you, weary warriors. Just as it is during battle, you do not get a reprieve for the night when a siege is laid upon your doorsteps. Neither did King Olaf who ruled these lands over a hundred years ago. The women are tired, weak, and their numbers greatly reduced. 'Twill be the male warriors who decide their fate."

Ceana's eyes widened, and the women surrounding her shifted uncomfortably. The men stiffened their backs. Macrath would protect her.

"The next game has been prepared within the woods, when the dark of night is even more oppressive. The women will step into the croft that has been built for the games, and the men are to remain outside. A battle will ensue, but do not think that you will simply fight other men. Nay, it would not be the war games if it were to be so simple."

Wolves, again. And assassins in trees. Maybe a bear or two. What other horrors could they unleash on them?

"Each male warrior will be provided with a shield and a single hand-held weapon of choice that you brought with you. If you did not bring a weapon, you will have to make do with your shields. No quarter given."

Macrath could use his father's claymore. Finally—a worthy weapon.

Lady Beatrice took the time to stare each male entrant in the eyes. Her gazed lingered overlong on Macrath. If he were less of a man, his bollocks would have been sucked up into his abdomen. "You will have exactly to the count of one hundred to get your weapons."

She raised her hand in the air, then swiftly brought it down. A drumbeat started the count, and Macrath leapt into action.

With only to the count of one hundred to dig up his father's sword, he had no time to waste. He shoved past several warriors, glad the guards did not follow him, and dove inside his tent. All the while, the sound of the drums made his heartbeat kick up a notch. He tossed his bedroll aside and started to dig into the cold, hard earth with his bare hands. With every passing second, he expected the guards to rip through his tent and hold him down so he didn't make the cut. But oddly enough, they left him alone.

Macrath dug until his fingers grew painfully numb, and then he felt the coldness of the claymore's hilt. He wrapped his fingers around it and tugged, the earth slowly letting go of its grip on the weapon.

Once free, he donned his back scabbard, secured his claymore between his shoulders, and charged out of his tent and ran at full speed back to the lines. A pile of wooden shields had been tossed in the center road, and the guards were ordering the men to grab one as they returned. Macrath grappled his up, catching sight of Ceana. He nodded, confident they would succeed in this next round.

The drum's pounding grew louder until finally it ceased altogether and the silence echoed like a night terror.

"If you have not returned to the lines, stay where you are."

Macrath took count of the men who'd returned. There appeared to be only a few who'd yet to reappear. He grimaced when he saw Aaron standing in line. He didn't trust the man at all. There was something odd in the way he looked at Ceana. Something beyond simple caring, beyond that of a guard. Aaron wanted her, but it was obvious the feeling was not mutual. And she was completely oblivious to his affection. There was a sinister twist of his lips. She was also unaware that her guard was capable of depravity, but Macrath could see it.

Macrath turned back to Ceana. She spoke discreetly with the woman beside her.

A loud, wrenching noise drew the entrants' attention to the gate as the guards raised the portcullis. The darkness of the void beyond the bridge beckoned them into death.

"Follow your guides. May the gods be forever in your favor!" the council shouted all at once.

Feet began to pound against the earth as the male and female entrants followed two guards on horseback through the gate and over the bridge. The guides carried torches, lighting the path over the moors. Macrath held back, waiting for Ceana, but Aaron did the same. The two of them scowled at each other as they flanked her—and she appeared unaware of their dislike of each other.

"I'll take care of my lady," Aaron said.

And he didn't intend for it to be said as an address of respect. 'Twas very clear to Macrath that the warrior was claiming ownership.

Macrath smiled. "I reckon the lass can take care of herself."

Ceana tried to hide her smile, but he saw it, if only for a second.

But the time for sparring was quickly taken over by the race to get under the gate. Though they would all be battling on the same team, that didn't stop the madness of the games from causing aggression in some of the entrants. Winners and discontents alike would fight side by side.

Dozens of running footfalls on the wooden bridge thumped, and the weight of them all running made the wood appear to bounce beneath their feet.

Macrath made a point to run slower, knowing that Ceana wouldn't be able to keep up with his longer stride—especially with a wounded leg. The moment he noticed her falter, he turned midstride and lifted her into his arms, one arm beneath her knees and the other behind her back.

She wrapped her arms around his neck. "Thank you," she whispered into his ear.

"As I said, we are a team." Macrath made sure he said the words low enough that Aaron couldn't overhear.

But even still, Aaron bumped into him several times, and he was certain it was on purpose, angry that Macrath had lifted Ceana. Angry that he'd taken that from him. Macrath had the distinct impression that this man was dangerous. And to Ceana. Jealousy bred evil. Even with his affection toward the lass, he was willing to hurt her to get to Macrath.

The horsemen disappeared into the woods, trailed by dozens of warriors. The light of their torches disappeared with them, leaving the men and women with only the moon and stars to light their path and prayers to the gods that they didn't step the wrong way. More than once, Macrath felt the edge of his foot hit a fox or rabbit hole, an uneven ridge in the ground. But he'd run enough in the dark—away from his stepmother's henchmen, his brother's drunken friends, and the demons that haunted him to power through it and keep his balance.

Moments later they were barreling into the forest. He held up his arm to block branches that were snapping back into everyone's faces by those who forged ahead of them; he didn't want them to hit Ceana. She'd already suffered enough for one day.

Forgetting his jealousy for the moment, it appeared, Aaron stepped in front of Macrath to hack at the branches with his sword. 'Haps feeling guilty for having almost caused his mistress more pain.

But the branches soon disappeared as they came to a well-trodden road. Twin yellow lights floated in the distance and appeared to be at a standstill. They weren't that far back from the horsemen—and their fate.

"We're almost there," Macrath said.

"You can put me down. I don't want to wear on your strength before the game begins."

"Och, lass, you are light as a feather."

They could hear shouts ahead as the guards ordered the women inside the croft. The clearing came into view. Macrath took in what he could make of the small building. Built of stone, the croft had a single wooden door which was flanked by two very small windows. Perhaps big enough for Ceana to climb through, but not wide enough for him nor a man of average size. A thatched roof was damp from the rain in the parts that weren't protected by the overhanging trees.

"I will protect the women, Macrath," Ceana said. "When our clan was raided, before I was laird, that is what I did."

"They should have allowed the women weapons." He frowned.

"They do not want the women to help you. They want us helpless. They intend to lessen our numbers further."

"How will you protect them?"

Ceana smiled. "With our wit."

He set her on her feet, wished he could kiss her, but settled for a squeeze of the hand. "I shall see you soon."

"Indeed, warrior. I will count on it."

Chapter Fifteen

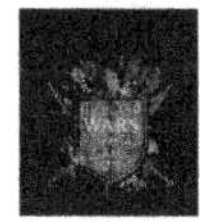

CEANA reluctantly left the safety of Macrath's arms. She wished him and Aaron luck before joining the women as they were bustled into the croft. Staying near the center of the line, she avoided the two guards—partially relieved she didn't recognize either of them as having been in her tent.

Inside the croft, several sconces held tallow candles, dripping wax down the wooden walls where it cooled in brownish-yellow streaks.

When the last of the women were inside, the guards shut the door, blocking the outside world from their view. Several dull thuds against the wood door set Ceana's nerves on alert. She lifted the iron handle, but the door wouldn't budge. They'd barred it from the outside.

"They've trapped us!" a woman shouted, which only caused mass panic among the other women.

Ceana turned and watched in amazement as alarm passed through the throng of women in a wave. They shoved her out of the way, and she caught herself against the wall, wincing at the pain of her jostled wounds. The frightened women pounded on the door, the walls. A couple tried to squeeze unsuccessfully through the tiny windows, falling on their arses in the process.

She was not unused to panic, having dealt with her clan women any number of times. But she was surprised at the women within the croft. This was all part of the games. Along the sides of the sparse and unfurnished croft were several other female entrants watching with dubious gazes.

"Lassies!" she called out, but still no one would listen.

She-muscle bumped up beside her, looking completely calm. "They've lost their bloody minds," she grumbled.

And they'd lose a whole lot more if the guards decided to settle them afore they could settle themselves.

"Lift me up," Ceana said.

She-muscle raised a questioning brow.

Ceana pressed a reassuring hand on her arm. "Trust me. If I don't get these women under control, they won't last through the night—or however long this game takes."

"All right. Come here." She-muscle bent down and hoisted Ceana up so she sat on her right shoulder, facing the trapped women.

"What is your name?" Ceana asked from atop her perch.

She-muscle gazed up at her and smiled. "Judith. And I gather you're not Bitch?"

Ceana laughed. "To most, no. My name is Ceana."

"Well, go on with it then," Judith said. She let out an ear-piercing whistle which had the desired effect of silencing the growing panic.

"Lassies!" Ceana shouted. "We are not trapped." Immediately, they went in on how the door was barred, but she cut them off. "Indeed, they've locked us in, but it is only part of the game. Did you not listen? This is the men's game. They are tasked with protecting the croft, protecting us. In order for them to do that, we must remain inside. We cannot be in the way of whatever the council has decided to throw at them. And indeed, why would we want to? We've fought already today. Let us rest inside the safety of these croft walls. If we panic, we are only going to distract the men. If they are distracted, they will lose. Then there is no telling what will happen to us. We must be silent. We must help."

They murmured amongst themselves, nodding.

Judith patted Ceana's leg. "You've got the right of it, lassie."

"You can put me down. I think they're calm enough to listen to reason now."

Once Judith set her down, Ceana spoke to the women again. "We need to form a plan. While this might be the men's fight, we must keep order for ourselves." She pointed at the two small windows. "With those windows, we can keep watch."

"But what if an arrow flies in?" someone shouted.

"We'll keep the shutters closed, and the woman who is on duty will chance a look every quarter hour."

"Who will decide who keeps watch?"

"We all will," Ceana answered.

Several outraged cries sounded from the back of the small croft as one particularly angry-looking female shouldered her way forward. "Who made you our leader?" she challenged.

Ceana was ready for such animosity. Was surprised it took as long as it did. With a bunch of frightened women intent on winning a single spot to rule, it was a given. "No one made me our leader. But Judith and I were the only ones who stood up to the chaos."

The woman didn't have an answer to that, simply nodded. Then she turned to the other entrants, her back to Ceana. "I say we do make her the leader for today. Once we leave the croft, however, she will have no power." She turned back around, her hard eyes narrowed. "Leaders are the first to die should we be invaded."

Ceana would have to keep a close eye on the woman. She'd not realized until that moment that she'd made an enemy—though she supposed in hindsight she should have. Every woman in here was her enemy. Even Judith should be, but she wasn't. They'd seemed to have bonded ever since the first day she'd met her outside the women's wrestling tent.

"So are cowards," Ceana replied, keeping her spine stiff and staring the woman straight in the eye.

Her lip curled. "What are you saying?"

Ceana shrugged nonchalantly. "Simply stating a fact."

"Don't go threatening the Bitch," Judith said. "There's a reason she's got the name. Let us get ourselves in order before the game begins."

Too late. The horn blew outside, and moments later the men began shouting.

"It has begun," Ceana said. "I will take first watch."

"As will I," said Judith.

Ceana hurried to one of the small windows and cracked open the shutters. Outside, it was not yet complete chaos. The men looked to surround the front of the croft in a half circle, their backs to the women, prepared to face the enemy head on.

"What is happening?" asked a woman.

A band of at least six men who could almost be classified as giants burst from the woods, brandishing swords, maces, and battle-axes. Their faces were painted a glowing white in the torch light, and they shouted war cries. They were easily a head taller than Macrath and wore tattered breeches and shirts—no plaids. Their hair was long and matted.

"They are being attacked by a bunch of limp-willies," Judith said.

Ceana smirked. Hardly. If she'd seen the band of brigands chasing her, she might have fainted.

The men took the attack in stride. Standing closer together, shields up, they issued a battle cry that shook the roof of the croft.

"The men are holding strong," Ceana said.

The giants were relentless in their attack. But so were the men. They had more to live for. They'd been put into the games for a purpose. They fought not only for life, but the chance to rule Sìtheil. There was something to be said about having more to live for than your next breath. They kept their shields up, blocking blows and then retaliating with their own weapons.

She marveled at Macrath's strength, holding her breath as he swung his claymore in an arc toward the head of one giant. The giant blocked with the handle of his ax and used his weight to push against Macrath. But her man was strong. He braced his feet and gave a mighty shove, knocking the giant to the ground. Several of the men pounced, and Macrath turned to take on the next giant, leaving the fallen one to his men. Seemed as though he too had taken a leadership role.

She searched for Aaron and saw him blocking repeated blows from a mace but saved when the leader of the giants shouted for retreat.

"They are leaving," Ceana mused. "But there will be more. I'm certain of it."

The men were not given long to catch their breath before a group of four demons rode in on horseback, swinging heavy iron-spiked maces at the heads of the warriors. They were dressed in all black—even black hoods covered their faces. Their horses wore metal armor on their faces, chests and forelegs.

The demons' weapons connected, shattering through the simple wooden shields and crushing four skulls. One of the demons was set upon by warriors, yanked from his horse, and hacked to death. The other three took out three more warriors—one crawled away, mortally injured, the other two lay dead.

Ceana sat in silence, horror filling her. It was brutal. A massacre. This was no game. But a thinning of the ranks in the worst possible way.

But even the three demons that still attacked were not safe. The men charged, slicing and cutting. One demon was able to escape, riding his horse back into the woods. The warriors took hold of the three horses left and mounted—Macrath one of them. They had a subtle advantage now.

Macrath stared at the croft, and she felt like his eyes connected with hers. Pride swelled in her chest. She wanted to shout out to him. But kept her words of encouragement to herself. She didn't want to distract him any more than she already was. He turned his gaze back to the warriors.

"Men!" he shouted, taking the lead. "Stand your ground. Return to your lines!"

Unlike the women with Ceana, the men were happy to follow Macrath's orders. He exuded power and strength of will. They pressed together in a line behind him, shields up, weapons ready. The men on horseback stood before the men on foot.

Her heart pounded, breath ceased as she waited countless seconds for the next enemy to attack.

The giants returned, but they did not charge. Instead, they stood on the edge of the forest, shouting insults at the warriors. Between them, two small trebuchets were pushed from beyond the trees. Thick, fat rocks filled wooden baskets.

"To the back of the croft!" Ceana bellowed.

The women did not utter one word of argument. Ceana slammed the shutter closed and rushed to the back wall, squeezing herself in with the women there. "Get down. Cover your heads."

Judith landed beside her, and they all crouched low, hands over their heads.

Outside the men shouted. She heard Macrath's voice carry above the others. "Trebuchet! Shields up! Women, be prepared!"

He'd thought to warn them. But she didn't have long to admire at his concern. The sound of cranking along with Macrath's bellow of "Incoming!" was enough of a warning for the women to brace themselves. But the stone did not hit the croft. The ground rumbled with its impact, and a scream that tore from one man's throat made her dizzy with terror.

"Again!" Macrath shouted, and the ground rumbled once more.

A dull thud sounded against the wall by the door.

"What was that?" Judith asked.

"Maybe a stone rolled into it?" Ceana asked, taking the time to look at her friend. She prayed it wasn't a body—or worse, a limb.

"'Haps."

Outside, the warnings for incoming stones sounded several more times, and each time it was followed by either a cry of agony or taunts to the giants for failing in their aim.

"Remain calm, lassies," Ceana urged. "They cannot have too many stones left. The men are strong. They will keep us safe. Pray to the gods they keep us safe and that not too many of the men are lost."

"How are you so calm?" Judith asked.

She feared her senses to violence had been dulled. "Our clan was ambushed often. 'Twas my duty to protect the women and children."

"Ah, I see."

"What of you, Judith? What did you do for your clan?"

Judith smiled as the wall shook with a little more violence than before. "Because of my size, my father didn't feel I belonged inside, embroidering with my dainty sisters. Nor did he want me on the list field with my brothers. So I was sent to the hills. He named me a shepherd."

"A shepherd?"

"Aye," she laughed. "Can handle a wolf just fine on my own."

Ceana smiled, but it was cut short when she heard the men shout. "Fire arrows!"

Without hesitating, she left her spot huddled with the women and went to the shuttered window. Sure enough, standing on the edge of the woods, the giants and trebuchets had been replaced by a line of archers, the tips of their arrows ablaze.

With her lips in a grim line, Ceana faced the women. "Be prepared for flames. We're lucky that it rained. Hopefully the thatch is wet enough to keep the flames doused, but there are certain to be parts that are dry." She turned to Judith. "Lift me up again."

"What are you going to do?"

"I'm going to climb out the window and take the bar off the door."

Judith blanched. "What?"

"If they shoot the arrows at the croft's roof, or even the walls, and it catches fire, we'll need to escape. We cannot be made to perish."

She nodded, but to be sure that she was not alone, Ceana spoke to the women. "I am going to go out the window and remove the bar on the door. Will you remain inside while it's still safe? We cannot allow our own panic to distract the men."

Silently, the women nodded, eyes wide as they stared at Ceana.

Ceana nodded at Judith.

"Be careful, Ceana of MacRae. You'll be unprotected should an arrow..."

She took a deep breath. "Aye, but danger is part of this game, and though I can fit through the window, not everyone will be able to. I have to do my part."

"I'll help you." 'Twas the woman she'd fought with by the barrels. The one who'd gotten her whipped by Beatrice. She should be angry, yet Ceana had been given a new gown and a strip of her mother's plaid for it. "I owe you that much for getting you lashed."

"I'll lift you." The woman who'd argued when Ceana first took the lead stepped forward to lift the smaller woman.

"Let us go at the same time, else one of us will be waiting unprotected outside the croft," Ceana said.

Once both of the women were situated at their windows, Ceana glanced out. Fiery arrows lit up the night. A few had made their mark in men's shields and bodies, but the majority lit up the ground, catching the slightest dry leaves and twigs on fire. Judith counted to three, and then they were both hoisted.

She gripped the top of the window edge and used her strength to put first one leg and then the other through. Her injury throbbed, but she pushed the pain away from her mind. She held her breath, her intent only to concentrate on making it through the window unscathed. Judith kept a hand on her back as she slid through, suspended in midair for a split second before her feet hit the ground with a bone-jarring crash.

She sat in a heap, momentarily stunned by the organized chaos that reigned around her.

The three men on horseback were still seated and systematically ordering men in the ranks to attack. Huddled together, using their shields as a barrier, the men were charging the archers. The bodies of at least a dozen men littered the ground. Their deaths a culmination of every attack that had been thrust their way. She searched the bodies for Aaron, cringing at even the slightest similar arch of nose, but he was not among them. Thank the gods. She felt a little guilty that she expected to see him dead.

Macrath caught sight of her, and panic flashed on his face. He started to turn his horse in her direction, but she shook her head, not wanting to divert him further.

"Bitch!" shouted the woman who'd joined her out the window, snapping her back to attention.

If she weren't in such a precarious position, she might have laughed and corrected her. She'd not shared her name with anyone other than Judith. But there was no time for that. An arrow whizzed past her, stabbing into the ground by her hand. A sign from the gods that she needed to move. She whirled toward the door and together they hoisted the heavy wooden bar.

"We need to keep this—as a weapon," Ceana said.

They burst through the door of the croft and slammed it closed behind them. Nearly two dozen sets of expectant eyes met theirs.

"What was it like out there?"

Terrifying. "The men seem to have a good handle on the attackers. I think they will be triumphant."

She met the gaze of her partner, and a silent message passed between them. There was no need to describe in detail the carnage. She'd wager a guess that at least half the women in the games had not witnessed battle before.

A great melee of clanging weapons and shouts of anger, cries of pain, filled the nighttime air. Inside the croft, the women were quiet save for their fearful, quickened breaths. So far, the threat of fire had not reached them.

"We are safe for now," Ceana said, her voice breathy, heart pounding in her ears.

Flashes of Macrath atop the horse, his face contorted in anger toward his enemies, passed through her mind. He'd shouted and pointed and swung his sword. And then fear for her had transformed him. She'd never seen a man look that way before. She wanted to rush outside and leap onto his horse, to tell him to run away from it all, that they had to escape. But doing so would only get the two of them killed.

"'Twill not be long now," she murmured mostly to herself.

Ceana dragged the bar over to the window, pulling back the shutter enough to peer outside. The men appeared to have taken out at least half the archers, but the other half still fired their blazing death points into the air.

And then the howling started. The wolves had been brought back into the fold.

Ceana shuddered, her knees quaking. The men had so many odds against them. If these horrors were only the third game, how would she ever make it through two more?

The first wolf came from the left, launching itself at a warrior just outside her window. His snarls and the man's bellows reverberated off the croft walls.

"Wolves!" cried the women.

Ceana slammed the shutter closed, afraid the wolf would catch the scent of their fear and leap through after he'd finished with his victim.

"Do you smell that?" Judith asked.

Ceana hadn't noticed her coming up beside her.

She sniffed. Smoke.

Holy mother of all gods, 'twas smoke. They'd been hit by one of the fiery arrows.

The other women began muttering and looking up at the thatched roof. Thin curls of smoke reached through the thatch and speared out in all directions, covering the ceiling within a few breaths in a blanket of dark, swirling fog.

"We were hit!" That was all it took for the panic to start.

The women started scrambling for the door, and Ceana and Judith leapt in front of it.

"There are wolves! You can't leave," Judith shouted.

"Get out of the way!" cried another woman, punching Judith in the throat.

Judith staggered backward, clutching at her neck and coughing.

Ceana lifted the board and swung it in an arch, nearly hitting several women. "Step back!" she warned.

"You're killing us!" Several women collapsed on the ground, coughing.

Their panic only made their coughing worse.

"Nay, you nitwits. I'm saving you! There are wolves afoot. You cannot run out without a plan!"

"We need no plan with wolves out there."

"But we have to," Ceana said. "We have this weapon," she indicated the board. "Who has the strongest swing?"

Judith raised her hand. "I do, lass." Her voice was tight. An angry, red welt had formed in the center of her neck where she'd been hit.

Ceana handed her the wood plank. "Then you'll be the one to fight off the wolves."

Judith smiled. "I'm good at that."

"Seems you are." Ceana turned her attention back to the women. "We file out one at a time. No pushing. A burning roof is the least of our worries if we're to go outside."

The women quieted, agreeing with her.

"We go behind the croft and remained huddled together, as far from the fighting as we can get."

Ceana cracked open the door, checking to make certain no wolves waited on their haunches, ready to pounce. It looked clear. As clear as it was going to get. "Do not look at the carnage," she warned.

She pushed the door all the way open, and they were at once hit with the brutality of war—game or not. Taking a deep breath, she led the women out of the croft and into the chaos. Despite her warnings, several women collapsed after taking in the bloodshed and had to be dragged by others.

Judith stood guard as the women filed around the side of the croft toward the back. A few of them screamed, drawing the attention of the men and a lone wolf. As his hackles were raised and he started toward them, teeth bared, Judith raised the plank, ready to swing.

A loud thundering came around the side of the croft in the form of Macrath on his massive warhorse. The charger's eyes were wild, and Macrath tugged the reins, a subtle hint for his mount to rear up. Taking his cue, the animal raised up and, forelegs swinging, he trampled the wolf beneath his hooves.

At the same time, a horn blew and the ping of arrows ceased. The male warriors shouted of the attackers retreat. Must have been the last of the wolves that Macrath and his horse flattened.

Game three was over.

Macrath had survived. She had survived.

Ceana didn't hesitate. She ran toward him, tears of relief flooding her eyes. Macrath leapt from his horse and lifted her up in the air, pressing his face into the crook of her neck. She breathed in his scent and squeezed him tight.

"We made it." Her throat was too tight with emotion to speak louder than a whisper.

"Aye, lass. We'll live to see another day." And then he kissed her, right there for anyone to see.

And she let him.

Game

Four

Chapter Sixteen

MACRATH never wanted to let go.

Never wanted Ceana to leave his arms.

His chest swelled, blood still pumping with battle rage and fear for her safety. She clung to him, lips warm and pliant, fingers curled tight on his shirt. The moment he'd seen her rushing toward him—alive—he'd leapt from his horse without a second thought.

"That was awful," she murmured against his mouth. "I'm so glad you're not..."

Macrath cupped the sides of her face and pressed his forehead to hers, their gazes locked. He had only eyes for her and none for the carnage around them. "We made it, lass."

Standing behind the crofter's hut, they were hidden from the guards and most of the entrants save the women. The dim light of the torches that had ringed the croft let off a soft, eerie glow.

"Might want to break apart now," the woman Ceana called She-muscle warned. She held a thick wooden bar in her hand and cocked her head toward the front of the croft. "Got company."

They'd been lucky not to have *company* before now.

To have kissed so openly where any of the guards could have seen was extremely dangerous. Reluctantly Macrath let go of Ceana and took a step away, hating every inch that separated them.

"Thank you, Judith," Ceana said to the larger woman.

She inclined her head, and Macrath found himself amazed that they'd been able to form a bond. At the same time, he regretted the sorrow Ceana would feel when she mourned her friend's passing—for they could not both win.

"Where is she?" bellowed her guard, Aaron, as he charged around the corner. Blood streaked his face, mostly that of whoever he'd fought against as there didn't seem to be any wounds readily visible. His eyes were ablaze and wild like a rabid animal. His sword was still drawn, causing a couple of entrants to take a step back and another to leap in front of him, warning to put the weapon aside, that the game was over.

Macrath might have been taken aback by the man's behavior, except he'd been waiting for it. Ceana, however, actually took a step closer to Macrath, her eyes wide and lips pursed as she watched her personal guard experience a breakdown of sorts.

Aaron scrutinized every person standing, though he did toss aside his sword. Finally seeing Ceana, Aaron quickly affected an expression of concern, but it had been plain for everyone to see his anger moments before.

"My laird, I was so worried." He scrubbed a hand over his face as he rushed toward her.

"As you can see, I am fine." She turned a smile at Judith and the other women. "We worked together, and no harm has come to us."

Aaron waved away her comment and came to stand beside her. Macrath watched in silence, finding it only slightly humorous when the man's hand twitched toward Ceana's. He must have thought better of it, letting it fall to his side. And good thing, because the part of Macrath that didn't find it humorous was infuriated enough to pick the whelp up and toss him as far as he could.

"I cannot say it was the same for the men." Aaron made a pointed stare at Macrath.

Macrath crossed his arms and stared the man down, daring him to say another untruth. The men had worked impeccably well together. Their formations, their willingness to let Macrath and the two others on horseback take the lead. Trusting them to see the game through. And they'd won because of it.

"Whatever do you mean?" Ceana asked, narrowing her brows.

Macrath was pretty certain she was about to get a taste of just how low her guard could go. He was also confident that she would see reason and understand that her guard was completely out of line. He'd seen her watching the men. She knew what they'd been through.

"Aye, Aaron, whatever do you mean?" Macrath said, challenging the man. A crowd started to gather, including the other horsemen.

"Only that—" But his words were cut short as the guards blew the horn and bellowed for the entrants to line up.

To his surprise, Ceana shifted forward, away from both him and Aaron in favor of walking beside her new friend, Judith. He frowned at her back and then at Aaron—it was his fault after all. The cowardly bastard would try to make him look bad in hopes of gaining favor with his mistress. Disgraceful.

The men and women waded through the bodies and trudged through mud formed by pools of blood mixing with the earth. They fashioned lines as they stood, not separating as they did normally. Judith stood between him and Ceana, and Aaron was on her other side. *Bastard.*

But the time for anger and jealousy abruptly came to an end as he took in the carnage around him. 'Twas a stark reminder of why they were there—and it wasn't to argue with a paltry green lad over a pretty lass.

"Entrants! We need to bury the dead. There." The guards tossed wooden shovels from a mule-drawn cart and pointed toward a burial cairn that they'd set up torches around. "Dig on the right side. Those who are injured need to be piled in the wagon."

Macrath was one of the first who stepped forward to pick up a shovel. Covered in sweat and blood, the rush of battle made him tremble as his mind tried to tell his body that he was still alive and the threat was gone.

To the right of the cairn was a flat piece of land that looked undisturbed. Around the left, the land rose and fell in subtle waves. That was where entrants of past games had been buried. With five years between, the grass had regrown.

Macrath struck the ground with the tip of his shovel, feeling it slice into the earth. He tipped his head, looking up at the stars in the sky, and whispered a prayer for those who'd died not only tonight but before as well.

"Have you buried someone afore?" Ceana asked, striking the ground with her own shovel.

"Aye, lass." *Too many*. "You?"

She didn't say anything. He paused in his digging to look at her, tears streamed down her face. He reached out for her, but she shook her head, offered a sad smile. She swiped them away. "I've lost many, but I've only buried one."

"What did you say to her?" Aaron snarled.

Macrath gritted his teeth, his patience growing thin. "Look, lad, I am not your laird's enemy. Nor will I ever be."

"But—"

"That's enough, Aaron," Ceana cut him off. "Macrath is my friend. You will treat him as you would a guest who's come to visit us at Gruamach Keep."

Aaron glowered at Macrath, but he kept his own expression blank. He refused to take part in any more pissing matches. As it was, at some point the lad wouldn't be around anymore. Either he'd die by Macrath's own hand or one of the other entrants'.

The moment was lost, and rather than continue to confess her losses to Macrath, Ceana kept on digging. Aaron jabbed his shovel into the ground, a satisfied smirk on his face.

Macrath put all his irritation into moving dirt, pounding the earth as he wanted to pound the whelp. The mounting tension between the two of them was palpable, and Macrath couldn't see it ending any other way than in violence.

About an hour later, the moon had shifted in the sky and all the dead were buried.

"Though it be not yet morning, Samhain is upon us," a guard bellowed. "Return to the castle. The injured shall be attended while the remainder of you rest and clean yourselves up. As it is a sacred holiday, you will be given a day of respite."

Many a breath was drawn in. Macrath had forgotten about Samhain. 'Twas the day that marked the end of the harvest and the beginning of winter. In Argyll, they would have celebrated it from sundown to sundown, with great bonfires, feasting, sacrifices to the gods, and the wine would flow. Men and women would dance and flirt and make love with abandon. 'Twas a day of merriment.

But the souls of the dead walked the earth on Samhain.

At Sìtheil, there were many dead. A century and more of death surrounded and clouded the lands and castle like a thick, ash-filled cloud, making it hard to breathe. How could they dance and laugh without restraint when shadows loomed all around?

To make matters worse, with his stepmother and half brother afoot, they would be certain Macrath did not enjoy even a moment of the celebration. That was if they got to him before Beatrice. He shivered.

He could still feel her bony fingers sliding over his nude skin. Her nails digging. Her whip lashing. The way she'd rubbed her breasts all over him. It was hard to suppress his shudder. Forced him to think of more pleasant things, like the way Ceana's lips melded to his. Or even just the way her eyes crinkled when she smiled or the splash of freckles on her pert nose. The strength that sat on her shoulders and the fierceness of her determination. *Those* things made him smile.

"So far away." Ceana touched his elbow, jarring him back. "Are you going to make a night of it at the croft?"

Macrath saw that nearly all the entrants had filed into a line down the darkened road, only the torches of the guides to light their path. Judith and Aaron stood a few feet away, and it looked as though the woman was trying to distract Aaron from Ceana.

"Nay, lass." Macrath smiled. "Was just thinking about tomorrow."

"Samhain?" Ceana smoothly tucked her arm in his elbow and steered him toward the road. She limped slightly, and he wondered if the stitches in her leg had come undone. When they returned, he'd take a look to be sure her injuries weren't becoming festered.

He kept his eyes ahead, not interested in the least in Aaron's reaction. "Aye. How did you celebrate at Gruamach Keep?"

"We always sacrificed to the gods—but we never seemed to have enough livestock to do it. We started the day with a hunt, and we'd sacrifice half. Then we'd sip whisky and wine, dance by the fires. It was a nice escape. Most years, our enemies left us to it." She shook her head, pulling herself from her reveries. "I fear 'twill never be the same again."

Macrath wanted to wrap her up in the protection of his arms and promise that he'd keep her safe. That in every year to come she could dance and laugh and not be afraid. That she could live her life until she was bursting at the seams with fond memories, and no more heartache would touch her. But sadly, even when they won, he could never promise her a life without strife. 'Twas simply not the way of it. To be human was to struggle and overcome the odds, whatever those odds may be on any given day.

"You had a lot of enemies?"

She nodded. "'Tis one of the reasons I joined the games."

"You've not spoken much about your reasons," he prodded.

Ceana kept her head forward without answering. Their feet crunched along the trodden path several paces behind the others. Aaron turned around every so often in a jerking move as if hoping to catch them at something. An owl hooted in the distance. A startling sound. So removed were they from reality, it was hard to fathom nature living on as though death did not blanket the land.

"Our clan lands were raided often," Ceana's voice broke through the mock tranquility of the woodlands.

"Gruamach Keep?"

"Aye. 'Tis a powerful stronghold—but we are isolated. Built on an island, there are only two ways off—the bridge and by galleon. Used to be that our enemies would block our path from the bridge, but we had enough resources to wait them out. Now we either starve, fight, or surrender."

"I take it you chose to fight?"

"My people are already starving. I just pray they have not suffered while I've been away."

"And when you win?"

"I will have enough resources to rebuild our clan, to replenish our reserves. We will be strong once more. And then no one can starve us out or raid us." Conviction punctuated every word. She may not have been laird long, but already she'd embodied that responsibility, and he was proud of her for it.

"Your people are lucky to have a leader as selfless as you."

Ceana let out a short laugh. "I've not been their leader long. Nigh on a month, 'tis all."

"Aye, I heard what you said about your brother when we left the healing tent. My sympathies for your loss."

"Thank you. That means a lot to me." She drew in a breath, and he thought she would speak again, but several breaths passed before she did. "He was a great leader. Kept us as protected as he could. We used to have great farming land. My mother was in charge of the planting and harvesting. But when she was taken from us, our enemies raided our crops. Took them all, burned the land. After that, it was never the same again." She let out a deep sigh. "Dougal was killed in an ambush while we were hunting. I killed the man who executed him, but that didn't give my brother breath. I had to return to the clan to let them know that he was gone. That I not only had no food for their starving bellies, but that our laird was dead and the enemy was afoot—minus the one. 'Twas not long after that I boarded a galleon and entered the games."

"You're very brave."

"What about you? Your stepmother entered you, hoping you'd die. And now she's here to make that happen."

"Aye." The reality of it left a bitter coating on his tongue. "She's hated me since the day I first drew breath."

"And your father? How does he feel?"

Macrath stiffened a moment, never having spoken to another soul about his familial situation—or his feelings, for that matter. He was a warrior. Warriors repressed all emotion, and yet when he was with Ceana, he was starting to feel things differently. Wanted to open up and share with her the deeper, darker, hidden parts of himself. What was more, he believed she'd accept him for who he was. He trusted her.

When he'd first saved her in the woods from the wolves during the initial game, and he'd kissed her, wondering if she would think he was good enough, he'd never expected to have… What? Fallen for her?

Was it love that had drawn him in?

Macrath shook his head.

He couldn't afford to love. Couldn't let such emotion block the way to victory or soften him to the games. Fierceness, ruthlessness. That was what would help him win.

So he kept his heart shielded. His emotions well hidden in the locked trunk encased within his ribs.

He cleared his throat as if that simple action would solve all his problems. "I know not what my father feels. Nor do I care to ponder on it."

Ceana knew the precise moment Macrath blocked her out.

She'd shared with him her troubles, her brother's death, and yet when she'd asked for a piece of himself, he'd worked triple-time to build up the stone wall that had come tumbling down at some point since they'd first met.

She wanted to be upset about it. To be angry that he didn't want to share.

But she wasn't.

How could she be? The man had been abhorred by his family what seemed like his entire life. His own stepmother sending him to his death. She couldn't imagine the heinous things done to him as he grew from an infant to a man. And she wouldn't force him to relive them only so she could be informed.

Ceana understood the need for walls. The need to protect oneself. Hell, they were battling every day to protect their bodies. It was a wonder any of them had thoughts at all to anything other than: eat, sleep, survive, repeat.

She tucked his arm closer, pretending to limp a little more just so she could feel the heat of him beside her.

Macrath may not know it yet, but he needed her as much as she needed him. And not in just the physical sense. When she was with him, she felt something. Was it wholeness? He filled all the voids and mended her soul together. Aye, she thought she could say it was wholeness. He made her feel complete.

She cast her eyes up at the trees, seeing breaks in the branches of the firs and nearly bare oaks, ash, and birch. Most of the woodland animals kept hidden, away from the human foot traffic and the nightmarish sounds that their battle had rent in the air.

"There is this place atop Creag na Faol near my family's lands. I'd sneak up there when we were at peace. Just sit and think. No one bothered me there. I think they knew where I was. I'm certain my brother had me followed at least once." Ceana smiled at the memory. "I had the best vantage point there. I could see the island our castle sat upon, the loch, the forest, and the road. There is something to be said about having a place you can go that is only for you. A place where you feel safe. I've found myself thinking about Creag na Faol often. Ironically, it's named because it used to be the home of wolves. But they are no longer there. Legend at Gruamach is that a wolf hunter lives in the caves and hunts them at night." She licked her lips. They were cracked, tasted metallic. "I don't know whether or not the lone hunter exists, but what I do believe is that sometimes there is someone there to fight our demons for us and other times we have to forge ahead alone."

They came to the edge of the woods. Across the moors, the castle lights sparkled like stars had landed on the stones. Shadowed black figures glided over the heath as the entrants made their way back to Sìtheil. Apparitions, nay, but just as connected with the afterlife as those who'd met their demise in the first three games and the years they'd left behind.

"I'm here to forge ahead with you, Macrath, whenever you're ready to let me."

Chapter Seventeen

CEANA woke with the dawn. Watched her tent go from a balmy gray to a dusky white. Around her, the world seemed to be moving at a slow and staggered pace. A shuffle of feet. A cough. Grouses and finches called out good morning, and a woodpecker hammered somewhere close by.

She blinked the sleep away from her eyes, rolled onto her back, and stretched. As it was every morning, her limbs were sore, muscles ached when forced to lengthen. Her toes, ankles, and fingers all crackled awake. Her eyes felt heavy, swollen. She sat up to examine her wounds. They'd been cleaned, a salved rubbed over them, and the bandages had been replaced upon returning from the middle of the night game. 'Twas a blessing that her wounds had finally chosen to heal.

Peeling back the white linen layers on her hand, she flexed her fingers and then made a fist. The slice over her knuckles strained against its new skin but did not break open. Even still, she rewrapped it, then looked at the stitches on her arm and leg. Bruises marred the skin around her wounds. The black crisscross of threads was crude, but done well. She'd broken the one in her leg open, but the poultice they put on it last night seemed to have aided in ceasing the bleeding and rejuvenating her skin.

Ceana stood slowly, wrapped her plaid around her shoulders, and stepped out into the morning. With the council giving them the day off, many were still abed, and she wished she was one of them.

But sleep had been something she'd not done well for years. Even when she finally did fall into a deep sleep, she was pulled out of it. Would lay awake, staring up at the ceiling. Thoughts racing.

With the coming of Samhain, autumn seemed to have disappeared overnight and brought with it an early winter's chill. She shivered, curling her toes in her boots. The sky was slowly turning blue, a yellowish-pink stripe on the horizon.

Ceana ducked back into her tent and made use of the chamber pot, then took it to dump by the moat near the front entrance as they'd been instructed to do. There were no guards awake at this early hour. No one about that she felt compelled to be wary of. She didn't know if that was more alarming or not. She felt awkward and unsteady without fear biting at her heels.

The scent of the moat was not as overpowering as it had been on her first day of arrival, perhaps due to the quickly dropping temperatures. She ducked beneath the entrance gate and took the stone stairs on the left to the small grassy and rocky patches along the shore of the slop-filled trench. Above her, the bridge was empty. Being alone left an eerie feeling crawling over her limbs as though she were the only one left in this desolate land. She hurried back up the stairs and beneath the gate to the inner courtyard.

Back within the castle walls, and most still abed, she returned the chamber pot to her tent and took a moment to analyze the massive stronghold. Soon to be her own. She wandered away from the occupied areas and through a gate where a kitchen garden had been mostly picked clean of its contents.

Only two more games she had to live through before it was indeed hers.

And, with hope, Macrath's.

"Good morning, lass." The gate squeaked behind her.

Ceana whirled to see Macrath standing there. Every time she looked at him, she was stunned by her own reaction. Dark hair hung loose around his stubbled jaw. Blue eyes stared at her with an intensity that set her heart to a rapid pace. A grin that promised so many things. Despite the lack of cleaning accouterments, his shirt looked as though it had been washed, and his plaid was neatly pleated around his narrow hips.

"Good morning." She couldn't help the smile of joy from coming to her. Seeing him was only a reminder that they'd overcome the odds so far.

Up to now, the gods had indeed been in their favor.

"'Tis probably dangerous for you to be wandering about without a proper escort," he said, low and smooth.

She nodded. "But there was no one about."

He flicked his gaze behind him over the wall. "Starting to rise now."

Ceana grinned. "And now you're here to keep me safe."

Macrath approached her, and she was again stunned by his sheer strength and beauty. How could a man be made so rugged and yet boast eyes that sparkled a beautiful blue and dark hair that glossed sleek and feather soft?

He leaned down and captured her in a deep and tender kiss. She sank against him, warmth filling her all the way down to her numb toes.

"What are you looking at?" he asked, his gaze roving over the dirt patches at their feet where some remnants of herbs still clung.

She shrugged, pretending she'd not just been greedily eyeing him. "Nothing, really. Looks to have been picked quite clean."

"Could you not sleep?" he asked.

She shook her head, already wishing they were kissing once more as the heat of their passion was overtaken by the chill of the coming winter. "Seemed a waste to spend the morning lying in my empty tent when I could be exploring the grounds."

She shivered and tucked her fingers tighter into the folds of her plaid *arisaid*, glad it had not been yet ruined. She'd chosen not to wear it during the games as the extra fabric only seemed to make her clumsy. As little as she was, she needed all the dexterity she could get from light clothes. But the night, it had simply been too frigid to go without it.

Macrath stepped beside her and tucked her against his side. "Your lips are turning blue."

"'Tis a little cold," she conceded.

"Shall we go to the tents and see if they've managed to give us a warm breakfast?"

Ceana laughed. "I doubt very much we'll find that."

Though even as she said it, the scent of bread baking wafted on the next chill breeze.

Macrath raised a brow. "We may both be surprised."

"Nay, we'll both be disappointed. My guess is the council is going to have a mighty fine morning meal. Maybe even the guards. But not us. We are mostly doomed to death. Not worth the waste of a good loaf."

Ceana giggled at Macrath's wounded expression.

"But what of good whisky? Will they think us unworthy of it? Because after the past several days, I could use a good nip."

Ceana leaned her head against his solid shoulder. "I could use a wee nip myself." And she normally didn't have a taste for the peaty, potent drink. Wine and ale, not a problem. But whisky? It burned a path to her stomach and took all sense from her mind.

She closed her eyes, breathed in Macrath's comforting, male scent. Bagpipes sounded on the wind. An enchanting melody that sank deep into the bones. With it came the distinct blow of the horn.

They were being summoned.

A shiver of fear volleyed up her spine and made her stomach drop at the same moment. Had they lied about it being a day of rest? Did they mean to take the exhausted survivors of games one, two, and three and push them right into game four?

Ceana swallowed, trying to push air past her lips and failing. Forcing her tongue to work, she whispered, "What do you suppose that means?"

Macrath looked down at her, his expression blank. But in his eyes… She could see everything—he feared much the same.

"I cannot even guess." Macrath raked a hand through his hair.

"'Haps they merely want to wish us peace for the day?"

Macrath's jaw tightened. "Whatever they throw at us, we can dodge it."

"Or catch it."

"Aye. We'll be ready."

Together they left the garden and walked around the inner courtyard, the sounds of the piper growing louder until they reached the tent field. Standing in the center upon a raised wooden dais was the piper, and behind him stood the five council members, clean and freshly pleated.

About half the entrants had already lined up. Others were still stumbling bleary-eyed from their tents, wiping sleep from their faces and wrapping plaids around their frigid shoulders.

"Do not trust what they say," Ceana whispered. In the game of war, the rules were constantly changing. She felt naïve for believing they'd be given a reprieve.

Macrath gave a slight nod. "Aye." They moved closer to the lines, Beatrice's angry gaze on them both.

"She has taken a disliking to you," Ceana said.

Macrath grunted. "She dislikes all things human."

She glanced up at him wearily, remembering every plane and angle of his chiseled features. "We must part here."

Turning to face her, he leaned close, and she was afraid for a moment he would kiss her in front of everyone. "Only in body. In spirit, I hold you here." He touched his chest, his eyes serious.

"We shan't part." Ceana walked away then, as quick as she could, afraid she'd not be able to let go of his arm, which would only give the guards cause to cut them apart.

They rejoiced in blood, and it wouldn't do to give them a reason to shed it.

She took her place in the back of the line of women. Across the path, Macrath kept his gaze rooted on her. His face was grim as the piper finished his song. Aaron stood not too far from Macrath, and he too regarded her. But unlike with Macrath, where she felt soothed by his constant stare, she was starting to feel uncomfortable with Aaron's attentions.

When she'd left Gruamach, he'd not been her first choice of guard. Boarg MacRae had. He was a cousin of her mother, gray streaking his hair with age, but still a fierce warrior. She trusted Boarg and had asked him to choose another warrior to join them. When Aaron volunteered, she'd not wanted him to come because he'd been so close with her brother. But the man had broken down, feeling guilty that he'd not been there for her and Dougal when they'd gone on the hunt.

Stated that he felt partly responsible and wanted to at least do right by her and her brother's memory by making sure she arrived at Sìtheil unscathed.

But there was something off about him now. As though a part of himself that he'd kept hidden was banging on the barrier he'd created to hide it. Shaking herself out of her own pensive state, she realized she'd been staring at Aaron this entire time and felt awkward.

What exactly was Aaron's purpose in escorting her? Why had he so readily joined the war games when the game steward had demanded a MacRae warrior enlist or else she'd forfeit her place?

"How's your head?" Judith murmured beside her.

Ceana glanced sideways at the mountain-sized woman. Her hair was pulled back in a wet plait down her back, and she stood at attention as she always did, even in a more casual situation.

"If you're referring to when you hit me with your cudgel, I am completely recovered."

"And if I'm not?" Judith raised her brows in question.

Ceana gave a grim smile. "Then I seem to be falling into a pit of darkness."

"Darkness?"

Ceana nodded, chewed her lip. "What do I have to be happy for today, when tomorrow another person will die?"

"Life." Judith shrugged, sounded so nonchalant about it, as though it were the most simple answer of all.

Life. It almost seemed absurd.

The simple reality of it struck her hard, leaching the breath from her lungs. "I am happy to be alive," she said, as though trying to convince herself, then a little louder, "I am alive."

"Then you should not let yourself fall into the blackness of evil's hands."

Judith was right. Ceana shifted her gaze to the council who stood behind the piper. All of them stared straight ahead, not one even bothering to look at the entrants. But she was particularly interested in Lady Beatrice. The woman stood tall. Lines creased her brow. And though she stared into the distance, her displeasure was evident. This woman had let evil take her in its grasp. She lived in the murkiness of her own life's discontent. She may have won her place on the seat of Sìtheil, but she'd lost everything that made up her humanity.

The back door of the castle opened at the same time the piper's song ended. A waif-thin woman scaled down the stairs on the arm of a handsome-looking nobleman. He did not wear a plaid like most Highlanders but a fancy-looking tunic of soft wool and a thistle design embroidered on the hem and around the collar. A thick, corded-leather belt was tied about his waist, and a sword hung at his hips. There was something imperceptibly familiar about his face, but she couldn't quite place it and was nearly certain she'd never seen him before.

"We have missed the opening piper's tune," the woman said, her voice rather high-pitched as she walked haughtily toward the council's dais.

The young noble beside her nodded but said nothing, his eyes hungrily scanning the lines of women. There was something criminal in his contemplation, and she was instantly on alert.

She happened to flick her gaze at Macrath. Though he stood facing forward, his entire body was stiff and he stood taller. Was this his stepmother and half brother?

Lady Beatrice stepped forward to address the warriors, ignoring the newcomers other than to give them a look of complete disdain. An older council member assisted the noblewoman and man in climbing onto the dais where they came to stand behind them.

"Warriors, today we celebrate Samhain. The souls of the dead will walk around us, among us. Through us. You have all survived the first three games. But you will not all survive the next two. Live today as though it were your last, because it might very well be."

A shudder passed through Ceana. By the gods, it would not be her last day. Nor her last sennight, fortnight, or month of moons. She'd be standing tall and proud as she was now come the end of the games—with Macrath by her side.

Lady Beatrice's gaze roved over the crowd of entrants, and Ceana had the distinct impression she was taking stock of who'd be left among them in the next few days.

Ceana refused to do the same. There were still women left—like Judith—who could swiftly bring death upon her head. But looking over the male warriors, Macrath was easily the strongest and fiercest among them. He stood tall and proud, his dark hair shifting in the wind, strong jaw stiff and eyes directed on her. His shoulders were square, muscled legs braced. His linen shirt and plaid were plain, but on his powerful frame, they could have been the king's clothes.

And then, with a guilty conscience, she looked toward Aaron. The man would be lucky to make it through the next round. She'd forever have his life on her hands—and yet she'd told him not to join. He'd insisted, and she was drawn back to her worries over what his motivations were. Had he hoped to rule beside her? Did his affections run deeper than simply being close with her brother Dougal?

"Think of today as a reprieve. A celebration of what you've accomplished. A chance to consort with the souls who will welcome you shortly into their ethereal arms." Lady Beatrice paused a moment, turning her back on the entrants. As if waiting for her to have said the last few words, a train of servants exited the kitchen doors of the castle.

How many times had they heard her speech before? But her questions evaporated with the steam coming off the various platters piled high with food. Following the food were servants carrying jugs, Ceana hoped, of wine.

"You will feast together today. For you have earned it. But beware. Come the dawn, the celebration will end, and game four will be upon you. *Slàinte*! May the gods be forever in your favor."

Lady Beatrice waited, and within a breath, the male entrants bowed and the females curtsied. She turned on her heel and walked regally back toward the castle, the remainder of the council in her wake. Macrath's stepmother and half brother lingered, eyes on him. She had to go to him, protect him as best she could.

The piper began another enchanting tune. The scents of the feast filled the air, and Ceana's stomach grumbled. She walked straight forward, not breaking her stride, toward Macrath. If they were going to be allowed to feast together today, then she would not waste another moment from his side. They were being allowed more time than she could have ever asked for. And with it being the games, the females were not required to have a chaperone. She wondered if that was one of the reasons the council had deemed it all right for them to dine together. There could be no distractions today. No games to play. And if the men and women chose to bed down together, who was to stop them? Who cared? Some of them would die virgins as it was.

Macrath held out his arm. "'Twould be my honor to escort you to the feast," he said.

Ceana slid her arm over his, sparks of anticipation and need firing over her limbs and centering in her middle. Macrath had put her off when she'd begged him to lay with her, but she'd not take no for an answer this time, and she hoped he wouldn't either.

"'Twill be my pleasure to spend the day with you."

Aaron started toward them, but she narrowed her eyes and shook her head. Today was about her and Macrath, and she wasn't going to let his jealousy get in the way. He turned away with a glower. No matter. She'd not let his sour mood spoil hers.

They entered the tent, a mass of bodies bidding for seats along the benches of the trestle tables. Roasted goose, stewed venison, lamprey pie, loaves of freshly baked bread, tremendous hunks of cheese, apple tarts, and honey cakes amassed the tables like a starving man's dream. Her mouth watered.

Macrath led her toward the back of the tent and the end of a table. Men scooted down, allowing them space to slide in.

"Thank you," Ceana murmured to the man on her right.

Macrath sat on her left side and filled her cup with wine. "To us. To survival," he said in a low voice that didn't carry.

"To us." She raised her glass to his and then drew in a long sip.

He began to pile meat, pie, bread, cheese, and sweets onto her plate. The feasts for the entrants after the initial games had been splendid, although separate, but neither of them compared to this display.

The tent grew loud with the excited voices of the entrants as they crammed one bite of tantalizing food after another into their mouths. Ceana could barely hear a word that Macrath said, but she felt complete with him beside her. As they'd been the last to squeeze in at the end of the table, Aaron was on the other side of the room, but she could feel him watching.

'Haps she had the wrong of it, and he was simply worried about her?

All of a sudden, Macrath stood. She glanced up at him, nearly melting from the smile he beamed down at her.

"Come with me. I have an idea." He grabbed up a flagon of wine, a loaf of bread, and a hunk of cheese.

Ceana followed suit, loading a trencher with tarts and honey cakes. "Where are we going?"

"The loch."

She'd yet to see it as it was beyond the gate. "Will they let us?"

He shrugged. "We will not know until we try."

For the first time in weeks, Ceana was starting to feel light of heart, though she had no purpose in doing so. There was too much sadness in her soul. She felt she didn't deserve a moment to be uplifted. But the way Macrath was looking at her, the cheerfulness of the entrants, the heady wine, and hearty food... The entirety of it was intoxicating. Dragged her into a happier place within her mind.

"Let us go, then."

They hurried from the tent, Ceana practically skipping. They marched with purpose and laughter down the center lane toward the gate. Guards were posted at the side, but they made no move to stop them, simply said to be back before dark when the gates would be closed, that the archers would be watching, anyone attempting to escape would be shot, executed without question.

Macrath led her around the left side of the castle walls—where she'd not yet been. Beyond the moors was a sand dune, and beyond that, Loch Eu-Dòchas. The sound of the water lapping at the edges of the sand traveled over the wind. However cold she'd been this morning, she no longer felt it. Only warmth.

And hope.

"You're not supposed to be up here."

Aaron turned to the guard who approached him atop the gate tower. He'd snuck up the circular wooden stair to peer over the crenellations at where the bastard Macrath had taken Ceana.

"Just looking at the landscape," he said casually.

The guard touched the hilt of his sword. "Leave."

Aaron shrugged. "I'll not do anything to distract you from your duties." He gazed toward the woods, hoping to see a flash of movement, but all he saw were the birds and a stupid fawn that munched on grass. Ah, a distraction for the numb-brained guard. "Wager you can't shoot that deer with your arrow." He smiled to himself, proud of his forward thinking.

The guard looked over the wall toward the woods and grinned. "Wager I can. But that's not going to keep me from throwing you over the side if you don't get your arse out of here within the count of three."

Aaron just so happened to gaze around to the left toward the loch, catching sight of Ceana's red locks blowing in the breeze and a hulking mass of arsehole beside her.

"As you say, sir." He moved around the guard but then found himself floundering through the air as he tripped over a purposefully extended boot.

"Lucky to only have fallen to your knees. Next time you go where you shouldn't, you'll end up dead," the guard threatened.

Aaron swiped at the warm, sticky blood seeping from his nose where he'd smacked it on the stone floor. Without bothering to respond, he ran toward the door leading down. This latest offense would be added to the list of reasons why he had to kill Macrath—least of all that he'd enchanted his lady away.

Aaron pushed through the door at the bottom and crossed under the gate. What better day to make sure Macrath made it to his maker than the day souls walked the earth?

Chapter Eighteen

FORGETTING for a moment just where they were, Ceana skipped over the dune, her boots skating over the rocky sand. To their right, a long pier stretched out into the water, and the gentle sway of the loch licked up the thick posts. There were no galleons moored, all of them being forced to leave the day the games began. The only way off the island was to travel miles and miles down the beach until the end of Sìtheil to a neighboring clan. The travel alone would take days, if not longer, and once there you weren't guaranteed passage, for who would want to wage war against the council by assisting in the escape of a discontent?

A salty, chill breeze blew off the water. Ceana closed her eyes briefly and breathed it in. 'Twas refreshing. She rubbed her arms, tucking the length of her *arisaid* tighter around her shoulders, and smiled at Macrath.

"I love the water," she said.

"Aye, me too."

"Do you have a loch near your home in Argyll?"

He shook his head. "We are on the shores of the Firth of Lorne."

"Sounds beautiful."

Macrath gave a bitter smile and sat on the sand, pulling her down beside him. He uncapped the flagon of wine and offered her a sip.

"Sometimes." Regret laced his response.

"And at other times?" Ceana hated to pry into what seemed like a painful upbringing, but she hoped he felt comfortable in speaking freely after closing up on her the night before. She took the offered wine, letting the heady contents warm her from the inside.

"You well know that my stepmother has a hearty dislike of me. And even that's an understatement. If she could have, she would have strangled me with my own birthing cord."

Ceana nodded.

"She did not make growing up easy."

Ceana couldn't even imagine. Her clan had been steeped in war since as long as she could remember, but the one thing she'd always had was the strength of her clan and family. To feel unprotected and unsafe as a child seemed the worst thing in the world. Even still, it had made Macrath who he was. A strong, dependable, intelligent man.

"But now you're all grown up."

"Aye," he grinned, "but age has not lessened her dislike of me, nor made my life any better, save for I can defend myself."

Ceana's heart ached for what he must have been through as a child. "And soon you'll show her exactly how well."

Macrath nodded and tore a hunk of bread off the loaf. She watched as he hollowed the piece, stuffing the soft, bready part into his mouth. Then he tore off a chunk of cheese and stuffed it into the center of his crusty shell. When he took a bite, a small smile touched his lips.

"I've never seen anyone eat their bread and cheese like that before," she teased.

Macrath glanced at her sideways. "Then you should try it. 'Tis the only way." He held out his cheesy bread, inviting her to taste.

Ceana did not hesitate. She leaned forward, sinking her teeth into the crunchy crust and then the softness of the cheese. It was amazing. Simple, but so good.

"I like it," she said.

Macrath tore off a piece of bread and cheese so she could make her own. They sat in a comfortable silence, munching on their food and staring out over the loch. They split the tarts and cakes, licking the honey from their fingers.

"Why didn't you tell me you were a laird?" Macrath brushed crumbs off his hands and casually picked up the jug of wine.

Ceana tossed the rest of her cake to a hovering seagull, watching it dive straight toward the sand to take ownership of its prize. "I was only just named laird prior to coming to the games. I suppose part of the reason I've kept it quiet is because I am still reeling from the idea. I never thought I'd be laird. Never thought my brother would be murdered. But he was. And now I am. In fact, 'tis the sole reason I'm here. When my brother was murdered and left me in charge, I suddenly had all these mouths to feed. As I told you last night, my people are starving. We are constantly raided. I had to do something."

"You're very courageous." Macrath looked on her with pride. He'd said as much when she told him the night before. And she believed him.

Ceana smiled, let out a short laugh. "I don't know whether I'm brave or just desperate."

"I think 'haps both. But you know, most of the people here did not choose to enter the games."

"Hardly anyone would be so foolish."

Macrath shook his head, put his arm around her shoulders, and tucked her close. "Och, I do not think it foolish, but noble. I would have done the same thing."

Ceana sank against his hard body, warmed by the heat of him.

"If we could, I would stay right here in this moment forever." She clasped her hand over his arm.

Macrath pressed his lips to the top of her hair. "Aye, lass. I would also."

Ceana tilted up to stare into his mesmerizing, blue eyes. "Thank you."

"What do you have to thank me for?"

"For being here. For being you."

Macrath stared at her intently, the force of his emotion dizzying. "There is nowhere else I'd rather be, nor anyone else I'd rather be with."

Ceana leaned up, pressed her lips to his, tasting the heady wine on his tongue. Macrath was intoxicating enough as it was, but the wine only seemed to enhance the sensations of his kiss. The soft swipe of his tongue, the tender brush of his lips. His thumb stroked along her cheek, and then she felt herself being lifted as he settled her on his lap.

Ceana trembled, shivering a little at the chill air and even more at the deliciousness of Macrath's embrace. Her limbs tingled, and her belly leapt. Nipples hardened, and between her thighs was instantly afire, yearning for the touch of his fingers.

Oh, how wanton she felt in his arms, and yet so natural.

Her heart pounded against her ribcage, and she clutched an arm around his neck, the fingers on the opposite side, holding tight to the coiled muscle of his upper arm.

When she was with him, she felt like she was floating, as if all burdens had been taken away and she could live out the rest of her days in peace and utter joy. And as absurd as those thoughts and feelings were, she clung to them as hard as she held on to this man.

With Macrath, the world *could* be a better place.

"I want you," she whispered. Words she'd uttered several times since first meeting him. "And 'tis not just because I'm afraid or because we may not live after tomorrow. I want you desperately because when I'm with you I feel at peace, happy, and hopeful." *Because I love you.*

She'd laid her heart open enough that he knew how he made her feel, but to whisper those simple words... Well, hadn't Macrath said when she'd snuck into his tent after the first game they should save some things to look forward to? She'd save those words for the day they won and not let him feel the burden of her heart.

"Och, lass. I fear I've not the power to turn you away, because I need you so urgently I feel I may wage war against the council just so I can keep you all to myself."

"There is no need for war. Just take me. Here. Now." Ceana moved to straddle Macrath's hips. The hardness of his arousal pressed against the apex of her thighs, sending a jolt of delicious warmth and desire spreading through her. "I know not how..."

"Shh... I know, and I will teach you." Macrath tensed, pulling away from her lips for a moment to survey the beach. Ceana laughed.

"You see? When it is just the two of us, the world melts away."

"Aye, lassie, it does." Macrath set her aside for a moment and then stood, holding his hand out. "Come with me."

Gripping his hand in hers, she allowed him to lead her up the beach just a little ways before he pulled her against a stony, earthen wall. A tree hung down over it creating a hollow. He sat down, his back to the natural wall, and tugged her down. Ceana straddled him again, rocking slightly at the insatiable pulse that built deeply and intimately with the touch of his hardness to her sensitive inner thighs. Macrath groaned, his eyes heavily lidded and locked on her.

"Come here," he said. Threading his hands around the back of her neck, Macrath tugged her mouth to his.

Zounds! They were going to make love, and she was desperate for it. Wanted to feel every part of his body. Wanted to kiss him like this forever.

Macrath gripped her hands and pressed them to his chest. "Do you feel how hard my heart beats for you, Laird MacRae?"

Ceana mirrored his movements, putting his hand to her breast. "And mine for you, Son of Fortune."

Macrath grinned. It was both endearing and wicked, and just for her. "I want to make your heart beat faster."

His thumb brushed over her puckered nipple, and Ceana drew in a deep breath as tingles shivered over her skin. "You already do."

"Not even close." He leaned up, capturing her mouth once more.

Ceana wrapped her arms around his neck, clinging to him. He explored her breasts, her nipples, ribs, and waist. He slipped his hand beneath her gown, sliding up the slope of her calf to the underside of her knee. Everywhere he touched, gooseflesh followed. As he caressed her, kissed her, he moved, arching his body along hers and then retreating. Ceana followed his lead, rocking her pelvis over his, gasping with each tease of his hard shaft. And she wanted to feel more. Wanted to know what it would be like for his naked skin to touch hers.

She tugged at his shirt, pulling the bottom from his plaid and running her fingers over his bare chest. The slight brush of hair tickled her fingertips. She slid her thumb over his nipple like he'd done to her. Ran her nails gently over the dips and curves of his muscled chest and abdomen. Marveled at the corded sinew of his shoulders and back. His skin was smooth, but rough, compared to hers.

Macrath pulled suddenly away from her, his hands cupping the side of her face, eyes serious. "I pledge myself to you, lass. Now and forever. I want you to be my wife."

Ceana nodded slowly. Both earnestly and emphatically, she said, "Now and forever, I want you to be my husband."

"And if a child is born of this, I will not make a bastard of it."

"As the gods are our witnesses, we are trothed to each other, and our child will not be named a bastard."

"Och, gods, lass." Macrath wrapped his arms around her, captured her lips in a demanding kiss.

With an arm around her waist and the other bracing himself on the side, he hoisted her into the air and rolled her onto her back, hovering above her. The sand beneath her back was warmed from where he'd sat, but even if it wasn't, her skin was aflame from the fire of his touch.

He settled his weight between her thighs and his lips to the side of her neck where her pulse beat wildly. She bit her lip, nervous. Her fingers trembled when she touched him. But this was what she wanted. This man. This moment. With her next breath, she let her inhibitions take flight with her fear. Ceana tilted her head, gasped at the flicker of his tongue, stroked her hands down his strong back.

Macrath continued to rock against her, over her, all around her. She arched her back, let her knees fall wider. This was what it had to be like in heaven, high up in the clouds in paradise. When his teeth scraped seductively over her collarbone, her eyes popped open as she moaned with pleasure.

The morning sky had cleared to a silky blue, nearly the same color as Macrath's eyes. Fingers of shining golden sunlight streaked in prism-like wonder. Almost as though the gods were shining down on them, blessing their union, their promise.

"I wanted our first time to be perfect. A feather-tick bed, roaring fire, sweet wine, and sweet fruit," Macrath whispered against her over-sensitized flesh. "I wanted to make love to you slowly, over and over again. But instead, I'm afraid to remove any of your clothes and freeze you to death. Forgive me?"

Ceana threaded her fingers through his hair, stroking him tenderly. "There is nothing to forgive. You're all I need." And she meant it. No amount of soft beds or sweets could make this moment any more perfect than it already was.

"You do not understand how much it means to hear you say it. Och, lass, *mo chridhe*... I want to keep you in my arms forever, safe."

I love you.

The look in his eye, vulnerable and filled with... If she had to swear on her own death, she'd say that Macrath loved her too.

"Shh... Let us live today as though it were every day. Today we are Prince and Princess of Sìtheil." Ceana lifted up, brushing her lips over Macrath's jaw, licking the scrape of bristles. She kissed his neck in the same place he'd kissed hers, feeling the way his pulse beat against her mouth. She tasted the salt on his skin.

Macrath nuzzled her neck and the slope of her breasts. He massaged one globe and then the other, tugging lightly at her gown and exposing the creamy swells one inch at a time until the pink tip of her nipple was free. He groaned and dipped his mouth to taste. The velvet heat of his tongue stroking her skin had her crying out, arching against him. She lifted her legs, tilted her hips, wanting so much more of the pleasure he gifted her.

"Oh, Macrath," she murmured. Was it possible to love him more with every breath?

While he laved at her breasts, he worked his fingers up her legs, leaving chills of anticipation racing up and down her limbs until he touched her center. He leisurely tugged her skirt up until it was bunched around her hips. Even the chill of the air couldn't take away from the heat of the moment. With the pad of his thumb, he stroked over the knot of flesh that sent spirals of heat careening through her. Her thighs quivered, womb contracted. Soft moans escaped her lips between pants.

What magic his touch was.

"You're ready for me, lass," he said.

"Aye," she answered.

Macrath untied his belt, and unraveled his plaid, pulling it over the both of them, capturing their heat within its span. He resettled himself between her thighs, the heat of his thick shaft making her shudder against him.

"Och, gods, you feel so good." Macrath pressed his lips to hers, teasing her with his teeth and tongue. He grabbed hold of her hand and brought it to his turgid flesh. "I want you to guide me in. I want you to be in control of bringing us together."

Ceana panicked a moment, unsure of what she was supposed to do. But his hand was still over hers, and so she guided him toward the part of herself that felt so delicious when he stroked her.

"Almost, love." He guided her hand lower until the tip of his flesh pushed against a barrier. "Are you ready?"

Ceana nodded. Macrath drew in a deep breath and then thrust forward. A pinch of pain throbbed as he speared her, and she gasped, eyes flying open to stare at the radiant sky.

"Are you all right?"

She couldn't answer. She was too shocked. It had felt amazing until that point. Now she wanted him to stop. She gritted her teeth, blinking away the dampness in her eyes.

"The pain will not last long, or at least that is what I'm told. Please, tell me. Are you all right?"

She met his gaze, and nodded meekly. The pain *was* beginning to subside.

"I'll not move until you're ready, love." True to his word, he kept his hips still but nibbled at her ear and kissed her neck. He brushed his lips over her mouth, making her forget all about the pain.

Love. He kept calling her that. He did love her. The thought lightened her heart and sent warmth rushing through her.

Ceana was the first to move, tilting her hips and gasping at how that subtle movement made sparks shoot through her.

"Wrap your legs around me," he said.

She pulled her legs up, tucking them around his hips, causing him to sink inside her another inch.

"Oh, Macrath," she murmured, pressing her lips to his neck, his shoulder.

"Does it feel good?" He rocked against her, pulling his hips back and then sliding slowly forward.

"Oh, aye..."

"Good, because I've never felt anything like this."

And neither had she. It was... tremendous, magically life-changing.

Macrath kissed her tenderly, threaded his fingers in hers, stroked a light and tingle-inducing line down her arm to her elbow and then back again. As he moved inside her, he kissed her fingertips, murmured encouraging words in her ears. Told of how she made him feel. It was enough to make her dizzy with passion. In her core, an unimaginable pressure grew, making her thighs shake, her insides quiver. He increased his pace, his soft moans and panting breath mingling with hers. She could barely breathe as he brought her higher and higher.

Until finally—it hit her like a Highland avalanche, whisking her up in its tumultuous tumble. Crashing down around her, startling and staggering, it buried her.

But he was right there to lift her back up. Cradling her hips in his hands, he drove inside her several more times, and then he too appeared to be tumbled. He thrust deep inside her, letting out a groan that made her quiver all over again.

Macrath slowed over her, pressing sweet kisses to her forehead and then her lips.

"You're exquisite," he murmured. "I've never known a woman like you."

"What's this?"

Ceana started from her haze of languid tranquility to see an unfamiliar face looming nearby. What was happening? When had he gotten there? How much had he seen?

"Victor." Macrath growled, his gaze on the man, then he roared. "Get out of here."

Ceana gasped, remembering at once the man who'd stood at the dais that morning. As she'd suspected, this *was* Macrath's half brother. There were subtle similarities about them—perhaps the color of their hair—but the way they carried themselves was completely different. She would not have been able to guess they were brothers other than Macrath's confession.

Victor tilted his head back, laughed, and clapped slowly, his vile gaze raking over their bodies covered by Macrath's plaid.

"Och, brother, 'tis you who ought to be getting out of there. Having a nice fuck?"

Macrath's entire body stiffened and seemed to go up about ten degrees. The vein in his neck pulsed.

Ceana pressed her hand to his chest, wishing to impart some sense of calm over him but knowing at the same time doing so was futile. Macrath was angrier than she'd seen him on the battlefield. She genuinely was concerned for Victor's life. From the sound of it, the arse needed a good thrashing, but doing so would only injure Macrath's future in the games.

"He's only goading you," she whispered.

Even still, Macrath slipped from beneath his own plaid and stood on the beach, his shirt going to his mid-thighs and covering the part of him that had just been inside her. Fists clenched, jaw muscle bouncing, through bared teeth, he said, "Best you get back to the castle, Victor."

"Och, but I'm having so much fun watching you. So's the sneak up on the dune." Victor tilted his chin upward.

Ceana glanced up, but could see no one. Either he was lying, or the beautiful moments they'd just enjoyed had been spied on by more than solely Macrath's nasty brother.

"Might do you well to return to the tents. I have some news for the council." Victor winked at Ceana and then turned on his heel.

A burning, nauseating sensation took up in her belly as she gazed between her fuming warrior and the retreating figure of his malevolent brother.

Chapter Nineteen

"BLOODY bastard." Macrath had gritted his teeth so hard his jaw pulsed with pain. Nothing was ever easy in his life.

The moments of beauty and peace he'd found had been interrupted, and a haze of black smoke choked him. Victor had gone back up over the dune and disappeared from sight. He glanced behind him where Ceana had pushed off his plaid and stood, smoothing her smudged gown. Fear pinched her lips and around her eyes.

"'Twill be all right," he said, knowing that he lied. He was going to be punished. Most likely by both Leticia and Lady Beatrice.

"I'm not naïve enough to believe you." Ceana stepped up beside him and held out his plaid. "Your brother wants to hurt you. He won't take anything less."

Macrath took the plaid and laid it out on the ground to pleat it. "He's no brother of mine. Blood doesn't betray blood."

Ceana bent to help him. "But I think it does. Think of past history. Brother fought against brother to rule clans. Father against son. Cousin against cousin. Mother against daughter. There is no shortage of blood feuds." She reached out and touched his arm, the contact soothing. "That does not make it right. There is nothing worse than being betrayed and believing you are utterly alone. But you are no longer alone. I am with you."

Macrath nodded, his mouth a grim slash. He didn't want her to get hurt, and he was terrified that her allegiance to him would do just that. Hell, she'd already been abused by the guards because of him. He donned his plaid and helped her to dust the sand from her hair. They walked hand in hand up over the dune. From outward appearances, with the piper's tune, the smoke of several bonfires, and the laughter floating on the breeze, one might have been tricked into thinking this were an actual clan Samhain celebration. But he knew better.

Though he held her hand now, Macrath was certain that if Ceana were to have a chance at making it through the games, he would have to put some distance between them. He hated how callous that would seem. That he'd taken her maidenhead and thrust her aside, but it wasn't like that at all. He just knew his family, and he'd caught more than a glimpse of Lady Beatrice's true nature.

Ceana would not last a day if any of them got their clutches on her.

Halfway across the marshy ground to the dirt-packed path, Aaron leapt in front of them, face red, chest heaving with his labored breathing. Ceana started, her hand tightening in his. Macrath narrowed his eyes, wondering if this had been the other person spying on them as they made love.

"How dare you!" he growled at Macrath and swung out his fist.

Ceana gasped, and Macrath caught the smaller guard's hand in his fist, crushing his fingers.

"What are you doing, Aaron?" Shock filled her words.

"Exactly what he's wanted to do from day one." Macrath spoke through gritted teeth, bringing his face close to Aaron's.

"You let this animal touch you?" Aaron seethed.

Ceana looked taken aback. "Excuse me?" Suspicions confirmed—Aaron had been the spy.

"You let him put his hands all over you. Rut with you in the sand like you're a common whore."

Before Macrath had the chance to react, Ceana's hand shot out, slapping Aaron hard in the face. Aaron reacted immediately, trying to wrench his hand from Macrath to hit Ceana. But Macrath wasn't going to let that happen. He gripped Aaron by the throat, lifted him into the air, and tossed him several feet away. When the man landed, red-faced and sputtering, he glared up at Macrath.

Macrath stormed over, putting his foot on the man's chest, and leaned down. "Do not ever speak to her like that again. Do not dare to even *think* about putting your hands on her. Ceana will be my wife, and you'll be lucky if I don't kill you this day myself."

Aaron looked crestfallen. He glanced past Macrath to Ceana. "You'd marry this bastard?"

Macrath turned around, suddenly fearing that she might change her mind. He was a bastard and she a laird, and he was likely the one who'd get her killed—hence the need for distance—but he still didn't want to hear her say no. Then again, maybe it would be best for her and for her safety. And if that was what kept her alive, he'd gladly back away.

"Aye. I will." Ceana came forward, pressed a soft hand to Macrath's shoulder, and nudged until he stepped away from Aaron. She reached out her hand to him, but Aaron wouldn't take it.

He pushed away from her and stood. "Dougal would be ashamed of you. All the MacRaes will be when they find out."

Ceana shook her head. Sadness filled her eyes. "The only disappointment right now is that a close friend of my brother's, my own personal guard, would harbor such ill will toward me."

Aaron reached out for her, but Ceana put up her hands. "Do not. You've already said your piece."

"My laird, I do not harbor ill will toward you." He clutched his hands together, pleading.

Her regard of him was flat and did not waver. "Your actions, your words, they say otherwise."

"I've only ever loved you. I wanted you to be my wife."

Ceana glanced toward the ground at his admission, his words obviously affecting her. "But that would never have happened. Don't you see? My brother had plans for me to marry another laird. To bring a strong alliance to our clan. He'd just not yet narrowed it down. There was never a chance for us to be together."

Aaron looked frantic now as his world crashed down around him. "There was."

"When?" She looked genuinely confused.

"I thought we'd win the games and then you'd *have* to marry me."

Ceana sighed. "If that had been the case, then after the five years I would have bid you farewell. I do not love you, Aaron."

"And you love this man?"

Ceana glanced at Macrath, and his chest tightened. Did she? For he loved her with every breath in his body. Her eyes were glassy with tears, intense with emotion. "I feel much for him. Yes."

She flicked her gaze back toward Aaron, but Macrath could not stop staring at her. She loved him. He loved her. A hasty courtship it had been, and yet they'd endured and survived more than any average couple ever would.

Aaron clenched his fists, bared his teeth. The man was certainly having a hard time realizing he'd lost. And Macrath couldn't seem to find his throat. There was so much he wanted to say, and yet he wanted to keep it all inside. There was still the very real fact that Ceana's life was in danger because of him.

"Run away, Aaron. In the next game, just disappear. You'll find a way. I'd hate for you to end up dead because of a notion you have about the two of us."

Aaron's glare hardened, and he shook his head. "Best of luck to you, then." Venom laced every word, lending to the idea he didn't truly mean it. He whirled toward the tents and charged away.

"Will he also cause trouble for you?" Macrath asked. The list of those wishing her harm was growing longer, and he was the central cause.

"Nay."

"How can you be certain?"

"He is angry, aye, but I don't think he will do anything to harm me. He cares about me deeply. Cared about my brother."

Macrath had his doubts on whether any of those reasons would hold the man back. If he thought it in her best interest, he may very well go through with a foolhardy plan. He didn't trust the guard. Not even the slightest.

"Even still, promise me you'll watch your back when I'm not with you." Which would be very shortly.

Ceana nodded. "And you promise to do the same."

Macrath grinned. "Haven't stopped since the day I could walk."

Ceana reached out and squeezed his hand. "Despite Victor's interruption, I still had an amazing time with you. And I meant what I said."

"Lass, meeting you has been, by far, the highlight of my life." He pulled her close and pressed a hard kiss to her mouth. He had an idea of what she wanted to hear, that he loved her, but he just couldn't say it yet. Not when he planned to push her away at least for the next two games. He'd keep a keen eye on her, but other than that, once they reached the tents, he'd not speak to her again until they won. "Let us go."

They walked at a slow pace back to the tents, neither of them wanting to reach there and hurry the punishment that was certainly coming. But all the same, when they walked beneath the gate, it felt entirely too quick.

"No matter what happens here until the end—I will see you on the other side. We are one, Ceana." Macrath's chest felt like someone had sliced right into him, shredding his insides deliberately, excruciatingly. His troth to her was not a lie.

"Now and forever," she whispered, then let go of his hand and took a few steps away.

The guards were waiting, snickers on their faces, just inside the gate. "Well, if it isn't the Bitch and her dog."

Victor and Beatrice were not in sight, but he had a feeling they'd be waiting for him inside.

The guards stepped forward, surrounding Ceana—the same who'd attacked her in the tent. "You're coming with us, lassie."

Bloody fucking hell. It was worse than he could ever imagine. They would punish her and not him. Macrath stepped forward, but the guards were expecting it, and the central leader—the one who'd actually attempted to violate Ceana before—pulled his sword, holding it against Macrath's neck.

"Believe you me, bastard, I want very much to slice this blade across your throat and watch you bleed to death. But I've orders not to do so. And I've also orders to escort this fine, luscious piece inside. So now you'll need to step back and let me do my job, lest you end up gutted and she ends up speared by my cock from arse to throat."

Macrath bared his teeth, loathing that he was completely without options. If he chose to fight, he'd only end up dead, and she'd still be dragged inside. He shifted his gaze to hers and was struck by the calm reflected there.

"Let me go, Macrath," she whispered. Her pallor had gone ashen, lips pinched tight and eyes glistening. But even still, she held strong.

He couldn't answer. Couldn't say, *all right, on with you, then,* because he didn't want her to leave with the vagrants. Didn't want to see her hurt, and he knew that was exactly what was going to happen. Tears pricked his eyes. Ceana put a calming hand on the guard who held his sword to his neck.

"Please, take it away. I'll go with you." She nodded at Macrath, mouthed the words *I'll be all right,* and then turned her back on him.

She walked willingly toward the castle, the other guards surrounding her. Voluntarily provided to her own punishment—*his* punishment.

Mo chreach, he was gutted.

The one with his sword to Macrath's throat remained a few moments longer. He laughed in his face and then removed the sword from his neck, but only to punch him in the gut with the hilt.

His vision went red with anger, and it was all he could do to keep himself from launching forward and pummeling the man to the ground. Macrath looked up, eyes bulging, and said with determination, "I *will* see you bleed."

"Ha! Not bloody likely." The vile man followed his cohorts, whistling as he went.

Ceana kept her body stiff as she was led into the great hall of the castle. Her face was placid, though it was hard to hide her shock at *not* being assaulted by the guards before arriving. She was certain she was about to be raped.

The great hall was lit with candles and warmed by a fire. She felt her bones starting to melt, and she'd not realized how cold she'd been outside. On the beach with Macrath she'd been warm, but the scene with Aaron and then with the guards had chilled her blood to the point of ice.

The guards left her alone in the empty hall to await her uncertain fate. Her knees knocked together, and she locked them tight to keep them still, which only made her dizzy.

She shifted on her feet, feeling a thousand eyes on her, and wondered just how many stared at her through spy holes in the walls.

"Apologies for keeping you waiting, Laird MacRae." The syrupy sweet voice belonged to an elegant woman who glided rather than walked from a rear door until she was within a few feet of Ceana. "I hope you've not been here overlong?"

Ceana shook her head, not wishing to speak as she was certain her voice would croak and show her weakness.

"I am the Countess of Argyll."

"My lady," Ceana managed to murmur, and dipped her knees to curtsy, swaying slightly. Rather than bowing to this heinous woman, she would have liked to scratch her eyes out and worse, tie her to a post and lash her as many times as she'd done to Macrath over the course of his life. But alas, 'twas not possible at that moment.

"Oh, my, you look positively awful. Are you feeling well?" The cruel smile she gave said she knew precisely that Ceana was indeed not feeling well at all.

"I am fine."

"Hmm… Well, in any case…" She clapped her hands together, giving the impression she was about to gossip with her, and whirled on her heels. There was something completely unstable about this woman. It was terrifying. "I have a surprise for you. Have you met my son?"

The countess's gaze flicked behind Ceana, and she could hear subtle boot heels click over the wooden-planked floor.

"Indeed, Mother, we have met." He slid up beside Ceana and patted her backside, which made her skin crawl.

"How wonderful. Now off with you two. Enjoy your day together."

"Wait, what? I'm not going anywhere with you." Ceana stabbed daggers from her eyes in Victor's direction.

Leticia gave a mock sob, drawing Ceana's attention back around. "Oh, but you see, my dear, you are. Today is a celebration day for everyone, and it just so happens that Lady Beatrice allowed Victor to choose the woman he wished to spend his day with. He chose you." The woman floated out of the great hall using the same entrance she'd used when she arrived.

Victor's fingers curled around her upper arms from behind, biting painfully into her flesh.

"No!" Ceana cried.

But he paid no attention to her lamentations. Victor propelled her backward, whirling her to face him, looming overly close to her visage. In her panic, there appeared to be two or three of him.

"Shut your mouth, wench, or I'll see it shut for you."

She didn't care for his words, and struggled against him. When she'd thought to be raped by the guards, she'd still planned to fight, abhorred the very idea of it, but by Macrath's own flesh? She would never be able to live with that. Victor slapped her hard on the face with the back of his hand, momentarily stunning her.

"What's all this?" Lady Beatrice's cool, calm voice broke through the churning of Ceana's terror.

"My lady," Victor said, amiably. "You gave permission for me to enjoy one of the entrants of my choosing."

"Not her. You'll have to do with another."

"But, my lady—" he faltered.

Lady Beatrice let out a great sigh. "Oh, all right. Now you may have *no one*. You see? I do not tolerate those who would argue against me. Now be off with you, vile creature."

When Victor remained rooted in place, his clutch digging bruises into Ceana's arm, Lady Beatrice shouted, "I said leave."

The boom of her voice shook the rafters and even made Ceana's knees knock together.

Victor hurried after wherever his mother had disappeared to, leaving Ceana alone with the woman who'd only the night before abused Macrath so cruelly.

"Come. You may spend the rest of the day and night sleeping on a feather-tick."

Ceana could have fainted. Maybe she had, for certainly her head was not receiving the right messages. She had to have heard wrong. "Pardon?"

"You heard the right of it, Laird MacRae." Beatrice smiled heartlessly. "Seems that having you in here is stirring up quite a bit of trouble outside with your bastard warrior."

Ceana did not comment.

"But I owe your mother enough to give you a nice night of rest before tomorrow. And I rather like that he's fuming madder than a cornered adder."

Macrath was nothing like a snake. He was more like a wolf, ready to tear into the guards who kept him separated from her. Ceana just prayed he didn't get himself killed in the process. A shiver stole over her, and she rubbed vigorously at her arms.

"Why do you owe my mother?" Ceana asked.

Lady Beatrice cocked her head and squinted her eyes, studying Ceana for a moment. "I do not wish to share that with you now. Follow me."

Ceana dreaded every step she took in the councilwoman's wake, but did not see that she had any other choice. She dared not argue either, fearing what the retribution from Lady Beatrice would be.

Up the winding stair they went and through an unlit corridor to the third door on the left. Beatrice swung the door open. "There you are."

Ceana stepped inside the cold room. The hearth was bare, no candles lit. An old bed covered in a dusty plaid blanket sagged against the far wall.

"You'll have to make do without a fire. After all, you've not one outside, but at least a good bed for you. Cannot have you spinning tales of cozy hearths and maids to wait upon you. Good night."

Good night? It was not nearly the nooning.

The door closed, and there was an audible click from the outside as Beatrice locked her in.

Chapter Twenty

"I need to speak with the council! Get me Lady Beatrice!" Macrath's face felt swollen and full of bruises. His lip was bleeding, and at least a couple of his ribs were cracked, but that didn't stop him from demanding entrance to the castle and access to the woman who held his lass prisoner.

Dear gods, but what had been done to poor Ceana? His love… She'd not reemerged the whole night through.

"Och, quit your whining, you cunt. We'll not be getting her for you, and best heed our warnings lest we beat you into a stupor again." The guards made rude arm gestures.

Macrath growled and returned the arm signals. "Fuck you, you limp-cocked arseholes! I'll not be leaving—"

"What is all this racket?" The heavy wooden door creaked open, and Lady Beatrice stepped onto the stone platform at the top of the stairs dressed as though she were attending a royal procession and not games of death. "Oh, I see." She smiled. "Why, Macrath, you've had a pleasant run-in with the guards."

"Where is Ceana?"

"Ceana?" She cocked her head, playing coy, only making him madder than hell.

"Where. Is. She." The crunch of his teeth grinding echoed in his ears.

"She's right here." Lady Beatrice opened the door, reached inside, and tugged Ceana out.

For the first time in his life, Macrath's knees buckled in relief. She looked a little scared, but there were no other marks on her other than what he'd seen the day before. He prayed that meant she'd not been hurt. Ceana made a move to descend the stairs when he reached out for her, but Beatrice held her back.

"Ah-ah-ah," she chided. "Men to their lines. Women to theirs. Game four begins."

Macrath pushed to standing, hungrily taking in Ceana's tiny form and the pleading look in her eyes. All the thoughts he'd had the day before about staying away from her had ceased to exist the moment they took her away.

The horn blew, and then there was a scrambling all around him as both the entrants and the guards hurried to their places, most suffering from illness caused by imbibing on too much wine and rich food the day before.

Lady Beatrice hooked her arm through Ceana's and took her down the stairs, marching her right past him, a crooked smile as she went. The woman was tormenting him. Ceana looked behind her, their gazes locking. *I am well,* she mouthed.

He was so relieved he could have seen double. His stomach rolled, limbs shook. He'd been coiled so tightly for just under a full day, and now it was all coming unraveled.

His booted feet were heavy as he slogged through the mushy ground. He slowly approached the lines, and the horn blew once more. He was rewarded with a swift kick in the rear from one of the guards, but he didn't falter, just added their face to his memory—the record he was making of all the guards who'd pay once he was Prince of Sìtheil.

"The time for celebrating has come to an end!" one of the male council members shouted.

Macrath searched the women for Ceana, finding her in the back of her ranks right where she should be. Judith was patting her tenderly on the shoulder.

Lady Beatrice approached the dais and addressed the crowd of entrants. "Today's game will see your numbers greatly diminished. Today is a day of reckoning. A day of being reborn. Today is your drowning."

Macrath's gaze shot from Ceana to the dais. His heart kicked up into his throat. Drowning? She couldn't be serious! But there was no smile on her face, nor that of the council members. He chanced a glance back at Ceana, and her eyes were wide and frightened.

Bloody hell... Lips in a flat, determined line, he nodded at her, hoping to give her some assurance that they would make it through, but all the while inside he was clawing his way out of an imaginary, frigid loch.

"As you all were enjoying Samhain, we went amongst you and chose pairs. There are two rounds in this game—the victim and the savior. Each of you will have your chance to play a part—that is, if you make it past round one. In each round, the victim will be tied at the hands and feet, weighted, and pushed into the loch. The savior must find the victim in the water, free them, and bring them to safety. If you pass round one alive, you will switch places. There are an uneven number of you, twenty-two females and twenty-five males, so some of you may count yourself lucky, or not, that you can wait to pair with someone whose partner has failed. If you should both survive, you will move on to the final game. If one of you does not survive, then you will be paired with another of the same fate. If you die... well, may the gods be forever in your ethereal favor. To the pier!"

The group of men and women trudged somberly through the arched gate, some murmuring that they knew not how to swim. Macrath would not be surprised if their numbers were cut in half, or more, before the morning was out. Forty-seven entrants to start; how many to end? He slowed, letting those in the back of the male ranks file past him so that he could walk beside Ceana.

"Keep it moving, Macrath. Do not fret over the lass. She'll be your partner," Beatrice said cheerfully as she rode by on a shiny brown mare.

Shock chilled his blood. He would have to save Ceana from drowning, and she him.

Unlike many of the days when they had clouds shadowing the sun, today the glowing orb burned bright, warming them. The water would still be cold. Enough to numb limbs. If left in the water for more than a few minutes, many would begin to take a chill that couldn't be thawed. He'd seen men die of the affliction in the firth by his father's castle.

But by pairing him to Ceana, Beatrice had given him a rare gift. He now had the power to save her. They walked across the moor toward the rocky shores of the loch, descending over natural stone steps. Down the beach they marched, toward the long pier that headed out to a deeper part of the loch. The five council members sat their horses in a row, gazing at the entrants. Four guards stood at the far end of the pier beside barrels.

"Four pairs at once. We'd not want to be at this all day." Lady Beatrice beamed with merciless smile. She nodded to her fellow councilmen.

One pulled a scroll from where it had been tucked into his belt and handed it to her. She unrolled the parchment and listed eight names. None of which were Ceana and Macrath. She'd make them wait, he had a feeling. Beatrice was like that, tormenting in any way she could. Hell, had she not kept Ceana within the castle all the night to tear him apart inside? After a night full of angst and no sleep, he should barely be able to function, but instead, a rush of energy was forcing its way through his veins. He wrenched his neck, trying to look through the small crowd of entrants for a tiny, red-haired lass.

Did Ceana even know? Just as he thought it, he felt her slide beside him. "We are paired," she said, answering his internal question.

He resisted the urge to tuck her close. Right now, Judith stood in front of her, hiding her from the view of the council, but any move from him would make it obvious. "Aye. We'll survive."

She sagged against him and let out a sigh. "Can you swim?"

"Aye, lass, verra well."

Another deep sigh. "Good, me too."

"'Tis more the cold and how long it takes me to get to you. The water looks murky."

"We'll survive." She repeated his earlier words. The backs of her fingers brushed over his, and he caught them in his grasp, squeezing tenderly.

"Aye. That we will. And then they will all pay."

"Aye." Grim conviction filled her voice. Once named Prince and Princess of Sìtheil, they'd be a force to be reckoned with.

They watched as the four female entrants were bound at their ankles and at their wrists behind their backs—the rope so tight it cut into their flesh. Two of the women sobbed. The other two looked on stoically, determined. After they were bound, sacks of rocks were tied to their wrists—heavy enough to cause one of the women to waver. Each male was handed a dirk to cut the rope and weights once in the water.

As soon as the guards were finished, they turned to the council members, waiting for the cue to continue. There was a moment of hushed, suspended silence. No one breathed, especially Macrath. This was it. Game four had commenced, and it was going to prove to be more brutal than the previous three.

One nod from Beatrice had the four bound females being tossed haphazardly into the water. Their bodies splashed, water spraying up on those standing on the pier, before quickly disappearing into the murky depths. Gasps sounded all around them, and prayers and curses too.

Gods help them… And gods aid him and Ceana in destroying these abominable games.

The men tried to jump in after them, but the guards held them back for the span of at least five heartbeats, and then the men too were shoved into the water.

"You'll have to hold your breath," Macrath said. "Hold it until it burns, and then keep holding it. Do not open your mouth in that water. Do not move, either. Remain still, lest you use up your air."

Ceana nodded, her face having gone pale. He squeezed her hand, trying to offer comfort, and when that didn't work, he wrapped his arm around her shoulders and pulled her in tight—guards and council be damned. Most of the entrants had their arms around each other, or at least clasped hands. How could they not? They were watching their fellow entrants plunge to their deaths.

One of the men splashed around in the water, shouting his terror. He could not swim. Macrath's gut clenched. His female entrant would die, and so would he. Instinct bade him run to the pier, leap into the water, and save the dying man, but self-preservation, the end goal of destroying the council, kept his feet rooted in place.

"Oh, gods save them," Ceana whispered, her face pressed to his chest.

He couldn't blame her for not wanting to watch. He tucked her even closer. But even holding her didn't lesson the agony of watching someone die.

But there were no gods that could. The man fell beneath the surface and did not return. A moment later, one of the males brought up his female.

"Swim to the shore," the guards yelled.

Another surfaced and then another. The only one who did not was the male who could not swim.

On the shore, the women coughed and shucked out of the remainder of their ties, shivering as they went. Their lips were blue, eyes haunted. The men wore mirrored tight-lipped expressions as they were called back to the pier for the second round. They were tied, weighted, and tossed. The females held back and then pushed in. This time only one surfaced. She worked hard, coughing and spluttering herself to get her male to shore. When they finally reached it, another of the females surfaced, shook her head, and swam to shore.

Out of eight entrants, only three had survived. Not very good odds.

The next set of names were called, and once more Macrath and Ceana were not among them. But Judith was.

"This is good-bye, Bitch," she said with a shy shrug. "Spend all my time up a mountain. I cannot swim."

Ceana reached out and tugged Judith in for a hug. "You can do it. You can. You must."

"I'll be swimming in spirit." Judith pushed away and stood tall. "It has been a pleasure fighting with you." And then she was gone, walking along the pier.

Ceana sobbed beside Macrath, and he would have done anything to take away her pain. Much the same occurred, though it was hard to stomach. Five survived—three males and two females—Judith not one of them.

When their names were finally shouted, Macrath could not move his feet. It was Ceana who tugged him along. Eyes swollen from tears bore intently into his. "We'll survive, remember?"

He nodded and gave a clipped, "Aye."

Ceana was tied, the ropes cutting into the pale, delicate skin of her wrists and ankles. She gasped as the guard roughly handled her, wobbled backward when the weights were attached. Macrath refrained from retaliating, from removing a sword from the guard's hip before tumbling him into the water, afraid it would only cause them to be split apart, and then there was no certainty of survival.

"Macrath." Ceana's breathing was heavy, and she gaped at him with terror in her eyes.

And then she was shoved off the pier.

The frigid water hit her body like a massive block of ice. The weights sucked her down and down and down into the murky waters. Ceana blinked, trying to see around the greenish fog, but it made her eyes hurt, it was so cold. She'd taken a huge gasp before the plunge, and while her lungs were uncomfortable, they did not yet burn.

Macrath was right about the cold. The temperature of the water seeped into her bones and muscles, nearly paralyzing her. She counted to five in her head, her heartbeat echoing slowly, and then heard the sound of the plunges from above, like an explosion echoing as the men were tossed in.

Her lungs were starting to burn. She struggled to remain still and calm, her body warring with her mind's choice and its natural instinct to survive. Not a moment later, she felt Macrath's hand on her shoulder. Her eyes popped open, and she could see his outline looming in front of her. He kissed her quickly on the mouth and then cut the weight off the rope at her wrists but not the rest. Instead, she felt herself being propelled upward, her head breaking the surface with a stinging slap of wind.

"Stay still, lass. I'm going to cut these ropes." He made quick work of slicing the ones at her wrist and then rolled her into the cradle of his arms as he cut the lines at her ankles. "We did it," he said.

"Not quite. We still have you, and I'm fr… freezing." She shivered, her teeth chattering.

The cold of the water did not seem to have affected him as badly. He rubbed her arms and legs vigorously, then tugged her toward the shore.

"Let us do this quickly," Ceana said, with confidence. She was certain she could do for him what he'd done for her. Mostly certain.

They walked stiffly across the pier, their limbs still numb from the cold. Ceana shivered while Macrath was tied and weighted. Took the dirk from the guards and prayed over and over again in her head that she could get him out of the water before he drowned. Of their group, only one other pair had made it back to the pier. She'd not noticed when she was tossed down, but she had been floating near the bottom with dead entrants.

Oh, gods! What if she couldn't find Macrath, but only one corpse after another?

Macrath was shoved off the pier, taking her mind away from its disastrous thoughts and focusing her energy on the task at hand. Seconds later, she too was thrown back into the icy-cold water.

At first, she was too shocked to move. Anger rushed through her at her body denying her orders to move. Her legs cramped painfully, and tears stung her eyes. *No! I have to do this! I cannot fail Macrath!*

She took a deep, shuddering breath and dove down toward where she thought he'd been dropped. It was hard to see. There were many shadowed shapes at the bottom of the loch. Corpses.

I am swimming with the dead.

Macrath would be still, as he'd told her to be, and so she couldn't truly discern him from the lifeless. But his size—he was easily bigger than many of those who'd already drowned. Ceana swam through the bodies, lungs burning, mind panicking. Had she gone too far? Had she dove in the wrong direction? Her foot bumped against one cold, motionless limb after another.

Where are *you?*

When she thought she'd have to surface to take another breath, she finally caught sight of him. There was no time for a welcome kiss as he'd given her. She slid the dagger along the length of cord and sawed through. When the weights fell with a muted *clunk* on the bottom of the loch, she tugged his arms as he'd done. But he was considerably heavier. She could barely get him to budge. There was no way she could swim with him all the way to the top.

Ceana cut through the ropes at his wrists, lungs near to bursting, so Macrath could at least help her paddle upward. Once they were at the surface, the cold air stabbing into her lungs, she went below the water to cut the rope at his ankles. They swam back slowly to the shore, muscles cramping, lungs burning—the only survivors of their round.

They huddled together with the other survivors, shivering in the breeze off the shore in their wet clothes. They didn't speak, didn't say anything. Aye, they'd lived—a victory to rejoice in, but so many had died.

By the end of game four, there were only five women left and nine men. Fourteen entrants out of one hundred sixteen originally entered into the war games.

And Judith was not among them. Neither was Aaron.

She and Aaron had shared a long, tension-filled stare as his name was called. Guilt had flooded her, and she shook her head, hoping he'd try to run. But he glanced at Macrath and then whirled toward the frigid water. He'd willingly gone to his death.

A sob escaped Ceana, and she flung herself into Macrath's arms, grief overtaking her. Macrath held her tight, and though he did not make a sound, there was a subtle shake of his back. They mourned the loss of so many, together.

The walk back to the castle was quiet. They'd been given instructions to go into the separate male and female large tents where fires had been set up to dry themselves by, and large plaids to keep warm. The women chose to undress and wrap themselves in their plaids.

Ceana stared into the flames. Her anger and hatred mounted.

Only one game left.

And when she and Macrath won, they would indeed make the council pay, for before she drew her last breath, she swore on everything she held dear, the war games would cease to exist.

Game

Over

Chapter Twenty-One

THERE were few certainties in life. But one of the most certain was death.

Fourteen pairs of feet trudged woefully across the wooden bridge away from the gatehouse of Sìtheil Castle and toward the beach. Fourteen pairs of eyes stared vacantly over the landscape. Fourteen mouths would not smile this day—nor many days to come.

"Keep it moving!" the guards shouted, rushing them even in this moment of lamentation.

Ceana felt as though she were being pressed to death with stones, the heaviness within her chest was so tangible. It was hard to breathe. Hard to think. Difficult to do much more than mourn the death of thirty-three men and women who'd died brutally just after sunrise.

Their deaths had not been quick, nor painless, nor without fear and hope for a rescue. For they'd either recognized that they'd drown for lack of knowing how to swim, or they waited patiently at the bottom of the loch for someone to free them, until the burn in their lungs became too much and instinctively they sucked in water when what they needed was air.

"I'm glad you stayed," she said to her guard Boarg. He could have easily returned to their clan rather than wait outside the walls unaware of her fate.

"I could never have left you here alone, my laird. My duty has been to your family since afore you were born."

Ceana shuddered, fresh tears stinging her eyes. And she prayed he returned to their clan with good news and not the sad news of her passing. She clasped her arms around herself, trying to ward off the gooseflesh that rose along her limbs.

Dried and as warm as they could be—for it was certain her bones had taken on a chill that only dissipated when making love to Macrath—they crossed over the moors, the grasses swaying gently and ironically peaceful in the breeze. Finches and grouses dove in and out of the forest, warbling as they made nests for the coming winter. Nature, completely oblivious to the destruction of mankind.

The world seemed to move on without a care. But it had stopped for Ceana. She'd not only lost fellow entrants this morning, but she'd lost her guard, Aaron, and her friend, Judith. She'd never forgive herself for having allowed Aaron to enter. There had to have been more she could have done to stop him. would be forever on her hands. And Judith... closed her eyes tight, her feet moving habitually over the fading heather-covered moors. Judith had saved her life, and vice versa. The bond they'd formed had been tight, and in the back of her mind, Ceana had wished they could both end this game alive. But it was impossible—especially now. Judith was one of the few who didn't know how to swim. Aaron had been victim to a savior who couldn't swim either.

Victims. Saviors. How cruel of the council to name them such.

After the winners had been warmed and fed, their companions were allowed back within the walls of Sìtheil Castle to mourn the passing of the departed—the ones who'd not made it past the drowning of game four, the siege of game three, the women's fight in game two, or the wolf attack in game one. The mightiest of nightmares and fears had been thrust upon everyone in less than a week's time. Though they'd only be able to bury those who'd died during the last game, they'd be allowed a moment to pray for all who'd passed.

As they neared the beach, she could see that three small boats, piled high with wrapped packages, were moored to the pier. Where had the boats been before? Waiting, hidden in a cove?

The closer they got, the more she could see exactly what the packages were. Bodies wrapped tightly in linen. She could make out the shapes of their heads, the roundness of shoulders, the length of legs and feet sticking up. Piled one after another, kindling surrounded the edges of the boats. Everyone before today had been buried. Were these the bodies of those who'd drowned? Who had fished them out?

Again she shuddered.

She stepped closer to Boarg. She needed the comfort of home as they neared the beach. "His family will blame me," she whispered.

"Nay, lass, they will not. They know Aaron came of his own accord. He died a warrior. 'Tis an honorable death."

Ceana tried to see it that way, but she couldn't. Aaron had come to the games with one purpose in mind—to win and marry her. If only she'd known his plans before they'd ever left Gruamach lands, she'd have insisted he stay and that someone else escort her. Furthermore, if she'd been aware that there had to be two entrants per clan, she would have made certain—

What?

Would she have willingly lured one of her own clansmen to his death? No. Would she have married one of them for five years before pushing him aside? Maybe. Because the winners of the throne of Sìtheil only had to pledge themselves to each other for five years, and hadn't it been her plan all along to bid farewell to whomever she was attached to at the end? To take precautions a child was not born of the union. To make certain she garnered enough wealth and power to protect her clan.

Things had changed when she'd met Macrath. She still wanted to protect her clan, but she also wanted to remain by his side the rest of her life.

She steeled a glance in his direction. Ever since the end of the game that morning, he'd been silent, brooding. Much like she was.

He walked silently beside her, tall, stoic. The marks of the guards' beating still marred his face. His broad shoulders were squared. A short growth of stubble lined his square jaw. Macrath was the epitome of manly strength. A true warrior. How many mourning ceremonies had he attended? Certainly more than she had. Gods, but she wanted to absorb his strength.

Her warrior did not have any servants or a personal guard. Ceana wasn't surprised, given his stepmother and half brother's extreme hatred of him. He'd said she'd shipped him and poor Rhona off without a crust of bread to sustain them during their fortnight-long journey. It was a wonder they made it to the games alive. And it was a certainty at least one of them would never leave Sìtheil breathing. Ceana's breath shuddered as a sob threatened to escape. Taking Rhona's life was a moment she would forever remember in the darkest of night terrors.

Ceana glanced around, confirming that Leticia and Victor were not present within the group of mourners. She supposed she shouldn't have been surprised. Neither of them seemed to care much about any of the entrants. They were only there to enjoy the bloodshed.

When their feet at last sunk into the rocky sand, Ceana braced herself to examine the boats filled with bodies. Her eyes counted the bundled and stacked forms, hoping and praying she wouldn't make out the outlines of Judith and Aaron's bodies. She couldn't tell where they were, and she didn't know whether that was worse or not. But there didn't appear to be enough bodies. Many more had drowned. What happened to the rest of them? Fear and more questions than she cared to have the answers to invaded her mind. When she was a girl, the clan elders told stories of monsters that lived at the bottom of the lochs and fed on the feet and hands of little children. As an adult, she liked to think those monsters were simply the imaginings of elders to keep children from swimming too deep. But…

The piper stood at the end of the pier and put his lips to the mouthpiece. Graying clouds met the far side of the loch, and in the distance the forest appeared to weep. His cheeks puffed with air, and then that first drone piped out before his mourning song filled the beach and carried on the wind. A song for the dead.

The council members dismounted from their horses and walked in a solemn line onto the pier, led by a stiff-backed Lady Beatrice. Though she was no longer Mistress of Sìtheil, she still carried herself as though she were. They were all dressed in their finest plaids with jeweled pins on their shoulders and gemstones glittering on their hands.

Beyond the piper's woeful dirge, silence reigned. Even the seagulls left them to their sorrow. A slight breeze blew off the loch. The air was cold, the sun covered by storm clouds, and Ceana wondered if she'd ever see brightness in the sun again, or if for her it would always be gray.

Let the storm hold out until the birlinns are far out to sea and burned to ash.

Beside her, Boarg was stiff and stared out over the loch, his ancient brows wrinkled, lips turned down. Ceana shifted her gaze toward Macrath. He'd vacated her side, and she shifted uncomfortably, searching him out and failing until she felt him step up on the other side of her. Warmth and comfort seeped into her. His strength. She needed it. She needed him. Without Macrath by her side, she would not have made it as far as she had.

The next gust of wind sent a spray of water flicking against her cheeks. She closed her eyes and breathed in deep. The air was tainted with the scents of death, peat fires, and the chill of autumn air.

The backs of Macrath's fingers tickled over hers, and she wanted to grab him, to have him hold her in his arms, but with their numbers so drastically reduced, any affection they showed each other would be noticed immediately.

"Stay strong, lass," he whispered. "They are free from fear now. Free from the brutality of this world."

Tendrils of the piper's tune swirled gently around them, easing into the clouds until the song came to an end. Lady Beatrice inclined her head to the musician and stepped forward, her gaze raking over the fourteen entrants and the many servants and guards allowed inside for the burial.

Palm upward, the councilwoman spread her hand out toward the small boats. "We gather this afternoon to say good-bye to the discontents of game four."

Ceana frowned. Even in death, Lady Beatrice saw the dead only as discontents and nothing more. She took away their very humanity by framing them that way.

"To let go of the memories of the discontents of the previous games. If you will repeat after me the Sìtheil Prayer for the Departed."

Surprise tightened her stomach, but she supposed for a place that saw as much death as it did, it made sense they had their own prayer for the dead.

"Blessings to those who have preceded us in passing;
Released from pain and dread;
Sleep now, and know we are not weeping;
For tears are best not wept for the dead;
Peace be forever now your everlasting;
And the gods protect you on this journey next led;
Through blessed moors and a castle for keeping."

Ceana mouthed the words but could not bring herself to actually say them. Aye, they were giving blessings to the dead, but she *did* weep for them. She wept for them all.

When the last of the entrants said, *keeping,* Lady Beatrice motioned to the archers on the beach who stood beside barrels of flames. The guards cut the ropes tying the *birlinns* to the pier and shoved the rims with their boots. The crafts drifted slowly out into the loch. Ceana's lungs constricted as she suppressed her sobs while watching the bodies glide over the murky waters.

Air broke in whispers as the archers let their arrows fly. Dozens of flaming shafts shot through the somber sky, landing in the kindling set up on the boats, a few fizzling in the water. Great flames burst where the arrows had buried themselves. As the fires grew, licking over the bodies, black tendrils of smoke curled and twisted into the sky.

The piper had once again taken up his playing. It seemed that each chord of his song weaved its way in and out of the flames and smoke as though he charmed the infernos himself.

They stood on the beach, feet rooted in the rocky sand, lips grim, eyes stinging, arms wrapped around themselves. Even the council looked a little more stiff-backed than usual. The previous burials had been quick, hurried, uneventful. There were no prayers. There were no ceremonies. But the council had said this mourning period would be different.

Not because of the brutality—the games had all been ruthless and bloody. Not the numbers, because the first game had seen their numbers cut by nearly half. 'Twas because this was the game before the last. Within the next couple of days, only two of them would be left, and after days of carnage and death, those left needed something to keep them going. Whether that be the thought of winning the crown or the idea that if they did not make it through the final game they would be mourned properly. They would be honored for giving their lives.

They watched until the *birlinns* were only tiny flaming dots on the horizon, and then the council walked off the pier and mounted their horses. "A mourning meal has been provided for you in the tents." Lady Beatrice led her council from the sands and back toward the castle.

Ceana walked numbly over the dunes and moors. Footsteps echoed softly on the wooden bridge, and then they filed beneath the gate. The iron portcullis was not pulled all the way up, its spikes low enough to threaten their heads as they passed through.

The lights of the candles inside the large tents glowed on the outside of the walls. Ironically enough, in the short time since they'd walked from the beach, the skies had gotten darker. Guards and servants alike were welcomed into the tents with the fourteen entrants remaining.

Macrath walked silently beside her, as did Boarg, and while she'd craved silence, now she wanted to hear their voices. Wanted to distract herself from the horrors of the past week. But everyone mourned differently.

Boarg mourned the loss of Aaron, who was his cousins' son. In a way, he might mourn her as well, unsure if she'd be able to make it through the next round. Macrath, besides nursing aching ribs, a bruised and beaten body, was also deep in thought. Planning how they would win? Or praying that the last game was not beyond Ceana's abilities.

And her? She preferred not to contemplate it anymore.

Death would come to them all. It was only a matter of time and circumstance whether she be a lass of nineteen summers or an elderly woman with a graying head.

After a week of observing and living in a deathly hell, Ceana wanted to float off into oblivion. Wanted to recapture those moments on the beach when it had been only her, Macrath, and the heated passion of their two rocking bodies.

She walked through the open flap of the tent, the air inside noticeably warmer. Wind whistled beneath the edges and slapped against the tent walls. The trestle tables were slowly filling with outsiders.

Outsiders?

Though they may have been servants, family, and guards of those passed and those still living, to Ceana they were outsiders, brought into the fold only after the horrors she'd witnessed were over.

They'd not had to experience death firsthand or kill another during these games. They'd not been submerged in freezing water, praying that the one to find you would indeed cut you loose. Or have to swim around bodies, knocking into lifeless flesh in order to find your loved one.

And yet, outsiders though they might be, she found their presence oddly calming and welcome. They brought with them something different than what was encapsulated inside the walls of Sìtheil Castle. An innocence of sorts that she wasn't willing to let go of.

"Let us get some wine," she murmured.

Boarg and Macrath both stepped forward to clear a space for her on a bench. She smiled an apology to the servants who were displaced, then slid along the wooden bench. Boarg and Macrath flanked her, each handing her a glass of wine at the same time.

"I suppose I may look like I need both," she said with a meek smile. And perhaps this was just what she needed, to drown away her pain in a cup.

"Apologies, my laird," Boarg mumbled at the same time Macrath said, "Och, I didn't see that your clansman had gotten you one."

"'Tis all right. I'll take both." She took both cups, sat one in front of her empty trencher and took a long sip of the other. It was a smooth wine, not like what they were normally served, and even better than the wine they'd been given at the Samhain celebration. It was sweet and heady at the same time.

"I see they've favored us with the Sìtheil mourning wine," Boarg said.

"Sìtheil mourning wine? You've had it before?" Ceana raised the glass to her lips again.

"Aye." He didn't expand further.

"As have I," Macrath murmured.

How was it that both men had tasted mourning wine before and she had not? "Appears I am the only one who hasn't."

"A good thing, lass," Macrath said, glaring into his cup.

"Aye," Boarg agreed.

Ceana was pretty certain she didn't want to know the reasons behind both men having been exposed to a wine that was obviously kept only for certain occasions. She just wanted to escape. But she realized there would be no escape. No getting away from the darkness that covered this place. That stain covered her. She glanced down at her hands, expecting to see the prominent veins beneath her flesh turning black and that blackness leaching out to cover her skin. But they remained the same. Unlike her mind.

"Will you share with me how you came to drink this wine?" she asked.

Both men were silent, and she glanced from side to side to see them both nod silently, brooding, their eyes ahead.

"My story is simple," Macrath said. "Leticia brought me to observe the games when I was a boy. I think it was her plan all along to have me entered. The mourning wine was poured, and she brought a cup to my lips and whispered that this wine would be the last taste upon my tongue." He set down his cup roughly, wine sloshing over the sides to spill on his hand. "I was sick for nearly a week after that cup. Poison. She was not pleased I lived."

Ceana swallowed hard, biting the tip of her tongue. The harshness of Macrath's story left her feeling hollow. She reached out with a napkin and wiped the spilled wine from the back of his hand.

"It will *not* be the last thing you taste," she swore.

"Enjoying the wine, I see?" Leticia's cold, smooth voice reached out and grabbed them both by the throats.

Ceana jerked her hand away from Macrath's. She turned slowly around to see Leticia smiling over her own cup of wine.

"Best be careful with that," Ceana said, letting all the cruelness inside her seep into her own smile. "Sìtheil mourning wine has been known to make some ill."

Leticia's face colored red and her eyes shot fire. "How dare you speak to me that way?" Even still, she eyed her cup wearily.

"Dare I? What allegiance do I have to you?" Ceana stated.

"I outrank you," the woman seethed.

Ceana shrugged. "Inside these walls, there are only two ranks—the council and the entrants. You are but an outsider, and you have no sway here."

Chapter Twenty-Two

"LEAVE her be," Macrath said to Leticia.

Leticia took a step forward, a snarl peeling her lips. Before she could speak, a cheer went up as servants filed into the tent carrying fried fish, pease porridge, and bannocks. Their entry momentarily distracted the dozens of examining eyes.

Macrath owed this woman nothing anymore. He deliberately turned his back on her. In a day or two, he'd either be dead or Prince of Sìtheil. She'd either bow down to him, or laugh over his corpse. At any rate, he was done with her overbearing nature. And if it caused him another lashing in Lady Beatrice's torture chamber, then so be it. But he suspected that the councilwoman did not look kindly upon his *loving* stepmother.

"And just who do you think you're talking to, bastard?"

He bared his teeth, sucking his tongue against the back, and pushed his wine cup away. Bracing his hands on the table, he rose slowly, feeling every bone in his back unfurl as he stood. Ceana touched his elbow, but he brushed her aside. She wanted to keep him safe. He knew that. But there was no stopping him. Too many years of anger, frustration, and torment had boiled over. The gods themselves couldn't have held him back.

Macrath looked his stepmother—his tormenter—in the eyes as he spoke in a low, threatening tone. "I said, leave her alone."

"And what are *you* going to do about it, Macrath? Nothing. You *are* nothing."

He clenched his fists and forced himself not to throttle her. "I have listened to your shite, the venom you've spewed since before I could speak, and I will not listen to it anymore."

"Oh, you will listen, and you will listen well." She stepped so close he could smell the herb-scented water she'd rinsed herself in that morning. The same that she always had—rosemary and lavender. Two scents that combined made him nauseous. Thank the gods Ceana's essence was more earthy and floral. "You were born a nothing. You grew up a nothing. You will die a nothing. And if you don't die during these games, I will see to it that every one of the Campbell allies joins forces against you. Believe you me, before winter ends, you will cease to breathe."

Macrath laughed then. A rumbling sound that started at the center of his abdomen and burst from his mouth. But the laughter didn't reach his eyes. He was mocking her. Mocking her grasp at authority, for he knew in truth she had none. Aye, she'd been able to torment him as a child, even as a man, but her power ended now. He cut his laughter short and leaned in so close the tip of his nose nearly touched hers.

"We both know my *father*"—gods, but it felt good to thrust that back in her face—"will never gather his allies nor his own warriors against me. I trained those men. They will side with me. Not with you. Your threats are empty. The only way for you to kill me is to sneak into my chamber and slit my throat yourself. But you'll not make it past my threshold without me waking, and if you draw a knife on me, I'll have no qualms about striking you down—and no remorse for doing so."

Leticia sucked in a startled breath and staggered back a step. "I cannot—"

"Save your breath, stepmother."

Victor approached, his face blotchy and red. "Step away from the countess," he ordered.

Macrath rolled his head, giving his hated flesh a long, calm stare. "Where have you been?" he asked. "You've missed our family reunion. We are brothers, aren't we?" This last part he said facing Leticia again.

The woman's lips had gone white, she pressed them so hard together.

Rage burned through his veins, and the tight leash on his control started to loosen.

"Ha!" Victor burst out a laugh. "There's no way to prove that. Your mother was a common—"

The leash dropped. Without hesitation, Macrath thrust out, slamming his fist into Victor's face. The vile maggot yelped, gripping his nose from which blood spurted, and faltered backward on his feet until he fell hard on his arse. Only Boarg's grip on his elbow kept Macrath from leaping forward to pummel the limp-wicked arsehole into the ground.

"Victor!" Leticia shouted, falling to her knees and reaching for her son.

Victor batted her away, striking her on her hands and arms, smearing his blood on her. Served her right that she had such a venomous child.

"Get away from me!" Victor shouted at her in his embarrassment.

Macrath snickered. The only thing worse than getting your nose busted in front of a room full of strangers was having your mother rush to your aid, or at least that's what he'd been told.

Victor turned his glare on Macrath. "You'll pay dearly for this." He pushed to his feet, whirled on his booted heels, hand still clutching at his nose, and shouldered his way loudly out of the tent.

"You will not get away with striking my son." Leticia stood, shoulders rigid. Her face had gone red and splotchy—a female version of Victor. He'd never seen her so angry.

Macrath didn't say a word. Didn't change his expression, simply stared at her. She was probably right. Lady Beatrice would have to punish him. But it had felt good to hit that bastard in the face. Damned good. And he'd do it again in a second.

He flexed his hand and reclenched his fist. His knuckles were sore, but it was an ache he'd longed to feel for years.

"Macrath." Ceana touched his elbow, her voice filled with fear.

He glanced down at her, grinned, and winked, hoping to ease her anxiety. He spoke in low tones, so no one could overhear. "Guess I was dreaming of the day we'll be crowned and the first thing I wanted to do as Prince of Sìtheil."

She licked her lips nervously. "Aye, and I bet it felt amazing."

"It did."

"Macrath!" Leticia shouted, trying to return his attention to her, but he only had eyes for Ceana.

"What do you think the council will do about it?" his tiny woman asked, eyes flitting nervously to Leticia.

"I don't know." He glanced behind her at her guard. "Best stay close to Boarg."

Ceana shook her head. "I can't let them hurt you."

"Do not ignore me!" Leticia bellowed her rage.

He flicked his gaze at Leticia, saw her make a move to step forward but hesitate at his glower. Macrath glanced toward the tent flaps and answered Ceana. "Won't be any worse than what they've given me already."

Ceana's eyes closed, and he watched her throat ripple as she swallowed. Slinging an arm around her shoulder, he tugged her in close but all the while kept his eye on Boarg. The guard gave him a silent nod. Macrath longed to press his lips against Ceana's hair, but with their audience… He was in enough trouble as it was.

"I will speak to the council about this!" Leticia continued to bluster while he ignored her.

"Do not fash over me, *mo chridhe,*" he whispered to Ceana. "Just remember we will soon rule this place. One more game and the throne is ours. Keep your mind tied to that. Do not look back."

"Macrath Mor! Son of the Earl of Argyll, turn around." Lady Beatrice's voice grated like a rusted blade down his spine, gripping his bollocks in her viselike grasp. She would be harder to ignore than his stepmother.

"Macrath," Ceana whispered frantically, clutching at his shirt.

"Shh, lass. All will be well. The lady… fancies me."

"Aye, bloody!" Ceana wouldn't let go, her eyes wide and locked on his.

"Bloody, aye, but not dead." He winked at her, hoping his bravado would seep into her. The last time they'd been punished, Ceana had been the one taken, but nothing had happened to her. He'd had the bloody shite beat out of him. But Ceana had been safe. "Be strong. I'll not let them break me. Don't let them break you."

"Macrath!"

He turned slowly. Leticia smirked, looking entirely too self-satisfied. He took in the severe tightness of Lady Beatrice's hair pulled in a knot at the nape of her neck. But the austerity of her hair contradicted the expressionlessness of her face. She studied them all with disinterested eyes and a flat mouth, making Macrath question whether or not the woman had a soul. Judging from how she'd treated the entrants, the way she brushed off death as though it were nothing but a foul stench, the mildness of her manner was flawed. And disturbing.

He would never underestimate her again. Not after she'd surprised him so many times. Macrath put his back to Ceana, inching her closer to her guard as he prepared to face down one of his enemies.

"My lady." Macrath bowed low, showing Lady Beatrice the deference she demanded.

The tent had gone silent when Macrath and Leticia had argued, but now they dared not breathe. Mugs and trenchers remained untouched on the tables as they waited to see what exactly the councilwoman would do. It wasn't out of the realm of possibility that she would punish them all by calling an end to their meal, forcing their servants and guards back outside the front gates and commencing with the final game.

"What, exactly, is going on here?" A chilliness swept over her words and snaked around his spine like snow from atop a mountain.

Her eyes did not leave his, and yet Leticia interrupted. She pointed at Macrath. "That bastard attacked my son."

Lady Beatrice held up her hand and turned a cold smile toward his stepmother. "I believe I was asking the bastard myself."

"I humbly beg your pardon, my lady, but you cannot mean to take his word over mine?" Leticia looked exasperated.

"Believe me, countess, when I say I would gladly take anything from him over you."

There was an underlying anger that seeped from her words. What history did these two women have? But even the words themselves… He had an idea she was referring to the moments she'd held him captive in her torture chamber, how she'd desperately rubbed herself all over him. He'd been nonresponsive, which had only angered her more.

Leticia stepped toward Beatrice, her head lowered to speak in confidence, but the silence in the room let her words be heard. "Bea, really, I understand your anger, but—"

Bea?

Lady Beatrice sucked on her teeth and hissed at Leticia, "Silence your mad tongue."

Macrath flicked his gaze between the two women. The familiarity used lead to them being old friends. No wonder he'd been brought to the games as a lad. Had the councilwoman helped his stepmother taunt him?

She pointed at Macrath. "You. Come with me." Then, changing her mind, she pointed at Leticia, Victor, Ceana, and Boarg. "All of you."

Macrath glanced at Boarg, a silent exchange for them both to protect Ceana. Leticia hurried to follow right behind Lady Beatrice, leaving the three of them trailing behind. The moment the tent flap closed behind them, the inside erupted into chatter—and he knew exactly what—rather who— the subjects of conversation were.

Instead of going into the castle, Lady Beatrice led them to the tent the council used. Once inside, she whirled on them, eyes bulging, and stabbed toward the ground with her finger, taking a menacing step forward.

"Just what in bloody hell do you think you're doing, disrupting a mourning dinner with your antics?" She glared at Macrath.

He kept his mouth shut, certain that stating he'd not been the one to start it would not solve anything.

Leticia was all too happy to fill in the space he left silent. "This little tart was insulting me, and when my son came forward to defend my honor, Macrath attacked him. He was trying to enrage the rest of the entrants into an uprising—to thwart the council's authority."

Beatrice studied Macrath, her eyes burning into him. He felt exposed, as if she could see every thought, every mark of pain, every ounce of joy he'd ever experienced. He kept his face placid, eyes cool. Hands tucked behind his back casually, he was still ready to strike if need be. Ceana stood beside him, equally still, and Boarg on the other side. None of them spoke for fear of making Beatrice mad. He'd not seen such strong emotion from her before.

The councilwoman was normally a cold-hearted tyrant. Went about her taciturn behavior in a calculated way. Emotions were ruling this moment, and he sensed it was mostly directed at Leticia.

Again he wondered, who was his stepmother to Beatrice?

"Is what the countess says the truth of it?" But her gaze slid to Ceana on the last word, as though she was asking her and not Macrath.

"No." Ceana kept the emotion from her voice. Good.

She could be diplomatic when needed, and that made him excessively proud.

"Tell it to me as you recall." Beatrice looked to calm a little.

"The countess was provoking Macrath, at which point I felt the need to step in. We exchanged heated words. Macrath joined the conversation, having taken offense, and when Victor saw the exchange he too added his piece. Macrath did hit him, but he was only defending his mother's honor."

"Mother?"

"Aye, his mother. Not the countess."

Beatrice nodded. "The three of you are dismissed. Go and finish your meal, for the final game begins before dawn. Lady Leticia, you will remain, if you please."

Before dawn? Macrath and Boarg ushered Ceana from the tent before the councilwoman could change her mind.

When they returned to the tent, they ignored the stares of others and sat in their same seats.

"Best eat as much as you can, and then we'd do well to get some rest. I've a feeling we'll be woken in the middle of the night." Macrath speared a piece of lukewarm fish.

Ceana hollowed a chunk of bread and stuffed a piece of cheese inside, just the way he'd shown her when they'd gone down to the beach. The reminder made him smile. That had been the best day of his life—the day they'd made love, the day he'd discovered she loved him and he loved her.

"What if they separate us? Like they did in the second game?" Ceana whispered her concern, but even those slight words were filled with panic.

She was a damn strong lass, but everyone had their breaking point, and he was certain she was close to hers.

"My guess, having gone off the way these games are progressing, is that you'll be together," Boarg offered.

Macrath nodded slowly. "Aye. The first game was a picking off of the weakest entrants. The second and third games tested us individually, and the fourth game tested us as partners. The fifth game I think will also see us paired. It will force us to choose allies, and only two will come out of it alive."

Ceana chewed, contemplating his words. "I can see that. I think you're both right."

The tent flap whipped open, and the guards filed in. "The mourning feast is over. Entrants to your tents. The rest of you rabble, get thee gone through the gates lest you incur the council's wrath."

Boarg tugged Ceana into a hug. The man had a fatherly aura about him. She sunk against the older guard. Macrath could tell that the man had been a source of comfort to her for a long time.

Macrath held out his arm to the guard, and he took it in a tight grip. "I'll look out for her."

"I know you will." Boarg left with the others, leaving the tent to the fourteen entrants and the game stewards lining the wall.

"Sleep well, warrior," Ceana said, standing beside him.

Macrath took her hand in his, not caring who was looking, and brought it to his lips. "Every dream will be about you, lass."

A sweet smile curled her lips—something he'd not seen often enough and one of the things he swore he'd see more of when they were crowned.

"Not much longer," he whispered. A flash of fear in her eyes made his gut clench. "Never fear, love. We will prevail. I feel it in my bones."

"I demand that you and your son leave the castle at once," Lady Beatrice said to her spoiled younger sister. Not a day had changed since the whiny little half-wit had been born.

"What?" Leticia clenched her fists and stomped a foot. "How can you demand such a thing?"

Beatrice's blood started that slow steady boil that meant she'd soon be lashing out. "You are a nuisance and a distraction. Victor has already raped half the servant girls in the castle while you turn a blind eye simply because you want to see your husband's bastard perish. I cannot allow it to go on any longer."

Leticia took a step back. "Bea—"

Beatrice held up a hand and closed her eyes searching for patience buried somewhere deep inside her. She couldn't find any. "Pack your things and see your way out, else I will lock you and your son in your chambers until the games have concluded. It is very unorthodox that I've allowed you to be as involved as you are. The rest of the entrants' family members, servants, and guards are kept outside the castle walls. I could have forced you to do the same."

"But we are not the same, Bea. I am not a family member of an entrant, but of you."

Beatrice laughed sharply. "Aye, but your son is a family member of an entrant, isn't he? And that just grates right along your precious nerves."

Leticia's face turned redder than a radish. "He is not—"

"Och, but he is. They share blood. Your husband's blood."

"Do not say such things."

"But 'tis the truth and the reason you hate the man so much. Shame really. He's quite a specimen."

Leticia rolled her eyes with disgust. "You always had a thing for brutish rogues."

"And what of you? Is not Macrath and Victor's father a rogue himself?"

Her sister's lips pinched tight. "I hate you."

"As does everyone else. Now get thee gone from my sight, lest I decide to become quite unpleasant."

Leticia dropped her gaze, sadness filling the lines around her eyes and mouth. "Bea, please… Being here with you is the only thing that makes me happy."

Beatrice clenched her teeth tight. Why did her sister have to try to make her feel bad for her? She didn't really. Leticia was pathetic, but she supposed it couldn't be helped. After all, Beatrice had been the one to practically raise the simpleton, given their parents didn't have the faculties to do so. Perhaps, this one last time… "I may allow you to remain until the end, if you keep yourself and your spawn hidden within your chambers. I do not want to see you again until the crowning."

Leticia pouted. "You've not warmed a day since you I was born."

"I'm not concerned with being warm, Leticia. I'm concerned with being obeyed and with keeping order. You are a hindrance to my focus."

Leticia turned on her heels and stormed from the tent. *Good riddance.*

Chapter Twenty-Three

CEANA woke to the sounds of drums beating a slow, rhythmic pace. At first she was bewildered, confusing the thrumming with the thump of her heart. Her tent was pitch-black, and she leaned upon her elbows, trying to discern if the pounding was in her head or truly occurring.

There were no other sounds, just that simple—*bump bump bump bump bump.*

It was a death call. A summons to the final game, of that she was certain.

Her heart skittered, stopping and then pumping hard. Lips numb and tingling, her entire body stiffened.

This was it. This was the moment that would determine her fate. Whether she lived or died. Whether she ruled here on earth or floated up in the heavens.

Terror filled her, and she couldn't move. Frozen in place, there was no forcing her limbs to move. No forcing herself to get up and go toward the sound of the drum.

She stared, wide-eyed, into the blackness and willed the drums to stop their beat. Willed herself back to Gruamach Keep. Willed her brother alive and this all a night terror.

But it wasn't a night terror. Dougal was still dead.

And she wouldn't be whisked magically back home.

The war games were all too real, and her reasons for being here unchanged. She had to save her clan. If time were reversed, she'd not have met Macrath. The games would be drastically different without him. He'd made every moment better, restored her. Kept her sane.

Slowly, feeling came back to her fingers, and she rubbed the sleep from her eyes.

"Ceana." She'd recognize Macrath's voice anywhere.

He slid inside her tent, a flash of torchlight lighting up the space for a moment before the closed tent flap blocked it out again.

His presence moved her body into action, and she tossed aside her blanket, lifted up onto her knees at the same moment he dropped down on his. The pressure of his fingers clasping her shoulders was a comfort as he hauled her up against him.

"The final game begins," he said.

She breathed in deep, his woodsy, masculine scent filling her. Ceana closed her eyes and wrapped her arms around him. Their chests heaved as one with each of their tortured breaths. "Do you know what they'll have us do?"

"Nay, love, I do not. As soon as I heard the drums begin, I ran for you." He pulled her tight against him, her cheek pressing against the hardness of his chest. His heart beat only a little faster than it normally did.

Ceana laid her hands flat on Macrath's warm, strong back and prayed. Prayed they'd both make it. Prayed that this was not the last time they embraced.

"We must go. We cannot allow them to come and look for us but must present ourselves as we will when this game ends. Together. Strong-willed." Macrath's hands clasped the sides of her face, the roughness of his palms a welcome scratch against her sensitive skin.

He was right. They had to. The last time they'd come looking, she'd ended up with a varlet's phallus in her face and vomit down his legs. She shook her head, needing to wipe that horrid memory from her mind. "Kiss me, Macrath. Kiss me the way you'll kiss me when this is over."

His lips brushed over hers tenderly, and she closed her eyes, imagining the sharp angles of his face, the brightness of his blue eyes. Ceana threaded her fingers through his soft hair and clutched him. Tasting the peaty whisky on his tongue. Leashed power trembled through him. She let herself be swept up by him, plunged into the whirling clouds of pleasure and fantasy that happened every time they kissed. Macrath's touch was magic.

The drumbeats grew louder. Faster.

"We will finish this kiss when we win," Macrath said affectionately. He pressed his lips to her forehead. "But I cannot go into this last leg of war without saying something to you, Ceana."

Their breaths and the drums blurred. She swallowed around the lump in her throat. "Tell me."

"I love you. I love you more than life itself."

Gods how she wished she could see into his eyes. "I love you too."

He pressed his lips hard to hers. It was swift, it was demanding, and it swept her up once more. "Let us go," he said.

Macrath pulled her up, his fingers laced with hers. Coarse palm pressed to her softer one.

Outside the tent, the night sky was clear—black with thousands of tiny, sparkling stars. The moon was large and silver, and without the light of the torches, they would have been able to see from its brightness.

The entrants were emerging from their tents, wrapped in plaids to ward off the cold. They trudged toward the center, prepared to line up for the final game. Twelve of them would die tonight.

The thought soured Ceana's stomach.

Hours left in a dozen lives.

Hours. That was all that remained of this heinous fight to the death. That was all that was left of this tragic and senseless loss of life.

"We have to do something," she murmured. "When we win, we cannot allow this to happen again."

"Aye, lass. My word as my oath, we will see these games come to an end."

Too bad they had to win first and they couldn't have vanquished the council and the hundred-year-old war games a week before—when everyone was still alive. But it took power to contest a royal council, a king. It took influence to make that drastic of a change, and winning would give it to them.

Standing on the dais were the five council members.

Leticia and Victor were absent. Thank the gods above. Ceana wasn't sure she could have kept her mouth shut if the woman had tried to prod them again.

The drummers lined the center road. Faces placid, they beat their sticks at a quicker clip until all fourteen entrants stood in line. Then they abruptly ceased their pounding. There was no rhyme or reason to the way the entrants lined up on this night. No men's side. No women's. They all stood huddled together, ready—and some not so ready—to accept their fates.

"Warriors," Lady Beatrice started. Her hands clutched in front of her a sword, point pressed into the floor of the dais. "You have fought valiantly over the past four games, and tonight we commence with the final game. Only two of you will survive, but know at this moment, we consider you all to be victorious. Twelve of you will receive a burial fit for a distinguished warrior. Twelve of you will be remembered throughout time. But only two of you can live."

A shiver went up through the crowd, and a woman on Ceana's left let out a harrowing sob before getting hold of herself.

"In a moment, the guards will step forward, bind you, blind you, and load you into a wagon. The wagon will take you into the woods, where you will be deposited—still bound—in an undisclosed location.

Your mission is to find your way back to Sìtheil. There will be many obstacles along the way. If more than two of you should find your way back to the castle, then there will be a final battle within the list field—hand-to-hand combat with swords. Be brave, and accept your fate with honor."

Lady Beatrice nodded, and at that moment, fourteen guards surrounded them, tucked hoods over their faces, and yanked their hands behind their backs. The cloth smelled musty and old. It sucked away the air from Ceana's lungs. How many countless others had the hood thrust over their faces? How many countless others struggled to breathe? How many panicked? Ceana counted to five, giving herself that short bit of time to regain her composure and figure out how to breathe.

The guards were rough, touched in places that they shouldn't, and laughed when the entrants shouted their anger. She had more than one fondle her breasts and pinch her buttocks. But she did not make a sound. Didn't want to give them the satisfaction, nor did she want Macrath to know.

Though she could no longer see him, she could still feel him standing silent beside her. Ceana kept silent too. She needed to save her energy.

Her ankles were bound, the rope threatening to cut off her circulation. Thank goodness there was a barrier between the rope and her hose, because the rope tied tightly around her wrists was already biting into her flesh. Another length of rope was tied between the binds at her ankles and wrists, causing her back to arch and her to fall to the ground. She wasn't the only one. Bodies thudded to the ground all around her amid curses.

Ceana was hoisted off the ground, her body bouncing uncomfortably, pain searing against the ropes, and then she was tossed on her side onto a hard platform—the wagon. She winced at the pain shooting from her leg and arm where she'd been stitched. Several bodies were tossed beside her, all of them providing heat to each other in the cold night air.

A moment later, the wagon started to move, the wheels cranking, and the boards creaked as it rocked. She bumped against someone in front of her and behind her, their lengths pressed tight together.

She tried to focus all her energy inward, using the ride to their destination to rest, but it was impossible. Her body jostled uncomfortably, and her feet and hands had started to tingle unpleasantly. She wiggled her fingers and toes, trying to keep the blood flowing in her veins, but it did nothing but make it worse. So she set to rubbing her hands and feet back and forth, working to loosen her bindings. When they were deposited, they'd still be bound, and she had no idea whether or not weapons would be nearby to cut them loose. They'd not been given much information beyond—return to Sìtheil.

"What do you think is going to happen?" asked a woman somewhere in the wagon.

Ceana remained silent. She had no idea and did not want to speculate, but rather to glean information and thought processes from the women who were essentially her foes.

"Think it will be the wolves again?"

"Or the giants?"

"I imagine it will be any and all terrors, and we will be left without weapons to arm ourselves."

Their conversation was downtrodden and left little hope for thinking positively. Their fears were real and were the same that Ceana had. But she knew she had to survive, and if that was what she was given, she would fight against it. She'd find a big stick and…

And what? Fight off a wolf with a big stick?

She'd just end up dying.

The only reason she'd not perished before was because Macrath was with her. And he'd be with her again, she hoped. But she also had to defend herself. Had to defend him. Had to pull up every moment of training she could recall her brother giving her. She couldn't always depend on him to see her through.

The rope at her ankles and wrists started to loosen, and feeling came back to her appendages. She dared not loosen them further, because the guards would still need to pull her out of the wagon.

Ceana listened to the sounds beyond the conversations being whispered in the back of the wagon, hoping to get an idea of exactly where they were being taken. The wheels had creaked over the wooden bridge and then sank into the earthen road. Sounded like there were two wagons. Judging from the conversations, female warriors were in one cart and the males in another, possibly two.

They were on the road a while, and then there were sounds of scratches and whips against the sides of the wagon—tree branches? They'd made it into the woods. Lady Beatrice had said they'd be left in the woods. All Ceana had to do was concentrate on how long they drove and decipher any turns.

She counted the minutes, and when they'd reached about eight, the wagon took a sharp turn to her right. Another three minutes, then a sharp turn to the left. Fifteen minutes passed before they turned right once more.

Seven minutes later, the guards shouted at the horses, and their whips cracked over the sounds of the wagons being hauled. Up a hill they went for four minutes. And then the wagons stopped on a crest.

"All right you mangy vagrants," a guard shouted. "You're about to be left to your own devices."

But they weren't immediately grabbed. She could hear things being tossed into a pile. Sounded like metal and wood—weapons?

And then her ankle was grabbed, and searing pain shot up her legs. The rope binding her wrists and ankles was caught up in someone's grip, and she was tugged free of the wagon, falling until her chest hit the ground and she grunted her pain. She smelled damp leaves. The forest floor.

Another body was dropped beside hers, and then she was being dragged, her gown catching on sticks, rocks, and roots, scraping mercilessly over the ground. The hood was yanked off her head, and she blinked, trying to adjust to the little bit of light the moon afforded. She was in a pile of squirming bodies on top of what looked like a creag. She watched the last of the entrants be removed from the wagons just as roughly. One of the women hit hard on the ground, enough that when they took her hood off she remained unconscious.

Ceana twisted to find Macrath, but the males had been laid in a pile behind her, which was blocked by another female entrant.

"It's so… dark here," someone whimpered.

"'Twill be light soon," another answered. "We need to stick together if we're going to make it."

"We are not all going to make it. Best head back on your own. Better chances alone."

"Best you all watch your backs, as I plan on winning," said yet another.

A foul group they had. One planned to murder them all, one wanted to run it on her own, one filled with fear, and another who looked for allies. And then there was Ceana, who kept quiet and to herself. She was going to find Macrath, and then they were going to go it alone back to the castle—because she had a good idea of how to get back. Down the hill they must go first, and if they ran, perhaps the time would be about one and half what it was to travel on the wagon. About ten minutes past the hill, they'd make a left, travel about twenty-two minutes, make a right. Five minutes, then a left. Twelve minutes to the edge of the forest. 'Twould be grueling.

The last of the entrants was tossed onto the heap, and then the guards jumped onto the wagons. "We bid you farewell, arseholes! May the gods be *never* in your favor." Gritty, nasty laughs followed.

The wagon wheels cranked amid their laughter as they once more descended the hill. As soon as they were out of sight, Ceana continued the efforts she'd made on the wagon, but the way they'd tugged at the ropes when they pulled her off, it seemed like they were only getting tighter instead of loosening.

Bodies writhed around her as everyone had the same idea.

This wasn't working. She'd heard them throw weapons. Where? She craned her neck, trying to catch sight of any glimpse of metal reflected in the moon's light. There! About fifteen feet away. Rolling onto her knees and forehead, Ceana took a deep breath. This was likely going to scrape the hell out of her face, but how else would she get there? Craning her head forward, she braced herself and inched her knees forward. She repeated the move, her neck straining.

Behind her, others had gotten the idea and inched forward too.

An excessive amount of time seemed to pass before her head clunked into the first weapon. Lying on her side, cheek pressed into the dirt, she glanced at the weapons. Swords, bows, knives. She scooted closer to a knife, and reaching behind her, grappled with nothing before her fingers hit against metal. A little too hard, she felt the sting as the blade made a small slice in her skin.

Biting her lip against the pain, she slid the blade against the ropes, but she couldn't seem to get a good enough grip to make any cuts. She grunted, cried out. Sweat covered her skin as she worked to get the rope undone before anyone else. Afraid to be left vulnerable when the woman who'd said she'd murder them all had already reached a weapon and was vigorously working the blade against her own ropes.

A moment later, a shadow fell over her, and her eyes flew open, certain she was about to die, but Macrath smiled down at her. He sliced through her ropes, and instead of relief, tingling pain flooded her limbs.

"Come now, lass," he said, reaching down for her. She grabbed his hand, and he hauled her up, thrusting a long dagger into her grasp and slinging a bow and a quiver full of several arrows over her shoulder. "Time for us to claim this as ours."

"Not if I can help it." It was the woman from the wagon. Ceana turned in time to see her swinging her sword in their direction.

Chapter Twenty-Four

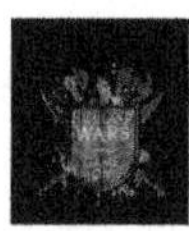

MACRATH brought his sword up in time to clang against the female warrior's. Sparks lit in the night where their swords met. She grunted against the strength of Macrath's sword arm.

Ceana scrambled to nock her bow and pointed the arrow straight at them, but she couldn't get a clean shot. They parried back and forth, but it was obvious Macrath was not putting all his strength into it.

Most of the other entrants had managed to inch their way to the weapons. Several helped each other to get free, but as soon as the fight began, they fled. Ceana would have helped the others to get untied, but she was now worried that someone else might attack them.

Keeping her feet braced, she observed the entrants still sawing through their ropes and those who stood trapped in fear, their eyes glued on Macrath.

In the darkness of night, everywhere she looked, she saw shadows. The black tree limbs swayed in the breeze, reaching toward her like giant's arms. The eyes of the owl looked like that of a wolf. What sort of dangers would be leaping out at them? Because if the final game meant only two winners, there had to be more to it than simply finding their way home.

A gurgling sound and the press of several of the entrant's hands to their mouths had Ceana whipping her gaze back to Macrath and the woman he fought against.

Macrath stood over her body. Ceana could barely make out the blood slipping from the woman's throat. A clean cut across her neck. A quick death. He turned his gaze to Ceana, his mouth grim. Even in the dim light of the moon, she could see he struggled with having to kill the woman.

"Go on, all of you," Ceana managed to say to those who watched with horror.

They didn't say anything but turned and fled—not all in the same direction.

Ceana tucked her arrow back in the quiver and met Macrath halfway. She wrapped her arms around him, but they were quickly reminded of what a precarious position they were in when an arrow whizzed past.

"That was close," Macrath said, grabbing her hand and running into the cover of the trees.

"We have to go down the opposite side," Ceana said.

Macrath shook his head. "Everyone is going that way, we should keep our distance."

"But how will we find our way back?" She chewed on her lower lip, heart pounding hard against her ribs.

"We'll circle back around but keep well away from everyone else. The forest is dangerous enough without having to deal with any more of the entrants trying to kill each other."

As the words left his mouth, a death cry filled the night air. Two down. Ten to go.

Macrath picked up his speed, their fingers entwined. Being so much shorter than he was, Ceana had to work twice as hard to keep up. Ignoring the shooting pains up and down her legs, she ran as fast as she could.

When her lungs felt like they would burst, she let Macrath's hand drop and stopped in her tracks, bent over to catch her breath. Her heart pounded hard in her ears, and she felt nauseated.

"We cannot stop. Not yet. Let me carry you." Macrath came to stand beside her, his palm resting on her back as he massaged her spine.

Somewhere in the distance a wolf howled, reminding her just how much danger they were in. Wolves. She hated them. Would hate them forever.

Ceana straightened, her lungs no longer spasming, and the nausea passing. She shook her head. "I can keep going." She couldn't let him carry her all the time. Doing so would only weaken him, and she would not leach away the energy he needed to fight.

"Are you certain, lass?"

She nodded. Macrath held out his hand again, a smile tugging at his lips.

Ceana marched forward, pulling him along. "Well, are you coming, warrior?" Every part of her body protested, but she couldn't let him down. Had to prove that she could keep up. They continued running down the opposite side of the hill, and once at the bottom, they circled around to the right, slowly picking their way through the trees. Whenever there was an owl hoot, or a stick cracking that hadn't been one they stepped on, they crouched low and listened, making eyes and nodding or shaking their heads at each other. Luckily, every howl of a wolf didn't sound close enough to be a danger.

They continued on like this until the first rays of orange started to break through the forest in streaks of glowing light.

"The creag is wider than I thought," Ceana murmured.

"Aye, but I think we'll have missed the other entrants."

Ceana nodded. They came over a small ridge, and perhaps seven feet below, they caught sight of the road, and lying facedown was the body of one of the male entrants. An arrow in his back. He'd not even been given the chance to fight.

A whistling cracked the dawn air, and an arrow pierced the grown beside her feet. "Archers," she hissed, jumping back.

Without thinking, Macrath tossed her over his shoulder and turned in the opposite direction. He ran back down the ridge and several hundred yards before ducking behind a fat tree. He settled her behind him, his body covering her from danger.

"At least we know where the road is," he said, an attempt at humor.

Ceana smiled meekly, but her eyes were drawn back toward the road, the vision of the dead man lying face down flashing in her mind's eye. "They've been picking off the entrants as they downed the hill. I'm glad we went the other way."

Macrath settled his hands on his hips, giving her a chance to admire his long, lean, muscled body. Even in a situation like this, she could appreciate his magnificence. "Aye, but it can't be as easy as all that. There has to be more."

"If we stay off the path, we might escape whatever it is." She swiped a flyaway hair from around her forehead.

"Aye. A leader never willingly walks into a dangerous situation they know nothing about. We've got no one to scout out the enemy for us, so we'll have to keep our eyes and ears keen to anything out of place."

Ceana nodded her agreement. "Should we go quietly back to the road and seek out the archers? We could take them out with my bow and arrow."

He reached forward and tucked another tendril behind her ear. "That would be a good idea in case they've also been charged with some other task down the line. They'll know the way back and could have a few other traps set up." He eyed her. "How good a shot are you?"

Ceana smiled, proud of her skill and eager to be of help in their last game. "I'm an excellent shot."

"Verra good." Taking survey of the lightening forest, Macrath said, "Follow me."

They crept over fallen logs, hid behind trees, ran when there was grass to soften their steps. When they neared the ridge before the road, they both stilled. Macrath made a hand signal for them to get down and crawl the rest of the way up the crest until they could see the road.

"Scan the trees," Macrath whispered.

Both of them scrutinized the limbs. The coming winter was on their side and made it easier to flesh out anything that didn't belong. Ceana nudged Macrath with her elbow, then pointed toward the other side of the road and westward. Sitting in a tree was a well-concealed archer. But the tip of his arrow had caught the light of the rising sun and glittered like a beacon to his hiding spot.

Macrath saw the man, nodded, and mouthed, *Are you ready?*

Ceana inclined her head and then nocked an arrow. She took aim, making sure her own arrow didn't catch the light, a deep breath, and then she let it fly. Her arrow struck the man in the center of his chest, and he fell out of the tree with a startled cry. Quick to nock another arrow, they were both immediately on alert for any other archers, but there was only an eerie silence. Even still, they waited to see if any arrows would fly their way or if another archer would leap from his perch to check on the downed man. When none came, they picked their way along the edge of the road, hidden by trees. By the time they'd made it to their first turn, the sun was out in full force, lighting the forest through the sparse tree limbs. A thin, trickling burn split through the forest, beckoning her.

Her stomach grumbled, and her mouth was dry with thirst. Her muscles ached, as did her wounds.

"Can we rest but a moment?" Ceana asked.

Macrath stopped, his eyes scanning their surroundings. "Aye."

Ceana dropped to her knees, sunk her hands in the cold water, and splashed it over her face, then sipped from her palms. Gods, but it was good and ice cold. Her stomach and throat were instantly appeased. And still she sipped more, savoring the water as though she'd not had any liquid in days. When she stood, Macrath bent down to drink, and she took up his watch, scanning the forest for any signs of man or beast—or one in the same. They appeared to be all alone. They'd not seen anyone since shooting the archer, and while on a normal day Ceana might have thought that was a good thing, today it only unsettled her.

Where were the other entrants? Where were the guards and beasts who should be stopping their trek back to Sìtheil?

"See anything?" Macrath asked, his voice low.

Ceana shook her head. "Not a thing. Isn't it odd?"

"Aye." He squinted his eyes as he turned in a slow circle. "They cannot have all perished, and there is no way in hell the council would let the journey back be so easy."

Ceana grabbed hold of Macrath's arm and sank against him, her limbs shaking from the rush of panic and the exertion of their journey.

"Not much longer," Macrath soothed, tucking her against him.

Not much longer... A cold knot settled in her stomach. She couldn't shake the feeling that something was terribly wrong. "We need to keep moving," she said. Her skin crawled, and though she was exhausted, her muscles itched to move.

The hairs on the back of her neck prickled. Someone was near. They were being watched.

"Macrath...," she whispered, her throat tightening. "We have company."

He pulled his sword from the scabbard on his back and tucked her behind him, but she had no place being shy. This was a game they would fight together. Ceana snatched an arrow from her quiver, nocked it in her bow, and pulled back the string, ready to shoot. Back to back, they turned in a slow circle. No sounds came from the woods, and no glints shined off weapons. Had her mind simply overreacted to their situation, fabricating a nemesis?

"They are close," Macrath murmured. "I can hear them breathing."

Ceana tuned out the rustle of leaves, the sounds of their own breathing. She jerked to the right, took aim and fired as a man leapt from behind a tree. Her arrow still in motion, she nocked another, ready to fire as her first shot sank into his abdomen. The man fell to his knees. She recognized him from the men's battle—one of the demon warriors, his face was still painted black.

"You'll... never... make it...," the man said, blood spilling from his lips.

Ceana hated that he was voicing her fears. For she truly wondered if they would make it. The odds were stacked against them. And yet, together they were more powerful. From what she could see of the other entrants, there did not appear to be anyone who had made allies, though several of them had run off together. They were bound to join forces somehow. It was simple human instinct—the survival rate was better in a group than alone.

"I do not think there are any more," Ceana said.

Macrath grunted. "There are always more of those devils."

Branches cracked on their other side, and they both leapt to face the coming foe. Her heart pounded, fingers twitched against the bowstring. But it was only a squirrel rummaging in the fallen leaves.

"Let's keep moving. No sense in remaining a target," Macrath said, his voice gruff.

Ceana took one last, longing glance at the burn, wishing they had a waterskin to fill. Macrath eased forward, holding his sword in two hands, and she kept her bow nocked and ready. They walked along the burn at a slow pace, stopping every so often to listen to the sounds of the woods. A bloodcurdling scream had Ceana's feet faltering, and she tripped forward into Macrath's back, nearly stabbing him with her arrow. Her heart skipped a beat.

"Steady, lass." The calm in his voice, the strength of him, settled over her.

"I'm so sorry."

"I know you wouldn't stab me on purpose," he said with a wink.

"Not unless you incur my wrath, warrior."

Macrath chuckled. "I'll be sure to stay on your good side then."

They ducked beneath low-hanging branches, their steps silent. From Ceana's estimation, they'd reached the next turn. The road itself bent in a curve, verifying she was right.

"We'll have to cross over the road to the woods on the other side," Macrath said.

They both crept toward the road, then knelt beside a tree surrounded by gorse bushes. Voices carried from over a rise, and moments later a man and woman entrant appeared. They were arguing about something. Hands moved animatedly, and then the male entrant grabbed hold of the female's arm, stopping her. He swung her around to face him, clutched her other arm and then backed her against a tree, grinding his body boorishly on hers.

The woman struggled, letting out a gurgled scream before the man slammed his mouth against her. She fought against him, kicking, bucking, but he held her tight. Was this a man who thought he'd win, demanding she give him what would be his right once they were wed? Did it matter? Nay, it did not. Rape was rape, and Ceana didn't care what would be his right. For it wasn't now, and she didn't think it would be ever. She raised her bow, aimed, and fired. Her arrow struck his back, just between his spine and shoulder blade—hopefully piercing his heart.

The man jerked backward, stumbling as he cried out with pain and tried to see just what it was that had struck him. Not waiting to see who had maimed her attacker, the woman turned into the woods and ran. But not fast enough. The man Ceana had shot whipped out a knife and hurtled it through the air, striking her in the back of her neck. She fell forward, unmoving, onto the forest floor. At least she'd been spared torture before she died.

Heart slamming against her chest, Ceana gagged. Bent over and heaved water from her belly.

Macrath rubbed her back and tugged her hair out of the way. "'Twill be all right," he cooed.

But she didn't believe him. She didn't think she'd ever be all right.

Not after what she'd witnessed and what she had had to do.

At least four entrants were dead now, that they'd seen, which meant there were possibly eight others still out there that they would have to defeat in order to win.

"We must move now," Macrath said. "I can carry you."

"I know you can." She glanced up at him, and gave a feeble smile. "But I'll walk beside you."

"Stubborn, wench." Macrath kissed her quick on the forehead and then tugged her forward.

She wanted to pull him back. To ask him to hold her for a little while, at least until her hands stopped shaking, but they did not have the luxury of recovery. Their only option was to move forward.

They ran, bent low, across the road, away from the bodies and out of sight. Once at a safe distance, they continued to walk cautiously. The wound in her leg throbbed. Studying the placement of the sun in the sky, Ceana nearly tripped over the body of another entrant. Looked as though she'd been hacked with an axe. That left only one female entrant besides Ceana and six other men besides Macrath unaccounted for. Make that four…

Two male entrants not far from the woman appeared to have fought to the death—killing each other. Had they fought over the deceased female?

The road to her left began a wide bend, hiding the rest of the road from view.

"Here, Macrath. I think this is where we must make the final turn." They'd have to cross over the road again.

Suddenly Macrath speared his sword into the ground and cupped her face. He stared intently into her eyes. She let her bow sling back over her shoulder, her arrow falling to the ground. "Ceana, know this. I love you with every breath, more than I could ever express."

Her chest swelled, and tears prickled her eyes. "I love you too."

He brushed her cheeks with the pads of his thumbs. "We have made it this far, and I believe we will make it to the end. We will be crowned the winners of these games."

Ceana sucked in a breath, nodded, her hands shaking.

"I also have a feeling that this last leg of our journey will not be easy, and I… I just… I needed you to know how much I love you, and that we will make it."

"Aye." Her voice trembled, and she licked her parched, cracked lips.

He kissed her softly then, just brushing his lips tenderly over hers, but it was enough to send energy sparking through her. Enough to tunnel her back to those precious moments on the beach when it had been only the two of them, and the world itself had slipped away.

Around them, the forest had grown hushed, as though the trees themselves held their breath. The sun threw shafts of light onto the road, glittering flecks of dirt and pollen catching the rays and making the road look as though it beckoned them.

Ceana reached up, squeezed Macrath's hands at her face. "We cannot dally any longer, lest I go mad."

Macrath chuckled and pressed his lips to hers once more. "I dare say, I do not want a mad wife."

He pulled his sword from the earth, and Ceana bent to pick up her arrow. Armed once more, they inched out, looking downward and listening for the sound of voices. All appeared to be clear save for a log fallen near the opposite side of the road.

"Go, lass. I'll watch your back."

Ceana kept her bow nocked, aiming it up and down the lane as she crossed, careful to keep her eyes on the forest ahead. She stepped over the fallen log.

And was suddenly falling.

She dropped her bow and arrow, turned to clutch at the fallen tree, one leg down in the hole, the other bent at an awkward angle over the log.

"Macrath!" she screeched.

"Ceana!" He was running toward her, the pounding of his feet, swishing plaid, all moving in slow motion.

She felt herself sliding, the slickness of her sweaty limbs not holding enough traction. Scrambling for purchase, her nails shredded against the bark, skin of her arms scraped. But all her grappling was no help against the weight of her body falling into a deep hole that had been covered with thatch and dirt.

But Macrath was there in an instant, hands reaching out and gripping her upper arms just as she lost her battle with the log.

"Don't look down," he said. Face grim, he pulled her up and over the log.

As soon as she was safe, she peered over the side at three male bodies lying at the bottom—more than a dozen snakes crawling over and around them—slithering over her fallen arrow. Her legs shook so hard she could barely stand upright.

She let out a breath, and nearly collapsed on shaking knees. If Macrath had been one second later, she'd be lying dead with those men. Throwing herself into his arms, she was unable to control the torrent of tears that gushed from her eyes. "Macrath…"

"Hush, love," he whispered, stroking her back. "You're safe now."

Are we?

"Who laid the trap?" she asked.

They both ducked, gazes darting into the trees, but no one came forward.

"I think we are safe, but we must keep going," Macrath said.

"There are two entrants left besides us—another male and female." She swiped at her tears.

"'Haps there are, but we cannot let that knowledge poison our thoughts. Come, we must be away. Your scream has likely brought every devil the council left to maim us." He bent and picked up her bow, which luckily had not fallen into the hole.

"I'm sorry." She slung the bow over her shoulder with her quiver.

"There is no need for sorry, lass." He swiped at her tears with the pads of his thumbs and looked into her eyes. "I would have screamed too."

Ceana let out a short laugh. "Nay, you would not have."

"I'm deathly afraid of snakes." He nodded, face all seriousness.

"Courtesy of your stepmother?"

He nodded grimly. "Aye. Likely, I would have screeched louder than you."

But she knew he wouldn't have. Macrath would have sliced through every one of those serpents with his sword. He would have vanquished them all, because that was who he was. He was a winner. He was a leader. He deserved to be crowned Prince of Sìtheil.

"We've not much further to go. Down the road and onto the moors. The castle will be in sight within the hour." Macrath lifted her into his arms amid her protest. "Just for a little while, lass. Until your legs stop shaking."

Ceana pressed her head to his shoulder and sighed. "You win."

"No, *we* win."

Macrath carried her for over a quarter hour. Despite the chill of the woods and the coming winter, they both had sweat trickling down their backs. Fighting to stay alive was exhausting.

"You can put me down now."

"Are you certain?"

"Aye."

Macrath set her on her feet and kissed her tenderly. "We're nearly there."

They could see down the road where the light grew brighter. The end of the forest.

"We have to run," Ceana said. "We're so close. I just want to be there."

Macrath nodded, and they picked up their pace, careful to only step on solid, undisturbed ground.

They broke through the trees, stopping short at the edge of the moors, the castle jutting out of the ground in all its imposing intensity. They could see the guards, tiny as they were from here, standing atop the gate towers and the battlements of the castle.

"They beat us," Ceana said, her breath catching.

Standing at the gate were the remaining male and female entrants. Waiting.

"We'll have to fight them in the list field."

Ceana nodded, terrified. At this distance, they couldn't see who they were. "I'm afraid my feet won't work."

"That gives me an idea."

She raised a skeptical brow. "What?"

"If I carry you, they will think you're weak, or injured. They will underestimate your ability to fight."

Fight. Battle to the death. She would have to kill again or be killed. Ceana stared over the gently waving grasses of the moors toward the gate doors where the two entrants stood stock still.

"You just carried me a long way, if you carry me more, you will only weaken yourself."

"Lass, I've enough energy to keep fighting for another month of moons if I have to. I mean to see us to the end."

She glanced up at him, taking in the sharp angles of his cheeks, the strength of his jaw, the glittering determination in his eyes. Macrath spoke the truth, and she believed every word he said. Trusted him implicitly.

"All right," she whispered, too afraid to speak as terror wound its way up through her middle. She wished she could be as strong as he was, but she was afraid she didn't have it in her. The horror of the past week, of her brother's death, and their clan's wars before that. It was catching up with her quickly.

"All right," Macrath murmured against her ear as he bent to pick her up.

She shivered and let her body fall against his, arms around his neck. "I love you so much."

"Och, lass, you've no idea how verra much I love you."

Chapter Twenty-Five

FEAR tunneled a path from Macrath's feet all the way to his head.

His fingers were cold, and his chest was tight.

They were so close to the end, and yet they'd not quite made it. Ceana trembled in his arms, and he forced himself to remain calm—at least on the outside. He didn't want her to know just how worried he was.

They closed in on the bridge. The male and female warrior turned to stare them down, sauntering away from the gate to meet them at the foot of it. Macrath assessed the male. He was one of the men who had ridden on horseback and fought beside him during the third game. Blood caked the exposed skin of his arms. He wore his beard long and braided, the hair a lighter shade than the red of his head. His plaid was dirty, ripped in places, just as his shirt. He looked rough, and the grin he wore was even coarser. Macrath had liked it a hell of a lot better when the man was on his side.

The woman was tall, tough, and she sneered at Ceana as they approached. Ceana would have trouble fighting her, he could tell. Not because Ceana wasn't skilled, but the woman was larger and meaner.

A quiet groan left Ceana's lips.

"'Twill be all right." Macrath tried to soothe her.

"Nay. 'Twill not."

Her quaking grew in his arms, and he sought to divert her from her fears. "Why, love?"

"That is the woman who fought me by the water barrels. If we'd not been interrupted, she would have won that fight too."

Macrath recognized her at once, several of her front teeth missing. She'd been the one to say Lady Beatrice was violating Ceana, touching her, and torturing her in that same chamber she'd taken Macrath. The warrior woman was brutish, vulgar, and had no honor. "She is no princess, love."

"But she is a warrior."

"I am with you. I will be right beside you. I can take them both."

"Well, if it isn't the little bitch and his cunt," the woman sneered.

Macrath tightened his hold on Ceana but said nothing. "Do not let them goad you," he whispered in her ear.

"Had to carry the little sloppy mess all the way back, did you?" she said, elbowing the man beside her.

He grimaced, obviously not thrilled that the woman to have made it back could be his wife. His eyes hungrily roved over Ceana. The warrior wanted her, and there was no way in bloody hell Macrath was going to let him take her away. Too bad for him, he didn't know better. The man puffed his chest and sent a lecherous grin toward Ceana.

"I see you've brought me my bride."

Macrath bared his teeth. "The only thing I've brought you is death."

The man laughed, pulled his sword from his back scabbard, and tossed it from hand to hand. "I wager I'm splitting her thighs afore the sun goes down—just after I split your skull."

Macrath set Ceana down gently, maneuvering in front of her. He pulled his sword from his scabbard.

"Ah, you arseholes are going to fight over that bitch?" the woman scoffed. "Looks like you're going to have to make do with me." She whipped out a knife and tried to lunge behind Macrath to stab at Ceana, but both he and the other warrior brought their swords down at once.

She fell to the ground, a deep gash in her back and another in her neck.

Ceana remained silent behind him, and he dared not look her way for fear of taking his eyes off his opponent. He trusted that she would stay safe. He did not trust his opponent to fight fairly. Nay, the man's tactics would be as dirty as his hands.

"Well," the warrior shrugged as he glanced down at the dead woman. "That's a relief. I couldn't have fucked her if my life depended on it." He chuckled. "But that piece," he pointed his sword at Ceana, "she's worth fighting for."

"Aye," Macrath growled. *And worth killing for.*

Every muscle in his body tightened, ready to pounce on the craven fool.

His opponent must not have felt the need to waste time. He lunged forward, arms arching and swiping down. Macrath whipped his sword upward, the metal clashing together with a piercing clang. They stood, pushing swords, both of equal strength. They might have been matched in power, but Macrath had more at stake than the pig he fought against. He was also a better swordsman—he was pretty damned sure of it.

Leaping backward, Macrath arched his sword again, parrying in long, sweeping, power-packed arches. He drove the warrior back until he gained his footing and advanced. Echoes of their ringing swords and grunts clouded the air. Feet slogging in the muddy road, it was hard to gain traction. They moved in a circle, both of them tripping more than once.

Movement caught his eye—Ceana. She'd moved the woman's body out of their footpath and stood to the side.

Attention back to the fight, he blocked a healthy blow from his opponent, and another circle they made, each of them pushing their swords hard and then jumping backward to parry again.

When Macrath crashed forward, sweat pouring from his temples, his foe's eyes widened, sword arm dropping, his movement ceased. But it was too late for Macrath to stop. His sword met its mark in the crook of the man's shoulder, crunching through flesh, muscle, and bone. The warrior opened his mouth as if to speak, but only a whooshing, gurgling breath released.

The moment seemed to last forever as Macrath stared into his opponent's eyes. This man was the last to die today. The last to die in these games. Ever, if Macrath had anything to say about it.

"I'm sorry, lad. So sorry," Macrath said.

He put his foot on the man's chest, yanking his sword free, and his rival fell forward to his knees and then onto his torso. Macrath's eyes widened. The man had an arrow in his back.

His gaze shot up to stare at Ceana. Grim lines creased her eyes, and her lips were turned down. A single tear slid down her cheek.

"We won," she whispered.

Macrath nodded, staggering backward, his sword falling from his hands. Ceana hurled down her bow and quiver of arrows and ran forward. She threw herself into his arms, wrapping herself around him. He gripped her tight, mouth crashing onto hers. Their kiss was hard, anguished, relieved.

"Och, lass, we did it," he said against her lips. Relief flooded through him, making him weak, unsteady. But her kiss, her hold, they gave him strength.

"It's ours," she answered.

"Congratulations." Lady Beatrice's voice broke unwelcomingly through their passion. "Come through the gates, this time as the new rulers of Sìtheil Castle and the lands with which it has been granted."

The new rulers…

Macrath pressed his forehead to Ceana's and breathed in deep. Emotions welled in his chest. Ceana clutched to him, her heart pounding against his.

"This cannot be!" Leticia's voice brought instant anger coiling inside him.

"Ignore her. You've won, and there is nothing she can do about it," Ceana whispered.

She was right. Leticia could no longer reach him. "I love you," he said.

"I love you too." Ceana cupped his face and pressed a soft kiss to his lips. "And now we claim what is ours."

Hand in hand, they walked over the wooden bridge. Lady Beatrice and Leticia stood on top of the gate tower. The portcullis raised, its chains grinding, the gate doors swung wide. Ceana flashed Macrath a triumphant smile, and the tension that had tightened his muscles painfully started to ebb. No longer would they walk beneath these gates and to their death—unless it was in defense of their castle, their people. Gods willing, they'd win every time.

"The gods have granted you this castle, its lands, its riches, and its people. Sìtheil Castle and all it holds is now your responsibility. Keep it safe from enemies who will wish to seize everything you hold dear. Do not let King Olaf and his son Gillemorre's lives and what they fought for vanish into oblivion."

Lady Beatrice stood upon the dais in the great hall of the castle. The guards lined the halls, and beyond that the family members, servants, and personal guards of past entrants filled the remaining spots. Boarg had a front-and-center view of the proceedings—as did Leticia and Victor.

Ceana could feel the pride of her clansman at her back and the hatred of Macrath's family.

They knelt before the dais, having been cleaned and dressed in finery fit for royals. Only an hour since their fight to the death. Two councilmen stepped forward, gilded and ruby-studded crowns in their hands. They raised them high and in unison said: "That with which the gods has granted remain in your hands and safekeeping until the time when your obligation is fulfilled. By the gods and the king, we name thee Prince and Princess of Sìtheil."

The weight of the crown being placed on her head, although slight, felt immeasurably heavy. A warmth seeped over her. She'd saved her people. Clan MacRae would forever be saved. Gruamach would not have to fear another siege, and her people would never go hungry again. And yet the weight of such responsibility—far greater than she ever would have imagined—overshadowed her triumph. It was up to her and Macrath now to save all of Scotland from the evils of the council and the games.

Beside her, Macrath gripped her hand, squeezed her fingers. But still they did not stand, for moments later a priest was brought forth to issue their wedding vows. But to them, it was simply a formality, for they'd pledged themselves to one another on the beach.

"The Prince and Princess of Sìtheil!" shouted the council.

The room erupted in shouts and cheers. Ceana and Macrath turned to face the crowd, and the first to kneel before them were those of the council. Ironic, considering they'd also pledged to each other to see the council disbanded and the games done away with. Their very enemies bowed before them.

One by one, everyone in the room stepped forth. When the guard who'd violated Ceana and beaten Macrath stepped forward, she could feel the rage rumble through her husband. She turned to look at him, seeing the veins in his neck bulging. She took a step to the side, certain she would not be able to quell his wrath. He glanced at her, and as if he understood her silent acceptance, he wrenched his arm back and then punched the man in the nose with such force blood burst in torrents down his face. There was an outraged shout from the guard, but no one else spoke. The man had deserved it. Deserved far more, but that would have to wait.

Last to approach the dais was Leticia and her son Victor, the latter with two black eyes and a crooked nose from the last time he'd encountered Macrath. They bowed and curtsied in silence, their eyes not quite meeting Macrath's or Ceana's. When they rose and turned, Macrath cleared his throat.

"We have not heard your pledge of fealty," he said.

Victor let out an outraged gasp. "We'll not pledge our fealty to you! We owe you nothing."

Macrath grinned. "On the contrary, I am your Prince and my wife your Princess. We'll hear your pledge or you'll not leave our lands alive."

Leticia scoffed. "You would threaten us? Your father—"

Macrath crossed his arms over his chest. "Will do nothing, just as he did nothing to thwart your attempts before. I'll not wait another moment."

Victor grudgingly took his sword from his scabbard and knelt before Macrath, the tip of his sword pressed so hard into the wood of the floor his knuckles whitened. His mother knelt beside him, repeating the same lines, save for her name. "I, Victor Campbell, son of the Earl of Argyll, by the gods do swear my allegiance to Their Majesties, the Prince and Princess of Sìtheil." Both sets of eyes glittered with hatred. "'Tis my oath that should I go against your rule, that with this sword you shall pierce my heart."

And Macrath gladly would.

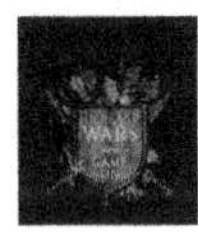

Candles gave off a soft glow in the master chamber in Sìtheil Castle.

Macrath carried Ceana over the threshold and kicked the door shut behind him. "Our bedchamber, my laird and princess wife."

Ceana nuzzled closer to his muscled heat. "'Tis magnificent."

The hearth was lit, warming the room. Tapestries telling the legend of King Olaf and his son Gillemorre lined the walls. An alcove was set deep in the wall, lined with three arrow-slit windows and a cushioned bench. The hearth was flanked by two large carved wooden armchairs with soft-looking embroidered pillows. But what drew her eye was the massive bed against the left wall. She'd never seen one as large as this. Each oak post was thick as a man's thigh and carved with swirling Celtic knots. A half dozen warriors could fit upon the mattress. The canopy was made of soft wool plaid, deep and rich in colors of reds and greens, matching the coverlet on the bed. A fur lined the bottom half of the bed, and woven rugs covered the floors to ward off any chill.

The room was greater than the one at Gruamach Keep, fit for royalty.

"And they've left us a feast," Macrath said.

Ceana looked to the left of the door, having missed the long table filled with wine and other delicacies. "Shall I feed you, husband?"

"Och, I believe the only morsel I'll be feasting on is you, lass." In two brisk steps, he was at the edge of the bed, and he tossed her down on top.

Ceana squealed, bouncing back onto the bed. She smiled up at Macrath as he crawled onto the bed and up the length of her. He sank against her, his mouth claiming hers as his hard body pushed her into the soft feather mattress. He tasted of sweet wine and desire. Her body came to life, tingling with delicious anticipation. She breathed in his clean scent and smiled into his mouth, relief and happiness overtaking all the gloom and darkness of the past weeks.

Sadness and despair had no place in this room. Their chamber would be for them, for joy, for celebrating life. For passion and pleasure.

She wrapped her arms around Macrath's back, muscles rippling beneath her fingertips. She held on to him, never wanting to let go. His ardent heat enveloped her, warming her muscles, making her pliant. She parted her legs, the pressure of his arousal causing her sex to grow damp and tingly. She shuddered, letting out a soft moan.

"Too many clothes," she murmured.

"Och, lass, but we must take it slow. Let it last forever." He trailed his lips over her chin, nipping at her earlobe, then slid a searing path down her neck to her collarbone. "I want to taste every luscious inch of you. And I want to savor it."

She wanted to savor him too. Naked. Ceana tugged the pin from his plaid, tossing it toward the table. It clinked and then fell somewhere on the floor. She giggled. "Best we not step on that."

Gripping the length of plaid flung over his shoulder, she slowly slid it off. Macrath pushed up on his arms, looking down at her, a devilish twinkle in his eye.

"Spoiled, lass," he said.

She shook her head. "Nay, husband. I but want to gaze upon you." On the beach there'd been no time for exploring. There'd been no time, period. They'd made love fervently, fiercely, and it had been heavenly, but they had not been able to relish each other like they could now.

"I like the way you think." He bent low, nibbling on her lips, and then knelt back on his heels.

With eyes wide and excitement rippling through her veins, Ceana watched as he tugged his shirt over his head, revealing a muscled chest she'd felt in the dark, felt beneath his shirt, but now could stare at openly in the glow of the candles and hearth. A light dusting of dark hair graced the ripples of his torso. She reached out to touch him, pressing her hand to his heart and then trailing her fingers between his nipples toward his navel. He sucked in a breath, his eyes growing heavy.

"I like when you touch me," he said.

"I like touching you."

He winked. "I want to touch too." Macrath plucked at the ties of her bodice. "Stand up."

He crawled off the bed and pulled her to stand in front of him, where he slowly divested her of her clothing, kissing and caressing as he went. When she stood in nothing but her hose and boots, she shivered—but not from cold. Nay, she was incredibly hot. She trembled with need, with being exposed. She felt beautiful. Every flaw she'd ever seen in herself disappeared in his heady gaze.

She reached out and grabbed his belt, giving it a little tug. Macrath grinned wickedly.

"You want me to take this off?"

She nodded, biting on her lower lip.

Macrath gripped the end of his belt and leisurely removed it. His plaid unraveled, falling to his booted feet. She stared at the hardened shaft jutting from a tuft of dark hair between his hips. She marveled at his size and how the length of it had fit so comfortably and deliciously inside her.

Macrath knelt before her. He unlaced her boots, removing one and then the other. Then he gradually rolled her hose down her legs, his fingers gently brushing her calves, tickling behind her knees. When her feet were bare, he lifted her right foot and kissed the inside of her ankle.

"You are so beautiful. And mine."

"All yours," she whispered.

Macrath kissed his way up to her inner thigh. Her knees shook, and she held her breath. His lips on her flesh made her want to weep from the pleasure of it.

He kept his eyes locked on hers as he trailed upward, his hot breath lingering over the apex of her thighs. Her sex pulsed, her womb clenched tight, nipples ached. Knees shaking, she threaded her fingers through his hair.

"Macrath," she murmured. "What are you doing?"

"Making love to you properly," he breathed, tongue flicking out to dance along her delicate folds.

She nearly fainted, forgot to breathe.

She watched him pleasure her, body trembling, eyes trying hard to fall closed. His hands held tight to her hips, tongue massaging her silken flesh in wild, blissful licks and suckles.

"Oh, gods..." Unbidden, her body was quick to spiral up that mountain, and the only way down was to fly even higher upon a thundercloud of pleasure.

Macrath was relentless in his pursuit of her release, and she let him take the lead, enjoying every moment of it. Fingers tugging tight to his hair and shoulder, she let herself go, let herself fall off the edge of the mountain. Panting and moaning, thighs quivering, she cried out when a burst of pleasure sprang free, followed by another and another. She rode the waves of intoxicating sensations until she couldn't move or breathe or stand.

He kissed her hip, her belly, and then her breasts, scraping his teeth gently over her nipples. She was powerless to move, which suited her just fine because the sensations he elicited from her were overwhelmingly wonderful. Macrath lifted her up, cradling her to his body, and placed her gently on the bed before coming down on top of her. Her musky scent was on his lips when he brushed them over hers, but she didn't care, somehow found it even more enticing.

"Tonight is more perfect than I ever imagined, *mo chridhe,*" he said.

"How often did you imagine it?" she teased, her toes tickling up his calf.

"Almost as much as I envisioned spending the rest of my life at your side, making you smile and laugh."

She pressed her hand on his heart then leaned forward to kiss the spot. "We'll never be separated again."

His hips settled between hers, the hardness of his shaft pressing against the heat of her. She tilted her hips, inviting him to sink inside her. She wanted him. Wanted to feel that glorious pressure again. To feel him moving within her. To be one in body and soul.

"I want you inside me," she whispered.

He kissed her neck. "Och, lass, the way you respond to me… It drives me to the brink of madness."

"Join me. I'm already there."

Reaching between their bodies, she gripped his hot, heavy, velvet shaft in her hand, running her thumb over the delicate ridge. Macrath groaned, his forehead falling against hers. He trembled above her, and she liked the power of knowing she did this to him. She guided him toward her center, tilting upward when the press of his erection slid along her flesh. Macrath reached down, his grip over hers, and pushed the tip inside. He gripped her hand in his and pulled it from between their bodies and over her head, entwining his fingers with hers.

Ceana wrapped her legs around his hips, and he surged forward, burying himself deep inside her. They both cried out, bodies tightening. She arched her back, tucked her legs up higher, wanting to bring him deeper.

But Macrath tormented her by withdrawing and then slowly easing his way back inside. Fire lit inside her, sparks flashing out into her limbs all the way to her fingertips and toes. Slowly, he retreated. Unhurried, he slid back inside. All the while, he kissed her lips, teased her with his tongue, nibbled at her neck. He kept their hands entwined above her head, instead using his body to arch over her, inside her, out of her, his mouth to taste and nibble. His chest brushed against her aching nipples until he licked and suckled them.

When both of them shook, when they were both slick with perspiration and desperate for release, he deliberately withdrew and then plunged back inside. He thrust and thrust and thrust until Ceana was crying out with pleasure and her body exploded in flashes like the thousands of stars in the sky.

Hearing her pleasure, Macrath murmured, "Dear gods, you are so incredible." He plunged harder, driving into her with purpose now. "I want you to find your release again. Soar with me, love."

And she did, crying out as the startling vibrations overtook her again. Macrath growled at the same moment, his mouth capturing hers in a demanding, heart-throbbing kiss as he too quaked and shivered.

He stilled above her, kissing her more tender now until both their quickened breaths subsided. Rolling to the side, he pulled her with him. He stroked the hair from her temples and kissed her lovingly. Ceana tucked her leg around his thigh and settled her head against the crook of his shoulder, her fingers dancing circles on his chest.

"That was even more magical than before," she said, a smile curling her lips.

His fingers trailed over her spine. "You forever amaze me, lass."

"I'm so glad we found each other." Without him, her life—or death—would have been drastically different.

His chin bumped her head when he nodded. "Aye, lass. The gods were looking down on us."

"Fate had plans for us." He entwined his fingers with hers on his chest.

"We'll change history, you and I. Scotland will not put us in a five-year box."

"Nay. The council will pay for all it's done."

"The End"

Well, *the end* for now…

Look for **Book Two** in the **Highland Wars** series,

Highland Sacrifice.

If you enjoyed **HIGHLAND HUNGER**, *please spread the word by leaving a review on the site where you purchased your copy, or a reader site such as Goodreads or Shelfari! I* *love to hear from readers too, so drop me a line at* authorelizaknight@gmail.com *OR visit me on Facebook:* https://www.facebook.com/elizaknightauthor. I'm also on Twitter: @ElizaKnight. If you'd like to receive my occasional newsletter, please sign up at www.elizaknight.com. *Many thanks!*

AUTHOR'S NOTE

Dear Reader,

First off, I wanted to thank you for reading the start to my new series! This was an exciting book to research and a dark world to build—but filled with hope and the opportunity for change.

King Olaf the Black, was an actual medieval king on the Isle of Mann (I moved him to the northern Scottish isles), however I did use creative license for how his reign ended, and what happened to the country following. Olaf's ascension and reign was brutal in its own right. According to several sites, he did have a son (born out of wedlock) named Gilhemoire (changed to Gillemorre).

Mac Rath, does mean "Son of Fortune", and I named my hero for a Pictish King, Giric, who was nicknamed such. Macrath's surname Mor, means "great", and I purposefully had his mother name him such because she believed that her son would do great things.

Throughout Scottish (and medieval) history, there were games, feats of triumph and tournaments in which great rewards were given to the winners—lands, titles, riches, spouses, freedom, etc… It was a chance for warriors (and sometimes not warriors) to show their skill, their power, their authority, to practice for battle, and to make something of themselves. The war games within this book are fictitious, obviously, but I did base most of them on some part of history.

We have to remember that while fiction glorifies battle and medieval life, that back in those days it was brutal, hard and stark. I tried to recreate a picture of that darkness within the book, but also to show that despite such hardship and brutality, that mankind and the human psyche has the power to overcome such harsh realities.

The HIGHLAND WARS series is ultimately a historical Scottish romance fantasy, based in part by the Highland games in history, the gladiatorial games of Rome, medieval tournaments of historic Europe, with a sexy, romantic, mysterious twist (some readers have likened it to an adult, medieval, sexier version of the *Hunger Games* series by Suzanne Collins or the *Game of Thrones* series by George R. R. Martin. I admit to not having read either of these series titles at this point, though I have enjoyed the movies and television sagas, and am flattered that readers would liken my works to such well-received prose.)

While most of my books contain battles, death, sorrow (and a brighter side, too!) the HIGHLAND WARS series is a bit of a deviation in that it is much darker than my usual writing. Despite this deviation, I do hope you are enjoying Macrath and Ceana's story, and that you continue reading the series to see their ultimate triumph in the end.

All the best,
Eliza

HIGHLAND WARS

You've just read *HIGHLAND HUNGER*, Book One in the Highland Wars series. Ready for Book Two: *HIGHLAND SACRAFICE*!

Victory was theirs. At least for a little while…

Ceana MacRae and Macrath Mor fought valiantly to win their temporary titles as Prince and Princess of Sìtheil during the bloody war games. A burgeoning love, countless hopes and dreams for the future of Scotland fill the daytime hours, and passion holds them at twilight.

Just married and given only five years to rule before the next set of savage games begins, Ceana and Macrath have vowed to take down the royal council in charge of the games, but before they can move ahead, they have to first conquer their enemies—and their own personal demons. With the ghosts of their pasts chasing them and their adversaries stopping at nothing to see them destroyed, ruling Sìtheil will prove to be a challenge not only for their reign, but also for their love.

May the gods be forever in their favor…

Have you read the Stolen Bride series?

The Highlander's Temptation
The Highlander's Reward
The Highlander's Conquest
The Highlander's Lady
The Highlander's Warrior Bride
The Highlander's Triumph
The Highlander's Sin

Like historical fiction?

Check out Eliza's Tales from the Tudor Court, written as E. Knight!

My Lady Viper

Prisoner of the Queen

ABOUT THE AUTHOR

Eliza Knight is a *USA Today* bestselling indie author of sizzling historical romance and erotic romance. While not reading, writing or researching for her latest book, she chases after her three children. In her spare time (if there is such a thing…) she likes daydreaming, wine-tasting, traveling, hiking, staring at the stars, watching movies, shopping and visiting with family and friends. She lives atop a small mountain with her own knight in shining armor, three princesses and one very naughty puppy. Visit Eliza at http://www.elizaknight.comor her historical blog History Undressed: www.historyundressed.com

Game One

116 started
- 37 dead
79 left (pg. 82) 37 women (pg. 176)
- 37
42 men

Game Two (women only)

[48 started (per Cona) pg174, nearly 4 doz.]

37 actually pg 176
- 15 died GII
22 left

36 woman died first 2 games
22 left
58 total women

116 total in Games
58
58 total men

Game Three - men guarding women

42

10
32 left

22
32
54

22 females
25 males
47
left for game 4

Game Four

47 total
22 females
25 males

5 women left (17 died)
9 men
14 alive
(16 died)

116
14 alive
102 died

Made in the USA
Las Vegas, NV
16 May 2021

23149445R00216